The Hawk and the Cup

The Island of the Mighty has been defeated. The shadow of the Eagle lies across the land. The Britons are a broken and defeated people. But hope lives in one man and one woman. The man is Merlin, Seer of the Island of the Mighty, whose quest for the ancient sword, Excalibur, kindles hope that the royal bloodline of Britain will one day be restored. The woman is the fiery-tempered red-haired beauty Boudicea, whose destiny it is to strike fear into the hearts of her Roman oppressors, and bring fire and blood to the cities raised by these foreign invaders.

This sequel to *The Hawk and the Wolf* continues the tales of Merlin and Boudicea, but paints a vivid tapestry of a defeated land, torn by betrayal and deceit, by political and religious factions. It is a land of war, a land of passion, a land of savagery; but it is also a land where, beyond all hope, can be found the one miraculous treasure that can restore peace to the land and fulfill the purposes of the gods of old.

The Grail.

Also from WestBank Publishing by Mark Adderley:

The Hawk and the Wolf

Praise for *The Hawk and the Wolf*:

"Intriguing and original . . . myth, legend, romance, and history are inextricably entwined" (Tom Shippey, author of *J. R. R. Tolkien: Author of the Century*, for *Arthuriana*)

"Drawing simultaneously from history and legend, Mark Adderley skillfully weaves realistic detail into the Arthurian mythos. His characters inhabit a very tangible ancient world, where magic must compete with the mud and smoke of the everyday. He gives us a young, struggling Merlin whose travels around the Britonnic Isles provide us tantalizing glimpses of the mature wizard he'll become. The result should prove satisfying for both scholars of Arthuriana and lovers of fantasy literature." (Nathaniel Williams, AboutSF, University of Kansas)

"A worthy addition to the Arthurian Canon" (Bill Tolliver, *Renditions of Camelot*)

"Merlin's Britain . . . is situated somewhere between the mystical world of legend and the cold world of modern historical imaginings. . . . Ripe reading material for Merlin enthusiasts and lovers of fantasy" (Jonathan Schindler, *The Englewood Review of Books*)

THE HAWK AND THE CUP

Book Two
The Matter of Britain

To Beth,
Happy Reading
Mark A[illegible]

Mark Adderley

10.9.10
Lander, Wyoming

Westbank
Publishing

This is a work of fiction. All characters and events in this novel are fictional

The Hawk and the Cup

Published by WestBank Publishing

For Information Address:
4408 Bayou Des Familles
Marrero, LA 70072

Cover Art by Floyd Alsbach

ISBN-13 978-0-9789840-6-9
ISBN -10 0-9789840-6-4

Printed in the United States of America

To Kit

I

The glade was quiet, save for the birdsong, the air full of apple blossoms, the soft grass carpeted with them. The sun shone softly. The sweet shower of early morning had left the petals of the flowers open, and added lustre to the glowing green life all around. Spring had been kind, and a narrow brook, dark fishes weaving through the pebbles in its midst, snaked left and right through the glade at its eastern end.

The thunder of hoofs, when it came, broke the stillness abruptly. A dozen men, all horsed on heavy chargers, their bridles jingling, their armour clattering, erupted from the western end of the glade, sending the birds flying in multicoloured clouds. The hoofs rumbled from one end of the glade to the other, and then they were gone again. Stillness returned. The birds once more struck up their paean to spring.

The horsemen, meanwhile, continued on their gallop through the forest. There was a faint track they were following, one that had been pointed out to them at the last village they had passed. Grim of face they were, their eyes flinty, and most especially, their leader. His boots were flecked with mud, like the flanks of his horse, and he let his cloak stream out behind him, heedless of the cool air blowing all about him. Beside him, and a little behind, rode his standard-bearer. The standard streamed out behind, the wind tugging at the white linen so that the crimson dragon seemed to writhe and gnash its teeth.

The leader of the horsemen held up his hand, and pulled gently on his reins. The horses slowed as they came to a wide avenue, apple trees on either side, that hugged the foot of a tall hill. Men and boys in robes turned to watch, wide-eyed, as they approached.

Coroticos, High King of the Island of the Mighty, had come to Afallach, abode of druids.

The High King swung himself down from the saddle, and pulled his gauntlets from his hands. Briefly, he rubbed the insides of his thighs, for they ached persistently. Several boys hurried forward to tend to their horses, leading them away with deferential bows.

One of the other riders moved up to stand beside Coroticos. "Is he here, do you think?" he asked.

Coroticos turned to look at the man who had spoken. "I don't know, Milwyr," he said. "I am here because I *don't* have second sight. Anyway, we must first deal with Archdruid Gwelydd."

"He's been quiet of late," commented Milwyr.

"He has," agreed Coroticos. "I don't think he feels the threat of Rome as do we who fight against the Eagles. You would think he would remember the Medway, for he was there. He was concerned enough then to leave us so he could tend after his druids here. I don't think he has left Afallach in all that time, eight years."

"Old birds stay close to their nests," remarked Milwyr.

A druid in his middle years coughed politely from a door in the hillside. "Archdruid Gwelydd is ready to receive you," he said, holding the door open for them.

Coroticos entered the Cave of Knowledge, stooping a little as he passed through the door. It took a few moments for his eyes to get used to the dark, but then he found himself in a large chamber with shelved walls, upon which rested many ancient volumes. The light came from torches and from a skylight above them. Gwelydd reclined upon what seemed to be a bed, but which was backed like a throne. His acolytes and senior druids were ranged about him.

"May the gods be good to the Chief Dragon of the Island of the Mighty," said Gwelydd; his voice, Coroticos noted, was shriller than he remembered it.

Coroticos bowed before the Archdruid. "May they favour the Archdruid of Britain also," he said.

"I hope," said Gwelydd, "that you will excuse my not getting up. My old bones, you see. You who are young cannot readily imagine what a relief it is to us who are no longer young to remain at rest. To be always acting is the curse of the young; to be always dreaming of acting, that is the curse of the old."

A druid in his mid-forties pushed a stool up behind Coroticos, who swept aside his cloak and lowered himself onto it.

"How have the years treated my lord Archdruid?" he asked.

"Indifferently," replied the old man. "Indifferently. But we hear great news of you, my lord. We hear of your forays past the borders of the province of Britannia."

"We do what we can," answered Coroticos, "and the gods have blessed us thus far."

"Thus far?" Gwelydd peered into Coroticos' eyes. Coroticos stared back. The old man's eyes had lost none of their ability to penetrate to the very soul, he reflected. "Do you fear for the success of your military enterprises in the future?"

"I begin to," said Coroticos.

Gwelydd shrugged. "Such must be always the care of a military commander," he said, "and such doubts do not lead one to visit the Archdruid of the Island of the Mighty. On what other matter do you seek my advice?"

"Very well then," said Coroticos. "It is told me that there is among you a Seeing One."

Gwelydd nodded slowly. "There is one, to be sure," he said, "but he is not under my authority."

"Will the authority of the High King summon him to this place?" asked Coroticos.

"You do not understand, sire," answered Gwelydd. "He is not under my authority, for he is no acolyte, and he is no druid. Sometimes, he dwells here to consult the books in this place, and he eats with us, tills our fields with us, and ministers to the sick of our community, and sometimes, he spends days or even weeks in contemplation upon the summit of the Hill of

Afallach. But at other times, he disappears from this place for weeks on end, telling none of us whither he has gone, nor for how long. He treads his own path."

"If he is here, and the Archdruid of Britain sends for him, will he come?" asked Coroticos.

"I think he will." Gwelydd whispered a few words to an acolyte, who sped off, and motioned to another, who brought a flagon of wine and two cups. Gwelydd and Coroticos drank.

"This man, this Seeing One," said Coroticos, "what manner of man is he?"

"Of mankind," replied Gwelydd. "He thinks the thoughts of men, and he feels the ills of the world as men do. More so, perhaps. He sees the ways of this world as the gods see them."

"If only he can help me!" said Coroticos. "My way has become cloudy."

"There is such a moment in the life of every man," Gwelydd told him. "If you recall, mine was upon the banks of the Medway."

"I have often wished to ask you about that," admitted Coroticos.

"I have often wished to explain it to you," said Gwelydd, struggling to sit upright. An acolyte moved forward to rearrange the cushions on his seat. "I hope, your majesty, that you have never taken our parting of ways as a sign that I had renounced my allegiance to you, or doubted that your way was the best."

"I cannot admit to innocence in that regard," answered the High King. "I was puzzled by your stance at the Great Council."

"I imagine so. I was stalling for time—the weak position, perhaps, but I did not like aligning myself with Cartimandua's policy." Gwelydd did not speak for a moment, relapsing into reflection. Then he said, "There is much about the invasion that I did not understand, and I understand little more now than I did then. Two things in particular surprised me. The first was that Cartimandua of Cameliard should advise war but provide no men to assist you. The second was Cymbeline's desertion. My intention was to travel here, and secure the defence of Afallach. From there, I meant to travel to Cameliard, and beseech Cartimandua of reinforcements. But by the time I was ready to set out, I heard about the defeat at Mai Dun, and I knew that the war would now be a defensive one. I looked principally to the defence of Afallach." He paused. "Your Majesty's escape from that battle was little short of miraculous," he observed.

Coroticos nodded. "I often wish I had died there," he said. "I spoke largely to my men of the virtue of dying in a noble cause, and no cause was nobler than ours. I should have died, too, had not that blow to my head stunned me."

"That is a tale I have not heard," said Gwelydd.

"There is little enough to tell," answered Coroticos with a sigh. "I was unconscious and taken as dead by the enemy, and removed from the field of battle by Milwyr and another of my men, who has since given his life in our struggle. But now there is something new, which may surprise you. Cartimandua has made offer of those men she withheld then. I think she sees that the Romans are a threat to all Britons."

Gwelydd's eyes were narrow slits. "Yes," he said, drawing the syllable out. "But be wary, O High King. Cartimandua is not to be trusted."

"In times of peace, I agree," said Coroticos. "But these are extraordinary times, my lord Archdruid, and I think she feels the threat even as we do. And there are my men to consider. They are weary of battle, and depleted in numbers. If there is any hope of swelling their numbers, it is a hope I must embrace."

"You must do what is necessary," said Gwelydd, "as all kings must. But behold: here is the Seeing One."

It was a man in his early thirties who stood in the doorway to the Cave of Knowledge. He wore dark robes, with nothing on his head, and a short beard covering his chin. Merlin dropped to his knee before the High King, who raised him up and indicated a stool, into which Merlin lowered himself.

"Health and success attend your majesty, all your days," said Merlin.

"And you," returned the king. "We have met before, I think."

"Your majesty has an excellent memory. Once, we met when I made a spectacle of myself at the Great Council; the next time, we spoke briefly upon the battlements of Mai Dun."

"I recall that," said Coroticos. "But I also recall a path of blood that one young warrior cut through his foes on the hill outside Mai Dun."

Merlin's eyes flickered down for a moment. "Sometimes," he said slowly, "I too think of that. I am ill-suited to the battlefield, I'm afraid." He shrugged, and turned his eyes directly on Coroticos. "But you, your majesty. You are not ill-suited to the field of battle. If report has been just, you have distinguished yourself many times in the eight years since Mai Dun."

"Long have been the years since Mai Dun," said Coroticos, reaching into a belt-pouch and drawing out a folded parchment, "and bitter the struggle. And we are not the only ones whose fame has spread. We have heard much of Merlin the Seer, though I did not know until now that I had met you before. Not a swain tending his sheep upon the slopes of Eryri, nor high-born prince of many castles does not know of the Seeing One of Afallach, he who sees what is yet to come. Is it a true gift?"

"In nature's infinite book," replied Merlin, "I can read a little. But the Sight is a fickle gift. Sometimes it gives, sometimes it takes; it is not mine to know when or where."

Coroticos moved over to the desk in the centre of the room. Merlin joined him. The High King moved aside the writing implements that lay upon the desk and spread out the parchment. It was a map of the Island of the Mighty, from the archipelago of Lyonesse in the southwest to the border between Cameliard and Lothian. Coroticos pointed to Caer Wisc, the principal stronghold of Cornwall, and traced a line north to Linnuis in Cameliard.

"This is Fosse Way," he explained. "It is the frontier between the Roman province of Britannia, and what remains of the Island of the Mighty."

"I have seen it, sire," said Merlin. "I have even traveled beyond it."

"Then Merlin the Seer has been places that Coroticos the High King has greatly desired to visit," said the High King. "In four years, not a Roman has dared to stir beyond Fosse Way. We have kept their advance in check, raiding their frontier forts, ambushing a patrol or pay-wagon, and then retreating into the mists, gone as quickly as we appeared."

"It is an excellent strategy," commented Merlin. "Perhaps it will be too inconvenient for Claudius to hold onto this particular province."

Coroticos gave a sneering laugh. "Emperor Claudius, we hear, is worshipped as a god in Camulod of the Eicenni. 'King' Prasutagos leads the worship, no doubt."

"But not his wife," snapped Merlin.

Coroticos looked at him with eyes narrowed to slits. "Perhaps not," he said. "Anyway, it seems that things are changing. Intelligence has reached me that the Romans are going to march upon my army, and force us into a pitched battle."

"You cannot win such a battle," said Merlin, shivering to think of the remorseless shield-wall at Mai Dun.

"I think perhaps I could," answered Coroticos. "I know their tactics now, and I can wear them down by ambush and night attack as they approach. I shall draw them in among the mountains of Northgalis, and finish them off there, once and for all. Better men than Suetonius Paulinus, this new governor, have foundered in those valleys."

"But your Majesty has not the numbers for a pitched battle," Merlin pointed out. "Why not continue to harry the enemy, without offering battle? It has worked so far. You cannot hope to reduce his numbers so drastically as to stand a chance in a full battle. All you can do is make his occupation of Britain too inconvenient to maintain. But when the day of battle comes, the final confrontation between the forces of Rome and Britain, then you will be wiped out."

Coroticos did not speak at once. His fingers clenched and unclenched. At last, he said, "The men who are with me now are but a small portion of those who have been promised me."

"By whom?"

"Cartimandua of Cameliard and Grwhyr of Cambria."

Merlin bit his knuckle thoughtfully. "How can his Majesty's humble servant be of assistance to him?" he asked.

Coroticos drew a deep breath. "Merlin," he said, "will I have the victory?"

Suddenly, Merlin felt the deepest pity for the High King that he had known for any man. He reached out and touched him on the shoulder, saying, "Whatever path you choose, your men will follow you."

"Aye," said Coroticos, "even to the death. That is the problem. I don't know that it is right to lead such men to certain death. I remember my words at Mai Dun, and I do not think I was wrong. But I do not think I could say them again." His head was bowed so low that his face almost touched the map before him. He squeezed his eyes shut, and slammed his fist into the table. "Claudius," he said between clenched teeth, "why do you, with all your grand possessions, still covet our poor huts?"

"This you know already," interjected Gwelydd. "Claudius' claim to the imperial throne was tenuous—he was elevated by his own Praetorian Guard, who had just assassinated his predecessor, Caligula. He needed a military victory to secure his power. And he cannot give up Britain and retain his power. Great King, do not forsake your plan. It is a good one. Once Claudius is succeeded by another, one who does not need to maintain Britain, the troops will be withdrawn. Make it too inconvenient for Rome to hold onto this poor little province."

But Merlin shook his head. "Claudius was old when he was made emperor; now he is close to death. But if reports be right, he is preparing another to take his place, a man called Nero, and this man is more like Caligula than any of the other emperors. He is a madman. And who can tell what a madman might think?"

"Do you suggest open war, then?" wondered Gwelydd.

Merlin bit on his knuckles again. "I do not know what to suggest." He looked at the High King.

Coroticos remained for a long while silent and stooped over the map, till at last he straightened up and looked across the map at Merlin. "What should I do, then, if I do not meet Suetonius Paulinus in open battle?" he wondered. "Should I disband my men, and dissolve before the Romans like mountain mist before the rising sun? Then, at least, we could come again together to continue the fight later. Or should I march south and east, picking up reinforcements from Cambria and Cameliard? What should I do, Merlin?"

Merlin fixed Coroticos with his eye. It gleamed in the torchlight, like the eye of a bird of prey. He said, "Unless I mistake my guess, his Majesty has already made up his mind."

"Yes," said Coroticos, with a slow nod. "It is to be reinforcements. But what of the victory? Can you see the outcome, Lord of Prophecies?"

Merlin was silent for a long time. He looked down and pondered the map, tracing lines back and forth across the face of Britain. He finished in Caermyrddin, where his finger stayed for long moments before he jabbed it with a decisive gesture.

"I cannot answer at once," said Merlin, "but I shall seek an answer from my attendant spirits, and tomorrow, at this hour of the day, if they give me an answer, I shall be ready to pass it on to you. But I should warn you, this gift of mine is fickle, as I have said. I do not know when or why the gods will speak to me, and sometimes, most of the time, they speak in riddles whose meaning only comes clear when the events to which they refer have passed."

"Any guidance is better than none," answered Coroticos.

"Then let us speak of these matters again tomorrow," said Merlin and, bowing, took his leave.

Not half an hour later, he was upon the crest of the Hill of Afallach, and his aspect was dark.

II

Merlin spent an hour in private conversation with the High King the following day, and none ever discovered what words had been between them; but when they emerged from Merlin's hut at the eastern end of Afallach, Coroticos inclined his head to Merlin, who bowed before his liege lord, and they parted company. Coroticos swung himself into his saddle.

"I ride east," he said to Gwelydd, who stood outside the Cave of Knowledge, leaning heavily upon his oaken staff. "I shall seek aid from Cartimandua. And yes, I shall be wary. I know her reputation of old."

"Go then," said Gwelydd, "and the gods go with you; the future of the Island of the Mighty is in your keeping."

Coroticos dug his spurs into his horse, and at once they were off, vanishing among the trees. Stillness returned to Afallach, as if the horsemen had never been there.

At the sound of another hoofbeat, Gwelydd turned and saw Merlin approach. "So, my son," said Gwelydd, "you too will leave us?"

"For a time," replied Merlin. "I shall return to Caermyrddin, where I have not been these eight years. I have a message to my uncle from the High King."

"What do your prophetic eyes see, Merlin?" wondered Gwelydd. "Do you foresee victory?"

"I see only what the gods choose to reveal to me," replied Merlin. "My advice must still be based upon likelihood, and I cannot guarantee success. I think we have little enough hope. But little enough is not none. Hope is not utterly dead until we are dead. Farewell!"

He shook the reins of his horse, and in a moment he too was gone. Gwelydd turned, an acolyte at his elbow, and with slow and painful steps, returned to the Cave of Knowledge.

* * *

Caermyrddin sat exactly where it had always sat, looking out over the Tywi estuary as its custom had always been. Nothing had altered from the image Merlin had long cherished in his memory. In the past eight years, he had traveled to many different places. He had wandered across the barren landscape of Hath Tír Iath, and crouched in the cold hall of the Lord of Ila. He had waded through snow that came to his waist among the Lorne Hills of Lothian, and swum the frigid waters of the River Dubglas to reach Dun Guinnion. He had stood on the windswept cliffs near Tintagil, and gazed out over the western sea, which men said had no end. He had even crossed the Narrow Sea to the archipelago of Lyonesse, which men shore up against the encroaching sea. And he had crossed the Fosse Way, and looked on the new cities, the cities with the straight roads and new buildings, and strange, new names: Camulodunum, Londinium, Venta, Durnovaria. It was good to look down upon Caermyrddin, and know that some things had not changed.

Merlin drew his hood over his head, and blended with the shadows a moment until he had passed by the guards and into the fortress. He strode into the great hall, and lurked for a while in the shadows of a corner, watching his uncle at work. The responsibilities of the throne had pressed many years upon the head of Grwhyr. For a moment, Merlin had almost thought he was looking upon his grandfather, and he shook his head sadly.

Merlin lowered his hood and stepped out of the shadows. Nobody saw him at first, and he did nothing to draw attention to himself. Then the man who was speaking with Grwhyr on some manorial matter caught sight of him out of the corner of his eye, and fell silent. Grwhyr followed his gaze, and his eyes fell upon Merlin.

Merlin stepped before the dais and dropped to one knee. "Your Majesty!" he declared.

Grwhyr continued to stare at him in wonder. "Arise," he said, "Emrys . . . is it?"

"It is, my lord," answered Merlin, rising to his feet, "and your humble servant, now as ever."

Grwhyr's face broke out into a smile, and he descended from the dais, clasping Merlin to himself in a firm embrace. "My nephew shall not be my servant," he said. "Meldred!" The man who had been speaking to him looked up. He was young, no more than sixteen or seventeen years old, and looked much as Merlin remembered Grwhyr in his youth. "Come, and greet your cousin." Meldred and Merlin shook hands.

"The last time I saw you," Merlin said to Meldred, "you were fighting the other boys with a wooden sword."

"I have graduated to iron now, you will observe," said Meldred, tapping the hilt of the sword that hung from a baldric slung from his right shoulder.

"It is too true," said Merlin wistfully. "Time goes ever as he will."

"Emrys," said Grwhyr, "we did not expect to see you again. Our last meeting was on a bitter occasion, and bitter too have been the years since then. What need brings you to Caermyrddin?"

"I come as a messenger only, my lord," answered Merlin. "Coroticos, High King of the Island of the Mighty, sends greetings to Grwhyr, king of Cambria. I am the instrument of his pleasure, the bearer of news, and a most humble supplicant to your Majesty."

"Then we must talk at once, and in private," said Grwhyr, turning to dismiss the men who had gathered about him.

* * *

Half an hour later, Merlin and Grwhyr sat opposite one another across one of the tables in the hall, a half-empty flagon of wine and two pewter cups between them. Grwhyr tipped the dregs down his throat and poured himself another generous cupful. Merlin held his hand across his own cup in refusal.

"So," said Grwhyr, "we put all our gold on one horse. Is that the way of it?"

"That is the High King's decision."

Grwhyr cast his eyes downwards. "It was also his decision at Mai Dun," he said, "where my father, your grandfather, fell."

"I was there," Merlin reminded him. "Our case now is not so hopeless as it was at Mai Dun. At Mai Dun, we hoped for death rather than surrender. Now, eight years of harrying the Roman frontier has weakened our foe. I think it will take but a minor victory on our part to make Claudius—or Nero, more likely—wonder seriously whether it is worth hanging onto the province of Britannia. It does not need to be a complete victory. A minor one will suffice."

Grwhyr looked penetratingly at his nephew. "Emrys," he said, "since the time of Mai Dun, stories have been told of a great prophet at Afallach, a man known as Merlin. I know not the truth of the matter, but if you are he, I understand you have great powers. I remember once, when you were a child, and you told me of a dream you had had. I said nothing at the time, but it seemed to me that the dream was a prophecy. You dreamed of two dragons fighting each other, and while they fought, an eagle swooped upon them and killed them both. Could you ask for anything clearer than that? And now it is coming true. One dragon dwells now with the eagle, for Cymbeline is in Rome. But what of the other dragon? Will Coroticos be slain or captured? He has avoided this these eight years, and now he changes his strategy. Why? Was it by your advice?"

"I give no advice," answered Merlin. "I tell the truth, and let men make up their own minds about what they should do. Do you think the gods speak clearly to me? Upon what foundation could I build my advice? Coroticos made up his own mind—it was made up before he consulted me, he merely wanted me to confirm his choice."

"But is his choice the right one?" asked Grwhyr.

Merlin gave the question some thought. Then he said, "It is the right decision because it forces a conclusion. He has chosen a path, and will no longer be hesitating at the crossroads. Whether other men will follow his path with confidence is a matter yet to be seen."

Grwhyr pursed his lips and narrowed his eyes. "Emrys," he said, "you have become skilled in not being pinned down. Were these times of peace, you would find yourself useful at court."

Merlin raised his cup in a salute. "I thank you," he said, grinning, "though I think that was an insult. All right, then, if you want my opinion: this course is most desperately taken, and the chances of following it to the end and coming home unscathed are small. But since the High King has committed himself to the course, I am trying to ensure that his chances of success are as high as they can be. I think he has a chance of success, if the armies of Cameliard and Cambria stand with him."

Grwhyr looked up. A light was beginning to smoulder in his eyes. "Can he do it?" he asked. "Can he unite his armies thus?"

"Even now," said Merlin, "he rides for Caer Ebrauc with what men he has. The offer has been made; it requires but yourself and the High King to meet there the army which Cartimandua has amassed. Together, my lord, we can perhaps shoot an arrow at the eagles, pluck a few feathers from their wings. At the least, we can make Britannia a costly province to administer."

Grwhyr looked away. The fire in his eyes went out, like someone stamping upon a campfire. Yet, Merlin thought, the embers were still glowing when he looked back at him. "This is a thing we must discuss in council," said Grwhyr. "In the meantime, nephew, you must be weary after your journey. You should rest. And I think your mother would be glad to see you again."

"Most noble king," said Merlin, rising from the seat and bowing, "I most humbly take my leave."

He turned and left the hall. Behind him, Grwhyr sat long in reflection.

* * *

The council met the next day, and on the day following, the muster began. Grwhyr sent messengers into all corners of Cambria and, one by one, they returned with the replies. Pwyll, Lord of Dyfed, promised eight hundred foot soldiers, two hundred men on horses; Maelgwn, lord of Gwynedd, promised four hundred men on foot, two hundred cavalry; Glynn, lord of Deheubarth, sent word that he would meet Grwhyr at Caer Ebrauc with three hundred foot warriors and eighty horsemen.

"Is not this a kingly company?" demanded Grwhyr, turning to Merlin. "What do you think? Shall we teach these Roman eagles how to fly?"

Merlin looked at the back of the messenger who had just come from mountainous Deheubarth. There were few people living in that central region at all, and Glynn's offer had been perhaps more generous than was truly in his power. And it was common, Merlin knew, for the offer to be twice as strong as the reality turned out to be. Merlin said, "We shall need more than this, my lord."

Grwhyr shrugged. "Well," he said, "it is fewer than half the messengers who have returned to us so far. And there are Cartimandua's men to be added to our number. No, Merlin. My father's shade shall sleep easy soon."

Merlin left the hall and went out into the sunshine of the June day. Men were practising arms outside, and the musical ring of sword on sword and the dull thudding as the blades pounded into the wooden shields mixed with the laughter of a group of men supping ale before the doors of the hall, and the clucking of chickens from the coop. Merlin watched the combat practice for a while. His mind went back, back over the years, and he saw in his mind's eye his grandfather, his eyes turned down to gaze in disbelief at the sword-tip that protruded from his chest, and Cathbhad the bard, crumpling forward over the Roman soldier's impersonal thrust.

Merlin's reverie was disturbed by a "pruk-pruk-pruk" noise, a pig-like grunting behind him. A raven was standing on the door-post of the great hall, regarding Merlin with a shining, intelligent eye. "On whom will you be feasting, I wonder?" said Merlin.

A new noise distracted Merlin from the bird. Another messenger had ridden in through the gates, and was even now leaping from the saddle to hasten towards the hall. Merlin frowned. There was something in the slope of his shoulders, the set of his jaw. It did not seem that he bore good news and, as he began to climb the steps to the great hall, Merlin put out a hand to stop him.

"From where have you come, friend?" he asked.

"From Rudglann," answered the messenger, avoiding contact with Merlin's eyes.

"What news?" asked Merlin.

"Very ill news, my lord, which I shall deliver to the king." The messenger disappeared into the hall, Merlin following him. The raven's beady eye followed Merlin into the hall.

The messenger dropped to one knee before the king.

"Rise, Ruthin," said Grwhyr, "and deliver your message. What news from the lord of Rudglann?"

The messenger took a deep breath. "Evil news, my lord," he said.

"What, will he not assist us in our need?" demanded the king.

"He will not, my lord, not one man, not one horse, not one weapon. But this is not the evil news I bring."

"There is worse?" Grwhyr's voice was a whisper, and the hall was completely silent. "What worse could there be?"

"My lord," said the messenger, "the High King is ambushed by the Romans, his men cut down, and he himself fled, alone and unaided, to Cameliard."

The expression on Grwhyr's face was frozen into an impassive mask. He sat silent for a long while. Then he asked, "When? Where?"

"A fourteen-night ago," answered the messenger, "near Dinas Eryri. This news I had from the lord of Rudglann, and this was why he refused to aid us. I believe he wants peace with Rome."

"So the lord of Rudglann would make alliances with our enemies, break the oath of allegiance he swore to us upon his very sword!" Grwhyr jumped to his feet. "May the gods rain down curses upon his head!" he cried. "May his wife be barren, his fields blighted!" Grwhyr looked down upon the messenger. "But are you sure the High King is defeated thus? You had only the word of a traitor that it is so."

"Nay, dread lord," answered the messenger, shaking his head slowly, "I returned home by way of Dinas Eryri, and saw the graves. And the grass all about was still stained with blood."

Grwhyr's eyes flickered. His moment of passion was over, and now there was nothing to reveal his emotions. He said, "Go now, and refresh yourself. These news are ill, but you have done your duty well."

"Thank you, my lord," said the messenger, turning and striding from the hall. Outside, the raven gave a deep croak, and Merlin heard the rustle of its wing-feathers as it took flight.

III

Hoofs clattered over the wooden bridge and echoed under the arch of the double gates of Caer Ebrauc. Citizens hauling on carts, driving beasts, or tending their meagre gardens stopped in their work to watch as a score and a half riders thundered into the city. At their head rode a man who wore a crown, and beside him, someone else—a man with dark eyes, thought the citizens of Caer Ebrauc; but the riders were gone before anyone could see much of him.

The way had been long for the Cambrians, through cold and treeless uplands, and over windswept moors clad all in heather and broom, but now they were arrived at Caer Ebrauc. It was not the principal city of Cameliard, for that honour belonged to Caer Luel, in the far north. But Cartimandua had spent most of her time here, for her third husband, Gwenutios, held sway in the north. As they rode, Merlin pondered the strange story of Queen Cartimandua of Cameliard. Her first husband had died in a hunting accident, and her second had been king of Cameliard. When he died under mysterious circumstances—some whispered about poison in the gloomy corners of Caer Ebrauc—Cartimandua had stayed on the throne and married one of Cameliard's most powerful barons, Gwenutios; but he had left her when he had found her in bed with his chief druid. That druid was still her consort, though he dared not call himself king. Gwenutios and Cartimandua lived in a perpetual rivalry of the kind that sustained itself. It was hatred, thought Merlin, that kept them apart, but hatred also that kept them alive.

Caer Ebrauc was not a big city, not an impressive city. The dwellings on either side of the road that led to the citadel were low, with roofs of dirty-coloured straw and wattle-and-daub walls. Mangy dogs and dirty children played in the streets. Winds out of the north were channeled along the streets, bringing with them a cold that chilled to the bone. It had rained recently, and muddy water had gathered in the wagon-ruts and hollows in the road. It seemed to Merlin that he was picking up more mud on his clothes than he ever had in the wilderness. He looked about him at the tough little huts, crouching against the elements, each with its small garden of turnips and other roots, occasionally a skinny pig or goat. What did one do in a place like this? Survival was hard enough, but why did one even *want* to survive?

Cartimandua stood on the steps of her citadel, flanked on one side by Coroticos, on the other by a man leaning on a staff of oak, a wolf's pelt draped over his shoulders. This, Merlin knew, was Felocatos, former druid to Cartimandua's second husband. Cartimandua had changed little since Merlin had last seen her, at the great council: a wild face, which had once been beautiful, and now was as lonely as the crags and windswept moors that surrounded her palace, but kept in check by a powerful will. There was power in the line of her jaw, and on her hip she wore a sword that some warriors could not wield. Merlin studied her face as the Cambrians drew rein before the palace, and wondered what it had been witness to. What schemes, what plots, what acts of hatred had those eyes seen, to which that calculating mind had carefully suppressed any response? She was a powerful ally, thought Merlin; but she would be a terrifying enemy.

Grwhyr, dismounting, threw himself at the feet of Coroticos. "My lord!" he cried.

Coroticos reached down and, very gently, raised him to his feet. "The gods give you blessings, Grwhyr," said the High King. "You come at the most desperate hour of all. Come, enter the hall. We have much to discuss."

* * *

The wine flowed freely at the feast that night, and there was great singing in the hall. Merlin watched the revelry with a sour expression, and withdrew himself into one of the alcoves set off the hall. It did not seem fitting to him that they should celebrate. The battle ahead was a desperate one, they had suffered a telling defeat once, and Merlin's Sight told him nothing of the likely outcome. He tried one more time to see into the future. Sitting in his alcove, Merlin closed his eyes and sent out the fingers of his mind, groping into the future.

At first, all was dark, all was misty. Then a shape emerged from the darkness, and became a woman's face. Her hair was as black as the berries of the nightshade, her skin pale as parchment. It was a face Merlin had not seen in eight years. He had almost forgotten about Morgana.

"Where have you been these many years, Morgana?" he asked.

"I have watched you, Merlin Emrys," replied Morgana. When her lips parted to speak, they glistened softly. Deep red they were, like blood on snow.

"I have been tardy. My will has slept these eight years, and I have but dabbled while the secret of Excalibur has lain hidden."

Morgana nodded. "You have wandered from your path, but I can guide you once more."

"I have sought the sword, in so many places, but I have not found that which I sought."

"Keep searching. This battle to come is nothing, less than nothing. Whatever sways you from your path is a hindrance, howsoever noble it may seem. The ways of kings will be but vanity until Excalibur is found. And then . . . and *then*, Merlin Emrys, you and I shall raise up a dynasty that will last until the ending of the world."

The vision faded, and Merlin was back in his alcove.

All the warriors of Cambria, all the bodyguard of Coroticos, were asleep. The silence in the hall, after the boisterous feast, was uncanny; yet the tapers burned still, and the hall was filled with light. Merlin felt his scalp prickle. Had his vision lasted so very long? Was the feast over, and the men gone to their rest? In growing alarm, Merlin scanned the hall with his eyes. Some of the Cambrians had collapsed on the floor. Others had risen from the board and walked a few paces before crumpling into a pile. Others had just put their faces down upon the table before them, and now snored softly. But the Cameliardi were awake! Merlin looked down at his own wine goblet, untouched before him, and slowly lifted it to his nostrils. He set it down quickly.

Cartimandua's men stood at the portals of the hall, surveying the slumbering Cambrians impassively. Their swords were unsheathed. Cartimandua made a quick motion with her hand, and the men began moving through the hall, plunging their swords into the sleeping Britons. Merlin almost cried out. His hand flew to his mouth, and he felt his stomach twitch. The Cameliardi worked meticulously and swiftly, plunging in their swords, leaning close to be certain that the life had quite gone before moving on and repeating the whole grisly routine.

Cartimandua spoke, and Merlin turned to watch her, aghast. She spoke in Latin, slowly, growling almost like a bear. Her tone was precise, but laced with contempt which threatened constantly to spill over into her words, but which never did. To her right sat Felocatos the druid; on the other side, immovable as the statue to the god Claudius that Merlin had seen in Caer Camulod, was a Roman general.

"This one is Coroticos," said Cartimandua, pointing, "and this one, Grwhyr, king of Cambria."

"Excellent," replied the general, "excellent. You have indeed kept your part of the bargain, Cartimandua. My emperor wishes for Coroticos to be kept alive."

"And the fine young Grwhyr?"

The Roman shrugged. "He might be useful." He snapped his fingers and beckoned, and half a dozen Roman soldiers stepped forward. At a curt command, the legionnaires set about binding Coroticos and Grwhyr hand and foot. The soldiers were ungentle in their handling, and Coroticos stirred as they bound his hands behind his back; but he did not awaken. Merlin shrank back into the alcove, a shadow among shadows.

"Wine, my dear Suetonius?" asked Cartimandua, pouring three cups out. "It is Gaulish—I get it from a trader who deals often in Cornwall. It has a very Roman flavour. It should not be too taxing to your palate."

"You Britons must become accustomed to drinking wines from all parts of the Empire," replied Suetonius off-handedly. They sipped their wine a few moments, watching the business in the hall in silence.

"Such sights as these cannot be unfamiliar to you, Suetonius," said Felocatos. "It is not, after all, much different from . . . what do you call that punishment you have for criminals?"

"Crucifixion," replied the Roman, flicking his eyes for a moment over at the druid. "Yes, crucifixion is a very great deterrent to rebels." They fell silent once more. After a while, Suetonius gave a small sigh. "Rome will reward you well for this service, Cartimandua," he said. "I think you will be allowed to keep your kingdom."

The queen nodded. "Thank you, Your Excellency. Your Excellency's generosity is without bounds. I shall be allowed to keep what is my own!" She paused a second. "Your Excellency is aware of the rest of my price."

Suetonius nodded. "I shall leave three of my best cohorts with you, and then you can seek out this wayward husband of yours, and deal with him as you will. Cameliard is your kingdom, after all. The Emperor does not wish to dictate policy to neighbouring monarchies. Only, do not shame my legion. They fight best using their own tactics. Do not insist on chariot races and such like."

"I shall use whatever means work best to destroy Gwenutios."

"Well, my officers shall stay with their men. You have them for the year, Cartimandua. Pray to whatever gods you believe in that your business be done by then, for the Emperor needs his legions, all parts of every one of them. The Hispania will be needed."

"Fear not, commander, that I will ill-use your soldiers." Cartimandua smiled. "I have seen battle before." She raised her wine-cup, and they drank a toast while the Cameliardi warriors slew the last of the Cambrians in their sleep and reported their duty done.

"Is that all of them?" demanded Cartimandua.

"Aye," replied the warrior, wiping blood from his blade with a napkin he took from the table. "None have escaped us."

“Where is the prophet?” asked Felocatos, rising from his seat.

“The prophet?” said Suetonius, interest in his voice.

“Aye,” said Felocatos. “The prophet is the most dangerous of them all.”

Cartimandua glanced at Felocatos, her eyes flashing a moment, and then back at Suetonius. “My loose-tongued druid speaks of the young man who made a scene at the great council before the fortuitous and most reasonable invasion of this land by Your Excellency’s army,” said Cartimandua. Suetonius arched his eyebrow at her sarcasm, but Cartimandua ignored him. She sounded irritated. “He was among the Cambrians.” To the warrior, she said in Brythonic, “Show me his body.”

“Show us his corpse,” said Felocatos, moving closer to the warrior, “or show us your own. He cannot be allowed to live. None of them can.”

Merlin’s throat was dry; he dared not move an inch. His breathing seemed intolerably loud in his ears, like the rasping of a file in a smithy.

The warrior shuffled his feet. “I knew of no druid, majesty,” he said. “I was careful to note every new face at the feast, and every one I noted lies cold in this hall.”

Felocatos made a contemptuous noise. “Then you missed one face,” he said. “A young man, with black eyes and a nose like a hawk’s.”

“Perhaps he was taking a piss,” remarked Cartimandua in Brythonic. “Anyway, he must have been outside the hall. He will not be unconscious. He might put up a fight.”

Felocatos’ eyes widened. “Perhaps he foresaw what would happen! Find him at once. He cannot have got far.”

Cartimandua nodded. Cameliardi warriors hurried from the hall, bowing as they did so. Suetonius threw the dregs of his wine down his throat with an air of finality, and stood, stretching his limbs so that they cracked. “The imperial—and divine—will of the Emperor is that Rome’s final victory over the province of Britannia should be celebrated with a parade through Rome. As our first ally in Britannia, you are entitled to attend.”

"What great pleasure it would give me!" said the queen in Latin. "But, alas, I have matters to attend in my own kingdom which, believe me, will also give me great satisfaction."

"Then I shall convey your greetings to the Emperor. My congratulations on successfully accomplishing our task." He motioned to one of his guards. "Bring the prisoners," he said, and strode from the hall.

Two legionnaires stepped forward and seized Coroticos and hauled him upright. Suddenly, his eyes opened, and he looked left and right, his eyes wide like those of a hunted animal. He froze and, slowly, his eyes pressed shut and stayed closed for a moment. When he opened them to look upon Cartimandua, they burned like gledes.

"Cartimandua," he sneered, "is there enough blood for you here, you damned witch? And is it you would make treaties with our enemies?"

Cartimandua regarded him for a long moment. Her frame seemed to quiver, almost imperceptibly. At length, she spoke. "No," she said with regal indifference, "only with *your* enemies." With a quick hand motion, she dismissed the legionnaires, who followed the general, dragging the fallen High King of the Island of the Mighty between them. Two more legionnaires picked up Grwhyr and carried him after. And then there were only Britons in the hall.

"This business is well concluded, your majesty," said Felocatos ingratiatingly. "Once we have finished off Gwenutios, Cameliard will be the most powerful kingdom in the Island of the Mighty."

Sunlight peered in at the window opposite Merlin's hiding place, and early grey light touched the cold shapes that lay in bloody sleep about the hall. A number of servants entered and started dragging the bodies away. Others swept the rushes, dashed water over the pools of blood, and mopped the stinking filth away. The shadows in the hall began to recede, and a pool of light crept across the floor towards Merlin. The queen sat still on her throne, the expression on her parchment face inscrutable. Merlin shrank further into the narrow confines of the recess where he had hidden himself, but the light was only an inch away from his foot. He cast up a prayer to Argante, to protect him until nightfall, when he could make good his escape, but the treacherous gold of the sun crept nearer until it touched his toe. Then his prayer changed: "Let me live, Argante," he whispered in his soul, "let me live until I can have my vengeance upon the witch-queen of Cameliard!" His limbs began to ache, but he dared not move; then the sun climbed beyond the upper rim of the window, and the shadows began to lengthen once more.

The queen had left the hall, but now returned to deal with the administrative business of the day. In the very hall where she had betrayed the last of the Britonnic warbands, and turned her High King over to the common enemy, Cartimandua dealt with the petty affairs of her kingdom. A peasant was wrangling with another over ownership of a cow; another wanted to build a fence on the edge of the land he held; a third had been accused of seducing the miller's daughter. The protective shadow about Merlin lengthened, but Merlin stayed stock still, his sinews screaming at him, the dread of discovery sweating from every pore of his body. He breathed a prayer of thanks to Argante, for most of the morning has passed, and no one had yet looked his way.

One of the warriors came back from the manhunt, bowing low before Cartimandua. "Majesty," he reported, "I rode as far as a man on foot could go in a day, and no sign did I see of the prophet. No horses are missing from the stable."

"Then perhaps another will find him," mused Cartimandua, and dismissed the man.

Merlin's body suddenly stiffened. Images began to crowd into his mind, and he felt his mind sliding away from him.

"Not now, Morgana, not now!" he whispered. "Send me no visions now!"

Was this Morgana's way of punishing him for his tardiness? he wondered. I must resist it, he thought urgently. He fixed his gaze upon a wall-hanging opposite his hiding place. It was a hunting scene, where brightly-robed hunters pursued a stag through a maze of intertwined branches. He concentrated upon it; but even as he did so, the shapes began to move, to change, and the tapestry grew until it surrounded him, until the flanks of the stag moved with its breath, and the leaves rustled in the breeze. Merlin clenched his fists. His nails dug into the palms of his hands.

"Poison!" he cried suddenly and shrilly. "Poison flows through the lair of the lioness!"

Every man in the hall fell silent and turned towards Merlin, who had jerked into plain sight, his arms twitching madly as if under the blows of some invisible assailant, his spine contorted and writhing. Cartimandua rose slowly from her throne. Felocatos' eyes were keen, and he watched Merlin intently.

"The hunters cannot take her by might," Merlin went on, his eyes glassy, "so they lay traps, to take her by stealth. It is the wolf who sets the trap, and its mate who pours the poisonous liquor down the lioness' throat, when the lioness lies bleeding in the trap!"

Merlin came to himself, drenched in sweat, and found that two servants held him securely before the throne of Cartimandua, queen of Cameliard. Her lip curled upwards, but her eyes remained blank. "So, there you are, prophet, lurking in my hall, while my leaden-arsed servants seek you through the land!"

Merlin sagged between the servants, for now, he saw, all was lost.

"Put him to death," ordered Felocatos. "Delay not, but kill him at once!"

One of the servants that was holding Merlin whipped out a dagger and raised it high to plunge it into his breast. Merlin closed his eyes, and waited for the end.

IV

The knife-point hung poised, high above Merlin's throat; the servant's hand twitched as he began to bring it down. But the blow did not fall.

"Stay your hand!" rang out a voice. Merlin's eyes snapped open. It was Cartimandua who had spoken. She had risen from her throne, and now descended from the dais and stood very close to Merlin. His nose wrinkled.

"To what or whom does the *wolf* refer?" asked the queen of Cameliard.

"Majesty," said Felocatos, stepping forward, "Cartimandua, this is Emrys, the unwanted brat of the daughter of the late King Rhydderch. You heard his ravings at the Great Council. Pay no heed to him."

"Was he not in Afallach?" demanded Cartimandua. "I think I should at least listen to what he has to say."

"He was in Afallach," admitted Felocatos, "but he learned nothing of the ways of the druid. This prophecy signifies nothing."

Merlin turned his eyes towards Felocatos and noticed, as he had when he had first arrived in Caer Ebrauc but not since, that the druid wore a wolf'-s pelt as part of his regalia. He wondered what on earth he could have said in his prophecy. *Tylweth*, he prayed, in the privacy of his heart, *mother of rhymes, give me a quick tongue.*

Cartimandua said, "If the prophecy signifies nothing, that will soon appear, will it not? Come, Felocatos. Make a guess as to how his words might be interpreted. Do it for me."

There was a long pause. Cartimandua and the druid regarded each other. There was a haughty coolness to Cartimandua, but Merlin saw that, slowly, fear crept into Felocatos' eyes, and there crouched, poised, ready to spring inward to maul his soul. At last, the druid reached a decision. He blinked, and the fear was veiled. "Well, whelp of Cambria," he said, his businesslike manner contrasting with his insults, "what is your reading of the prophecy? What does the wolf signify?"

"You are a druid," sneered Merlin in return. "Cannot you say yourself?"

Felocatos stiffened, and looked long and hard at him. "Ignorant boy," he said, his lip curling, "innocent in the ways of the world! To challenge the wisdom of one who has twice your experience! I had my schooling under the shadow of the Sacred Hill—where you lived and learned little. Oh yes, boy, I know your history, and a good many other things!" He took a step backwards. "This is futile, majesty. It is clear the boy knows nothing—he is a dreamer."

Cartimandua held up a hand to stay his speech. She resumed her seat upon the throne. Felocatos, with his back to her, seemed to cringe. A nerve in Cartimandua's cheek twitched, as if she were pressing down upon a heavy weight that threatened to consume her. She said, slowly and deliberately, "I have still not been satisfied, and I should like to know what your great wisdom, Felocatos, can reveal to us about this young man's prophecies. I would like to hear from both of you. And I wonder, Felocatos, whose explanation will please me most?" Leaning forward in her throne, she inquired sharply: "It is told me you have the Sight, young man. Is that true?"

"I do, dread queen," answered Merlin.

"Then how do you explain your prophecy about the wolf?"

Merlin delved into his mind, rummaged through it with mounting desperation. He could remember nothing of the prophecy—he seldom could.

"He is a charlatan," insisted Felocatos, turning to face Cartimandua. "He learned nothing in Afallach, and rejected the druids' ways. His ways are nothing, nothing at all!"

"I will hear an interpretation of this prophecy," Cartimandua swore, quiet danger lacing her voice as the sleeping draught had recently laced the wine of the Cambrians. "And I will hear from you first, Felocatos of the deep wisdom."

Felocatos' mouth opened and snapped shut two or three times. Then he drew himself up, and his voice took on a learned and indifferent air. "The intention of the prophecy is transparent enough," he said. "The lioness is your majesty. The wolf signifies some Briton whom this knave threatens will attempt to slay you with poison."

Merlin became suddenly quite calm. He could feel a coolness spread through his limbs, soothing, calming. Indeed, it was with an effort that he suppressed the urge to smile, for Felocatos had revealed enough of the prophecy that Merlin could feign a knowledge of it.

"And you?" asked the queen, turning to Merlin.

Merlin wet his lips. "Majesty," he said, "my prophecy is true, as all my prophecies have been; but this man lies as to its true meaning. For in my prophecies I see no fixed future, but warn of dangers that might be. It is true that the lioness refers to your majesty, but more as a warning to beware of traitors in your midst. Beware of the ambitious one, who wears the wolf's pelt, seeking to slay the lioness and take the throne himself." He paused a moment. "Felocatos," he said, "has taken a new lover."

"He lies!" cried Felocatos. "How can you doubt my love for you, Cartimandua? Do not listen to the jealous rantings of this whelp of Afallach!"

"I have no doubts about your loyalty, my dear Felocatos," said Cartimandua. "Not any more." She was silent for a long time, her eyes upon Merlin. At last, she rose, saying, "Young man, you speak the truth about traitors close to me. Did *you* not come hither with my enemy? And would you dare to suggest that Felocatos, my most trusted advisor, and most intimate, would be untrue in my service?" Felocatos, moving in close behind her, was openly gloating as she drew her sword. Merlin, knowing the end was near now, stood up straight and held his chin high. He drew in one final breath of sweet air.

Cartimandua turned to Felocatos and, reaching up with her free hand, pulled his face down to hers, kissing him long upon the lips. When they drew apart, a string of saliva hung, glistening, between them. "Felocatos," she said softly, "sweet have been the hours we have spent together. You have been, and are, my true love."

Merlin saw first the face of the druid convulse; next, the crimson point of Cartimandua's sword, protruding from his back. Felocatos twitched again, slumping forward against the queen, who twisted the hilt of her sword with a single, muscular action. The druid's eyes popped up at her. The whites were visible all around the pupils.

"I speak the truth," said Cartimandua, in tones that almost caressed. "I love you, and always will." She kissed the druid again, but Felocatos lost his strength, and their lips drew apart. He sank to the wooden floor among the reddening rushes. Cartimandua looked down at him for a long while. Her fists were clenched. Slowly, she released the tension in her fingers and turned to look at Merlin.

"Many years has this druid served Cameliard," Cartimandua said coolly, "but he served my husband ere he served me, and one can never be sure of those whose allegiance changes so. Long have I suspected the treason of which you speak truly."

Merlin let out his breath, but he did not speak. He regarded Cartimandua with loathing. She stepped up close to him, examining his face minutely. Merlin's nose wrinkled in disgust at the smell. The queen said, "You, though, I trust. You have never switched allegiance, for you have never sworn allegiance to me. There might be a use for you." She walked away, her hand upon the pommel of her sword. She seemed to be thinking deeply upon something. Quite suddenly, she said, "Well, prophet, prophesy. I am about to embark upon an expedition against my former husband, Gwenutios. Shall I have the victory?"

Merlin closed his eyes and stretched out his mind's fingers. He saw an army, marching, a chariot at its head and, standing proudly in the chariot, a woman. But it was not Cartimandua. It was one whom Merlin had not seen in eight years, except at a great distance, and his pulse quickened to behold his beloved Boudicea. How long had it been?

"Is the prophet struck dumb?" sneered Cartimandua.

Merlin opened his eyes. He felt light-headed, as if he were about to pass out. He opened his mouth, and words tumbled out, but he heard them indistinctly, like noises under water. He ceased, and fell backwards against the servant who had been poised to kill him; now the man's hands caught him and guided him gently to the floor, where he sat in a daze, blinking.

Cartimandua nodded, a slow smile spreading across her lips. "Victory to the lioness," she said. "Well, I care not if the fox shall threaten me, and the eagles rescue me, so long as, in the end, victory is mine." She fixed her eyes on Merlin. "Of course," she mused, "you might have said that without having any prophetic powers at all. What shall I do with you, Merlin the Prophet?" She pondered for a while in silence, while Merlin waited, gasping for breath on the floor, his hatred for her growing all the time; at last, looking at the servant, Cartimandua snapped, "Confine him, but do not damage him." She indicated the curled form of Felocatos, the blood drying about it now. "And have that cleaned up," she ordered.

Merlin felt hands grasping him by the arms, yanking him to his feet. A moment later, he was being propelled through the doors of the hall and down some steps into a dreary subterranean chamber.

* * *

The cell into which Merlin was cast was large enough to count three paces either way, and contained a hard cot, a small window, and nothing else. The jailer spat upon the ground where Merlin sprawled, and sneered, "I hope you like your accommodations, prophet." Then he turned and left. Merlin dragged himself out of the filth, sat upon the edge of the cot, his face in his hands, and took stock of the situation.

He was alive, but that was little enough advantage when his king was taken captive and the best men of his nation put to the sword, while he had looked on and done nothing. Merlin flinched under repeated blows from his stinging memory. His fingers closed in slowly, quivering, and his nails dug into the palms of his hands. Beads of blood squeezed out slowly. Quickly, and with bestial movements, Merlin licked away the blood. Some of it smeared across his cheek.

Nothing. Was there nothing he could have done? He remembered the Beltane sacrifice, all those years ago. The pungent smell was still vivid in his memory. He remembered the slaughter of Mai Dun, the twisted arms and legs, the eyes staring up at him vacantly, not like men at all, but like the husks of men, their insides scooped out, the windows of their souls open, revealing nothing. And now, the massacre in the hall of Caer Ebrauc. And was there nothing Merlin could have done? He should have died, his claws in the throat of one of the murderers.

Merlin leaped up from the cot, threw back his head, and let out a terrible wail, a mournful note, ululating through every chamber of the dungeon. He threw himself upon the filthy floor of the cell and let out another pitiful cry.

A clatter of footsteps sounded outside the cell. Merlin's head snapped around, and he let out a feral snarl. At the sound of a key turning in the lock, the jailer barreled in, his eyes wide with fear as he sought the source of the terrible noise.

Merlin sprang at him. The jailer shrieked. Merlin's head flashed downwards, and he sank his teeth into the man's throat. He squealed, the screams bubbling and gurgling as he sank under Merlin's weight.

Merlin fought like a mad beast, ripping with his fingers, biting and tearing with his teeth. The man ceased to struggle long ere other jailers arrived to drag the corpse away. They heaved the door closed with a heavy thud, and turned the key in the lock. Merlin hurled himself at the door, gouging deep lines in the wood with his fingers. His howl shook the dungeon to its roots. Then he sank to the floor, and darkness descended upon him.

* * *

When Merlin came to his senses, he looked down at his hands, and saw them to be smeared with dirt and blood. His eyes widened. What had happened? He rose and cast himself upon the cot.

A moment later, the keys rattled once more in the lock, and the door opened to admit a man almost as large as the doorway. His face was dark with wrath.

"You killed him," he said. "You killed Gwaessaf!" The man grabbed Merlin by the front of his tunic and hauled him to his feet. "It may be that her ladyship wants you kept alive," he said. "And, oh, I'll keep you alive, all right. But only just."

Merlin felt the blow when he was already flying backwards against the wall. He didn't have time to scramble to his feet, before the big man landed a kick on his stomach. Merlin doubled up. Then the blows came fast and heavy, one after another, without any comment from the man at all. When he had finished, the man stepped backwards, panting with the exertion.

"If you think you're in pain," he said, pointing a stubby finger at Merlin, "just think what you did to Gwaessaf!"

Then he left, and the keys rattled once more in the lock.

* * *

There was no food for Merlin that day, nor the day after. On the day after that, a little hatch at the foot of the door snapped open to admit a plate bearing hard bread and cheese, and a cup containing water. Merlin guzzled them down, though they left him almost as hungry as before. The food came regularly after that. It was never good—scraps from the hall, dried or mouldy bread—but it fed the vengeful soul in Merlin's breast. From waking up in the morning to shutting his eyes at night, he had nothing to do but reflect upon what he would do to Cartimandua, if ever he could get out of prison.

The days turned into weeks, the weeks into months. The little square of sky darkened as the year grew old, and Merlin stood under it to freshen his face with the rainwater. But the cell was leaky, and dirty water began to seep in and cover the floor. Merlin huddled on the cot and pulled his knees up under his chin.

His thoughts were not always filled with revenge. Sometimes, he thought of Boudicea, and wondered what she was doing. In the last eight years, when his studies had taken him beyond Fosse Way and into the Roman province of Britannia, Merlin had seen her twice, both times at a great distance, and he had not dared approach closely to speak with her. Age had matured her already considerable beauty, and she had become powerful and self-possessed. It was hard, though, to think of her as he had seen her in his vision, at the head of an army, for Roman rule of Eicenniawn was iron, and the Eicenni had had their weapons confiscated. What was it like, Merlin wondered, to live under Roman rule, when your spirit was wild and untamed, as he knew Boudicea's was?

Then his own spirit would fly about the narrow confines of his prison cell, and he would rattle the bars and rail at his captors; and when he was done railing, he would know that he had done so, but be able to recollect nothing of what had happened.

Then, one cold afternoon—Merlin estimated that it was December, close to the midwinter feast—he heard the tramp of mailed boots outside his cell. His ears pricked up. A voice said, in a harsh form of Latin, "Swords out!" and there was the sound of scraping metal. Keys jangled in the lock.

Merlin shrank back against the grimy wall as the door swung open. There, framed in the light of guttering torches, stood four Roman legionnaires, their swords drawn, their lips parted back from their teeth.

"Seize him," barked their Principal.

The four legionnaires moved into the cell.

V

The legionnaires seized Merlin, hauled him to his feet and shoved him before them, out of the cell and up the gloomy stairs. He could feel the prick of a sword-tip in the small of his back. It was a moment before Merlin realized that they had not killed him, and as they marched him along the dimly-lit passageway, he wondered what was going to happen to him. A door opened before them. Merlin flinched from the brightness of the light, and gasped to suck in a lungful of fresh, cold air.

Snow was on the ground in patches, here and there, and the birch tree in Cartimandua's courtyard was bare and spiky, like an old woman who fancied her allure greater than it was. A raven watched him pass by from among its roots, its eye ironical. Merlin felt like kicking the foul creature, but could not get close. Roman legionnaires stood or sat in small groups or individually throughout the courtyard, stamping their feet or holding their hands out over campfires or braziers full of glowing coals.

What was this all about? Merlin wondered, as the legionnaires took him away from the dungeons. Was this to be his execution? He had no recollection of killing the jailer; was he to be punished for that? Or did Cartimandua want to interrogate him for more prophesies? He thought of Felocatos, lying in a twisted pile in a pool of his own blood, months ago. Was that where Merlin was going?

One of the legionnaires pushed open the door to the hall, and propelled Merlin across the floor to the dais. Merlin raised his eyes.

Cartimandua and Merlin regarded each other for a long while in silence. She had laid a sword across her knees. The blade, Merlin noticed, was notched, blunted by much fighting, but it was bright—it had not neglected its duty. Merlin studied it intensely while the silence grew between him and the queen, and he suddenly understood that this was the sword of Gwenutios, Cartimandua's erstwhile husband, onetime king of Cameliard. He looked up into Cartimandua's eyes.

"Have you the Sight, young man?" she asked him, leaning forward in her throne.

"I have, madam," answered Merlin curtly, "as I told you before."

Cartimandua did not speak for a long while, but gazed at the blade of the sword, her brow creased into contemplative furrows. She looked as if she were reading a message there, hidden from the sight of ordinary mortals, but visible to her. The meaning was obscure, and she puzzled over it while Merlin watched her, his loathing for her growing. At last, she took it by the hilt and thrust its point, quivering, into the wooden planking of the dais. She rose and descended from the dais so that she was, once again, inches from Merlin, thrusting her leathery face into his. The faint odour of rottenness emanated from her, and Merlin flinched in spite of himself.

"The fox is dead," she said, "and the eagles will fly home to their master. Your prophecy was true. So was your prophecy about Felocatos—I have had all the young women of his acquaintance drowned in the Humber."

Cartimandua's words fell upon Merlin like leaden blows. He turned his head down a moment, closing his eyes; then he looked up again, his gaze steadfast. He said nothing.

"Felocatos called you the runt of Afallach," Cartimandua went on. "Did you complete your studies? Are you a druid?"

"Is it a druid that Cartimandua wants," asked Merlin, "or is it a priest to Claudius the God?"

One side of Cartimandua's mouth twitched upwards in an ironic smile. "Wise is the prophet," she sneered, "in the ways of prophecy, and far do his eyes see into future events. But he is a dolt when it comes to politics." She resumed her seat on the throne, and went on, "I am queen of Cameliard, and a Briton. I rule my own kingdom because I sold the High King to the Romans. Now they will leave me alone. And now, there is not even my late husband to worry about any more. I am the supreme ruler in Cameliard and, for all intents and purposes, I am the High Queen, the Chief Dragon of the

Island of the Mighty. The power has shifted, prophet, and it has shifted away from Logris and Caer Lundein to Cameliard and Caer Ebrauc. Did you not foresee that this would happen?"

Merlin let her gloat a while, and then said, "What does your Majesty want of me?"

"I need," said Cartimandua levelly, "an advisor, since Felocatos' demise."

Merlin took a breath. "You have killed or sold into slavery my friends and my king, and you have imprisoned me for many months. You have made an enemy of me, my lady. Why would you want an enemy for an advisor?"

Cartimandua raised her eyes to the heavens for a moment, and then said, "Don't be fond with me, young man. I know you think you are my enemy. But when you understand a little more of the ways of the men and women who rule this world, you will understand that such distinctions are irrelevant. You are my enemy, and you hate me. Gwenutios was my husband, and he loved me. And I loved him too, I suppose. But what does that matter? Politically, he was an opponent, and to secure my power, he had to be destroyed. There is only power, boy. Nothing else matters."

"Why do you think I will be a good servant?" asked Merlin.

"Because you hate me," replied the queen. "I know a little of the ways of Afallach, young man, and I know that one with the Sight cannot lie about what he sees. And you will not run away. You want to stay close to me, because you think that, one day, you can kill me, and avenge those friends whose loyalty you prized so highly."

Merlin said nothing, but he felt that a gulf had opened under his feet. Had Cartimandua the Sight?

"Of course," said Cartimandua, her voice changed oddly—it sounded like a blacksmith's rasp, covered with silk, "you might have another motive for staying." She rose from the dais again, and stepped up close to Merlin, turning her face upwards to look at him. Her eyes were dark, her skin leathery, her hair the colour of iron; and her breath still reeked. Every sense of

Merlin's rebelled against her being so close. He felt like vomiting, but did not want to back down from her either. She reached up, and traced the line of Merlin's jaw with her finger. "As my advisor," she crooned, "there are certain privileges you might enjoy."

Merlin could feel his gorge rising. He stammered, "The kind of privileges your Majesty has in mind are impossible for one with the Sight. My powers are bound up with my purity."

Cartimandua looked down for a moment, and stepped backwards. "We do not wish for you to lose your powers," she said, "not yet. Still, all prophets become useless eventually. When it is time for you to surrender your powers, it is my body that will take them from you. In the meantime, you will be useful." Cartimandua motioned him away. "Go now," she said. "Bathe. Dress properly. You are advisor to the queen of Cameliard now."

Merlin was escorted to a narrow chamber containing a bed and a chest, over which had been draped garments of scarlet and blue. A tub of hot water had also been placed in the chamber, the scented oils that had been poured into it filling the room with their gentle fragrance. Merlin was not surprised to hear keys rattle in the lock behind him, and he stood for a moment, doing nothing, contemplating his fate. Cartimandua had spoken truly, he reflected. While there was a chance of revenge, he could not die, and could not escape. And, although he could twist his prophecies to whatever end he might choose, he certainly could not lie about their contents. Resistance to Cartimandua, he concluded, was futile. He quickly removed his old clothes, and lowered himself into the bath.

Half an hour later, servants entered to empty the bath and remove it from Merlin's quarters, and he sat on the chest and looked out of the window. It was too narrow for escape, even if he starved himself, he observed wryly. It commanded a pleasant view of the courtyard. The birch tree stood there, the raven still strutting back and forth among its roots. Beyond the walls, he could see the tops of pale hills, rolling away into the distance.

Three times, Merlin watched spring clothe the birch tree with luscious foliage; three times he watched the leaves flutter to the ground and carpet the courtyard with gold; three times he watched little ledges of snow gather on the twigs, and icicles hang from the tips of its branches.

Merlin found no ally among the inhabitants of Caer Ebrauc. Indeed, few of them wished even to speak with him. This puzzled Merlin at first; but then he remembered Cartimandua's murder of all the girls associated with the druid, and he could understand the Cameliardi's resentment of him.

At first, Merlin felt the guilt of this keenly, and in his loneliness late at night, he castigated himself for having drawn innocents into this circle of death, simply to preserve his own life. But as the time passed, his guilt waned, until he thought little about it.

He thought instead about Excalibur. He watched the birch tree unleaving, and gathering snow, and budding and burgeoning, and he thought of ranks upon ranks of Romans, marching in straight lines about the land of winding valleys and swelling hills. At times, he would pace frantically about the little chamber Cartimandua had given him, his mind working over what little he did know about the Sword's whereabouts. At others, he sat himself upon the edge of his bed, closed his eyes, and sent out his mind throughout the land, searching, seeking. But nothing did he see of Excalibur, and he began to wonder if he would ever be able to resume his search.

Escape, however, was not a possibility. He was locked into his chamber at night, and guards were posted night and day. When Cartimandua wished to consult him, he was escorted by guards into her presence. She treated him cordially, and he sat with her at feasts; but always, the guards were waiting to escort him back to his own chamber at night, and always, the door shut behind him and the key turned in the lock.

Sometimes, Cartimandua would summon Merlin so that he could accompany her hunting in the nearby forest, or else hawking on the moors. On one of these occasions, when the hawks had glutted themselves and were no longer any use for hunting, Cartimandua had paused to look curiously at a dead tree springing from a rocky overhang.

"That," she said to Merlin, pointing, "is where Mathreu died." She gave a sigh. "He was the only one of my lovers whom I didn't kill." She smiled, looking ironically at Merlin. "Who would have thought it, eh? Cartimandua, that wizened old scarecrow, enjoying a long line of lovers! Well, I did, you know. I was very beautiful when I was young, and I had plenty of lovers. Mathreu was my first. I would have loved him all my life, if it hadn't been necessary that I marry elsewhere. Poor Mathreu. He never understood politics."

Frequently, especially in the first year and a half, Cartimandua would send for Merlin in the dark hours after the feast was ended and the Cameliardi slept on their shields in the hall. Merlin would be shown into Cartimandua's private chambers, and he would be asked to prophesy. Sometimes, he did; at other times, he invented things. Sometimes, when Merlin reached the queen's chambers, she would say nothing to him, but sit silently staring into space while Merlin waited, the curl of his lip speaking of his hatred.

On one occasion, Cartimandua spoke without asking for a prophecy.

"You remind me," she said, "of Cyngen, my first husband." She had been drinking heavily: her lip was wet with wine, and a single purple drop hung forgotten upon her chin.

"Why?" asked Merlin, then let the silence grow.

Cartimandua quaffed off her wine and poured another cup. Merlin's lay untouched on the table before him. "Cyngen did not need me," she said. "He was not like the others. He was self-sufficient." Her smile, like her words, looked slurred over the wine cup. "They talk a lot," she said, "about what women want most. What they want is men who don't need them, but want them anyway."

"And this Cyngen," said Merlin, "he wanted you?"

"Not particularly," answered Cartimandua. "I think that's why I loved him most. Not like poor Felocatos—I loved him too, but in the same way a wretched virgin loves a puppy-dog. No, that's not right—he was a puppy-dog, but I was flattered by him. I could think myself young again." She studied her distorted reflection in the curved mirror of her wine goblet for a moment. "Can't fool myself about that any more," she remarked. "Now, Cyngen, he was a man." She drank some more wine and reflected silently for a time. "Such a pity he couldn't handle his horse better," she said.

Shortly afterwards, she dismissed him. She treated him no differently from usual the next time she summoned him, nor the next time. But infrequently, from then on, Merlin would have to listen to drunken reminiscences, and then be escorted to his chamber and lie awake on his bed, wondering what on earth it all meant.

* * *

News reached them one night that Emperor Claudius had died, some said by poison, but it was true that he was advanced in years. Not long after, news reached Caer Ebrauc that Merlin found more personally interesting: Prasutagos, king of Eicenniawn, had finally died.

Cartimandua looked directly at Merlin. "I wonder greatly," she said, "that my prophet saw not these things ere they came to pass. What say you, Merlin?"

"That Roman Britain is now in the care of two capable women," answered Merlin tersely.

"Yes," said Cartimandua musingly. "Queen Boudicea." She turned to the Eicenni messenger. "You are welcome to Caer Ebrauc. Will you stay tonight, at least, and feast with us?"

"Madam, I shall," said the messenger, a man in his early twenties with dark hair and eyes. As servants escorted him to quarters that had been assigned to him, he looked straight at Merlin, and their eyes met. Merlin frowned, for he had never set eyes on the man before. Then the messenger was gone.

The messenger seemed to be something of a drinker, for that night, he drank with the meinie, and particularly with Merlin's guards. Every now and again, Merlin found the man watching him curiously, though every time

Merlin looked in his direction, his eyes slid away. When the food and drink had been cleared away, Merlin's guards appeared at either elbow, and he rose to retire to his chamber.

He lay awake long that night, staring at the ceiling. The guards who were normally posted outside his door had managed to smuggle a flask of wine away from the feast, and as the night wore on, they grew louder and more raucous. Merlin dozed, but his sleep was fitful.

Then, all at once, he awoke, and his senses were sharp. Something, some noise, had awoken him, and he waited, not daring to breathe, for its repetition.

There came a quiet scraping of metal upon metal, and a quiet creaking. A ribbon of moonlight from the window fell on a man's form as he quietly shut the door behind him. Merlin lay still, his muscles tensed.

VI

The man paused for a moment, evidently waiting while his eyes got used to the dim light. The moonlight gleamed on his eyes as his head turned left and right. At last, he moved, creeping with stealth towards Merlin's bed. He reached out with a hand.

Merlin reacted as quickly as a flash of summer lightning. He had the man's wrist in his own grip, and twisted it outwards, so that the man fell to his knees, and arched his back. He gasped in pain.

"Who are you?" demanded Merlin. "What are you doing here?" His voice was harsh, but he whispered—no need to let everyone in the palace know what was going on.

"Release me!" gasped the man. "I beg you, release me! I come with no evil intent!" With a start, Merlin recognized the voice as belonging to the messenger from Eicenniawn. "To you also I bring a message, Master Emrys," he said through gritted teeth.

Merlin released him. The man retired a couple of paces, massaging his wrist and flexing his fingers.

"Speak," said Merlin.

"Can we be overheard in this place?"

"Cartimandua trusts no one," answered Merlin. "I am watched constantly. Outside this door are two guards. Why did they let you in?"

"They are not listening," answered the messenger with a wry smile. "They have drunk deeply, and now rest in the arms of sleep. They were very grateful for the wine—they think I am their dearest friend—but they will pay for the pleasure they have taken tonight with thundering headaches tomorrow."

Merlin narrowed his eyes. "Then none may hear us, for there are only those guards within twenty yards of this room."

“Very well.” The messenger reached into his belt-pouch, and drew forth a gold ring. It was slender, and mounted upon it was a large gemstone the colour of still waters. “I bring not only the message of my lord’s death, but also this token to you of my mistress’ affection. This ring she bade me give you, my lord Emrys.”

Merlin took the ring, admiring the gem as it flashed and scintillated in the moonlight. But he was frowning as he slipped it onto his finger. He looked up at the messenger. “What does it betoken?” he asked.

“My mistress,” said the messenger, “wishes to know whom you serve. The Romans, their whelps, or the people of the Island of the Mighty? She wishes you to know that the gem-stone is hollow, and contains a powder so venomous that a single grain would bring low the tallest warrior in the realm before he could drain the cup into which it was poured. She says that you may use it in any way you see fit, but she bids you remember the fates of Coroticos and his comrades.”

Merlin put a hand to his temple. He felt a little giddy, but he heard a voice in his ears: his own voice. “Poison!” cried the voice. “Poison flows through the lair of the lioness! The hunters cannot take her by might, so they lay traps, to take her by stealth. It is the wolf who sets the trap, and its mate who pours the poisonous liquor down the lioness’ throat, when the lioness lies bleeding in the trap!”

When he opened his eyes, he understood that that had been the first prophecy he had uttered for Queen Cartimandua of Cameliard, the lioness; and he knew, now, who the wolf was—the she-wolf who would destroy Cartimandua through her lover.

Merlin inclined his head to the messenger. “I am,” he said, “her servant and Britain’s. Tell her that a hope lives, which I long believed dead.”

The messenger smiled and bowed low before Merlin. “Your Majesty,” he said, and left the room. Merlin stood for a moment, still trying to take in this new turn of affairs, while the key once again turned in the lock and slid out. He heard a quiet rattle as the messenger returned it to the guard’s belt, and then soft footfalls receding from the door.

Merlin lowered himself back onto the edge of the bed, and looked down at the gemstone on his finger. Peering closely at it, he could indeed just perceive a crack, as fine as a baby's hair, running all about the base of the gemstone, a little above the mount. He held it up to the light, and the moonlight flashed again from its multifaceted surfaces. But now the light was cold, like light on a distant world, where an alien race obeyed laws that Merlin could not fathom.

He took the ring off before returning to sleep.

* * *

It was many days before Merlin got close to Cartimandua again but, as he had predicted, eventually she sent for him. A fat candle squatted in a pile of its own wax in the middle of the table, its flame leaping first left and then right in the draughts that blew under the door and through the cracks in the window shutters. The flagon of wine was already half empty before the queen, and she was staring with dead eyes at the cup that rested between her bony hands. Merlin took his seat at the opposite end of the table, as usual, and waited.

"Look into the future, prophet," said Cartimandua. "Tell me what you see."

Merlin closed his eyes. He ran his fingertips across the hard corners of the gemstone on his finger, just for reassurance. "Death," he said. "There is blood."

Cartimandua gave a wry smile. "Blood," she said. "There is always blood. Do you druids see nothing in the days to come but blood? Is there truly so much blood in the world? Blood, blood, blood." She paused, and her eyes alighted upon Merlin's hands. He quickly covered his ring, but it was too late. "That is a new ring," said Cartimandua. "Where did you get it?"

Merlin stiffened. He took his hand away from the ring so that the candle-light flashed from its facets. "It was a gift," he stammered. "It came from one I knew in childhood."

"From the Queen of the Eicenni?" Merlin nodded. "Favoured is the prophet of Cameliard," crooned the queen. "Let me see it."

Like one in a dream, Merlin rose and pushed his stool back from the table. He walked along its length and put out his hand to Cartimandua. She looked at the ring, examining the gem closely as if she were a jeweler who would appraise it. She turned the angle of his hand to get a better view, first one way, then another. At last, she released him.

"It is a fine ring," she said, looking up at Merlin. "Her majesty must be a very good friend indeed."

"We grew up in neighbouring cantrefs in Dyfed," said Merlin, "and knew each other well as children, but I have not seen her in many years."

"And you loved her," observed Cartimandua. Her smile stopped just short of mocking. "You still love her. They say she is the most beautiful woman in the Island of the Mighty, and the wisest of prophets loves her but may do nothing about it, for he is a sworn virgin. Well, we all have our burdens to bear. You can sit down."

Merlin resumed his seat. Cartimandua did not say anything further, but she studied him impassively for a long while.

"Blood," she said at last. "There is always blood about a queen, or a king. Always blood. The throne is awash with blood, the sceptre rests in a pool of blood, the crown is smeared with it. Blood everywhere." Cartimandua took a long, reflective sip from her wine. "It was not always so," she sighed. "There was a time when there was no blood, when there was wind in my hair and soft grass beneath my feet. What has become of all those days and long years? Where do all the past days go?" She was lost in reflection so long that Merlin wondered if she had not fallen asleep. But then she raised the wine-cup and poured a long draught down her throat, wiping her lips afterwards with the back of her other hand. She reached out to the flagon, and poured herself another cup.

"I remember that," she said at last. "I remember what it felt like to have the sun fall gently on my arms, to feel the muscles of the earth through my toes. But no one is as free as the wind. What would it . . . " But her voice trailed off before she could complete her thought, and she took a long gulp of wine.

Now her eyes were on Merlin. He felt his skin prickle, as it would beneath heavy clothes on a hot summer day, though the December wind rattled the shutters to remind him of the season. His heart fluttered in his breast. Why did she stare so at him? Was it today that Cartimandua would decide she no longer needed his powers of prophecy? He fingered the gemstone on his ring.

Cartimandua stirred. She looked up at her servants, lingering outside the pool of shifting light that the candle cast. Merlin's guards sat in a corner, conversing with each other in low tones. They fell silent, feeling her eyes upon them.

"You can all go," she said, waving a hand. "All of you. Go. Go now. Go to sleep. By the gods, don't you want to sleep? *I* want to sleep! I haven't slept through the night in . . . well, the gods know how long. Go!" The servants began to move slowly out of the chamber. Merlin rose. "Not you," barked Cartimandua. "You stay. But you can go," she added, pointing at the guards. "You may take the night off—go and carouse."

Frowning at one another, the guards rose from their seats. But they dared not disobey. When the door had banged closed, only Merlin and Cartimandua remained in the room. Merlin dropped himself back onto the stool, his stomach hollow with sickness and fear.

Cartimandua sat in silence for a spell, sipping her wine while the candle-flame flickered and the wind hurled itself against the shutters. At last, she gave a sigh. "I have been very strong," she declared, "very strong." She looked up, directly into Merlin's eyes, and leaned forward across the table. "Not everybody could have done what I have done," she explained. "To rise so far—I was the daughter of a minor nobleman in a backwoods cantref of a remote province of Britain. And now? Now, I am Queen Cartimandua of Cameliard. The last of the free sovereigns of the Island of the Mighty. I answer to the Emperor of the World, and to no one else! That's a long way to come. It wasn't easy. I had to be strong."

She stopped talking. Her eyes rested on Merlin's ring. He slid his hands off the table and rested them in his lap, and watched Cartimandua without speaking. Cartimandua's eyes rose from the table where Merlin's hands had been to his face. Their eyes met, and now Merlin's did not flinch.

"You have to be strong," repeated Cartimandua. "That's the kind of world we live in. You can't be weak. Remorse must be pushed down, it must be squeezed out, it must be entirely eliminated. What on earth can you do, if you feel sorry for everything? 'Oh, I'm so sorry I had to execute you. You were a traitor to me and my realm, but I wish I didn't have to have you executed.' And they don't let you go—the ghosts of a thousand men hedge in about a queen, but what could you have done? Sometimes, watching in the dark hours, I see the face of Mathreu, the welts bright on his throat, or Cyngen, my first husband. But what is love anyway? A fire in the blood for a few moments, nothing more. The poetry of an idiot. A distraction—sweet, of a certainty, but to no practical purpose. Better suppress it now, and not have to deal with it later."

Cartimandua reached out with a wavering hand, picked up the flagon of wine, and poured herself a new cup. She sipped it a few times, her eyes wide and staring into nowhere.

"I loved Mathreu, and he loved me, and he dangled from the branch of the dead tree on the moors. I loved Cyngen too, and his horse threw him, and I watched him strike his head against a stone, and I saw the blood come out. It was deep red, deeper than I had expected, almost purple, almost royal purple. But Cyngen wasn't a king." She drank deeply and reflected for a long moment. "Cyngen wasn't a king, but Cloten was king of Cameliard. I became a queen, and I made Gwenutios a king. Cyngen taunted me. He said I had nothing, that everything that I possessed had become his when we had married. But when I married Gwenutios, I was already a queen, and *I* made *him* king of Cameliard. He would have been nothing without me.

And now I have once again made him nothing." Cartimandua raised her wine cup. Merlin watched its base rise above her face. She brought it down, very deliberately and gently, a few inches from the flagon.

"Now they're all nothing," she said. "Mathreu, Cyngen, Cloten, Gwenutios, even dear Felocatos. They're nothing, nothing, nothing. They sleep the eternal sleep, and don't have to wake up every morning and be strong, and be strong, and be strong. Who can be strong for ever? Where can you find the strength to face the sunrise tomorrow, and tomorrow, and tomorrow? Wouldn't it be better, after all, just to sleep, and never worry about what the daylight will reveal?" Cartimandua dredged up a deep sigh. Her eyes alighted for a moment on Merlin's ring, then rose slowly to his face. Their eyes met. Merlin felt a cold shiver run down his spine. Her eyes looked at him as if from out of a grave. She said, "Pour me some wine, prophet of blood."

Merlin did not move immediately, but continued to stare at her, his brow furrowing. She looked back, her face impassive. But behind her eyes, there was something else, a darkness, like a deep pit, and death was at the bottom. Slowly, Merlin rose from his seat, picked up her cup and poured the wine into it. It was all that was left in the flagon. He placed the flagon between the cup and Cartimandua, so that it blocked her view of his hand as he quickly tapped the gemstone of his ring. The top sprang open, and a whitish powder fell into the cup. His other hand passed smoothly over the top, and the gemstone clicked shut again as he extended his hand to Cartimandua. She took the cup without looking at it. She was looking at Merlin.

"I think you are strong," she said. Merlin had not sat down yet, and she looked up at him, her eyes empty and dark. "You can probably remain strong for another few years. Twenty, perhaps. Then you will be as old as I am, and you will drink wine every night until you can't even piss in a straight line. What will you do with your strength, Merlin? Whom will you serve?" Merlin looked down at the cup of wine that rested on the table before the queen of Cameliard. She looked at it for a long while, resting between her hands. The air was thick in the stuffy room, thick with the fumes of much wine drunk and melted wax and the dry rushes on the floor. Merlin was suddenly seized with a violent longing to dash the cup to the floor and scream at Cartimandua, to yell out loud that it was a poisoned cup, but he mastered the urge, digging his nails into the palms of his hands. Cartimandua had not moved except that now, her tongue licked her lips quickly, and then disappeared. She looked up again at Merlin, and suddenly, he understood.

She knew.

A faint smile played across the queen's lips, like the smile of a man who has struggled long, but can now rest, or a master who has striven for many hours, and at last his pupils understand. "For whom will you use your strength, prophet?" wondered Cartimandua. "And what will you do?" She picked up the cup and, without taking her eyes off Merlin, drained it to the dregs. She put a hand to her chest, as if troubled by a little indigestion, and then she looked up at him again. "Go," she said. "Leave me."

Merlin slipped out of the chamber noiselessly. The light was poor in the passageway outside, and it was a matter of little effort to slip unseen past the guards. A few moments later, he was a shadow passing under the birch tree in the courtyard, and then on the battlements. After that, he blended with the other shadows of the moors of Cameliard, and Merlin was gone.

When Cartimandua's servants discovered her the next morning, her cold face pressed against the table-top, they searched everywhere for the mysterious prophet who was her last known companion; but he had long gone from Caer Ebrauc.

VII

Merlin hastened away southwards, away from Caer Ebrauc. He paused a moment, looking back. The walls rose solid black, but he could see the sentries' fires flickering in braziers along the top. He should have stolen a horse, he thought; but then it occurred to him that he would never have been able to ride through the gates. His plan, such as it was, had depended on stealth, not speed. He turned his back on Cartimandua's city, folded his cloak more closely about his body, and strode off into the south.

The night was a bleak one, and the wind that had rattled the shutters in Cartimandua's palace howled down upon Merlin as he trudged southwards. The clouds were thick, and the night therefore dark as pitch, but still he went on, one heavy foot before the other, towards Eicenniawn. He could not stop. He must go on, for Cartimandua's servants would discover her body soon, and descend upon him quickly. By the time the sun rose, he must be as far away from Caer Ebrauc as human legs could take him.

The wind buffeted him, flattening his cloak against his back, and whipping his long hair forward so that he was constantly having to brush it from his eyes. It was not a horse he needed, he reflected grimly, but a hat. The wind was damp, and it was icy, and the cold began to seep into Merlin's soul. He stopped for a moment to take stock of his situation. Caer Ebrauc was behind him—he could still see its fires glimmering dimly in the ocean of darkness that surrounded it. He knew that nearby was a river that ran due south. If he could find it, it would guide him truly. If he turned a little to his right, he reasoned, he would find it soon enough.

He felt the soft, freezing touch of snow on his lips. The wind, which had been but cold until now, was beginning to bring swirls of snow. Merlin adjusted his cloak over his shoulders and went on.

Soon, the air was full of snowflakes, lashing into his back and leaving a cake of ice over his shoulders, gathering in his beard and on his moustache. He soon ceased wiping it away—it gathered so fast that the effort was vain. The wind wailed in his ears like some fell beast seeking its cubs.

Then he heard another noise, faint at first but growing stronger as he plodded forward. It was the rattle and clatter of water over a stony bed, and he knew he had found his river. Merlin picked up his pace. He could feel his feet crunching through a thin covering of snow. He looked around. Dimly, he saw grey clouds of snow all around him, darkening as night approached, but nothing more. He pushed himself to his feet and went on, following the river into the south.

Merlin staggered onwards, one hand shielding his eyes, the other holding his cloak closed over his chest. But the wind tore it continuously from his hand, and blew under it, freezing his thinly-clad body. Ice had formed in his beard and hair, and his teeth rattled against each other.

Merlin looked down at his feet. They seemed a thousand miles away, and covered with a grey blur. He looked left and right. The same grey blur extended out in all directions, wide and flat like the sea. Above was a black blur. Somewhere up there was the moon, somewhere beyond the thickly-piled clouds. How long had he been walking? Merlin wondered. But there was no way of knowing.

Merlin fell to his knees. He swayed once or twice, and then pitched over to the side. He found himself tumbling, rolling down a steep incline towards the river. His arms and legs flailed, rocks he had dislodged bounced along with him like little fish dancing along after a whale. He hit something hard, and snow fell all about him.

Merlin laughed. Silently at first, groveling in the snow, his shoulders began to quake with mirth. Then he opened his mouth, threw back his head, and guffawed. The noise of his laughter mingled with the lupine howling of the wind, and there was little to tell them apart.

At length, a calmness came upon Merlin, and he reached out to touch whatever had broken his fall. It was an old dead tree. Feeling about with his fingers, he discovered an opening. It seemed wide enough. He dragged himself towards it, feebly pushing himself inside.

Once he was within the tree, the noise of the wind subsided considerably. He crouched there in the darkness, his teeth chattering, his body quivering. And yet he did not feel cold any longer. In fact, he felt comfortable, almost warm, one might say. He began to feel drowsy . . .

* * *

Merlin's eyes opened suddenly. He was no longer in the old tree, but on a wide expanse of snow. It lay even in all directions, uninterrupted by tree or hill or rock. Above him, the white sky bulged, heavy with more snow to come.

Before him stood a pale, wild wanderer, cloaked in dark colours, a staff in his hand. His beard was grey, his eyes so pale that he almost looked like a blind man. The paleness of his complexion seemed to be intensified by the darkness of his robes, so that in himself he seemed to encompass all shades, from the palest light to the dunnest darkness.

"There is no path through the snow," he said.

Merlin crouched in the snow, wrapping himself up in his arms and shivering. He could not say anything.

The pale wanderer leaned downwards. "Do not fear," he said. "I have come many miles, many miles, through the trackless wilderness, across the pathless sea. When there is no path the eye can see, the soul can still find a way."

"I have no guide," muttered Merlin.

"You are cold," observed the wanderer. He held out a cup to Merlin. "Drink," he said, "and be warmed." The cup was gold, wide at its lip, and almost as wide at its base. Gems of many different colours were set into it, just below the rim. Its lines were simple and unpretentious, its craftsmanship flawless. Merlin had never seen its like. It was itself like a vision of perfection. He reached out and took the cup. He could not tell what was within it, but it was rich and sweet and spiced. Its aroma wrapped him up as if in a warm blanket. He took a sip. It was not hot on his lips, and yet he could feel warmth flowing through his body, even to his fingertips.

"Follow me," said the wanderer, "and I shall steer you to a safe harbourage."

He reached out with his hand. Merlin took it, and felt himself pulled to his feet. The pale wanderer turned, and began to move off through the snow. Merlin followed, stumbling. His footsteps were slow at first, and uncertain. But as he watched his companion ahead of him, striding with unfaltering step through the snow, certitude grew in him, and his limbs waxed strong, and before he had gone twenty paces, Merlin was able to keep up.

How long they strode through the featureless wilderness, Merlin had no way of telling. Time seemed to have no hold over them, wherever they were. But at length, the pale wanderer stopped.

"You will be safe in this place," he said.

"Who are you?" asked Merlin.

"I am the servant of the servants of the lord," he answered.

"Will we meet again?"

He nodded; it was almost a bow. "We shall," he said. "But not for many years, and your path is a harsh one until then. Take comfort. The path of righteousness is ever a steep one, and fraught with dangers."

"What does it mean to be righteous?" asked Merlin.

"When you too are the servant of the servants of the lord," answered the pale wanderer, "you will not need to ask that question. But now, rest. Drink again, and rest."

Once again, Merlin took the cup, and once again he felt the liquor's warmth spread through his limbs. But this time, it made him drowsy—the healthy drowsiness of rest among loved ones after a day of long labours. Merlin folded upon himself and, as he curled into a warm ball, sleep stole upon him, sleep of such restfulness as he had never known.

* * *

Merlin awoke, his nose twitching at the aroma of roasting venison. Slowly, other sensations called for his attention: a hard bed under his back, a soft pillow under his head. The acrid smell of a peat fire. The sound of the wind, distant and muted, the crackle of flames. And the sound of tuneless singing. The melody meandered, and the words seemed to be in a foreign tongue at first, but it was not.

Juice of leeks, fresh goat's gall
For loss of hearing help it shall.
Two parts of juice, the third of gall,
Diced up fine and warmed withal.
In nose or ear, this brew's so pure,
The headache it will swiftly cure.
Broken bones it soon will knit,
And vicious sores away will flit.
Leeks and salt the same way made,
Staunches woman's blood or maid's.
It's good too for a drunken man—
To chew on leek will ease his brain.

Merlin turned his head. The singer was a man, aged somewhere in his fifties, with heavy jowls, a bulbous nose, and a florid complexion. Locks of grey hair were flattened untidily over his head. He wore an ankle-length robe stitched out of deerskins. Merlin let his eye rove beyond the man. Animal hides hung on the walls—deerskins, fox pelts, the striped masks of badgers, even the great skin of a bear. But there were also shelves, and on them books, dozens upon dozens of books. Some of them were bound in leather, the titles written carefully upon the spines. Others were in scroll cases. One was heaped upon a desk, and the man was evidently in the process of sewing the folios together.

The singing had stopped, and Merlin directed his attention to the man, who was now peering closely at him.

"So," he said, "the dreamer awakes. Welcome back to the real world. Or at least, welcome back to the material world. You have perhaps been wandering through another, more wonderful world these past few days."

Merlin put a hand to his chest. "Has it been so long?"

"Thrice," declared the man, "has the sun warmed this little home of mine—feebly, I admit, but thrice, since I found you in the old tree by the river. You were at the extremity of hardship—but an hour more, and you would have been released from this miserable world."

"You make it sound as if that would have been a favour to me," said Merlin.

"To be released from the world of this ugly stuff," said the man, gently pinching the flesh of Merlin's arm, "is a blessing, though I think it unkind to go before one's time." He held out a hand. "I am Morfryn," he said.

"Merlin Emrys," replied Merlin, shaking his hand. He looked around the interior of the hut. "So many books!" he breathed.

"Can you read?" inquired Morfryn sharply.

"Yes," answered Merlin. "I was trained in Afallach."

Morfryn rubbed his hands together. "Oh, that is very good!" he announced gleefully. "That is very good indeed! We can have such talks!" He stood up. "But now," he said, "we must tend to the natural appetites of our animal natures. Would you care for some venison?"

The meat turned out to be excellent, lightly seasoned with thyme and tenderized with mead. Merlin commented on the food's excellence, and Morfryn chuckled modestly.

"I should have expected far less," observed Merlin, "considering your scorn for our animal appetites."

"That man should have a body is an embarrassment," sighed Morfryn. "Think on it: when we are minding our own business, pondering on ideals or observing the gods wheel their courses about the night sky in their jeweled chariots, our bodies will suddenly awaken with noise and the movement of gas, things that are not under our conscious control, and which we would suppress if we could. Or perhaps we have taken a stroll, in order to reflect on the lives of the long-lived ones, and why they do not commonly appear to our senses. A young lady walks by, and our bodies respond without our having even said good-day." Morfryn gave a deep sigh. "The body is an irksome companion, and I would do away with it at once, were I certain, with Plato, that my soul would not perish at that instant. But there is so much to do, so much to read, so much to reflect upon!"

"But . . . the meat?"

"Yes, yes, the meat," answered Morfryn. "Food is a pretty sordid sort of thing, its purpose to satisfy that base creature, the body. Venison is awful stuff. But soak it in mead for a while, sprinkle a little thyme upon it, and an almost alchemical transformation overcomes the modest little meal. Now it satisfies our minds and our souls, and well as our bellies! Mere feeding is for animals—good food elevates us above that level."

Merlin nodded. "You have a point," he said. He took another bite. It practically dissolved on his tongue, it was so tender.

"Can you read Greek?" asked Morfryn suddenly.

Merlin shook his head. "I can read but Brythonic and Latin," he said.

"I shall teach you Greek. And then, what a world will open before you! Plato and Aristotle and Homer are but the beginning! Have you read of Jason's quest for the golden fleece? Or the terrible fate of Oedipus, king of Thebes? Do you know how Heracles throttled the snakes that crept into his crib when he was but a year old? Or how Achilles gained his invulnerability, except for the weak patch on his heel?"

Merlin had to admit to his ignorance of these topics. "But I am engaged upon a journey," he said. "I must get to Eicenniawn."

Morfryn made a wry face. "It is the midst of winter," he said. "You cannot travel until the spring. Stay here with me, and learn the wonders of the mind and soul."

Merlin had already been more than half inclined to do so. "Very well," he said. "Teach me Greek."

Morfryn smiled broadly, his eyes lighting up as he reached for a heavy volume on a nearby shelf. "Let us begin with *The Iliad*," he said.

VIII

Morfryn set Merlin to work initially upon Homer. Merlin's head resounded to the clash of arms in *The Iliad*, and his heart yearned with Odysseus for a return to Ithaca. At first, Morfryn sat by his side, interpreting the strange characters. At night, with the wind howling outside, they would talk for long hours about what they had read, and Morfryn would read from other books, mainly by Plato. Eventually, when Merlin had worked his way through *The Iliad* and *The Odyssey*, Morfryn lovingly handed him a small volume called *The Republic*. It was a grey afternoon in February, and though the snows had retreated, rain poured from the grey and featureless sky, pounding on the roof of the hut and streaming from the eaves. For a long while, the only sounds were the crackling of the fire and the turning of pages. The afternoon wore on and, somewhere behind the solid clouds, the sun set.

Merlin closed the book softly and raised his eyes. Morfryn sat on a stool on the opposite side of the fire, his eyes shining, his hands clasped in his lap before him. He had long ago set aside his own book, and was regarding Merlin's progress with keen interest. "Well?" asked the philosophic man.

Merlin shook his head slowly. "I feel as if Plato just reached into my soul, took out its contents, and cast them upon the parchment."

"You see yourself in this conversation, then?" prompted Morfryn.

"Not yet," replied Merlin. "But I see everyone I have ever known." For a moment, Merlin closed his eyes. The book had been nothing, nothing —men talking of justice on the night of a festival. They had disagreed on how to define *justice*. Yet, to Merlin, the men had had faces, and the faces of those he knew, and they spoke with voices he recognized.

Morfryn cleared his throat. "What is justice, then?" he asked. He was trying to start the conversation, Merlin knew, but images were crowding in the shadows at that moment, images that could not be shaken off or shouted down. He saw the kindly face of Gwelydd, his life spent in service of the people of the Island of the Mighty, and the gods; he saw Coroticos, jealous in his defence of his friends, and Boudicea, her chin held proudly, her lips parted as if to shout some command; and he saw Cartimandua, her eyes dead, clinging onto the power she had gathered to herself over a long and unpleasant life with fingers that would no longer grip.

"Merlin?"

Merlin blinked, rushing back to the present and shaking himself as a man who has just swum a river shakes off the excess water. "You have not spoken. Speak. What is justice? Or let us put the question differently. These people, what or whom do they serve?"

Merlin drew a deep breath. "Themselves," he said. "One of them grows near the grave, and seeks a blissful afterlife by returning his debts. To him, that is justice—honesty. To another, rewarding friends or seeking vengeance is justice. It's a kind of balance—good to the good, evil to the evil. This one here, Thrasymachus, he thinks that justice consists of obeying the law, and he takes pride in obeying the law; but he is a ruler. He can change the law so that he can justify whatever action he deems necessary or desirable. Justice serves the law, but the law is made by whoever is in power. It all comes to the same thing—they serve themselves."

Morfryn almost looked disappointed. "Yes, you have it," he said. "But what is the alternative?"

But Merlin's mind was on other things. "What is the afterlife?" he asked. "I have seen the souls of the deceased. They went into a cave, a dark cave. It was cold, and it was dank. The very breath of the dead rolled out of its mouth. But what did these souls find there? Did they find their way to a happy land, some eternal banquet, or are they still in limbo? Did they cease to be? What man really knows what will happen when the earth is thrown over his head?"

Morfryn was silent, for once. He let Merlin talk.

"Gwelydd is a fine man. He had the respect of the King, the Chief Dragon of the Island of the Mighty. His life has been one of service to the people of Britain. But will he get his reward? Will there be rest for him, or merely oblivion? When I stood outside the cave of the dead, I wondered about that. And now, I wonder if there is much point in carrying on. I have another thirty years of life, perhaps, and then I shall be no more, and all my achievements will come to nothing. Perhaps there really is nothing more than pleasure in this life."

"Does that seem correct, to you?"

"No," answered Merlin, after a pause. "No, it does not seem correct. It seems that there is something more than that. But I cannot see what it is. The path has grown cold. Snow has fallen on it, and I can no longer see my way ahead."

"You have spoken of Cephalus, the old man; but what of the others? What of Polemarchus?"

"Reward and revenge," mused Merlin. "It seems almost too mechanical, too balanced for real life. Coroticos fought for his friends, that much was clear. He loved every man in his army, and would have shed his own blood to save any one of them even from discomfort. But his friends betrayed him. Coroticos lives on a straight street in Rome, in a square house, and his great heart swells, and would burst out of those corners to fill the universe. There is no faith in men. They are fickle."

"So, there is no certainty of an afterlife, and trust in men is hopeless," said Morfryn. "What is left?"

"Power, and joy in the present moment. That was Cartimandua. She had spent her life building her power, at whatever cost to her, those around her, those she loved. I think she *did* love. Always, she hunted greatness, and if its pursuit required the deaths of those she loved, she was prepared to make that sacrifice."

"What greatness?" inquired Morfryn.

Merlin shook his head. "I cannot tell," he said. "At least . . . well, it seemed to me that what she wanted was power over others. Now. Always.

Always, her eyes were on this world, not on the next, like Gwelydd. And when the present moment began to slip away, when old age stole upon her like that, what then could she do?"

"What was her reward?"

"She was a miserable, sad old woman," answered Merlin. His chest rose and fell with a great exhalation. He had not told Morfryn the fullness of Cartimandua's death, though he had recounted his other experiences in detail, but he thought of her eyes, resting on his ring, and then rising to meet his own eyes. He said, "I think she knew she was dying. I think that her death was a blessed release from perpetual torment."

"Then what is left?" Merlin did not answer his philosophical friend, but let the howling of the February wind outside the hut work upon his mind for a while. What was left? What was the point of action at all, when death hovered ever at one's elbow, to sweep away the accomplishments of a lifetime in a single motion? Why did anyone do anything?

"Let me tell you what is left," said Morfryn, unable to restrain himself any longer. "Justice herself is left."

"Justice herself?" repeated Merlin, returning to the present with a mild shock of surprise. "Is she a goddess?"

"There you go once more," replied the old man with an emphatic hand gesture. "Every concept must be a god or a goddess. What a materialist you are! Merlin, don't you understand? The most important things, the highest, the noblest things in life have no physical existence, yet they still exist. Do we really *need* a goddess of justice, to whom we must pledge our undying allegiance? Cannot we owe fealty to the *ideal* of justice?"

"The ideal of justice?"

"Certainly. Cannot we behave justly because it is the right thing to do?"

"I don't see the profit in that," answered Merlin slowly. "Why not pledge obedience to a different ideal—to evil, or to love?"

"Aye, why not?" retorted Morfryn. "Love, hate, evil, good, justice—these are all greater than any human simply because they are ideals, because you cannot touch them, or smell then, or taste them. Look at the book you hold—it's several hundred years old. The pages are yellowed and brittle, and the edges are frayed. It won't last. Already, the binding has broken on some of the leaves, and I suspect that it won't survive another hundred years. Look at my body: old and wrinkled, inclining to corpulence, and soon for the grave. It's where you will soon be, my lad. You don't think so, the young never do. But before you know it, you will be an old man, teaching young men. The body wears out, and we die. So do all things beneath the moon. But ideals are not subject to decay and corruption. Justice now is the same as it was when Socrates discoursed upon it, four hundred years ago. And you can't do anything to destroy it or diminish it. Would you rather serve the servant, or the master? It is matter that serves the ideal, not the other way around, as a servant serves his master. It's better to follow an ideal than an appetite. There's more constancy in it. Look around you. All the ills our world endures this day are due to concerns for physical matters. Rome does not value the Island of the Mighty for its way of life or its laws or its poetry. Rome covets the earth upon which we tread. Rome wants all the mud in the world to belong to Rome. But the philosopher, now—you take away the earth he lives upon, but you still have not subdued him." He paused, and his eyes bored into Merlin. "What troubles you?" he asked.

Merlin shrugged. "I understand what you say," he said, "and I do not disagree with your reasoning. It just seems so cold, to follow an ideal, and not a man, not a god."

Morfryn considered for a moment. "You are still young," he said, "young enough to be my son, if I had one. We cannot all be philosophers, though the world would be a better place if more of us used philosophy than currently do. I am thankful that I have had the privilege of devoting my life to thought. What use you may make of Plato, I cannot tell. But you have told me you have the Sight. Look now, and tell me, what do you see in your own future?"

Merlin closed his eyes. He could feel the warmth of Morfryn's fire prickling his skin but, for a moment, he could see nothing but the darkness behind his eyelids. He stretched out with his mind and heart, and vague images, blurs of light, began to coalesce. They danced and swayed before his eyes and, for a moment, became clear. For a moment, a sharp image stood before his mind. Then, in a moment, it dissolved, leaving him again in the dark. He opened his eyes.

"I saw a boy," he said. "He was perhaps fourteen, perhaps fifteen years old. He held a sword, and he stood in the midst of a lake."

Morfryn nodded sagely. "I know little of such things," he said, "but I think, perhaps, the boy is he into whose hands you must place Excalibur."

"But who is he?" Merlin frowned. "Why is he a boy? I had expected a man, like Coroticos. Is he truly to be so young? Who could he be?"

Morfryn gave a crooked smile. "The philosopher king," he answered. "Imagine that! If you could find Excalibur, and place it in the hands of a high king, untainted by the sordid business of politics that has destroyed the realm in our days, if that king were raised to understand that justice is its own end, not the servant of personal interest, what a king that would be! What a realm! The world would not forget such a king! Why, they would be telling his story a thousand years later!"

Merlin's eyes were wide, his nostrils flared. He rose to his feet, pacing about the hut and biting his knuckle. At last, he stopped, and asked, "What is the significance of the lake?"

Morfryn shrugged. "That I cannot say," he answered.

Merlin bit on his knuckle again. "The Ladies of the Lake," he said, at last. "The Morforwyn. They dwelt upon this island before the coming of men. Cathbhad told me stories of their deeds, and Gwelydd knew much of their lore. I have met Morgana, but there were others—Tylweth, Argante, and others. Time was, they used to mingle with mortals on this island. The story goes that it was Argante who fashioned the sheath of Excalibur, in the dawn of days, while Arawn forged the blade. The lake is the clue, if only I could read it. Tylweth would know, or Argante. But how can one consort with goddesses?" Merlin frowned, for something else occurred to him now. "Why have they not spoken to me?" he asked. "Morgana has spoken to me, but none of the rest of the Morforwyn. Why Morgana, and no one else? Why not Tylweth, or Argante?"

"I cannot help you with that," replied Morfryn.

"And who was the pale wanderer?" Merlin asked, but less insistently. "He led me to this place, through a field of ice, but him I had never seen before. Who was he? What did he want me to do?" Morfryn made no answer, and Merlin subsided into a silence that lasted for many moments. "Why are there no answers?" he asked. "When I was young, I had questions, but I was patient. I thought I would learn the answers as I got older. But life raises questions faster than it can answer them. A dying man must be the most inquisitive soul in the universe."

But the philosopher said nothing. Indeed, it looked from the expression on his face as if unanswerable questions were in his mind too.

* * *

The rains eventually ceased, and the drought of March blew in on the dry breath of the western wind. Buds began to appear on the trees, and the daffodils burst into golden flower. Merlin read on with Morfryn, but his soul began to yearn, and his eyes to linger on the southern horizon. When at last April arrived, he said farewell to the old philosopher.

"It is to your lady that you must go, then," said Morfryn.

"It is," replied Merlin. "I have tarried overlong, and she will be anxious to see me. I thank you for your hospitality this winter, and for the shelter and food you have given me."

"Thank you for your conversation," countered Morfryn. "An ample price you have paid for your lodging." He took something out from behind his back and held it out. It was a book. Merlin took it, recognizing it as *The Republic*. "When you find the boy king," said Morfryn, smiling, "I shall be long dead, no doubt. But read this with him."

"You do not need it yourself?" inquired Merlin.

“It is here,” answered Morfryn, tapping his head. “Those books are best that we pass on to others. Take it, and remember our conversations.”

“I shall,” said Merlin, tucking the volume away in his backpack. “You shall be ever the father of my thoughts.”

Smiling, Merlin turned and strode off into the south, towards Eicenni-awn.

IX

The journey towards Eicenniawn was not so hostile as the night Merlin had set out from Caer Ebrauc. As he trudged southwards, more and more flowers blossomed on either hand. Occasionally, grey clouds would gather overhead and sprinkle the earth with life-giving liquor; but the showers were not long-lasting, and for the most part, the weather was warm and dry. Merlin was delayed a day finding a place where a ferry could take him across the River Humber, but it did not seem unpleasant to be so delayed. At last, he found a ferryman, and they pushed away from the wooded shore, where the birdsong and the buzzing of bees joined to make a jumbled melody, into the silence of the river.

The ferry slid smoothly across the surface of the stream. The slap of the water against the boat, and the occasional pop as a fish broke the surface, lulled his senses. Merlin blinked. His eyelids felt heavy. The southern bank, upon which he had fixed his gaze, began to blur, and he suddenly saw Boudicea before him. She raised her hand and crooked a finger at him, then turned and walked into the south, casting glances at him over her shoulder. Merlin followed.

With a bump, the ferry ran aground on the southern shore of the Humber, and Merlin was shaken from his vision into the present. He paid the ferryman and struck off again southwards, but his step was light.

After a little over a week, meeting hardly a soul on his journey save a solitary shepherd, Merlin reached the city of Linnuis. This had been a mighty fortress in the old days, but the timber stockade had been replaced by a stout wall of stone, and the bronze helmets of the guards that paced them with measured steps bore the scarlet plumes of Roman legionnaires. At the northern end of the town, where the High King had sometimes held court in the summer months, straight rows of barrack houses now stood.

This was Linnuis no more, but the garrison of Lindum, northernmost outpost of Nero's Empire.

As he was leaving Linnuis, Merlin caught sight of Fosse Way, the great road of the Romans, stretching like a knife-cut through the forest to the horizon. For a moment, it took his breath away, so arrogant was it, so brash, youthful, unapologetic, and unspeakably modern. It was so straight, Merlin thought he could just make out Caer Wisc—Isca Dumnoniorum, as it was now called—at the end.

Merlin rubbed his eyes. A Britonnic chariot was clattering along the cobbled pavement of Fosse Way. He stared at it for a long while. The four horses were white, their heads held proudly, and the charioteer's whip flicked over their backs, cracking and snapping without actually touching them. The charioteer turned her head, and Merlin saw her face.

It was Boudicea.

Merlin's heart raced. The chariot turned south, made across the wide space that bordered the road, and plunged into the forest.

Merlin dashed after the chariot, but when he reached the point at which the chariot had left the road, he found no tracks to say where it had gone. Behind him, a file of Roman legionnaires trooped past, their nailed boots ringing on the pavement. Merlin shrugged, and struck out across the open land. In a short while, he was in the forest, surrounded by the twittering of the birds and the smell of humus. There was no chariot, and no Boudicea, and he went to sleep that night under the spreading boughs of an oak tree without having glimpsed her again.

But over the course of the next few days, he saw Boudicea more and more often. Sometimes, she was ahead of him, leading him on, beckoning, laughing over her shoulder. Sometimes, he would awake and find her at his side beneath his blanket. She would smile and reach out for him. Merlin would take a deep breath, and then wake up again in the cold morning.

The further south he got, the more often these visions came to him. He was moving through a flat landscape along a narrow path, with shallow water and reed-beds, pools and mires on either side. But he barely noticed, for ever before his eyes danced the phantasmagorical image of the Queen of Eicenniawn. When a bittern boomed suddenly from quite nearby, Merlin did not flinch, nor make the sign of the evil eye, as was the wont with visitors to these parts, for he had not even noticed it. He met more people here than he had in the north, for the fen-people were crowded onto small islands and a narrow silty ribbon of land around a large bay. He passed those who were digging for peat, or others who were hauling in a variety of fish, glittering in the sunlight, from the waters, and every now and again, a shallow-bottomed boat with large sail would drift slowly by him. But he saw them not. All he saw was the hair like fire and the eyes like the summer sea, and the moist lips parted.

Then, one day, the vision spoke to him.

"How long has it been, Emrys, how long? How have I yearned for you these long years past! Come to me, Emrys, and take your place beside me on the throne, beside me in my bed." And she held out her hands to Merlin.

Merlin stopped on the path. The wind was sighing in from the sea, flattening the wiry grass around him, and the mournful gulls cried from above.

"Are you a dream, my love?" Merlin asked.

"A dream or a nightmare," replied she, and she pulled Merlin to her and held him close. He felt her warmth, he felt the strength of her body against his own, and he put his head upon her shoulder. As he did so, he caught the fragrance of sage and rosemary, and suddenly, he knew that it was she and no vision. He gazed into her face, the face that had driven him from the cold hills of the north to the windswept fens of the south. But the face was real, the body was under his hands.

"Can it be true?" he said in wonder.

"Believe it, my love," replied Boudicea. And they kissed. And it was such a kiss as Merlin had not known could be, for it was as if, through their lips, their two hearts met in a blaze of light and warmth, and became one. "Believe it, my love," said Boudicea again, when they parted and gazed once more in each other's eyes. "I am yours, now, until I die."

"And I yours, to death and beyond," said Merlin. He mounted the horse she had brought for him and, the hoofbeats of Boudicea's meinie drumming upon the peaty earth, they rode side by side for the fortress of Bran Dun.

* * *

When they arose the next morning, after a night of dozing and lovemaking, Merlin took a bath and clad himself in the robes of one of the Eicenni. Then Boudicea took him out onto the battlements of Bran Dun. To the north, the sea stretched out grey and featureless, its flat surface dotted with fishing boats; to the south, the fens stretched out green and flat, save where the fen-dwellers moved, gathering their peat and reeds. The wind blew in stiffly from the north, bearing the tang of salt upon it.

Boudicea and Merlin walked hand-in-hand along the palisade, looking out over the sea and land, Merlin wondering all the time that this was real, that he could truly feel the warm palm of her hand against his, her fingers curled about his own. He looked at her often, at the fiery hair that poured from her temples, at the proud chin lifted high. He thought of their lovemaking last night, and he rejoiced that they had no longer to hide their love. After all the hardships of the last few years, it was difficult to believe that this was not one of his visions, that a woman of flesh and blood had loved him last night, and walked beside him this morning.

"Boudicea," he said, a thought suddenly striking him, "How did you know where to find me, and when? How did you know I was coming?"

Boudicea looked confused. For the first time since Merlin had known her, her eyes were troubled and uncertain. She said, "Perhaps I too have the Sight in some measure, for I saw you at a great distance. I saw you in my dreams, and last night was the first night I had not dreamed of you in many weeks. I saw you traversing great plains, or passing between the shoulders of mighty hills, or crossing the wide streams of swift-flowing rivers. Three nights ago, I saw you in Eicenniawn, struggling like a blind man along the

Wash, and I feared that you would put your foot wrong and sink into one of those mires we have in these parts."

Merlin took her in his arms and kissed her tenderly upon the lips. "I am the falcon, you are the falconer," he said. "I could not have reached you, except that you guided me. O my love, it fills my heart to the brim to know that we shall never be parted in this life!"

"It is what I have always wanted, what I have long striven for," responded Boudicea, pressing her body against his and drawing his lips down upon hers once more. "And I am glad," she added, "that that traitor Cartimandua is dead."

They parted, and leaned against the parapet to gaze out over the grey sea. "I think," said Merlin quietly, "that she was glad herself. It is easy for me to say such a thing, of course, for it was I who killed her, and to say she welcomed death is flattering to my conscience. But life had become wearisome to her. She had herself murdered all those she loved, in the name of power. To live is pain when you are a traitor. It is but love that makes life worth bearing."

"Then stay with me, Emrys, king of the Eicenni, and be loved," said Boudicea, reaching across and kissing him again.

"With a will," replied Merlin, kissing her back on the lips, on the throat, and along the collar bone. "It is but death can divide us now."

"I would not wager on Death either," smiled Boudicea, kissing him again. Still smiling, she parted from him and turned her back on the sea, leaning against the parapet and surveying the wide courtyard beneath them. "This is but one of our fortresses," she explained. "Caer Wenta is our principal seat, now that Caer Camulod is become Camulodunum. I should not like to live, in any case, in any place where the Roman Emperor was a god." Boudicea clenched her fist and struck the wooden palisade with it. "Who do they think they are?" she hissed. "Do they think they can make a new god by a vote? Do they think all things can truly be so because a gaggle of white-haired men raise their hands one way rather than another? Who are they to challenge the gods?"

“They have challenged the world, and won,” observed Merlin.

“They have won bodies and dirt,” replied Boudicea. “They have not won our hearts, or our spirits. Nor shall they ever. It is not for all time that they dwell upon the Island of the Mighty. The day shall come when we drive them back to the seven hills they are so nostalgic for. It has been done before; we can do it again.”

Merlin smiled inwardly to look upon her. Her jawline had clenched during her brief speech, and there was a tenseness in the muscles of her arms. She had changed little in the eleven years since last he had met her (for he counted not the glimpse he had got on his travels years ago). Her hips were a little broader, her breasts a little fuller, her arms had developed muscles beneath the smooth skin. She was a woman, and no girl. There was yet no lightening of her hair to tell the passage of years, and her eyes glittered with the youthful fire with which he had fallen in love nearly thirty years ago. He wondered how he must look to her.

She noticed his gaze, and smiled. “Well, Emrys, prince of Cambria,” she said, running her fingers down his chest, “you are a king at last, albeit king of a small and unprofitable territory. As my husband, you are king of Eicenniawn. How do you like that?”

“It has ever been my wish to be your husband,” answered Merlin. “If I must endure being king to be so, then I must say that I have endured greater torments for lesser pleasures.”

Boudicea reached up and kissed him lingeringly on the lips. Her eyes were shining with pleasure when they parted, and she said, “Sometimes, my hawk, I could wish to be anything but a queen. When I am with you, it is enough to love a man and be content. Sometimes, I wish I were no queen. I wish I could be but a wife, and a mother.”

“Where are the girls?” asked Merlin suddenly.

“Girls?” Boudicea smiled again. “They are in their twentieth year, and seeking husbands.”

"Twentieth year!" exclaimed Merlin. "Of course, I could have performed the arithmetic, I should have known. But such things pass one by. So much has been happening."

"There is more," said Boudicea, pointing. Below them, in the courtyard, a boy of about ten years was fighting with some other boys using wooden swords and shields. Their delighted battle-cries came up shrill to the battlements.

"You gave Prasutagos an heir," observed Merlin. "At least he died a happy man."

"Fool," replied Boudicea, punching him gently on the shoulder. "To think that you have the Sight, but cannot see! I gave Prasutagos no heir. Do you think we women are complete fools when it comes to our bodies? We know when to give and when to reserve, when to be open and when closed. Look at him. Is he not a fine boy?"

With growing wonder, Merlin looked down into the courtyard, and followed the antics of the boy as he dashed back and forth with the youthful host. There was no need to ask which he was: he had his mother's fiery hair and self-assured attitude. For a moment, the boy paused in his game, and raised his hand to wave to his mother. He waved with his sword hand, and Merlin gasped.

"What is it, my love?" asked Boudicea.

"It is nothing," replied Merlin. "Something that would perhaps trouble a child." But he was thinking of his vision in Morfryn's hut: the boy king, the philosopher king, who bore Excalibur. His eyes narrowed as they followed the boy from one end of the courtyard to the other.

"I named him Gwenddolau, after your great-grandfather," said Boudicea. "I did not think you would want me to call him Rhydderch."

"It is a good name," said Merlin. His mouth was dry, and he could barely form the words. "I should like to meet him."

X

Boudicea and Merlin descended from the palisade into the courtyard, Boudicea calling her son to her. He immediately dropped his wooden sword and flew into his mother's arms. He had her red hair, Merlin noted, but his eyes were darker than hers, dark almost like a hawk's, and his nose more pointed. He was a fair lad to look upon.

"Gwenddolau," said Boudicea, "I want you to say hello to this gentleman. His name is Emrys, and he will be staying with us for a while."

"The gods' greetings to you, Emrys," said Gwenddolau, bowing low.

"And to you, Master Gwenddolau," returned Merlin.

"My mother told me you would be here," said the boy. "Did you have a pleasant journey?"

"It was long and arduous," replied Merlin. "I am glad that it is over, and I am glad to rest in Eicenniawn with your mother."

Gwenddolau flashed a smile at them both. "Eicenniawn is the most beautiful place in the world, is it not?"

Merlin thought of the aspiring peaks of Cambria, and the rugged coastline of Cornwall that he had explored with the folk of Habren, so long ago. "Eicenniawn is fair to look upon," he said.

"You must return to your companions," said Boudicea, kissing her son on the forehead.

"I shall," said Gwenddolau, skipping away and picking up his wooden sword. "Shall I see you again at supper, Emrys?"

"You shall!" replied Merlin. The boy waved and plunged back into his game. They watched him for a while in silence.

"He is a fine boy, is he not?" asked Boudicea.

Merlin moved his head from side to side in disbelief and awe. "I can hardly believe," he said, "that I have a son."

Boudicea slipped her hand through the crook of his arm, and reached up to plant a kiss upon his cheek. “He will be such a king as this land has not seen since the days of Brutus,” she said.

“And he shall bear Excalibur,” said Merlin firmly.

Boudicea looked up at Merlin and, for a moment, she looked very much like the little girl who had sat with him, listening to tales of Brutus in the hall at Caermyrddin.

“The Island of the Mighty,” she said, “can rise again. You think that Gwenddolau can be Chief Dragon?”

“When I had just left Caer Ebrauc,” said Merlin, “I had a vision of a boy of perhaps fifteen years, standing in a cave, with Excalibur in his hands.”

“The boy was Gwenddolau?” Boudicea’s eyes were shining.

“Well, the boy was somewhat older than Gwenddolau. It is difficult to tell, and the vision is no longer clear in my mind.”

“You are not sure,” said Boudicea with some bitterness. “What use is a vision, if you can’t be sure about it?”

“If our son is to be High King,” said Merlin, “and drive the Romans from our land, if he is to bear Excalibur, then I have not long to accomplish my work.”

“What must you do?”

“I cannot tell yet,” said Merlin quietly. His eyes were on a windhover, floating on the upper air-currents, the fens far below it. He brought his eyes downwards, and they met Boudicea’s. He pulled her body to his, and kissed her fiercely on the lips. For a long while, they held each other tightly, like tired swimmers clinging to a rock. “Will you and I ever know peace?” he murmured.

Boudicea bent her eyes up at him. “Do you desire peace?” she asked, surprised. “Do you wish for a respectable life, calculating our taxes to Rome, worrying about the reed harvest? Do you want to spend quiet nights, sitting about the fire and listening to the songs of others’ deeds? If that is what you want, I have misunderstood you all these years, Emrys.”

Merlin drew in a deep breath. "Sometimes," he confessed, "that is what I want. To love you is an adventure quite sufficient for any man." She smiled at the compliment. "I should like to know peace," he went on, more quietly, "and love, and companionship. But I fear that our world affords very little opportunity for these things. And I do not fear to embrace the quest. I think I have been destined by the gods for the life of the road." For a moment, the image was imprinted upon his mind's eye of the pale wanderer, his dark robes vivid against the snow. Then he was back again in Eicenniawn. A crease had appeared upon Boudicea's brow.

"I wish I could come with you," she said. "There is so little to do here!"

"But you are a queen!"

"Yes, but one tires of commanding men to do nothing but arrest a thief or help with the harvest."

"You would rather command them in war?"

"I would."

"To what end?"

"For glory!" declared Boudicea. "For glory, and an everlasting name around the hearth-fires of the Island of the Mighty, from now until the ending of days!"

"It may be," said Merlin slowly, "that the world will forget about Merlin Emrys and Boudicea of the Eicenni within a generation of our deaths. It may be that they remember High King Gwenddolau far longer."

* * *

It was not long after this that they were married, and though Merlin knew he would soon have to part from his new wife and take up the quest for Excalibur again, he did not leave at once. Indeed, although he resolved to leave before harvest time, he did not do so, but lingered in Boudicea's chamber and dallied with her in warmth and security. The Roman Empire seemed very far away, and Excalibur even beyond that. What was real was the warm body beside him each morning as he awoke, the smouldering eyes of the Queen of Eicenniawn, and her arms about his neck. And so the harvest came and went, and winter set in, and Merlin resolved instead to leave in the springtime. But the spring came and went too, and Merlin told himself that he had no clues, and he stayed with Boudicea in Eicenniawn.

Gwenddolau grew and throve, and Merlin watched him intently. One day in early summer, Merlin sat in the green shade of a tree while blackbirds gave throat to their cheerful melodies above his head. The book Morfryn had given him was open upon his lap, but he had begun to doze, when he heard a boy's voice asking, "What is that?"

Merlin's eyes snapped open, and he saw that Gwenddolau was pointing at the book. Merlin patted the ground beside him. "Join me," he said. Obediently, Gwenddolau sat down. Merlin's heart was pounding. He felt as if he were on the brink of a moment of world-changing import. "This," he said, "is a book, given to me by a dear friend, who lives very far away."

"I've never seen a book before," said Gwenddolau. "What's it for?"

Merlin took a deep breath. For a moment, he was taken back in time to a morning when the leaves were budding, and the Spring of Tylweth was chattering away nearby. "What is a word, little merlin?" asked Cathbhad, from across the years.

"A book," said Merlin, "is a thing by which men make their thoughts lasting. A man called Plato, who lived many hundreds of years ago, put his thoughts into a book, and now others can share his thoughts."

"Then it is like a drawing."

"Yes, very much like a drawing."

"What are the thoughts in that book?" asked Gwenddolau.

Merlin looked down at the book in his lap. "This is a story," he said, "about a prisoner. He was in a cave beneath the ground, which was reached by a long passageway, through which light from outside came. He was chained by the neck so that he could see only what was in front of him, and there were many people with him, who also were so chained."

"What had he done?"

"I beg your pardon?" asked Merlin in surprise.

"Why was he in prison? Had he led a rebellion against a king? Was he a thief?"

"No, he had been there since childhood. This was all he knew of life."

Gwenddolau's eyes grew round. "That was all he knew? A cave and a passageway and a chained head? What could he have done, to be punished so as a child? My nurse once made me stay in a tiny room in the palace when I had spilled some flour in the kitchens. She made me stay there for a very long time, and it was dark and smelly in there. But she didn't chain my head. This person must have done something really bad."

Merlin was struck dumb for a moment. "Yes," he said at last. "Yes, you're quite right. He had done something very bad indeed. He couldn't help it—in a sense, it wasn't his fault. But he had done a bad thing. He had offended the gods. Perhaps we are all like that. None of us lead blameless lives. The cave is like the world, and the man is like each one of us, imprisoned for reasons we cannot comprehend, in a prison that is everything to us. But the outside: what is on the outside, Gwenddolau?"

But Gwenddolau shook his head. "You haven't told me the story yet," he said.

"Of course not," agreed Merlin. "Well, this man was chained as I have told you. And the light from the passageway shone on the wall before his eyes. And people used to walk up and down this passageway, talking and carrying various objects, like the figures of men and animals."

"Why?" asked Gwenddolau again.

"The story doesn't say," replied Merlin.

"It should," said Gwenddolau. He yawned.

Very rapidly, Merlin said, "All that the prisoners could see of these objects was the shadows cast upon the wall before them. And the cave had an echo, so that it seemed that, as the people behind them spoke, in reality it was the shadows that spoke."

"Do the prisoners speak to one another?" interjected Gwenddolau.

"I suppose so," answered Merlin, beginning to be a little impatient. "But they had little to talk about, since all they knew was the shadows and the echoes. They played games, like guessing what object would be carried past their vision next. They praised those who were able to see patterns in the behaviour of the shadows, and to predict what would come next."

Gwenddolau twisted his lips into a wry shape. "I suppose," he said, "that if you had nothing else to do, that might be entertaining. I think I would sleep." He looked with sudden urgency at Merlin. "How did they eat?" he asked.

"What?"

"How did they eat? Surely they must have eaten. Did jailers bring food to them? If so, they must have seen the jailers, so the shadows weren't all they could see."

Merlin took a deep breath. "They didn't see their jailers," he said, "because their food was lowered to them in baskets on long ropes, from above, where there were many winches and pulleys. The jailers stayed behind and above them. They could see the shadows of the jailers, however, and knew as soon as they saw them, that their food was about to arrive."

"Like dogs," assented Gwenddolau. "I have a dog called Bach, and he knows when I am about to feed him. He wags his tail and barks and drools."

"No doubt the prisoners drooled too," said Merlin. "But one day, our prisoner was released, and brought to the real world. He did not go willingly. For him, whose entire reality had been the shadows and the cave wall, it was like death. And at first, the light blinded him, so that he could not see. And he saw the people that, to him, had been but shadows and echoes. And he beheld the vibrant colours, and the preciseness of shapes. And men spoke to him, and told him that what he had seen before was all but meaningless shapes and sounds, and that here, here was reality. What do you think his response would be?"

Gwenddolau shrugged. "He would be surprised, I suppose."

Merlin nodded. "And he saw the world as it really was. But he could not see it all at once, for it was painful to his eyes. At first, he could see but the images of men and things reflected in water and, later, the things themselves—things that were not painful to look upon. Then he raised his eyes to the night sky, and he contemplated the courses of the heavenly bodies. And, after a long while, he looked upon the sky in daylight, and saw its beauty and its brightness."

"What did he do?"

"What did he do?" repeated Merlin. "He began to think. And he realized, at last, how the world really worked: he saw that the sun produces the seasons, that lit the whole world and gave life to it."

"Did he go back and free the other prisoners?"

"He tried to, for he was deeply sad when he thought of the dark and narrow world in which they lived; so he went back. And, at first, he himself, who had seen so much, could make out nothing. The other prisoners were still guessing at what shadows would come next, and he spoke to them, and told them of the sun and moon, of trees and hills and flowers. But they would not believe in the world that he had seen. It did not match their experience. They laughed at him, saying that what he told them was folly. But he persisted and, in the end, they killed him."

"How? I mean, if they were all chained up like that, how did they kill him?" Merlin was speechless for a moment. Then Gwenddolau went on, "I suppose it's a good story, but I prefer the story of Bran, and how he killed the dragon, and lost the Cauldron of Garanhir. Or the story of the Death of Arawn. Those are good stories. The heroes died, but they died nobly. That's what makes a good story." Gwenddolau got up and stretched his limbs. Something far away across the courtyard caught his eye. "I have to go," he said. "Caileag and Ifor are going swimming, and I should like to go with them. Farewell, Emrys! Tell me another story another day!" And he raced across the turf to his gesticulating friends.

An hour later, Boudicea found Merlin still beneath the tree, the book open at exactly the same place as before. It was a moment before he even noticed that she was there.

"What troubles you, my love?" she asked.

"The philosopher king," answered Merlin. He shook his head. "It may be many years before he is ready," he said.

XI

Over the next few weeks, Merlin kept his eyes open, watching Gwenddolau intently, though from a distance. He watched as the youth swam or went hawking with his friends, or practised with sword and spear in the courtyard. He watched when Boudicea's aged druid, Tasgetios, spun his web of enchantment in the evenings with stories of elder days, or of the more glorious battles of recent years. Once, Tasgetios sang an elegy for the fallen of Mai Dun.

Men of Britain rode to battle, blades athirst,
Protectors of their people, proud men of war,
Britain's mightiest, mounted, impetuous,
Mettled men on long-maned mounts,
High-stepping horses, harnessed for heroes,
Sent by Coroticos, king of conquerors,
Into unequal battle, a hundred against a host.
Rhydderch and Rhocardd strove against Romans,
Gwgawn and Gwiawn gave way to no man,
Cynfan and Caerpre were cut down in conflict,
Youths' years yielded to ravens' glut.
Shields were shattered, swords were slashed,
Blood burst, corpses scattered,
Pale the faces of the dead.

Merlin looked across the hall at Gwenddolau. His eyes were riveted on Tasgetios as the last harp chords reverberated into another world. For a moment, it seemed as if Merlin looked on himself, thirty years before, listening to Cathbhad's tale of Brutus, with Boudicea beside him. Had so many years passed in truth, and had he made so little progress towards the goal he had declared to her then? His eyes slid from the youth to the queen, and he saw that she was regarding him as she had all those years ago. He reached across and kissed her gently upon the lips, but lingeringly, so that their breaths entwined. He gave a sigh.

"I cannot long remain here," he said.

"Is it upon your quest that you must go?" asked Boudicea.

"It is," answered Merlin.

"Stay a while longer," urged Boudicea. "There are times when the affairs of a nation must wait upon the needs of a woman and her man."

Merlin kissed her again, and squeezed her hand. Tasgetios was the central focus of a group of youths now, and he was relating in detail the events of Mai Dun, though Merlin knew he had not been there. Then again, nobody in Eicenniawn knew that Merlin had fought that day. Nobody knew anything about him, except that he had grown up in Cambria, and that he was beloved of their queen. Gwenddolau did not know that Merlin was his father, although every day, the two of them resembled each other more, and before long the conclusion would be unavoidable.

"I must free myself of these silken fetters," thought Merlin, as Tasgetios began to sing of another battle he knew only by report.

* * *

Some weeks later, when the springtime buds had burst into leaf and flower, Merlin and Boudicea were spending some moments alone in the orchard, when the sound of steel on wood came to them through the hedge that enclosed their bower. Merlin raised his head, listening. He could perceive the voice of Ieuan, the Master of Spears, instructing the boys of the castle in the use of their weapons.

"Do you want to listen to Master Ieuan," asked Boudicea, "or make love to me?"

Merlin looked down at his wife. Her bare shoulders shone like ivory in the early summer sun, her throat was stretched like a swan's, and her eyes, half-closed against the brightness of the sky, were teasing and alluring. Merlin pressed his lips against hers, moved his body against hers. For the moment, the whole world was within the narrow bounds of the hedged wall of their bower, a world of sweetness and warmth, roofed by the brilliant canopy of the sky.

But at last the time came for them to leave, and they walked hand-in-hand through the avenues of pear and apple trees to the gate. Boudicea drew out her key and unlocked it.

Ieuan was still drilling the youths of Bran Dun outside. The lads were drilling their shield defence: one would thrust, the other would avert his point with the shield and counter-attack to the throat. A miscellaneous pile of weapons lay at the edge of the practice ground, and Merlin recognized a Roman scuta lying among the round Britonnic shields. At Ieuan's word, the boys ceased their practice and, panting for breath, listened to his new instructions.

"It seems," Merlin mused, almost to himself, "that Gwenddolau will listen either to the very young, or the very old. He takes the word of his friends, and of Ieuan, seriously, and when Tasgetios tells a tale in the hall at night, Gwenddolau is all rapt attention. I am neither young nor old. I may be precisely the right age to ignore."

Boudicea laughed. "Concern yourself not overmuch about it," she said. "When was it said of youths that their fame was for heeding their parents?"

"He doesn't even know I'm his father," returned Merlin. "I overheard him the other day, disclaiming me to one of his friends."

"He will not be able to deny it long," said Boudicea, becoming serious. "He favours you. Perhaps we should tell him."

Merlin did not speak at once, but at last, he said, "How would the Eicenni respond to the knowledge that neither their queen, nor their king, nor the heir to their throne has Eicenni blood in him?"

Boudicea did not reply; her eyes had turned inwards. She and Merlin strolled a little closer to the youths, and Ieuan's voice became clearer.

"It was discipline," said Ieuan, "Roman discipline that won the day at Mai Dun. If we are eventually to drive these southern eagles from our land, we must meet discipline with discipline. We must become Britonnic legions."

"No!" cried Merlin, dashing forward and releasing Boudicea's hand. She strolled up behind him. Seeing their king and queen approach, the boys and Ieuan all bowed.

"Your majesty?" said Ieuan, an eyebrow cocked. He was a small man, wiry and muscled, with dark eyes that saw things far off.

"Roman discipline," explained Merlin, "is their greatest weapon, but it's also their weakness. It's mindless discipline. They don't learn the fullness of the fight, only enough moves to overwhelm an enemy. Ieuan, can you fight like a Roman?"

Ieuan nodded, puzzled, and took up the scuta and a short sword that resembled a gladius. Merlin said to the boys, "Remember that you will meet the Romans without your shields, for the first thing they will do is cast their spears at you. Each legionnaire has two pila. They are thin-necked so that they bend upon piercing a target, and become useless. You cannot throw a pilum back. If a pilum hits you, you will be dead; more often, it will hit your shield, rendering it useless. You have to find a way to meet the Roman attack without a shield."

"What's the point of taking a shield into battle at all, then?" asked Gwenddolau.

Merlin caught his eye. "Your shield will save your life from the flight of the pilum," he said. He turned to Ieuan. "Behold. This is how a Roman wins his fight."

Ieuan attacked. With terrifying precision, he swept Merlin's blade aside with the scuta and thrust at his unprotected chest with the sword. Merlin felt the prick of the sword point, right over the heart.

"Notice," said Merlin, "that Ieuan holds the blade of the sword parallel to the ground, so that it slides easily between the ribs and out again, without catching on anything. The huge shield that the Romans carry, the scuta, easily sweeps your sword aside. And rank upon rank of these legionnaires will be moving, slowly but remorselessly, towards you, fighting in unison like ants. Ieuan, again."

Ieuan attacked again. But this time, Merlin stepped back, disengaging his sword from the scuta. The point of his sword dodged up under Ieuan's blade and hovered over his throat. A gasp of admiration went up from the boys.

"The Romans have no imagination," said Merlin. "Do what's least expected, and you will kill your man every time."

Ieuan looked at Merlin in wonder. "Where did you learn that?" he asked.

"At Mai Dun," answered Merlin.

Gwenddolau looked puzzled. "I did not know you had fought at Mai Dun," he said.

"I seldom speak of it," answered Merlin, "but Coroticos and I, and Rhydderch of Cambria, we all fought that day and, though we lost, many a youth of Rome will never see the sun rise over the seven hills again on our account."

Gwenddolau opened his mouth to speak, but was interrupted by an outcry from the direction of the gate. They turned as one, to see a guard rushing towards them. He stopped, threw down his shield and, cupping his hands about his mouth, shouted, "The Romans! The Romans are coming!"

Merlin felt a sudden coldness steal upon his heart. Beside him, Boudicea called back to the guard: "Come they in peace, or in war?"

"Armed," returned the other, "but not in warlike array."

Boudicea took in a deep breath and smiled grimly. "And I think I know why they are here." To Ieuan, she added, "We had best hide our arms."

"Aye, lady," replied Ieuan, and began issuing sharp orders. The courtyard became suddenly a flurry of activity. Not just the youths who had been practising, but all sorts of people were dashing to and fro with their arms full of swords, spears, axes, and other weapons. Merlin watched uncomprehending, as the pile at Ieuan's left hand grew steadily like some monstrous birth.

"The price of occupation," remarked Boudicea sardonically. "We are not allowed to carry weapons. In a most friendly fashion, the procurator informed me that we would have no need of them under the Peace of Rome."

Ieuan was examining a patch of turf minutely, as if searching for a lost trinket. Finding what he sought, he pulled, and a whole section of grass opened up like a trapdoor. There were evidently steps leading from the trapdoor's edge, for Ieuan descended into the pit and reached up as Bran Dun's youths passed him down armfuls of weaponry.

Boudicea snorted with contempt. "And my husband," she said bitterly, "was so enamoured of being king, that he would agree to this."

"We should rebel, mother," said a voice, and Merlin looked round to see that Gwenddolau had joined them. A deadpan expression on his face, the prince of the Eicenni stepped up to the edge of the pit and tossed his sword into the darkness. Returning to his mother's side, the boy noticed something about her, reached up, and pulled a leaf from her hair. He looked at it for a moment, dry and yellow, like a leaf of autumn, and then let it go, so that it drifted by circular paths to the turf.

"We should rebel," repeated the queen, quietly. "We should rebel."

The last dagger had been laid in the secret chamber, and Ieuan had just closed the trapdoor and smoothed the grass around the edges, when the tramp of boots was heard beyond the gate.

"Emrys, come!" cried Boudicea, and she hastened across the courtyard towards the hall, her skirts flying behind her. They hurtled up the steps and through the hall to the dais, where councilors and other noblemen were gathering. One of Boudicea's women fluttered about, dusting her face with some kind of make-up, pulling and tugging at the hem of her dress. Another placed a crown on her head and one on Merlin's. And then the fuss died down.

Servants hauled on the doors at the end of the hall, and the light from outside framed a Roman officer, flanked by subalterns and accompanied by half a dozen legionnaires. Behind them marched the standard-bearer, holding aloft a silver pole to which was attached all the medals and images that the legion had won. A dog, which had been drowsing by the door, looked up and growled, raising its hackles as the soldiers marched past.

The Romans halted before the dais and bowed their heads before the king and queen of Eicenniawn. Only the standard-bearer did not bow. The officer's eyes flicked uncertainly from Merlin to Boudicea and back again. "Your majesties," he said, "my message is to Boudicea, queen of the Iceni. We did not know that there was a new king of the Iceni."

"This is Emrys, prince of Cambria, king of Eicenniawn, my husband," replied Boudicea. "You may treat with him as you did with Prasutagos. And who are you?"

The officer snapped to attention, thumping his chest and flicking his hand out smartly in salute. "Hail, Caesar!" he cried. "I am Aulus Tullius Britannicus, Tribune of the Ninth Cohort of the Ninth Legion Hispania." He was a young man, probably in his mid-twenties, with fair skin and dark hair that showed as faint stubble on his smooth chin. His eyes were restless, ever roaming, like a beast that knows the hunters outnumber it.

"Ninth of the ninth?" repeated Boudicea. "An auspicious number. And, some would say, a fortuitous name. What would you with us?"

Tullius reached into a satchel at his hip, and drew out a scroll. He held it out to Boudicea, who ignored it, her nostrils flaring slightly. Merlin took it, broke the seal, and unrolled it, while Tullius summarized the contents.

"Know then, dread sovereign of the warlike Iceni, that as part of his last will and testament, your celebrated husband of valiant memory left to the Roman Empire one half of his fortune. This document is at this moment in Camulodunum, in the keeping of Catus Decius, the procurator. Catus extends his greetings to your majesty, along with his sincere commiserations for your husband's death. Now that a suitable period of mourning has passed, however, he wishes to remind you of the terms of your husband's will, by which half the gold in your treasury is to pass to Caesar."

Merlin ran his eye down the letter. Tullius had summarized it well—there was more detail in the written document, but the substance was identical. He looked across at Boudicea. Silence had fallen upon them, and remained like a heavy blanket for some moments before anyone spoke.

"We are grateful to you, Aulus Tullius Britannicus, for reminding us of our duty to Caesar," said Boudicea at last. "This last will and testament you mention, we are very curious about it."

Tullius blinked. "It is in Camulodunum," he said. "I have seen it myself. Catus Decius showed it to me himself, and I perused the contents. There is nothing irregular about it."

"Sure we are that you are quite correct, Tribune Tullius," replied Boudicea, with a sweetness that one who knew her better would have feared. "How did our late husband ratify this document?"

"By the royal seal of the Iceni, madam—even that which you carry upon your finger." Tullius pointed.

Boudicea looked down upon the seal, then up again at Tullius. "We shall in all our best intents obey the worthy procurator," she said. "Our husband, though, was advanced in years, and may not have understood the terms of the contract. Accordingly, we should like to see it, so that the wisest of our councilors can examine its contents and judge of its veracity."

Tullius looked affronted. "It is a legal document, madam," he said, rather pompously, "witnessed by senators of the gravest dispositions and irrefutable honesty."

"We are certain of it, Tribune," said Boudicea. "But we have grave and wise and honest men here, who we are sure would like to view this document ere they make any commitment of gold to Caesar. Have it brought here, and we shall in good faith pass our judgement upon it." Rising from her throne, she began to descend from the dais. "In the meantime, Aulus Tullius, you are welcome to Bran Dun. Our servants will show you to your quarters. You must stay with us tonight, our chiefest guest, and share our repast."

"Madam, I should not like to trespass on your hospitality . . . " began Tullius.

"Nay!" interjected the queen, stopping in her tracks to address the officer directly. "By your account, Britannicus, you already own half of my inheritance. Half of what is mine is yours, so enjoy it freely, and do not fear trespassing upon our hospitality. We insist you stay and enjoy the feast." She started to leave, then hesitated again. "Of course," she said, "we shall take the cost of feeding you and your men from *your* half of the kingdom's possessions, not our own." And she swept away from him and out of the hall. A servant stepped forward and waited for the Roman to gather his wits together.

XII

The Romans left the following morning, and Boudicea called together the Council of the Eicenni. They gathered together in a circle about the central hearth, which guttered and spewed smoke like a wheezy old man, themselves a circle of silver heads, nodding slowly as words of wisdom went this way and that.

"Caution is best," advised one old man. "These Romans dominate the world. Not a nation on earth but is swayed by them. Half of Prasutagos' wealth is, after all, a small price to pay for peace and security. When the wolf is at your door, better feed it your sheep than your child."

"But fight, my queen!" cried another. "If we should die, at least we will not have lived as slaves. Let us live and die as men and women of Eicenni-awn, not as slaves of Rome."

"But think!" urged another. "The payment is great only if we pay all at once. Let us pay a little now, a little a year from now, and so on. Very soon, it will be more effort to collect than benefit to the Romans, and they will neglect it. The Romans have a legend. They say their city was founded by one who was suckled by a wolf. I say, give the wolf enough to keep him happy, and perhaps he will terrorize other beasts."

"You do wrong," said Merlin suddenly, "to compare Rome to a wolf." The old men fell silent; all turned their heads in his direction. "Romulus and Remus lived long ago," said Merlin. "They are not now as they were then. A wolf is untamable, and lives wholly upon its appetite. It thinks of its belly, of its physical wellness, all the time. It is impatient, and swallows whatever is nearby. Rome is no longer a wolf. She can wait—she has waited, for many years, ere she completed the conquest of these islands. She can go hungry for many years too, if it will get her what she wants in the end. A wolf can never wait. Rome is full of guile, more like a fox than any other creature."

One of the old men spoke up. "My lord Emrys—his Majesty—does well to correct our imagery," he said, "but his point is one of poetic style, and what we seek is a practical solution to our problem."

"Yet Emrys is right," interjected Boudicea, speaking for the first time during the council. "Rome is not the wolf. I am the wolf, Eicenniawn is the wolf, the whole Island of the Mighty is the wolf. They have wrested our food from us, they have stolen our cubs, and what are we to do? We cannot stay in our cave and lick our wounds. It might be the wise thing to do, but it would not be right for us. It would not be our thing to do. A wolf must act like a wolf, and not like a sheep. Wise or not wise, it makes no difference. We must be who we are. This council is at an end. We shall decide what we shall do, and inform you of it ere nightfall. We bid you all good day, and thank you for your many pains."

The councilors rose slowly from their seats and began to drain from the hall. One of them, Segofax, a fellow whose barklike skin contrasted with the whiteness of his hair, lingered. "Madam my queen," he said, "I would urge you to consider well of what I have said. Your husband, of honoured memory, was wont to trust in my word. We flew the hawk together as children, and navigated the waterways of Eicenniawn in a wherry we built ourselves. He and I, we knew the people of the fens well, we understood their hopes and their dreams, and . . . "

Boudicea reached out and placed a comforting hand on his arm. "I shall not abuse the trust that the people of Eicenniawn have placed in me," she said. "I know I am a newcomer to these parts. I was raised far away from here, among the mountains in Cambria. But I shall not betray the Eicenni. You have the word of a queen."

To Merlin's surprise, the aged man stooped and, with much labour, went down upon one knee, bending his snowy head before his queen. "The gods rain blessings upon the Lady of the Eicenni," he said. "Whatever path you choose, know that Segofax of Caer Rhydd is your man in life and death."

Boudicea reached out to him and raised him up gently. "Segofax," she said, "we know your loyalty well, and doubt it not. Go now and return to your people, and tell them, their queen will not abandon their hopes."

The old man kissed Boudicea's hand, turned, and hobbled from the hall. Merlin did not speak for a long time, but stood marveling at Boudicea. Eventually, she turned, and noticed him.

Merlin dropped to one knee before his wife. "You are every inch a queen," he said, almost in a whisper. "My love and my mistress. I did not know until this moment what it meant to be queen."

Boudicea's smile flashed for a moment, and she struggled for several seconds to conquer it. She said, rather brusquely, "Love is a useful tool; people will obey you if they love you."

"If they fear you too," said Merlin, "but you are no Cartimandua, my love."

"Please arise!" pleaded Boudicea, shaking herself and pulling on Merlin. "You are my Emrys, my love, my husband. It is I should kneel to you. This is base and servile. Do not so!"

Merlin was on his feet, and he suddenly drew her to him and clasped her close, burying his face in the soft warmth of her hair. "What are we to do?" he asked.

Boudicea drew away and looked up at him. "I am your queen?" she said earnestly. "For life or death, you will do my will?"

"I shall."

"Find Excalibur," she said. "I can stall the Romans by paying them piecemeal, but I do not think they will be fooled for more than three or four years. Then we must fight. But only with Excalibur can we hope to win."

Her words fell upon Merlin like blows from a sword, and he stood mute for many long moments. "My love," he said, reaching up and brushing her cheek with his fingers, "I cannot deny that the quest for Excalibur is the great quest of my life, and yet to leave you now . . . "

"Emrys," replied the queen, "there will be a time of peace for us, when we can love one another as man and woman should. But there is work to be done first. It is the Romans will not let us have this time, and they must be thrust out."

Merlin nodded. "It has long grown in my heart," he said, "that this was but a brief sojourn, and that I must sooner or later be about my work once more. But it grieves me more than I can say to leave you."

They embraced, plying kiss upon kiss as if they were departing one another's company for ever. At length, their lips drew apart, and Merlin said, "It was you, many years ago, who first set my feet upon this path, and now you do it again. I shall return as soon as I may. In the meantime, know that I love you, and while I live, I shall love no other."

Boudicea's eyes shone with tears. "It is not for ever, my love," she said. "There will be a time, when the needs of the Island of the Mighty have been satisfied, when Boudicea and Emrys too can be satisfied. There will be a time for us."

Merlin blinked. For the briefest moment, quicker than it takes to wink, he saw blood upon the snow, and the great grey carcass of a she-wolf. Cold he felt, but he pushed his feelings down, and said, "There will be time for us, my love. But now I go to find again my path. I must speak with my old master, Gwelydd. He will know how I can pick it up once more. He will know. Perhaps there are secrets the Sacred Hill will reveal to me. I must visit other places, but I must begin at Afallach." He drew a deep breath, like a swimmer about to dive in. "So now," he said, "I must go once more and seek the sword of kings, so that our son can take the throne of the High King."

"Go, my love," she said, "and the gods go with you."

* * *

Merlin left early the following morning, before the sun had begun to scatter its grey light over the brackish waters of the fens. He kissed Boudicea on the cheek, the neck, and the shoulder, and she stirred a little in her sleep but did not awaken. He paused awhile, fixing the image of her sleeping face in his mind, like a clerk writing down carefully a thing he wishes to remember. Then he turned and passed out into the hall.

Gwenddolau slept in the hall, beside the door to his mother's chamber, and Merlin hesitated a moment as he passed the boy.

An old story had caused him to hesitate, a legend spoken by old wives at night to send their children off to sleep with a tale of ancient days. The High Kings of Britain, they said, the Chief Dragons, bore a hereditary birthmark, a dragon's head, on their shoulders. The true High King would always be known by this birthmark. The ancient ones of Caermyrddin had always insisted on the legend, late at night in the taverns. Merlin had forgotten it until this moment. And Gwenddolau slept in such a way that, just by raising the blanket a little, Merlin could see it, if it were there. Merlin stood debating a while. Slowly, carefully, feeling almost embarrassed to do so, Merlin reached out and lifted the blanket.

There was no birthmark, of course, just the smooth skin of youth covering the shoulder-blade. After all, it was only a legend. Merlin dropped the cover, and strode through the sleeping forms of Boudicea's meinie and through the doors, into the wakening world.

* * *

The course Merlin initially took was the reverse of that by which he had arrived in Bran Dun, over a year before. The weather was much the same, even, with cool, salty breezes blowing in from the north to take the edge off the strengthening sun of early summer. After two days, he left the coastline behind and found himself moving almost due west, through hills and past villas. Two more days brought him to Fosse Way and, after that, he left the Roman province of Britannia behind him, and struck off into the misty hills of the Island of the Mighty.

The terrain was tougher in the midst of the realm, for he was passing through the foothills of the Penines. It was over a week after crossing Fosse Way that he finally saw the sea again. But this was the Eirish Sea. He stood for a while amid the sand dunes, gazing out over the iron-grey expanse, while the puffins bobbed on the light waves or waddled to and fro at the margin of the sea. Somehow, he reflected, it smelled different from the other sea. It smelled like home. He looked westward, along the coast. If his eyes had been keen enough, he knew he would be looking at Afallach. With a lighter heart, Merlin adjusted the weight of the pack on his back and strode off along the coast.

He finally found himself approaching Afallach at the height of summer, when apples were swelling on the branches, and the wind sang its whispering song through the leaves while it tugged at the unreachable clouds that stretched across a sky wrought from one huge sapphire. Merlin stood for a moment, drinking deeply of the smell of the earth. Some things, he thought, never changed.

"Merlin!" cried a voice. Emerging from the forest, a basket of oak galls on his arm, came Aled. "Merlin, it *is* you! I thought so! Where have you been!" Setting down the basket, Aled clasped Merlin in his arms and embraced him tightly. "The gods be good to you, Merlin, and welcome back to Afallach!"

"I am happily repaid for the toils of the journey by seeing you again, old friend!" replied Merlin. "There is more grey in your hair, I see, than the last time we met."

"And yet my head does not lack," rejoined Aled, swiping merrily at the balding top of Merlin's head. Aled took up the basket and they started walking together into the druid settlement. "We druids may exert many powers over the natural world," he said, "but we cannot yet turn time backwards. If it could be done, I believe Dergen would find a way."

"To recall the past is to relive it," said Merlin quietly, recalling one of the axioms by which Dergen taught memory. "But recalling my full head of hair does not make it grow again. How is Iorwerth?" he asked.

"As well as ever," answered Aled, "and as verbose as ever."

"You do him an injustice."

"Not at all," answered Aled. "I speak only from affection. Many are the words of Iorwerth, and each of them individually, and all of them together, worthy."

"How is it that you still dwell in Afallach?" asked Merlin. "I was certain you would have moved on by now, to one of the noble houses of the north, perhaps, since you know their ways so well."

"It has fallen to me to tend Gwelydd in his age."

Merlin nodded. "I knew in my heart that he lived still," he said. "Had he died, I feel sure I should have known."

"He is weak," Aled explained, "and cannot now leave his bed. Few live to the age he has attained. Do you know, he can remember Cassivelaunos as High King?" There seemed nothing Merlin could say to this, so Aled went on: "He will be pleased to see you. I wonder if he didn't know you were coming. He has seemed, these last few days, to be waiting for something. He speaks of death, as he was not wont to do before, but he speaks as if Death were a servant, whom he has ordered to wait for him." Merlin frowned, but still said nothing. Aled said, "I will not tell you, *Do not tax the great druid's strength.* I think he has been gathering his strength for this. Seeing you might be the effort that will sever his spirit from his body—he, who has guided so many souls to their final destinations—but I think that many of his efforts might well be meaningless if I prevent you from seeing him. And," Aled concluded, with a smile, "when you are as old as he, seeing old friends is more important than drawing out a few more moments in this world."

"Should I go and see him now," asked Merlin, "or should I wait until I have washed?"

"If you were he," replied Aled, "which would you rather?"

They had reached the Cave of Knowledge, and Archdruid Amon stood outside. Evidently, someone had noted Merlin's approach, and run to him with the news. Amon held out his hands and embraced Merlin.

"Merlin Emrys," he said, "we are honoured that you choose to visit us."

"I am happy to be among friends once more," replied Merlin.

“I trust your time has been successfully spent since you left Afallach?”

“I have had my share of joys and troubles,” answered Merlin. “You will have heard of Cartimandua’s betrayal of Coroticos?”

“It was not entirely unexpected to those who knew her character well,” said Amon, “and I believe you warned his Majesty that it might be the case.”

“That does not lessen the bitterness of the betrayal.”

“Well, Cartimandua is with her gods now,” remarked Amon. “She is past our judgement. Is it to see Gwelydd you have come here?”

Merlin nodded. “I seek his advice.”

“He is within.” As Merlin passed, Amon put out a hand to stay him a moment. “He is not as you remember,” said the archdruid. “We look for each day to be his last. Few among men have seen his years. Many of the oaks from which Aled gathers the galls were but saplings in Gwelydd’s youth. Perhaps it would be better if one prepared him, let him know of your arrival, before you went in yourself. That would also give you a chance to wash and rest a little, and perhaps eat a light repast. You must be weary after your journey.”

“I am,” said Merlin, “and I thank you for your kind attention. But there is haste upon me and, I think, upon him too.” Merlin smiled. “Fear not,” he said. “I shall not tax Gwelydd beyond his strength.”

“It is nothing short of miraculous that you should arrive at this moment,” said Amon. “He might have died without ever seeing you again.”

“The gods have blessed my path,” said Merlin, and entered the Cave of Knowledge.

The interior was well-lit, as always, and several acolytes, scratching away at curly-edged parchments, looked up as Merlin entered. The smell of warm wax and ink was heavy upon the air, but welcome to Merlin, for whom it had been but a memory for several years now. Merlin nodded a greeting to the acolytes, who returned the greeting and went back to their work.

Gwelydd, Merlin knew, would be in his private chamber, next to the Chamber of Sleeping. Merlin bowed his head and went in.

Gwelydd had always been old, as long as Merlin had known him, but he had been hardy, robust, powerful. The power was gone. He was the husk of a man, as if the vital force had been sucked out of him, leaving his limbs bony, his cheeks hollow. But his eyes shone brightly in the dim light and, seeing Merlin enter, he pressed his lips into a smile.

"So," creaked the voice of Gwelydd, former Archdruid of the Island of the Mighty, "you are come at last. Well, I knew you would—a dying man is granted some measure of the Sight, you know." He wheezed a few moments with laughter. "You are not the only prophet in this room," he remarked. Setting his head back against his pillow, he breathed easily for a while. "Well, now I can get on with this business of dying. If you had been but a little while longer, this pedant, Death, would have had me away." He smiled, in a tired sort of way. "He is so particular," he said. "I am late doing the work he has set me, and he taps his foot and looks always upon the hourglass."

Now that Merlin could see his former teacher, he felt his chest quiver, and tears roll down his cheeks. He rushed forward to the bedside. "Master Gwelydd," he said, "you should be resting."

"Nonsense," returned Gwelydd. "You sound like Amon. If going to a little effort hastens my death, well, all I can say is that I have lived a very long time. A few hours, a few days, even, is little compared with the long years I have seen. But you came here for information, and I have stayed alive so that you could ask me what you will. There are things that are troubling you, Emrys, things that you do not understand about your quest. Ask. In what measure is granted me by the gods, I shall answer." And he sat up in bed, an acolyte hastening to arrange pillows behind him. His eyes glittered, like a vein of gold in a darkened shaft. His body was dying, but his mind was alert and alive.

XIII

Gwelydd's hand reached out, wavering, and the acolyte handed him a cup of wine, which he lifted laboriously to his lips, sipping a few times before returning it to the acolyte. Merlin knew what he wanted to ask, but the sight of his former master's weakness had silenced him. A tear, which he would have suppressed, had he the power, squeezed out of one eye and rolled down his cheek. He brushed it away furiously.

"Do not fear the approbation of a dying man," said Gwelydd. "Tell me what troubles you."

Merlin sat down upon the edge of the bed, and taking up Gwelydd's hand, stroked it gently. The skin was as dry as parchment, and cold as earth. He said, "Master, I still do not understand the gift the gods have sent me. I have not found Excalibur, nor have I found any clue to its whereabouts. Time is running out for me. When will I find the answers I seek? I have a family now—a wife, a fine son, and two beautiful daughters. Must I desert them for ever in pursuit of a dream, a wisp of nothingness?" Merlin beat his fist against his palm. "Will I never be done with this quest?" he demanded, a snarl in his voice. But then he saw the face of the dying man, and struggled to contain his frustration. "I have completed four decades upon this earth," he said, more quietly now, "and I know no more now than I did as a child how to master the gift that the gods have granted me."

"No more did Llygat, the last druid to be possessed of the Sight," answered Gwelydd. "He learned to control it—you have read his book."

"That is not what I do not understand," said Merlin. "There is another matter, one which troubles me sorely." Gwelydd waited patiently, while Merlin sought the words. "My quest is to find Excalibur," he said. "I know so little about it—that it was forged by Arawn, King of the Morforwyn, in the dawn of days; that Argante, his consort, wove a sheath strong in enchantment to go with it. I know that Morgana wants Excalibur, and I think she sends me visions that spur me on my way. But I have heard nothing from Argante, or from Arawn. Why is that?" Merlin took a breath, and continued. "Many years ago, when I left Afallach the first time, I was taken to Morgana's fortress in Annwn. She said she wanted to find Excalibur and return it to Britain. It did not sound unreasonable to me." Merlin sighed deeply. "What side should I be on? Is there any real difference between good and evil? I understand nothing!" The frustration was back in his voice, and in the tense lines of his shoulders, but now he did not seek to hide it.

Gwelydd spoke not for long moments; so long, in fact, that Merlin wondered if he had not fallen asleep, or worse. But at last, the old man stirred, and raised his aged eyes to Merlin's.

"You have learned much in Afallach," he said, "but you have not learned all, because you chose another path. You chose not to become a druid. And so, your knowledge could not be complete. Tell me what you know about the forging of Excalibur."

"Only what I have said—that Arawn forged it, and Argante made a sheath for it. When Brutus the Trojan arrived on these shores, Argante gave Excalibur to him. He passed it on to his son Locrin, and so on, down to Cassivelaunos, who gave it to Belinos for safekeeping when Julius Caesar invaded."

Gwelydd coughed, a hand fluttering to his chest. He seemed for a few seconds to be in the midst of a coughing fit, and the acolyte raised his wine cup to his lips. Gradually, Gwelydd overcame the fit and fixed his eyes again on Merlin.

"Your knowledge," he said, "is incomplete. The deepest, most closely guarded secret of our order, no one here can reveal to you. Why is the blood of men required by good gods? Why do not the Morforwyn speak to you in your visions? Why does only Morgana speak to you?" Gwelydd pressed his eyelids together for a moment, gathering his strength. "Blood is the secret. Blood. There is no god but Morgana, and she must have blood," said Gwelydd. "That is why life is one long scream, terminated by oblivion. The gods of old have deserted us and what remains demands blood."

And Merlin felt as if he were suddenly on the edge of a deep precipice, the point of a knife in his back.

But he was not finished yet. He could yet get a hand-hold, cling to the cliff, and perhaps clamber up it once more. He said, "This cannot be, master. Where did Excalibur come from, if not from Arawn and Argante? Are all the stories untrue? Where did Brutus get his sword?"

"There is one tale yet," said Gwelydd. "None here may reveal it to you, and it was never set in writing. The gods are dead, and only Morgana lives."

"Gwelydd, you can tell me." Merlin clasped his hand, held it tightly. "What is there for you to lose?"

"You are right." Gwelydd smiled, multiplying the wrinkles in his face many times over. "A dying man stands to lose nothing. But even a dying man is bound by the oaths he has sworn, or else he is but a beast, less than man. And I have sworn to keep the secrets of my order. Now I go to join those who came before me. Lay me out in the Chamber of Sleepers, Merlin Emrys. I cannot take my long rest among the druids of past ages, if I am not worthy to do so."

"You are worthy, Gwelydd," Merlin assured him, lowering his face so that Gwelydd could catch his words. "You are worthy, for you have kept the rules of your order. And you are worthy, because you have been as a father to me, and I have loved you." But ere Merlin had ceased to speak, he felt the cold breath on his cheek, and a stillness came over Gwelydd that no mortal could disturb. And Merlin wept, shedding bitter tears upon the stiffening hand of his old master.

"Master?" Merlin looked up. He had forgotten about the acolyte, who was now bending over the still form of Gwelydd, his face beginning to contort.

"The Master has gone," said Merlin.

"Oh, no!" wept the boy. "No, no, no!" And he fled the chamber, the door slamming behind him. Merlin stayed with his old friend and tutor, his head bent upon the old man's chest, shedding furious tears.

At a noise behind him, Merlin turned, and saw that Aled and Amon were framed in the light of the doorway.

"So, he has gone at last," said Amon. "Thus passes the greatest of us."

"Peace be upon him, wherever he is," added Aled.

Merlin got to his feet slowly and brushed away the tears. Gwelydd's face did indeed look peaceful. But he had left behind him strife in the breast of Merlin Emrys.

* * *

Merlin stayed for another week, while Gwelydd's body was prepared for interment, and then they laid him in the Chamber of Sleepers. He no longer looked like Merlin's old friend, but like a mockery of him. He had become an object, a statue of Gwelydd sculpted by one who had never seen men. Merlin stood beside him for a long time, his head bent, but his eyes unseeing. At length, he turned upon his heel and left the Cave of Knowledge, emerging into the incongruous sunshine of an August afternoon. A knot of druids stood outside.

"Gwelydd is still alive," said Dergen. "He has done with this body, but he will take up residence in another, probably nearby."

"Dergen the optimist!" said someone Merlin did not recognize.

"Many of us believe in transmigration," said Dergen defensively. "My studies assume it. Imagine it! If we could so train our memory that we could recall events not just from early in our present lives, but also from former lives, why—"

"Well, Gwelydd is gone," said Amon, interrupting Dergen with deliberateness. "He is gone from among us, and we must somehow continue to do our work." The druids began to disperse, leaving Merlin and Aled strolling slowly along the path.

Merlin looked left and right. Somehow, everything seemed wrong. He seemed to have passed from one foreign land into another, from the land of death into a land that had been transformed utterly by his sojourn elsewhere. Strange were the faces of the druids and the acolytes they passed in their walk, and strange was Aled's face when he turned to look at him. It was like seeing Aled underwater.

"Will you stay any longer?" asked Aled, and his question seemed almost ingenuous to Merlin. For a moment, Merlin was nonplussed; then he shook his head.

"I must continue to seek Excalibur," he said. Merlin focused on Aled's face, trying to force it into familiarity. The other's expression was blank, noncommittal, almost inhuman. "Perhaps, though," said Merlin hesitantly, "you can help me."

"In any way I can," replied Aled, though Merlin could see that they were utterly divided from one another, like two travelers following parallel paths, who might see each other from a distance, but never shake hands or embrace, for their paths never converge. "You have only to speak," said Aled.

Merlin thought for a moment. "One of the last things Gwelydd told me," he explained, at length, "was that the gods of old were dead, and only Morgana is left. Do you know any more of this?"

Merlin's remark was greeted by a sharp intake of breath. Aled stopped in his tracks. "He told you that?" he said.

"He said that none here would be allowed to tell me," said Merlin. "But I implore you, by all the ties of old friendship, as the only real friend I have in the world, Aled, tell me what you know of the death of the gods."

A change had come over Aled's countenance. His eyes had grown wide, and blood had drained from his face. One of his hands clutched at his throat. "It is forbidden," he whispered. "It is one of the deepest secrets of our order. None may reveal it."

"Oh, for the gods' sakes!" cried Merlin. "There is more at stake here than your stories—the fate of our kingdom lies in our hands."

Aled shook his head slowly, the corners of his mouth turned down. “It would mean death,” he said, in a strangled sort of voice. “Death for the one who reveals it, death to him to whom it was revealed.”

“Aled.” Merlin took his friend by the shoulders and glared directly into his eyes. “With Excalibur, and only with Excalibur, can our people drive the Romans out of the Island of the Mighty, and live free once more. Have you been south of Fosse Way? Our people are in chains. This is more important than the oath you swore to your brother druids. It must be—can you not see that?”

Aled shook his head again. “It is not,” he said, and Merlin felt his shoulders vibrate with the words, as if it was Aled’s whole soul and body that were speaking in unison. “You seek only to protect a nation,” said Aled. “But Morgana is more powerful than the Emperor, more terrible than lightning.”

“You fear her?”

“Of course I fear her!” Aled shook himself free of Merlin. “Of course I fear her,” he repeated. “Who does not fear death? But I love her too, and it is the love that silences me. Merlin, my friend, seek not to know more, but shun this knowledge. Shun it, run away, and hide.” He opened his arms to indicate Afallach. “We are the only hope for the Island of the Mighty,” he said. “Who else do you imagine can shield the crofters and the herdsmen and the wives and maidens of Britain against the wrath of Morgana? You, with your books and your visions? The High King, with his square house and shorthaired friends in Rome? If a leaky dyke is your only defence against the sea, Merlin, you had best repair the wall, rather than seek to tear it down.”

Merlin felt giddy—it seemed to him that the whole world, Afallach, Aber Alaw nearby, all of Cambria was swinging about him in a lazy circle that grew steadily faster and faster. He put out a hand to a tree to steady himself, and the giddiness evaporated. He bit his knuckle, his eyes staring vacantly at the dappled green shade of the apple tree.

At last, he turned upon Aled. "Morgana killed the gods herself," he said. "How did she kill them? How do you kill a god? You tell the world it is not so, because . . . why? If there are in truth no gods, how would that—"

"I can tell you nothing, Merlin," Aled interrupted him bitterly. "All I can tell you is what you already know—that life is a long scream—"

"Terminated by oblivion," cut in Merlin. "Yes, I know. I've heard it. But a part of this story is missing. I cannot even tell if what Gwelydd said was true, or just a lie to protect the Order." Gwelydd, he knew, would not lie; but how clear had his mind been, with the mist of death descending upon him? Merlin's eyes snapped on Aled's. "The Order is finished," he said. "One way or another, it has been a lie all this time, all these centuries."

Aled recoiled at Merlin's words. He drew himself up tall, his nostrils a little flared. "It is but our Order that stands between Morgana's wrath and the people of Britain," he said. "But you will find no further help among the druids. Follow other paths to seek your wisdom, Merlin of no father. Go to your philosophers in Greece, or go to your books in Lundein. Go to the Romans, for all we care, but go. You seek what you can never find as you are. You would tread a path upon which you have long since turned your back. Farewell, Merlin." Aled wheeled about and strode from the shadow of the apple tree.

"Aled!" called Merlin; but the other did not look back. Merlin cursed inwardly. With slow steps, he made his way back to the hut where he had dwelt all those years before his captivity in Cameliard. It had stood empty long, but over the last few days, he had breathed a little life into the gloomy surroundings. Dust still covered his books, his maps, and his instruments.

Suddenly, Merlin felt unaccountably tired, and he stretched his limbs out on the narrow cot in the loft. His eyes were heavy, and soon he drifted into a dreamless sleep.

And yet it was not quite dreamless; for at the deepest, darkest moment of his sleep, a vision came to Merlin, and he saw Boudicea all armed, Gwenddolau at her side. She was covered with blood, a sword held high over her head, the Eicenni swarming around her like ants. Around her were the ruins of a shattered city, the broken shells of buildings spouting fire and smoke. Merlin could hear the roar and crackle of the flames, and the acrid smell clung to the insides of his nostrils.

His eyes snapped open. He lay in the cot in his hut in Afallach, but the sound of flames and the smell of smoke lingered still. He sat bolt upright.

Flames were licking up the inside of his walls. The thatch of the ceiling had already caught, and the manuscripts on his table were aflame. Merlin cried out in anguish, leaping down his ladder and rushing over to the fire. Water! He needed water. He looked around. Normally, he kept a pail in the hut, but since his return to Afallach, he had neglected to do so. The well —that was it.

Merlin's hand was upon the latch of the door when a prickling sensation along his spine stayed him. He stood a moment, frozen, while brands of fire tumbled from the ceiling. He looked up. It was past remedy. Once the thatch had caught, everything in the house was done for, he knew that.

Cautiously, Merlin leaned forward and set his eye to a gap in the window-shutter. He peered out into the night.

Bathed in the glow of the fire stood a line of druids. He recognized Aled, and Amon—even Dergen and Iorwerth were there. Most of them carried firebrands, but some had already tossed theirs into Merlin's hut.

With a shock that felt like a blow to the heart, Merlin realized that it was his own friends who had set his hut afire.

XIV

The whole roof was aflame now. The roof-beam began to creak and groan, and Merlin saw instantly that it would not last many more seconds. He cast his eyes about the hut that had been his Afallach home for so long. The druids were ranged upon the north side of the house, since that was where the means of egress were—a door and three windows. They knew that Merlin favoured north-facing windows for the evenness of the light; but he did build one south-facing window, and now wondered if they had remembered that. He dashed across the room, raising his hands over his head to fend off the fireballs that were dropping from the roof with increasing regularity. He fumbled with the latch, and peered out into the night.

The apple trees were close, and rising, for there, above his head, reared the great black form of the Sacred Hill, lit for the moment by the lurid light of the burning hut.

But there were no druids that way.

Merlin flung the shutters open wide, and snaked through the opening. He dropped to the ground, rolled, and was on his feet in a trice. Four swift paces brought him to the edge of the trees, and he swung himself up into the lower branches of one. He felt the twigs scratching him, catching at his clothes. To his surprise, he found that he was singing, crooning a soft song as he pulled himself from branch to branch.

Sweet apple tree spreads its boughs through the smoke,
Its virtue hides me from the men of the oak.
A swarming crowd at its base, a host about its roots
And I a treasure concealed from those who search at its foot.
Now Aled loves not me, no welcome from Amon,
Iorwerth reveres me not, I am hateful to Dergen.
Swelling with fruits, sweet apple trees,

Hide me, hide me from my enemies.

In the midst of the tree, the bole divided, and Merlin squatted at the fork, looking back at the flaming mass that had been his home. The smoke belched upwards, blotting out the stars.

Suddenly, it seemed to Merlin that time had gone backwards and, a youth, he hid on the edge of a clearing, listening to the drums and watching as the wicker man was consumed by flames.

But then he was back in the present, and it was his home, not a sacrifice, that was sending its smoke up into the heavens.

With a terrific noise, the roof collapsed, sending a mushroom-shaped cloud of smoke, lit eerily from beneath, up into the night sky. Even in his concealment, Merlin felt the wave of hot air rush over him. The south wall teetered and fell, a mass of charred beams. The druids began to circle the house completely, still keeping their distance. The closest of them was Aled —Merlin could see the top of his head distinctly. If he had had a sword, he could have hacked it in two. But Merlin had brought nothing from the hut. He smiled grimly. And they said he had foresight!

The fire had died down now that most of its fuel had been consumed, but the heat remained as a barrier that Merlin could almost push with his fingers, as pliable as clay, but searing. He watched for a few moments. The druids were starting to douse the fire with buckets of water, and the thick pall of black began to be flecked with paler clouds of steam.

For the first time, the fact began to sink in that the druids had sought to kill him. His fingers tightened about the branch of the apple tree. But he was alone and unarmed, and they were many, all bearing the sickles of their profession. Flight was his only chance. Merlin turned away from the dying blaze. The trees grew thickly, and he was able to pass from one to the next like a squirrel, leaping on occasion, but mostly reaching out and swinging himself across the narrow gap.

Merlin made his way from tree to tree without looking left or right, and he did not notice that he had been climbing steadily upwards until the trees ran out and he looked over the bald patch of grass that surmounted the Sacred Hill. No one was about. Merlin clambered down the tree and climbed the few remaining feet to the summit.

Above him, the firmament was spread out in spangled brilliance, marred to the north by the blotch of smoke. The world was in darkness, but Merlin could see it: he could see the ploughman asleep beside his wife in Aber Alaw, the king with eyes starting in Caermyrddin. He could even see Coroticos, his hair shorn, his clothes ill-fitting, in his square house on a straight street in Rome.

And then he saw Morgana, robed like a queen, and seated upon a throne. And the seat of the throne was wrought from a single piece of marble, and the characters of an ancient language were etched around its edge. Merlin knew that that was the Siege Perilous, the Seat of Danger, and that one who sat upon it knew all things. The Siege Perilous, the source of all knowledge. The Sight, the gift of the gods to a selected few among mortals. Merlin looked upon the throne, and he knew whence came his visions, and he fell to his knees before Morgana.

"So, you see it," she said, descending from the throne. "At last, you know the truth. There are no gods. There is only me, Morgana, Queen of the Morforwyn and of the Island of the Mighty. I am the Lady of the Lake, the mistress of the hearts of a hundred thousand men and women. All pleasure, all hatred, all that is good, and all that is evil flow from me. It was I who brought life to the lifeless shores of Albion in the dawn of time. Love me and fear me, for those who do, do not die."

"It's a lie," said Merlin, though he knew he could neither prove nor defend his words. "None of this is true. It can't be."

"Here we are upon the crest of the Seeing Hill, the Sacred Hill of Afallach," said Morgana. "And here, you see before you the Siege Perilous, wrought so that who sits upon it may know all things. Take your place, Merlin: see all things, know all things. You will know the truth then."

"I am not worthy to do so."

"You will not be worthy if you dare not do it," answered she. And she cast down her robes, and stood before him in a simple shift, arrayed in all her beauty and magnificence and terror. She held out her hands towards him, her fingers long and beckoning, and Merlin felt his limbs move in response. His knees jerked straight, and one foot lifted.

"This is not it," he muttered. "It cannot be this. It is only my body—my mind is free! I have escaped from the cave."

He bent his will against the force that drove his limbs, but still his feet moved inexorably towards the marble slab.

"Why resist?" asked Morgana. "This is what you always wanted—you wanted to *know*. The Siege Perilous can tell you all you wish to know. It can tell you how to find Excalibur. Resistance is foolish. Give in, and rule with me."

"If this thing can tell me how to find Excalibur," said Merlin, between gritted teeth, "then why have not *you* found it yet?"

And, bending his will utterly upon his own body, he lurched around to face her.

There was doubt upon the face of Morgana; for a moment, her will ebbed. Merlin fell away from her clutches, and stumbled into the Siege Perilous. He glanced against it, and then spun to the ground, his fingers sinking deep into the earth.

For a fleeting moment, as he had touched the Siege Perilous, he had had a glimpse of what it could reveal. All of creation flashed before him, pressed down upon his head and his shoulders. He could still feel the weight upon him—it had knocked the wind out of his lungs.

He looked up. Morgana was gone. The Siege Perilous was gone. The morning breeze blew in from the sea, and scattered the last rags of smoke from the conflagration below. The druids began to disperse. Merlin took to his heels and dissolved into the forest.

* * *

Merlin fled into the south, through the gentle hills of Ynys Mon, across the Straits, and along the coast of Cereticiaun Bay, the mountains of Eryri marching majestically on his left. But he strode along as one pursued by unseen demons, looking constantly over his shoulder. He saw not the brooding mountain-tops, nor the sparkle of the late-summer sun upon the wave-tops. Images crowded his mind—images of violence, of blood and fire and broken buildings. His feet seemed to find their way without the help of his eyes, and he walked—sometimes, he ran—like one pursued. When the coast curved westwards, he struck off among the forests of Dyfed. He knew he was not far from Caermyrddin.

That night, as night was falling, Merlin came across a hawthorn, its branches thick with its dark green leaves, but spotted with rags of cloth. People from a nearby village had, according to their tradition, cast their old clothes upon the hawthorn tree as soon as May was finished, as a way of bidding farewell to the unlucky season. Merlin rested his head against a nearby rock, and kept one eye on the ill-fated form until sleep overtook him. And then he dreamed.

He dreamed of a man, who wore a plate of bronze on his chest and a helmet plumed in white upon his head. Behind the man, ships were drawn up on a sandy shores and from their topmasts fluttered pennons bearing the charge of a horse's head. The man knelt before a woman, who was handing him a sword—*the* sword, Excalibur. But the image was a fleeting one. Now he saw Boudicea, riding her chariot, her plaids flying behind her, a spear in one hand, a shield in the other. Beside her stood Gwenddolau, and he grasped Excalibur before him, its blade flashing red in the rays of the dying sun.

"I am dreaming," thought Merlin. "I must see more."

He saw the man again, to whom the woman had given Excalibur. He was dark of complexion, and his hair and beard hung in tight curls about his head. His eye was fierce. About him stood other men, dark of face and hair, stern of countenance, though none quite so fierce as he. And there were women among them, fair of face and lithe of body, and it seemed a light like the sun on moving water played about them.

Merlin wanted to see more, but the scene shifted again, and his ears filled with the cries of battle, the clash of sword upon sword, the shrieking of horses. Above the press, Excalibur swung in a glittering arc, carving the helms of the Romans who came before Gwenddolau.

"But how can I find it?" wondered Merlin. "Where is the sword now?"

The battle raged on. Boudicea fought alongside her son, her face and arms thick with blood. And then she paused, and turned her face towards Merlin. The eyes glared, yellow by some trick of the light, and her lips were pulled away from her teeth. For a moment, she did not seem human. Merlin screamed, and threw his hands up over his face.

He was awake in a moment, panting heavily, cold sweat springing up on his skin. He grew suddenly still, and turned his eyes towards the hawthorn. He could see a faint glimmer in the darkness, like little yellow lights beneath its branches. Merlin peered closely. To his amazement, it was a wolf, which had caught a coney and was devouring it at the foot of the tree. Merlin's throat was dry, and his fingers groped for his sword.

Of course, he had left it in Afallach.

The wolf ceased its repast, and turned its indifferent gaze upon him. The faintest growl, like distant thunder, rose from its belly. Then it returned to the coney, tearing the last few shreds of flesh from the bones. The wolf rose to its feet, stretched its limbs, and padded off into the forest.

Merlin breathed again. Was he in truth awake, or was this part of his dream? He looked around. Everything appeared to him as it had been when he had gone to sleep. There was the hawthorn, a pathetic scattering of blood and bones beneath it, and here the rock against which Merlin had rested his head. He could hear, nearby, the brook from which he had taken a little water last night.

Merlin waited, but nothing changed, nothing happened. Convinced at last that this was no vision, but waking reality, Merlin curled his arm and rested his head in the crook of his elbow. But when he drifted off at last, his sleep was full of disturbing dreams.

* * *

He plodded away southwards, through the forest of Dyfed, but he noticed little of the trees, which would have been familiar to him if the visions did not come to him in almost every waking moment: Boudicea, her eyes alight with vengeance, her fantastic hair flying like streams of fire, her sword dancing, and the Romans falling before her, their bodies twisted and mangled like the roots of ancient oak trees. Sometimes, he saw her in a city, and flames leaped from the buildings all around while bodies lay heaped in the streets. At other times, he did not see people at all. He saw a she-wolf beset by eagles, and a hawk flying at the eagles in a desperate attempt to deflect them from their attack. But the eagles were successful, gouging first the she-wolf's eyes, then tearing at her flanks and, as she sank to the earth, at her belly. The hawk flew off into a nearby forest.

Merlin hastened on his way, across the Dyfed Peninsula, and past Caermyrddin—he was so distracted that he did not stop there. He hit the coast and began to stagger eastwards, towards Logris. The land was relatively low-lying, though he could see mountains rising inland, and he crossed river after river. Merlin staggered onwards, as if the Wild Hunt were on his heels, and he heeded not whither he went, until one morning, a little over a week after leaving Afallach, he saw some fishermen on the beach below him, and stopped to watch them carefully.

In his mind, Merlin went back over the years, to his sojourn in Habren. He remembered Gwyden, who had loved him noncommittally. Now he stood on the low cliffs of southern Cambria, looking down upon the fishermen as they mended their nets, and he thought about Gwyden, her honest face, her clean limbs. He remembered her voice: "Who are you, Emrys?" she had asked. "Who is it stands in your shoes, and walks along your path?" Merlin looked almost sullenly back the way he had come. His feet had pressed a barely visible path into the grass, but it was rising back to its former height now, and the trace of his passage was almost gone.

"If there is no god but Morgana," he said to himself, in a whisper that was quieter than the hushing sound of the waves on the beach below, "if she is the only divinity in the Island of the Mighty, then to serve the High King is to serve her. There is no escape from Morgana. She will have her will." Merlin sighed. Above him, seagulls cried and mewed; below him, the fishermen joked and told salty stories. Perhaps, Merlin thought, perhaps I should return to Habren. Perhaps, if I hide away somewhere very obscure, no one will ever find me, and I shall not have to play a part in the drama of kingdoms.

He heard a sound behind him, and spun upon his heel.

Behind him stood a warrior, fantastically arrayed in white robes, a bronze helmet high on his head. His spear was leveled at Merlin's midriff. With a gasp, Merlin realized that he had wandered into Morgannawg.

He was in the middle of Morgana's own country.

XV

More warriors, dressed like the first, emerged from the forest behind him. One by one, they lowered their spears at Merlin. He looked around; save by jumping over the cliff or braving the spears, there was no escape. The first soldier he had seen, a flat-faced fellow with muscles bulging in his upper-arms and beneath the thin linen of his robes, stepped forward, his eye roving up and down him in an appraising fashion.

His hand lashed out. Merlin doubled over, pain erupting through his stomach. The warrior's hands swung through the air once more, and Merlin felt the haft of his spear crash across his shoulder blades. Another blow fell, and another. The others joined in, kicking, smiting with their spear-shafts, until Merlin's body was racked with pain. He curled up into a ball, his hands over his face, and waited for darkness to take him.

Then, all at once, it ceased. The flat-faced warrior pulled Merlin to his feet, yanked his hands roughly behind his back, and secured them with some rough twine. He gave Merlin a push towards the forest and, in a moment, Merlin found himself being propelled along a forest path. His body throbbed with pain all over, and he could feel his lip swelling and taste the blood in his mouth. He laboured up a steep gradient through trees that seemed too old to be alive. They hung on to their grey leaves jealously, like old men guarding medicinal drinks.

The soldiers talked as they marched him through the forest, but at first Merlin could make nothing of their speech. Gradually, like the hulk of a storm-tossed ship emerging from the night into the lights of a port, their language became clearer, and he realized that they spoke Brythonic, but a dialect so strange that it was virtually another tongue. He concentrated hard, and ascertained that they were speaking of the value their prince would place on his capture. The king, he learned, was on his deathbed and, somehow, their capture of Merlin could put them in the prince's graces.

All his life, Merlin had heard Morgannawg named with awe and fear. No one knew what horrid rites they practised, but it was common knowledge in Caermyrddin that those unfortunate enough to wander too close to their borders stood a good chance of being seized and sacrificed to their twisted gods. Their merchants came to the market at Caermyrddin, and sold fleeces—there was no finer wool than that sheared in Morgannawg—but, though the wives would purchase their wares, no man invited them into the taverns when their merchandise was sold, and they spoke to none all day, wending their way home alone through the gloaming. In Afallach, Merlin had learned a little more: under the renegade druid, Morgannawg, almost a thousand years ago, the Morgannawgi had separated themselves from the druids of the Island of the Mighty. Morgannawg had claimed to have the Sight, and to be communicating directly with the gods. Merlin had been unable to discover the nature of his heresy, for it was one of the secrets of Afallach that only a druid could discover. Now, as he emerged from the trees and entered a shabby-looking village, he wondered if this hadn't been the secret the druids could not tell him. Were the Morgannawgi, after all, right?

He felt the butt of a spear in the small of his back, and limped on.

The village was stretched out along the path and, rising above it, out of the side of a mountain, was a citadel of hewn stone, a single tower, tapering slightly towards its top, with a palace ranged behind it. Statues of a pair of huge cats flanked the gate at which the party stopped for a moment.

Merlin's captors exchanged a few remarks with guards on the gate, while Merlin peered past them into the courtyard beyond. The conversation over, the flat-faced warrior pushed Merlin along again. A quick march across the courtyard brought them to the palace, the door of which they reached by climbing a flight of wide steps and crossing a terrace. There were a few people, mainly clothed in white, conversing in knots, but the day was growing chilly, and most had retreated indoors.

The doors were opened by door-wards, and Merlin and his captors passed quickly through an anteroom and through another pair of doors at the far side.

Inside, the palace was surprisingly warm—hot coals glowed in many braziers, and steam rose from a rectangular pool in the middle of the room. There were people all around—conversing, dangling their feet in the pool, eating or drinking, reclining with their eyes closed, some making love slowly and languidly. They were of various ages and in various states of undress: a small group of young people, beside the pool, stood completely naked, and most of the women were clad only from the waist down. Some had thick hair on their heads; most were completely bald, though Merlin could tell from the hint of a shadow upon some glossy heads that they were shaven.

At the far end of the room was a dais, upon which stood an empty throne. Beside it, on a magnificent chair, which was nevertheless much smaller than the throne, sat a young man wearing what was obviously a wig, the thick black curls woven with golden threads. He wore loosely-fitting linen robes of white and gold, and sandals upon his feet. One of the soldiers struck Merlin in the back of the knees, and he fell down before the young man.

The man regarded Merlin for a moment, and then looked up at the warrior. His eyebrow was raised curiously.

"We found him on the cliffs, your highness," said the warrior with the flat face.

"And what of him, Sekhrey?" asked the young man.

The soldier looked shiftily about, and lowered his voice conspiratorially. "We thought your highness might be able to use this person for the Samhain Games."

A light went on behind the young man's eyes, and a smile turned the corners of his lips upwards. "Of course," he said, drawing his syllables out long. He turned his attention to Merlin. "Our laws thou hast transgressed," he said. "Forbidden it is that an outsider should come within this realm, lacking permission from Modron, king and living god of the realm of Morgannawg. I am Kenen, son of Modron, and I speak for him."

"Let me speak to the king," said Merlin. His lips were fat from the beating, and his words slurred. "I wish him no harm, but I am on an errand of the utmost importance, and would not be stayed." Merlin's mind was racing. *What does this peacock want to hear?* he wondered.

Kenen made an impatient sound. "Harm thou hast already done," he said, "for thou wast taken within our borders. Thy life shall be forfeit."

"Wait!" cried Merlin, opening his eyes wide to simulate fear. He started breathing heavily, and cringed before the tyrant. "For my life, I rate it at nothing," he wheedled, "but for my quest—that I value highly. Spare me, highness, and show your people what mercy belongs to a king!"

Kenen did not speak at once. "Mercy," he said, as if testing the word out on his tongue. "Mercy is for the weak. And I am not a king—that is not even within my power to choose. Not now, at any rate. I am but regent. But there is this much merit in that thou speakest . . . hast thou any skill in the hunt?" As he asked, the faintest smile played about his lips.

"A little I can do," replied Merlin. "I have lived in the wilderness long enough. I can find food for myself. My skills are your highness' to command."

"Admirable," answered Kenen. "Canst fight with sword and spear?"

"Aye, dread lord."

Kenen thought for a long while, so long that Merlin feared lest he had forgotten his business. But at last he reached a decision, glancing sideways at the throne. He said, "Blame us not thine entertainment here is so meagre, but rather applaud our generosity that we spared thy life." He looked past Merlin's shoulder at the warrior. "Sekhrey," he said, "see this fellow well lodged. And see that he is fed so that he may wax strong."

Sekhrey motioned with his spear, and Merlin moved as indicated, his eyes sullen. Where were they taking him? Already, Kenen's eye was resting upon one of the unclad women sitting beside the pool; she rose and went to join him as Merlin and the warriors left.

“That’s ill!” hissed one of the soldiers, as they marched along a passageway.

“What?” asked Sekhrey.

“He is not king yet—what business has he with his sisters? It’s not right.”

“And who art thou to question his highness’ actions?” demanded Sekhrey roughly. “Or his choice? Remember who thou’rt.”

They reached the top of some steps, and Merlin paused. The light was dim down there, and a damp smell rose from it.

“Down!” snarled Sekhrey.

And then Merlin realized where they were taking him. His eyes grew round, he gritted his teeth, and he leaped at the nearest warrior. His fear of being imprisoned again seemed to have given him superhuman strength, for he knocked the man over, and his spear clattered away along the flagstones. But a moment later he felt a blow to the back of his head. He saw darkness with bright spots of light scattered over it; and then he knew nothing more.

* * *

Merlin awoke in a cell that had been dug out of the solid rock beneath the castle, and smelled of damp and urine. He had been chained to the wall.

In prison, one more time, he thought darkly. He pressed his eyelids together, and wept silently. The last time had not been so bad—he had felt sure that Cartimandua would release him sooner or later anyway. But now he had so many things to be doing. There was Excalibur to find—he had to find his way to Caer Lloyw and begin searching the coast, looking in every cave until he found the ship—and there was his wife and his son, growing to manhood. There were other unanswered questions: the Morforwyn, for example. Could he find out anything useful by finding the place of their confinement? The books he had read in Afallach said that they were confined to a place called Avalon, in the Summer Country. Could he find the place? Could he learn anything there to help him find Excalibur? He clenched his fists until he felt the nails biting into his palms. He wanted to scream, to vent his frustration somehow.

Slowly, he opened his eyes and took stock of his situation.

There were several others chained to the walls with him, Merlin saw. In the corner was a high-backed seat, wrought entirely of metal. There seemed to be spikes all over it—protruding from the back, from the arms, from the seat—and leather straps dangled at the sides. In the middle of the room stood a table, upon which were arranged a number of strange instruments. Merlin felt his heart sink. He knew what kind of a place he was in.

"Why art thou here, stranger?" came a weary voice. Merlin turned his head. The man squatting next to him was emaciated—the bones almost poked through his flesh at the joints, his hair and beard were long and grey, his skin dark and leathery.

"I am a foreigner," answered Merlin, "and that may not be, it seems." His eyes searched the walls and ceiling for any clues about how to escape. Almost off-handedly, he asked, "Why are you here?"

The prisoner did not answer at first, and he looked puzzled, as if he were trying hard to understand Merlin's words. At last, he said, "The fault of it is mine alone; I paid not my taxes, and die in here I shall, or else at the Games."

"The Games?" Merlin remembered the guard mentioning something about Samhain Games.

"Aye." The prisoner wheezed a little—Merlin could not tell if he were short of breath, or laughing. "Th'art a stranger, thou'lt know nothing of the Games. Shall I tell thee?"

"Please do," answered Merlin, though he did not really want to know.

The prisoner wheezed a little. "What is thy home, stranger?" he asked.

"I am from Caermyrddin," replied Merlin absently.

"Ah, then thou know'st of Morgannawg from thy childhood days, I ween. What hast thou heard?"

Merlin fixed the prisoner with his eye. “That it is a strange place, with inhuman customs. The very name conjures up fear in the heart of every man, woman and child in the cantref of Dyfed.”

“Inhuman, is it?” mused the prisoner in his creaky voice. “Inhuman.” He seemed to be playing with the sound of the word, testing it against the insides of his mouth before letting it escape into the air. “Inhuman is what we call the other man’s custom,” he said. “The gods demand blood of us all—you, me, the friend thou think’st a clean fellow of his hands, whose fingers are dark with blood.”

Merlin nodded. “Life is a long scream,” he said.

“Thou know’st what ’tis to be alive,” agreed the other. “Our custom in Morgannawg is a blood-price at Samhain.”

“And that is to be me,” said Merlin.

“Like enough,” said the prisoner. “But a chance th’hast to live. For they’ll not kill thee, but hunt thee, and if thou canst kill thy pursuers, thou’lt live. And not only live—thou’lt be elevated, thou’lt be a noble, as thou weren’t before. ’Tis counted an honour amongst us, to be selected, for then our family may be ranked amongst the nobles. But of late, the princes have selected only the weakest quarries, the easier that they may slay them.”

“Perhaps it would be better just to let them kill me,” said Merlin. “I don’t think I want to be a Morgannawgi nobleman.”

The prisoner shrugged. “Please thyself,” he said. “To be alive is better than to be dead, for what canst do if thou’rt dead? Life is a long scream, as thou say’st, but ’tis better than oblivion.”

He did not speak again, and Merlin’s head sank gloomily onto his chest as he pondered what his fate was likely to be soon enough.

* * *

The light without the window faded into darkness, and Merlin saw a few stars pricking the veil of night outside; then greyness spread through the heavens, and a dim light came to the moaning wretches in the dungeon. A jailer entered and lit the torches, while another threw down pitiful food before the prisoners—stale hunks of bread, water, mouldy cheese. They did not immediately feed Merlin, and he wondered, as the other prisoners fell to, why he was being deprived. It did not bother him—he was really not very hungry, in spite of all—but he was curious.

One of the other prisoners, chained in the far corner, began to moan louder. "Food, food, food!" he cried. "Give me food or take my life now! Have mercy on me!"

"Why has he no food?" Merlin asked the prisoner next to him.

The prisoner looked up briefly from his repast. "That is Heset," he said. "He was the Steward and Butler to the King's Pantry. He raped one of the king's daughters, and they will starve him ere they kill him."

"Raped?"

"The lady was willing, quoth he, and that's like enough," replied the prisoner. "Better than share her brother on the king's death."

"Share her brother?"

The prisoner looked at Merlin through narrowed eyes. "'Tis little enough thou know'st," he said in amazement. "At the death of the king, there can be only one brother, and he taketh all his sisters for wives. Know'st not that?"

"I do now," replied Merlin, feeling a little sick. "So, now she has to share her brother anyway?"

But the prisoner shook his head. "'Tis clean they must be, if they are to live as the king's concubines. They slit her throat and cast her into the sea. But he's to be th'example for all. When he's naught but a skeleton, he'll endure the same as his lover, but they'll kill his spirit first. That will put fear in the people."

"It puts fear in me," muttered Merlin.

They were interrupted by the jangling of a key in the lock. The door creaked open, and the jailer entered, bearing a platter of food. Steam rose from it, together with the wonderful smell of roast beef. He set the platter on the floor beside Merlin.

“Thou’rt to have special rations,” he said, and left.

Merlin looked down at the plate: three thick slices of roast beef, still pink in the centre, with turnips, onions, cheese, and bread. He stared at it, dumbfounded, for a moment, then looked up. All the other prisoners were staring at him, slack-jawed and silent.

Merlin picked up the platter and passed it to the prisoner next to him. “Take what you want,” he said, “but make sure there’s some left for Heset when it gets to him.”

“Thou’rt sure?” gasped the prisoner. Merlin nodded. With reverence, the prisoner took a tiny slice of meat and passed the plate on. So did the next, and the next, until the plate reached Heset. The fellow was weeping. He looked around at his comrades, and fell to at once.

“Hey, new man!” cried one of the prisoners. “Thou shalt not starve!” And he tossed Merlin a piece of his bread. Merlin tore off a piece and chewed it thoughtfully. It was dry and thick, and he could barely swallow it, but he got it down in the end.

Within a few minutes, all the prisoners were talking. Merlin learned that the man next to him, the one who had not paid his taxes, was called Shesep, and he had been a thief in a minor way all his life. The one who had thrown his crust to Merlin was called Depet, and he was a ship’s captain by profession, trading with the ports in northern Gaul. But he had brought back a wife from his latest foreign voyage, and the king, suspecting him of sedition, had seized his goods and money, and cast him in this dungeon. He dared not think what had become of his wife, but fell to weeping at the conclusion of his tale.

Their conversation died away when the keys rattled in the lock.

“The plate, quick!” called Shesep. Heset tossed it gently, as one would throw a discus, and Shesep caught it and set it down beside Merlin just as the door opened and the jailer entered. He took up the plate, utterly clean as it was, and fixed Merlin with his eye.

“My compliments to the cook,” said Merlin. Nodding, the jailer left.

XVI

By the time Samhain came around, Merlin had become well-liked and respected among the inmates of Morgannawg's dungeon. On the night before the Samhain Games, the jailer brought Merlin's food as usual, and, as usual, Merlin passed his plate to Shesep. However, Shesep refused and, from across the room, Heset said, "Thou'lt need thy strength on the morrow-eve."

Merlin looked around at the bearded faces, all turned towards him. "'Tis not I need strength," said Shesep, "if it is for the Hunt thou'rt doomed."

Merlin frowned, looking down at his plate. As usual, his food was hearty. "It is as if they wanted to keep me healthy for the chase."

"Aye," said Depet, "and so thou may'st prove better sport."

"Nay," replied Shesep, "for, of late, they have chosen but the weakest—not sport, but to protect themselves is their aim."

"The king is dying," put in Heset. "Soon, all but one of them will be dead anyway."

"That is so," said Shesep, his mind now working on the problem. "Merlin, who consigned thee to this suffering?"

Merlin shook his head. "A prince," he said, "I do not remember his name."

"Was it Mesha?" asked Heset. Merlin shook his head. "Kheftey? Wereryet? Sesmet? Kenen?"

"Yes!" cried Merlin. "That was it—Kenen."

There was silence for a few moments among the inmates. "Strange, that is," said Heset. "Kenen is not the oldest of the brothers, the natural choice would not fall on him. Nor is he the strongest, for it is Kheftey who has served among the warriors of Morgannawg. But he is the most cunning.

Why would the guard bring thee to him, and not to Mesha, who is the eldest, and most natural to succeed his father?"

Their cogitations were interrupted by the arrival of the jailer, who took away Merlin's plate.

"What canst thou do for's when thou'rt free, Merlin?" asked Shesep.

"I cannot say," answered Merlin. He smiled at them. "I shall do my best to return to you, and free you from bondage."

"Nay," said Depet. "When thou'rt free, take thyself as far away from Morgannawg as thou canst. Stay not to look over thy shoulder, but fly."

"Shall I abandon my friends, then?"

"If thou valuest thy life at aught," answered Depet. "Thou couldst never attain this place again, once out, unless thou fought'st the guards, and thy strength, though better than ours, is not great, I ween. To die for us were foolishness."

"A fool may often guide a wise man," said Merlin quietly. And nobody else spoke.

* * *

The following night, half a dozen armed guards arrived to escort Merlin from the dungeon, and they marched him through a maze of passageways to the open. He drank in the early evening air as a man just come from the desert drinks water: sweet it was, and with a cold edge. Merlin was dragged into the courtyard of the fortress and there, pawing the cobblestones with their fore-hoofs, stood more than a dozen great horses, some white, some of the dunnest black. Astride them, some standing by their heads and holding the reins, were dark-haired men in white robes, ghostly in the darkness of early evening. A baying of hounds came from somewhere behind them. As Merlin got closer, he saw that the white robes were of wool, chased with silver that sparkled in the light of the torches. And they wore gold jewelry—torques, arm-rings, great rings set with ambers. Their faces were strangely angular; most of them had high cheekbones, and their eyes were oddly outlined in black. Merlin recognized Kenen amongst them, and guessed that these were his brothers.

"Thou art a stranger," said the nearest of the brothers. "By rights, thy life is forfeit, but if thou givest us good sport this night, thou art a free man. Thou shalt have until these sands run out." He inverted an hourglass and set it upon a wall. "When the sands are out, we shall pursue thee, and kill thee if we can; if thou escapest us until the rising of the sun, thou art free, and a nobleman of Morgannawg."

"Run, as far as thou canst, and as fast as thou canst," said Kenen, leaning forward in his saddle.

And Merlin ran. He dashed for the gate, hearing a smattering of laughter from the Morgannawgi brothers behind him. His feet clattered as he fled through the passageway towards the gate, and towards the dark forest beyond.

A blow struck him squarely in the chest, and he was flung to the ground, sprawling, the wind knocked out of him.

Over him stood the guard who had captured him, Sekhrey. He held a spear. Merlin's soul cringed. Was this some way of crippling him, so that he would be easy to catch?

But Sekhrey held out the spear and, gingerly, Merlin took it.

"I only ask that thou killest not Kenen, my master," said Sekhrey. "If thou meetest another, kill him; but spare my master, stranger."

Merlin stared at him in disbelief. "Why are you doing this?" he asked.

The warrior's eyes flickered a little in the dim evening light. "I pity thee," he said, and disappeared into the gloaming.

In a moment, Merlin was on his feet and running once more; but now his mind was running with his feet, and the ashen haft of the spear was a comfort in his hands.

The wall of the castle turned in towards the mountain against which it was built, and Merlin followed the defensive ditch around this corner. There, the trees grew closer to the wall, reaching over the damp ditch like dancers forming a bridge. Merlin cast a glance over his shoulder, but there was as yet no pursuit in sight.

The trees were apple trees.

Merlin leaped for the nearest of the trees, thrust the sole of his foot against the knobbled bole, and propelled himself up amongst the branches. He was hidden amongst the leaves in no time.

Wherever he looked, the branches were heavy with golden fruit. His heart rising, he reached out and took one, biting deeply. It was rich and sweet, and the juice ran from the corners of his mouth. For a moment, fear of his pursuers was gone. It seemed a lifetime since he had eaten such a delicacy.

> Sweet apple tree, and sweet your fruit,
> My enemies about your roots.
> Secret you grow in forest deep,
> Home of owls and squirrel's leap.

He set his spear athwart some of the upper branches, so that he would know later where to get it, then braced himself against the trunk and thrust himself towards the next tree, reaching out and grasping the next branch. He swung himself into the neighbouring tree, then the next, and the next. When he had disappeared thirty yards into the depths of the nighttime forest, he felt safe enough to enjoy another apple, and wait for his pursuers. He laughed, quietly, his shoulders shaking just a little. Not even the dogs would scent this path!

It was not long ere he heard the yapping of hounds upon the sharp October air. They had gathered at the place where he had first climbed the tree, but they could not follow him further. Merlin stretched out the fingers of his mind. What were they saying? What were the lords of Morgannawg asking about him? Did they suspect where he had gone? Could they perhaps see the spear where he had left it?

At first, the Sight revealed little to him: he heard Kenen's voice, advising them to split up, to search the woods more thoroughly that way. They went off—some innocently chasing after their quarry, others with some apprehension. Merlin wondered at first why this may be; and then he realized that they did not trust Kenen. The king was dying, and could have only one successor. In a flash, Merlin knew why Sekhrey had handed him the spear: the hunt was Kenen's way of ensuring his own succession. Mesha, the eldest brother, had remained behind with Kenen, and now Merlin heard his voice as clearly as he would had he stood beneath his tree.

"Well, brother, here thou art, and here am I too," said Mesha. "Wilt thou not search the forest for the quarry?"

A slow, unpleasant smile grew across Kenen's lips. "No, brother, for I have another task in hand."

"Ah, wilt thou kill me, then?" sneered Mesha, without surprise, and drawing his sword.

"Thou wast ever a fool, Mesha," said Kenen. "If we fight with swords, all in the forest, and half in the castle will hear, and know thy foulness."

"Whereas they already know *thy* foulness," retorted Mesha. "I shall say I drew in self defence, and who will say me nay? Defend thyself, an thou wilt; if not, prepare thyself for death!"

Kenen drew, but Mesha's first swing knocked the blade from his unprepared hand. It landed with a soft splash in the ditch. Kenen dodged under the arc of Mesha's sword and thrust his hands at his brother's chest. The two of them hurtled through the air, striking the bole of an apple tree with a shock that shook it to its topmost leaves. A shower of apples tumbled from the tree, puttering all around them. Merlin's spear also dropped from the branches, striking Kenen on the back of the head and then rolling onto the turf. Kenen cried out, but seized his opportunity anyway. Mesha leaped to his feet, swinging his sword around, but too late. Kenen thrust the spear-point into his brother's chest and heaved with all his might. The point buried itself in the living wood of the tree, while Mesha's life ebbed out with his blood. The spear bowed under Mesha's weight. Kenen heaved on the haft, dragging the point from his brother's body, which slumped against the tree. He looked thoughtfully at the spear, then up at the tree, considering. Then he dropped the spear beside the body of his elder brother, and clambered down into the ditch to retrieve his sword, wiping it on the grass on his return. He looked up at the upper branches of the trees all around, but evidently could see nothing, leaped upon his horse and rode off between the trees, so that the darkness of the forest swallowed him up.

He galloped past the foot of the tree that was sheltering Merlin, but did not look up. Merlin listened to him depart, then crept along the branch upon which he sat, and swung himself from tree to tree until he came to the cooling body of Mesha. He took up the prince's fallen sword and surveyed the land.

A little further along, the trees grew very close to the wall indeed, and he thought he might be able to get back into the castle unseen. It would not be what his pursuers expected, and he could perhaps free some of his comrades in the dungeon. He tucked the sword into his belt, and was about to set off in his attempt to break into the castle, when he heard a sound behind him, and spun around.

It was one of the brothers. He swung himself from the saddle and advanced upon Merlin, his mouth distorting into a sneer. "So, thou hast killed Mesha," he observed. "Well, thou hast saved my trouble, at least. But thou wilt slay no more of my kin."

Merlin drew his sword and stood at the ready. He measured the distance between them, and saw it was a good fighting distance; then he took one small step backwards.

The man lunged. Merlin dodged. The blade missed him, and his attacker was over-extended, temporarily unable to recover. Merlin swung his sword, and brought its edge crashing down onto the man's wrist. He cried out and staggered backwards, clutching the stump of his right hand. Blood was flowing freely between his fingers and onto the ground.

"What hast thou done?" cried the man. "I cannot be a king and thus marred. 'Tis that hand should have commanded, and fought, and taken my sisters to queen." He looked up at Merlin. "Slay me," he said. "Thou hast but done half thy job—finish it now."

Merlin looked down at the man, and saw him for a moment in one of the castle's private chambers. He saw his hands reach out to one of the girls of the fortress—one of his sisters, whom he had known already, thinking himself certain to be chosen king upon his father's death. In a flash, Merlin returned to the present. The man quivered before him, and Merlin stared at him, seeing into his soul. Murder and incest were painted there, and Merlin's lip curled in disgust. He had no compunctions. He drove the sword into his chest. It caught on one of his ribs, and he had to struggle to withdraw it. Then he wiped the blade on the grass, and tucked it into his belt.

He paused a moment. Far off in Eicenniawn, he knew, Boudicea awaited him. He could disappear into the forest now, go south, easily elude the other brothers of the Morgannawgi, and resume his quest.

Except that, he had said he would return.

But they had not expected him to do that—they would understand.

Merlin pressed his eyes shut. Then he opened them, took a deep breath, and dashed off along the treeline. He went north.

He soon found a tree that would do for his purpose, and snaked up it. He crawled along one of the outstretched branches, until he could almost reach out and touch the stone wall of the palace.

Just a few more inches, he thought.

He pushed a little further with his toes, the branch bending under his weight. He reached out with his fingers. They touched the cold stone, he scraped it with his fingernails.

A voice rang out behind him in the forest, and a dog yelped. They had not spotted him, but he was exposed in this position, and it would not take them long to find him.

What had he heard in the heroic poems recited in Afallach? He had heard of the hero's feats—the Spear Feat, and the Rope Feat, and the Hero's Leap. Could he do a thing he had only heard of?

"Andraste, Queen of Victories," he prayed, dismissing what Gwelydd had told him about the gods in the urgency of his situation, "if you indeed can shape the lives of men, give me strength!" He coiled back and flung himself into space.

For a second, he was flailing through empty air. He spread his arms wide, stretched his neck forward. For a second, it seemed that he was a hawk, a thousand feet above the hard earth, the air bearing him upwards, pressing up on his pinions. Then he hit the palisade, knocking all the air out of his lungs. His arms curled about the wall, his fingers scrabbling. He could feel them slipping, and pressed inwards with the palms of his hands. His feet kicked, his lungs screamed at him. Behind him, he heard one of the hounds barking again, as if it had picked up a scent.

Merlin became still. He closed his eyes for a moment, summoning his strength. He slowed his breathing down, taking deep breaths that filled his lungs as much as could be. He pictured his hands and his arms, the muscles in them contracting, the bones, great columns of strength, moving together and apart. He put out his will, as he would when trying to hear a distant conversation.

Merlin's fingers flexed; the muscles heaved on the bones, his arms bent, and he leaped lightly over the wall and onto the battlements.

"Thanks to you, Andraste," he muttered. "And to you, Tylweth, Mistress of the Sight!"

At the far end of the palisade, he heard a footfall, and saw a guard approaching him, making his long, lazy way from one tower to the next as his duty bade him. There was no cover, nothing behind which Merlin could hide, but he pressed himself backwards into the shadows, drawing the sword silently from his belt.

Suddenly, the guard froze, his eyes fixed upon Merlin. Merlin saw his chest puff outwards as he took a breath to shout out his discovery, his hand fly to the hilt of his sword.

Merlin flung his own sword. It had only a short blade anyway, and was weighted in the tip, so it flew well. The point embedded itself in the soft flesh between the man's jawbone and his throat. He was still thrashing in his death agony when Merlin drew it out and passed on without even glancing back. Silent as a cat, he padded along the battlements to the place where some stairs descended to the courtyard.

The main entrance was guarded, but there was a postern door in the west wall, reached by a flight of wooden steps. In a moment, Merlin was up the stairs, through the door, and in the palace.

He found himself in a long passageway, with doors on either side; at the end was an opening, barred by stone railings, like a balcony.

Merlin's heart was beating fast and, it seemed, loudly in his ears, as he crept along the passageway towards the balcony. That was indeed what it was, and it looked out over the hall—the one into which Merlin had been conducted when he had first been captured by the Morgannawgi. The humid warmth rose to him from down there, bearing heady perfumes. Most of the men were missing, he noticed—they were presumably Kenen's brothers, and were currently on the hunt.

Merlin spun around at a noise behind him, and melted into the shadows. Two men emerged from the room, closing the door softly behind them.

"How long?" said the first of the men.

"He will not last a week," said the other.

"His sons must know," the first said, more to himself than to provide information.

"Let them enjoy the Samhain Games first; perchance some will meet an evil fate this night, and thus save Pehtey his labour and the sharpness of his axe."

"The election will light on Mesha, I ween."

The second man, evidently a doctor, crooned, "What hath election to do in these matters, man? If thou hast made any friends among the brothers, be thou distant now. Thou canst not avoid the axe by thy friendships. Better to avoid than embrace."

"What wilt thou do?"

"I shall depart with haste."

"Wilt thou then leave the king to his death?"

“A stronger hand is pulling him thitherward than I can exert to pull him back,” answered the doctor. “Now I must leave, and avoid the blame. Fare thee well. I shall return for the wedding feast.”

The other man nodded nervously, then went back into the room. The doctor opened another door, and Merlin heard his footsteps receding down some steps before the door closed. In a moment, Merlin had opened the door softly, and was descending after him. At the bottom of the steps, a doorway led into the main hall, and the wet warmth billowed over him. But Merlin saw some more steps, descending below the earth, and he knew it was down those he had been hauled when he had first arrived in Morgannawg. Merlin drew his sword softly once more and crept down the steps.

They seemed to go on for ever, down and down through darkness. The warmth of the great hall dissipated quickly, to be replaced by a clammy cold. Merlin began to wonder if ever the steps would come to an end.

But even as he was wondering this, they did, and he stood at one end of a long passageway. At the far end, he could see a square of yellow light, the opening in the door to the guardroom before the dungeon. Muted, he could hear the rough voices of the jailer and guards. They were, he knew, discussing the outcome of the hunt, but he could not be bothered to listen to specifics. He could see that there were four of them in all, and each had a weapon within easy reach.

They stood between him and those he would rescue and, to Merlin, the odds seemed great indeed.

XVII

Merlin stood silently outside the door to the guardroom for a while, pondering his next move. The chatter of the four inside came to him through the iron grille, which also spilled yellow light geometrically across his face. He could not peer through the grille, lest he be seen by those within, and so lose any advantage which taking them by surprise might have had. So he closed his eyes, and pushed the Sight through the grille and into the room.

They were seated around a table, upon which stood a large pitcher of ale. One of them sat on a tall stool, and would be on Merlin's right. He held his mug in his hand, and leaned his back against the wall. His spear was only inches away from his hand, and he would seize it quickly, so he would be more dangerous than the others. The other three sat at the table. One of them had his sword out and on the table, the hilt a hand's span from the mug, which he was currently refilling from the pitcher. The other two had sheathed swords. They would have to draw and stand up from the table, a difficult manoeuvre. Merlin's mind raced. This was not the kind of fighting he liked, he reflected. Then again, one so seldom had the opportunity of choosing.

Merlin opened his eyes. He drew his sword and reached for the door-handle, slowly and quietly depressing the latch.

Before he could push the door open completely, the sound of a foot rang out at the far end of the passage. Merlin spun round. Two guards, come to relieve their comrades in the guardroom, had reached the foot of the steps and taken two paces before noticing Merlin at the door and freezing in their tracks.

The lip of one guard curled, his nostrils flared with contempt. "What manner of thing art thou?" he demanded.

Merlin flew at them before they had had a chance to draw. He thrust his sword at the first guard's belly. The man responded by leaping backwards, but not far enough. The sword-point pierced the soft flesh and clove through his guts. The other guard cried out in alarm. Merlin placed his hand on the dying man's chest and pushed to get him off the blade. He could feel the blade jarring against the man's lower rib all the way up to his elbow.

The other guard had his sword out of its sheath, while Merlin's blade was still stuck. He swung with his fist, bringing the heel crashing into the guard's face. The guard staggered backwards against the wall, his free hand rising to clutch at his face, the sword rising to defend him from Merlin's attack. Merlin's sword was free now, and he leaped at his opponent, pushing his sword-arm away with his free hand, driving the point into his throat with the other. The man gave a hideous gurgling sound. His eyes, inches away from Merlin's and staring straight into them, bulged obscenely. Then his body went limp, and he slumped.

But the sounds of the combat had alerted the guards inside. Merlin looked up from the still bodies of his victims in time to see a spear hurtling towards him. He ducked and rolled, the spear clattering against the wall and floor. Then the first of the guards was upon him.

Merlin was still on the floor, amongst the filth and the steaming blood. He lashed out with his blade, swiping at the feet of the nearest. The man grunted as the blade struck him on the ankle. The edge bit through flesh, but jarred on the bone. The guard toppled over backwards, clasping his foot in both hands and groaning. Blood gouted between his fingers.

Merlin's mind registered that one was no longer a threat. He sprang to his feet, ducking his head to avoid a sword-swing. His sword thrust upward, under his attacker's defences. The point made contact, pierced the thin leather jerkin and the soft flesh beneath. The man staggered away, blood flowering over his stomach. He tripped over his already fallen comrade and writhed on the ground in his death agony. Merlin leaped over him, planting his feet firmly on the further side. His sword was raised, his free hand out for balance, his knees bent a little. His lips were parted, and his breath rasped through his teeth, making a sound like some fierce serpent.

Metal rang on stone, and Merlin saw, to his surprise, that one of the survivors had thrown down his sword. The other, who had cast the spear, had raised his hands from his sword-belt.

"Peace!" one of them pleaded.

Merlin nodded. There was a bestial look on his face, his eyes wild, his teeth bright in the gloom. "Open the dungeon," he said.

"'Tis he hath the keys," said one of the men, pointing. Merlin looked down at the jailer. He was clutching his bloody foot now, but Merlin recognized him as one who had frequently brought him his food.

Merlin nodded. His sword was steady. "Get the keys," he ordered. "And help him into the dungeon."

The two who had surrendered picked up the wounded man; the other was already dead, his leg still twitching a little, but his eyes glazed, his chest still. The three Morgannawgi lumbered into the guardroom, Merlin directly behind them. They lowered the wounded jailer into one of the chairs at the table and he, his sullen eyes ever on Merlin, slipped the key-ring off his belt with bloody fingers and tossed them over to Merlin. Merlin did not move: he knew that if he stooped to pick them up, if he turned his back on the Morgannawgi to open the door and liberate the prisoners, he would be vulnerable. He took a step backwards and jerked the point of his sword downwards.

"Pick them up," he said.

One of the guards bent down, picked up the keys, and slipped one into the lock. Somehow, Merlin thought, the sound of the key in the lock had a different timbre on this side of the door.

The dungeon door swung slowly open, and a slab of yellow light fell across the gloomy interior, catching Shesep, who blinked at them. Merlin waved his sword and bade the guards enter. He followed himself.

He was amazed at what a change his perceptions had undergone in only an hour, perhaps a little more, of freedom. He had not noticed the defeat in the eyes of the prisoners with whom he had been incarcerated, but now he saw how it lay over them all like a thick fog. They looked up incuriously at the guards as they entered; then, as they recognized Merlin, the fog dissipated, and hope began to gleam.

"Why hast thou returned?" asked Heset.

Merlin grinned. "I said I would."

"Many are the promises I have heard," returned Heset, "but ever it is but the easiest word that is kept."

Merlin gave a curt command to the guards, and they began to free the captives. When it came to Heset's turn, he said, "No, leave me here. I am weak—thy food these last few weeks hath restored me, but I fear too little for what is now in hand. Leave me here, and make good thine escape."

"What foolishness is this?" Merlin asked. He shook his head and said firmly, "We will not leave you." He removed his manacles, and Heset rubbed his wrists and ankles.

The prisoners secured the guards, then rifled the guardroom for weapons. Mostly, they chose spears for preference—few of them had been trained to use a sword. Depet looked back into the gloomy confines of the dungeon, at the guards chained up in there.

"We should kill them," he said, fingering the head of the spear he had taken from the corner of the room.

But Merlin shook his head, moving past the erstwhile merchant and into the cell. He bent down over the wounded jailer, who was beginning to mutter in delirium. He examined the wound, turning the foot gently one way and then the other. It was clearly broken, and very close to the joint. If the bone knit at all, he would walk with a pronounced limp for the rest of his life; it might not knit unless he received care. Merlin found a cloak in the guardroom and tied up the wound as best he could. Then he left, locking the door behind him.

The prisoners were waiting for him. He bit on his knuckle and then looked up at them, smiling apologetically. "I have no plan for escaping," he admitted.

But Heset said, "I know a way. There is a passage from the buttery to the outer wall. It is used to bring in casks of wine, but there will be no traffic along it during the Samhain Hunt."

Merlin put a hand on his bony shoulder. "And if we had left you behind," he said, "who would have shown us the way?"

A few moments later, they were ascending the stairs silently, Heset confidently taking the lead. Reaching the hall, they paused and surveyed the scene.

The king's daughters and sister-wives lounged about, reclining on couches or immersed in warm water, sleeping or conversing. Some of the women were evidently in their sixties; some were as young as twelve or fourteen years. The buzz of conversation was underscored by slow, dreamy harp music, and it suddenly occurred to Merlin that it was over a year since he had himself played the harp. A few guards stood at the periphery of the hall, leaning on their spears with mostly bored expressions. Around the perimeter of the hall ran a colonnade, for the most part in shadows. Some of the women, and a few noblemen, snored gently upon couches placed in the shadows of the colonnade.

The prisoners made no noise as they padded along the wall, keeping as much as they could to the shadows. Only Merlin among them was shod at all; he knew they smelt bad, but the air was heady with perfumes, and he doubted that they would be detected, unless a guard by chance turned and saw them.

The first of the guards was very close now. Merlin motioned them on, sliding the sword silently from his belt and waiting, the point leveled at the guard's wide back, until the escapees were past. Then he ran after them.

By a miracle, no one noticed them as they skirted half the length of one side of the hall and reached the buttery, which was screened from the hall by oaken planking, dark with age. Within the buttery were dozens of casks of varying sizes, a neat line of amphorae containing wine, some trays, shelves full of pewter and stoneware cups, and a little food. It was mostly simple fare—a few loaves of bread, golden from the oven and still giving off a rich fragrance in warm waves, some cheeses, rosy apples and pears and other fruits. A ham hung from one shelf, black from roasting on the outside, pink within where it had already been sliced. Momentarily arrested by the wealth of food and drink, the prisoners paused, their eyes wide.

"Take what thou needest," said Heset, "but come quickly."

There was a moment's pause, as if the prisoners had not heard what he had said; then they reached out and seized what they could carry. Heset had found the door he had spoken of, and now he pushed down on the latch, drawing it open slowly. The hinges creaked, and all the prisoners tensed. But the sound brought no one. The prisoners slipped into the darkness, each of them seizing on some item of food on the way. Last of all, Merlin took a torch from a sconce beside the door and the tinder and flint from the shelf beside it and, when Heset had closed the door behind them, and they were in the inky darkness of the tunnel, he kindled a flame at its tip.

The flickering orange light showed them to be in a tunnel cut out of the living rock, rough-walled but of a very even floor, descending at a shallow gradient away from the door.

"Come," said Heset and, ripping a mouthful of bread from the loaf he had taken, he led the way down the tunnel.

The walk was longer than anyone had expected, for the buttery was at the north end of the hall, and the passage curved first east through the mountain against which the palace was built, and then south. It had to be long, Heset explained, because it could not be steep—the vintners had to carry or push the barrels along it without beasts of burden.

Their walk was a long one, for they could not move swiftly, in spite of the danger. Their limbs were stiff from long confinement, and all save Merlin walked with a limp. Heset had to pause frequently to rub his feet. Presently, they came to a dead end and a pair of doors.

"I have no key," said Heset forlornly, rattling the handle.

Depet spat on the ground in his frustration. "Why would anybody lock up a tunnel along which only wine travels?" he wondered.

"Because whatever normally comes along it, an open tunnel is still a way an enemy can get into a fortress," replied Merlin. He grinned. "Or out," he added.

"Stand aside," said Shesep, moving past Merlin and stooping to peer at the keyhole. He cracked his knuckles, flexed his fingers, picked up a stick, and jammed it into the lock. For a few moments, he turned the stick this way and that, a slight frown producing a crease between his brows. Then he gave a smile of satisfaction, stood up, and pushed the door open.

"If all that standeth between a thief and his freedom is a lock," he said, "there needeth no wondering if he cannot be confined."

Merlin patted him on the shoulder, and they all moved out into the night. The tunnel emerged in a rocky place, its entrance concealed behind a mossy boulder. A rough path picked its way through the trees.

"I know this path," said Depet. "It leadeth through a defile to the coast. There, we may find a ship."

"Lead on," said Merlin, and they plunged into the trees, Depet in front, with Shesep behind Merlin and Heset bringing up the rear.

A cry rang out, the sound amplified by the stillness of the night, and the four escapees froze for a moment.

"The hunt!" cried Merlin. "We must go faster!"

But it was too late. Behind them came the sound of drumming hoof-beats. They had been spotted.

"Run!" yelled Merlin. The prisoners hobbled along, as swiftly as they might, and Merlin began to feel frantic at their slowness.

The horseman came out of the shadows of the night, spear held high over his head. The moonlight brought out the whiteness of his robes and the wicked glitter in his eyes as he raised his spear and flung it at them.

Heset gave a grunt and pitched forwards, the spear-head lodged under his left shoulder-blade.

At that moment, the horseman saw the three others, and urged his horse forward to the fallen man, reaching out to take the spear. Merlin flew at him, swinging his sword in a downwards arc. Blood flew through the night air, the horseman let out a cry of pain. The horse whinnied and reared. The man pitched from the saddle and struck a tree, and the horse galloped off into the forest. The rider was slumped in an ungainly pile at the foot of the tree, his head lolling at an awkward angle that told them that his neck was broken; Merlin had also lopped off his arm.

Merlin dashed to Heset and rolled him onto his side. He gasped with the pain of the movement.

"I'm sorry, Heset!" wept Merlin. "I'm sorry." He clenched his fist, so that he could feel his nails dig into the palms of his hand. Tears had sprung from his eyes, and he wiped them away with a rough motion. "This is all my fault," he said bitterly.

"Nay, friend," replied Heset, through laboured breath. "Death in the dungeon, death out here—'tis all one. I thank thee that thou shared'st thy food with me." He took a deep breath—it was evidently painful to do so. "Now, draw forth the spear," he said, "and let me go."

Shesep knelt down beside them. "Farewell, Heset," he said and, grasping his friend by the shoulder, drew out the spear-point. Heset gave a great, shuddering sigh, and sagged in Merlin's arms.

They arranged Heset's body neatly beneath some stones, but had no time for particular funeral arrangements. The hunt was still on, though dawn was showing grey through the trees to the east.

"Thou hast thy noble estate, shouldst thou desire it," observed Depet.

Merlin looked at him wryly, but did not reply. A moment later, they were off once more, following the path through the trees as it descended towards the beach.

It took them most of the morning, but they found a fisherman willing to take them a little way along the coast, out of Morgannawg. Merlin sat in the shrouds, hugging himself for warmth, for the breeze blew briskly out on the water. He thought of the collapsing weight of Heset in his arms, and he wept silently to himself.

XVIII

The fisherman whose services they had engaged dropped them off at the mouth of the River Wysg, and they followed the river inland a few miles. At times, the forest was so thick that they had to seek a path further away from the waters, and they lost sight of it altogether. Above them, the bare branches of the trees formed a fantastic latticework against the iron-grey of the sky.

At length, they came to Caerleon, of old the hilltop stronghold of King Belin. It arose on the northern bank of the river, where it turned abruptly eastwards. At the foot of the hill, men had hewn the forest down for grazing land, and thrown up a wharf and some small warehouses. It was this port's existence that had drawn Depet hither, and now Shesep announced that he would accompany him henceforward.

"After all," Shesep said brightly as they stood beside the wharf, "a thief and a merchant are good company for one another, their business being almost identical."

"How will you buy merchandise?" asked Merlin. "Your goods and gold were confiscated by the king of Morgannawg."

Depet shrugged. "I shall ply my way as a seaman at first," he said, "and use what gold I earn to buy goods. I have done this before. But thou—what wilt thou do?"

"I shall sing," said Merlin, "and if that is worth some little gold, I shall use it to sail across the Sabrina into the Summer Country. Perhaps I shall learn the answers to some of my questions there."

"I wish thee good fortune in the seeking of thine answers," said Depet; "but I hope also that thou hast some questions still when thou'rt done, for a life without questions is not a life."

Merlin smiled with half his mouth. "I have never been without questions," he said, "and I yearn to rest."

Depet held out his hand, and they shook. He said, "Only Death answereth all. Good fortune go with thee!"

Merlin bade them both farewell, and turned his face northwards, along the road that led to Caerleon. On either side, hedgerows grew shoulder-height, the meadows beyond empty, grey and forlorn, for the cattle had been withdrawn into the winter byres.

Merlin climbed the winding pathway up the side of the hill. The wind grew more insistent as he approached the summit, and he shivered miserably, wishing that he had been able to bring a cloak from Morgannawg. Above him rose the wall, and ahead of him stood the great double gates, flanked by a pair of guards.

He was two paces from the guards when it happened.

It suddenly seemed to Merlin that the whole place was transformed before his eyes. Instead of the timber palisades, he saw whitewashed walls of stone. Great towers rose before him and above him, and within the courtyard were assembled brightly-clad and happy denizens. Many comely lords, the best of liegemen, celebrated with joyous abandon there, singing carols, dancing with gorgeous ladies. All the meat and the mirth that men could devise was there—such merrymaking and glee that it was glorious to hear. Happiness sang through halls and chambers, the dearest lords and ladies in the world. With all the health in the world they dwelt together, the most renowned warriors in the world, and the most beautiful ladies that had ever lived, a fair folk in the prime of their youth, and youngest and fairest among them was their king. Not twenty years of age was he, and a beard had hardly formed on his chin; but at his side he bore a sword that made Merlin's heart stand still, for he knew he was looking upon Excalibur. And the king's heart, though joyous as his company's, was wise beyond his years, and stern too.

The vision faded, and Merlin found himself sprawled on the ground in the gateway of Caerleon. One of the guards had stepped forward to help him up.

"What is your business, fellow?" he asked.

"I have come to sing," said Merlin shakily, "and earn a crust for my supper, or perhaps a little gold."

"Where is your harp, then?" asked the guard.

Merlin sighed and examined the guard for a moment. He was a young man, not much more than a boy—perhaps eighteen or twenty years of age, with dark hair and eyes. Half my age, perhaps less than that, thought Merlin. "Lost," he said aloud; and then he smiled. "But the human voice," he added, "is the loveliest of instruments given to men by Tylweth."

"Tread carefully, friend," advised the other guard, a somewhat older man, perhaps Merlin's peer. "The rains have made the ground slick."

Merlin nodded his thanks, and started to enter the courtyard; but a thought suddenly stopped him, and he turned back to the guards.

"Is that all?" he asked. "You are not going to examine me, interrogate me, search me? This is a frontier fortress—are you just going to let me in without any further hindrance?"

"I don't think you'll do us any harm," remarked the second guard. "You don't look like a Roman, or dress like a Roman, or speak like a Roman."

"He might be a spy," suggested his younger companion, a hint of teasing in his voice.

"If I am," answered Merlin, "it is the secrets of the kitchen I would learn!"

The older guard smiled and laid a hand on Merlin's shoulder. "Refugees from the south are welcome here," he said. "Go in, eat. Perhaps you can serve the rebellion against Rome."

So that was it. They had observed his broken-down appearance and incorrectly surmised that he had fled from the Roman invasion of the south. They were not very observant, Merlin thought wryly, as he crossed the courtyard. They had not remarked upon his accent, which was from Dyfed, fifty miles to the west, in unoccupied Cambria.

On the other hand, he thought as he entered the hall, I have spent many years traveling, or dwelling in other parts of the land. Perhaps I no longer speak in the accent of my boyhood!

Once inside the hall, Merlin fell in with a group of bards, borrowed a harp and earned a crust and some pennies singing songs before returning the instrument to its astonished owner.

He stayed a week in all in Caerleon, slowly earning enough money by singing to pay his way south, and discovered that the fortress was the focal point of a Cambrian revolt against the Romans. But Merlin watched the warriors gathering with great sadness. Wrapped in their furs, they sat at council and pounded the tables before them, declaimed in strident voices, swore vows to empty the land of foreign invaders, to tweak the beard of the Emperor himself in Rome.

Merlin winced at that one—he had met many Romans, and could remember none who wore beards. It was bombast, he knew, but it was not founded on a knowledge of the enemy, just on stirring desires and nostalgia for Britain's greatness, a greatness that was now gone for ever.

Unless, thought Merlin, I can find Excalibur.

The week wore on, and he watched the leaders of the revolt gathering. None of them sounded like Coroticos, or had the warrior's liquid movements, like Rhydderch. They moved like boys who had seen warriors, but who had never wielded swords except in play. Those drawn to the rebellion were few, and young, and Merlin saw that they would be crushed, remorselessly, utterly, the first time they met a legion. He did not speak of this; but when he had earned enough money for his passage, he quickly slipped out of the fortress and found a ferryman who would take him across the Sabrina. The man struck out due east and, before long, the contours of the coastline resolved themselves into shapes that were familiar to Merlin. It had been fifteen years since last he had felt these waters beneath the keel of a boat, but this was where he had learned to sail and to fish, and he would never forget Habren.

Then he saw the coombe, the lights of the houses twinkling in the early darkness of late November. It was like balm to his soul, to think of the blissful existence of a fisherman, with naught to worry him but the swelling of the waves and the buffeting of the wind. Once again, the thought swept over him, that it would be a fine thing indeed to abandon the company of kings, the quest after the unfindable, and blot out his thoughts with the everyday routine of manual labour.

But Boudicea. The image of her face returned to his mind, and of Gwenddolau. And Boudicea had commissioned him to find Excalibur. Perhaps there would be a simple family life for him, in Eicenniawn, once he had completed his quest. He must bend every sinew in his body, he concluded, to finding the sword.

The boat's prow crunched on the sand. Merlin paid the ferryman and strode off into the town.

Habren had changed very little in the fifteen years that had passed since his last visit, and he gazed with great fondness upon the familiar shapes of the fishing vessels drawn above the tide line and the huts climbing up the sides of the coombe. Merlin trudged up the path between the huts, his eyes glistening as they turned left and right, searching for the place where he had dwelt, so many years ago.

"Is it you, Emrys with his eyes upon the stars?" came a voice and, turning, Merlin stood face-to-face with a woman about his own age, silhouetted by the light that spilled from the door of a hut from which she had just emerged. Gwyden was as beautiful as he remembered, but in a different way: she had depth, she had dignity, she had wisdom. She had children too, he noted, looking past her, through the door into the lighted hut.

"It is I," answered Merlin, smiling, and letting his small bundle drop to the ground. "Am I welcome in Habren?"

Gwyden could not help but smile, and she stepped forward to fold Merlin in a chaste embrace. "You are that," she said. "Do you still seek that boat of yours?"

"I have not found it yet," replied Merlin.

Gwyden looked him up and down. "How thin you are!" she remarked. "How ragged your clothes!" She smiled mischievously. "Is this Merlin the Kingmaker?" she asked, with a wry grin.

Merlin shook his head, suddenly overwhelmed by weariness. "No," he said, "this is just a very tired and hungry Merlin, who would trespass upon your hospitality for one night only, before taking up his quest once more."

Gwyden's eyes widened for a moment, like one who had forgotten a duty. "Forgive me," she said. "Come inside. Meet my man, and my children." And she ushered him into the hut, where he joined in their repast of fish stew with onions, bread and ale.

Gutor, Gwyden's husband, was a rugged fellow with a deeply tanned face and an unkempt shock of black hair, who regarded him through narrowed eyes as they shook hands. They had three children. Their oldest, a boy, worked the boats now with his father and grandfather, Agor. Their middle child was also a boy, almost old enough to work, their youngest a girl of two years.

Agor was delighted to see Merlin, sitting next to him around the fire and confiding in him all the gossip from a decade and a half. Merlin felt his belly full of hearty food, and he looked around at his simple surroundings, at Gwyden carefully steering her daughter away from the fire, the boys tussling in a corner, and he sighed.

"Will you stay long?" asked Gwyden's father. Agor had changed little—his head was somewhat snowier, his face more seamed than Merlin remembered it, but he had neither gained nor lost weight, and he was in full possession of his wits.

"I do not wish to put you to any trouble," answered Merlin.

"Ach, man, it's no trouble to put up with old friends—especially one I taught to handle a rudder and a net! You *must* stay with us, I insist!"

Merlin snatched a glance at Gutor, and noticed the hint of a scowl vanish from his face as their eyes made contact. The boys were giving him their rapt attention, their eyes occasionally sliding towards their mother or father. Merlin drew a deep breath. "I cannot stay long," he said. "Certainly not past the springtime. I have business that will not brook delay in the Summer Country."

Gutor poured more beer, and they drank to it. Merlin stretched out his toes to the fire. It felt good to have nothing to do for the moment.

Gwyden said suddenly, "Why is it, Emrys, that to the Summer Country you must go?"

Merlin looked up at Agor and Gutor. Their eyes were keen over the rims of their cups, and Merlin was struck for a moment at how comic it was to see them both arrested in their movements when they were doing the self-same thing. Four eyes peering over two curved rims. When they saw him observing them, their movement resumed. Gutor took a deep draught and Agor put his cup down before him.

Why indeed? wondered Merlin, gazing forlornly into the fire. "I did not choose my life," he said quietly. "It was chosen for me, by the gods, I think. Were I to choose, I think this is the life I would live. But a path has been placed before my feet, and though I look to the left and to the right, I cannot but follow it wherever it leads me."

"What is it you seek in the Summer Country?" asked Gutor.

Merlin looked up at Gwyden. She knew the answer to that question, and looked away from him to resume her chores. Merlin sipped reflectively at his ale, and said at last, "Some of you know already that I seek Excalibur, the sword of kings, forged by Arawn of the Morforwyn." Agor and Gwyden nodded; Gutor raised his eyebrows, and Merlin plunged on. "There are . . . some things about the story of the forging of Excalibur that I do not understand," he explained. "These are things I cannot speak of here, things I learned recently, whilst visiting Afallach. I have questions, and I need answers. The druids could not give me answers that satisfied me, and so I must seek them elsewhere."

Merlin paused, to take another draught of ale. It had been brewed by Gutor himself, and it was fine ale, full-bodied and rich in flavour. The hut, he noticed, was silent, save for the girl's babbling. The boys had ceased in their rough-and-tumble to hang upon his words. It must be a fine story for boys, he reflected.

Merlin wiped the froth from his upper lip and went on: "There was a time when the Morforwyn mixed freely with mortals. At that time, they helped men, even married them. Argante herself, Queen of the Ladies of the Lake, married Corineus, king of Cornwall and friend of Brutus. By him, she had a daughter, Gwendolyn, whose own marriage to Locrin was so luckless. But, about a thousand years ago, the Morforwyn stopped mixing with mortals. They receded elsewhere—no one knows where—and they were not seen by mortal eyes again. These are the gods we worship—the goddesses, rather, for the Morforwyn menfolk were slain, every one of them, in the wars that Morgana waged upon them.

"In the early days, the Morforwyn dwelt most in the Summer Country. Of this, I have read in the books in Afallach. Men called their island home Avalon. I believe that, if I can find Avalon, I might find more clues to the story behind Excalibur. When I know more about Excalibur, I will be better able to find it, and put it in the hands of the High King. With it, he will be able to free the people of the Island of the Mighty from Rome."

There was silence for a moment, then Gutor said hesitantly, "You seek a path through the Summer Country?" Merlin nodded. Gutor pressed his lips together in a thin smile. "Dydwch," he said.

"I beg your pardon?"

"Dydwch is one of the fenlanders. He lives in Godney, a township some miles south of Badon, in the midst of the fens. He is a strange fellow; he seems almost to come from another world. He comes this way once in a while, peddling axe-heads and knives, and the best fish-hooks I have ever used. If anyone knows the fens, it is Dydwch." Gutor sat back, smiling, and took a deep gulp of his ale.

"Does he come here often?" asked Merlin.

"Two or three times a year," answered Gutor. "He does not like to travel far from his home, but our river flows eventually into the fens, many miles from here."

"How many miles?" asked Merlin. "How long would it take?"

"Nay, I know not," shrugged Gutor. "I have never traveled so far from Habren."

"You could not sail there yourself," said Agor, "if that is what is on your mind. It would be a hard trip in the winter, and once you got to the fens, you would be lost without a guide. You should wait for Dydwch. He will know all the paths through the marshes, and he will know how to avoid the dangers, for it is a treacherous place, full of rank pools and evil spirits."

"But," said Gutor, emptying his mug, "if your business takes you there, there you must go."

"I must indeed." Merlin picked up the pitcher, and poured Gutor another measure of ale.

XIX

But the weather was worse that winter than in living memory. Snow fell in the coombe, even on the beach, and the river froze. Gutor's eyes began to be sullen when Gwyden served Merlin a fourth part of their precious winter stores and so, one morning, Merlin found a villager who owned a bow, took it out, and brought back an eight-point stag at nightfall. He spent the evening butchering it and distributed small gifts of its meat through the village before hanging the remainder in Agor's store-room. That eased tensions a little.

One day, a trifle warmer than the weeks previous, Merlin found a piece of driftwood lying upon the grey shore. It was willow, and somehow twisted into a horseshoe-shape. Merlin picked it up and wondered at it. He fitted it against his shoulder—a little knobbly, perhaps, but quite comfortable. With a sense of mounting excitement, he turned about and flew into Habren.

An hour later, one of Gwyden's boys found him behind their hut, surrounded by wood shavings and tools borrowed from the village carpenter. He had shaped the outside curve of the branch so that it was a little more regular in shape, and had begun scooping out wood from the inner curve, so that it would be hollow.

"What are you doing?" asked the boy.

Merlin looked up, saw who had spoken to him, and returned to his chisel-work. "I am building a harp," he said. "Mine was destroyed, and I need a new one, so I am building it from this piece of driftwood I found just this moment."

The boy stepped closer, fascinated. "How are you going to do it?" he asked.

"Well," said Merlin, "first I shall scoop all the wood out of the middle of this piece of wood, so that the sound of the strings will grow greater when they are plucked. I shall find some planking, and steam it so that I can warp it into the right shape, and fit it into the hollow that I have made. I shall drill holes, and fit strings into the holes made from catgut or horse-hair. Then I shall smoothe the outside, sand it and varnish it and decorate it with pictures to make it look grand. Look at that grain there." Merlin pointed. "See how it curls around, like a wave? That will be beautiful, when I have finished."

"How long will it take?" asked the boy.

"Most of the winter, I should think," answered Merlin. "Then, if I work well, I shall be able to sing for you before I leave for the Summer Country."

"Do you need a harp to sing?" inquired the boy.

"No, but it helps."

The boy watched him in silence for a few minutes, then said, "My mother bade me fetch you in to dinner."

Merlin looked up at the sky. It was already a deep blue, and the air was chilly, now that he thought about it. He gathered up his tools and his harp, and followed the boy indoors.

* * *

Dydwch did not pay a visit all winter long, and spring had come again before he was sighted. He was an old, grizzled man, with bushy hair and a beard, standing a head shorter than Merlin. His long cloak was girded with a red belt. When Gutor introduced him, he ran his eye skeptically up and down Merlin's length, and spat upon the ground before thrusting his hand out. Merlin gripped him by the elbow, and was surprised by how tightly the fingertips clamped down upon him. When he withdrew his hand, Merlin saw pale circles on the skin of his arm.

Reluctantly, Dydwch agreed to guide Merlin to Godney, but expressed his doubts that the king would allow him to stay. So it was that, the next morning, Merlin bade farewell once more to Gwyden and her family, slung his harp, sealed in a waterproof case of canvas, over his shoulder, and stepped into Dydwch's flat-bottomed boat.

They rowed at first along the river that emptied itself into the Sabrina Estuary at Habren, camping that night on its bank. The low hills were silhouetted behind them, to the north. Merlin took out his harp. He had stained and varnished it, strung it with horsehair, and busied himself about tuning it while Dydwch watched him with dark eyes. Merlin nestled it in the crook of his arm, and ran his fingers lightly over the thirty-two strings. The sound rippled, like water.

The next day took them into the Summer Country, a land of brackish waters, where the languid beat of the heron's wings brought shining droplets from the glassy surface of the pools, and the grim willows overhung the complex network of rivers with their grey, knotty arms. Their going here was slower, and Merlin had time to take in all the details. He saw all manner of waterfowl—not just herons, but moorhens, sandpipers, and all varieties of duck. Once, he heard the booming voice of a male bittern, and scanned the reed-beds for a glimpse of the elusive bird, but he could see nothing.

Noon came, the sun drawing out clouds of midges. The boat slid on through the brown waters, the reed-beds near enough for Merlin to reach out and touch.

"It doesn't look deep," he remarked aloud. "I feel as if I could just step out. It wouldn't come much further up than my waist."

"Ah," agreed Dydwch, "but you'd sink past your foolish head into the mud iffen you tried." With that, he fell silent once more.

The afternoon wore on, and Merlin's stomach began to grumble. He turned his eyes up towards Dydwch, and wondered what motivated the man. He seemed hardly human—a fen creature, silent and knowing. What did he look for with those dark eyes? Merlin followed his line of sight.

A mallard, its emerald head held high, was floating past. The river had widened a little, and the duck would pass, Merlin noted, about six feet away. He caught a sudden, economical movement out of the corner of his eye. Dydwch had reached under his seat, produced a hollow wooden tube, and placed it to his lips. His cheeks puffed out for an instant. Merlin turned his eyes upon the mallard. It made a deflated sort of noise, and turned over in the water. Dydwch put away the blow-tube, and paddled the boat over to the stricken duck. He hauled it out of the water by its webbed feet and held it, dripping, in the air. Merlin could see a small, grey-feathered dart protruding from its neck.

"This'll make a nice supper," announced Dydwch, and fell silent once more. He didn't speak again until the sun was almost set, and they brought the boat ashore.

The night air was cool as they feasted on the mallard, but as the darkness closed about them, Merlin grew apprehensive.

"Is Godney nearby?" he asked.

"No," replied Dydwch. "Godney be half a day's rowing still, maybe more."

"Then what are those lights?" Merlin pointed; even as he did so, however, the light wavered away into nothing. A few moments later, another appeared. When it had likewise vanished, Dydwch remained still for a moment, looking at where it had been. Then he returned to the meat he had been enjoying.

"Marsh wisp," he said, as if that cleared matters up.

"What is a marsh wisp?" asked Merlin, when enough time had passed to indicate that Dydwch would not explain the term further without prompting.

"A marsh wisp be's the soul of one who's passed beyond the world," explained Dydwch, glancing around at the darkness and huddling down within his cloak. "Thirty, forty sunsets the soul wanders after a man's died." He gave an ironic grin. "The marsh wisp don't knows he's dead. He's tryin' to get back into his body, but that scares him so bad, he goes away again."

"Where to?" asked Merlin curiously.

Dydwch shrugged. "Maybe the shaman knows that, maybe not."

Merlin watched as another wavering flame appeared, far off in the darkness. "Do they talk?" he asked.

“Ah, but them’s poor guides, marsh wisps,” said Dydwch. “You speak ’em nice, and they help; you speak ’em bad, they lead you into quicksand. Never tell ’em they’re dead, else they get nasty right quick.”

Dydwch fell silent after this, and Merlin could not get another word from him on the topic. Soon after that, they settled down for sleep.

They arose before the sun the next morning, and rowed once more through the sluggish fen-waters. The day grew warm, and flies swarmed on either side of the boat. More than once, Merlin saw the surface of the water break as a fish snapped up one that ventured too close.

As midday approached, and the sun beat down through the budding branches of the willows, the water-course began to open out and, without any warning whatsoever, they found themselves sliding out into the middle of a lake. But more important, before them lay the town of Godney.

The banks of the lake were crowded with trees, mainly willows, and Merlin had to peer carefully at first to distinguish between living trees and the timber from which the town had been constructed. It was built over the water, supported on massive columns made by binding together four or more straight tree-trunks. A wooden stockade, fifteen feet high and built with embrasures so that the defenders could fire missiles or throw spears from relative safety, ran all the way around the town’s circumference. As the boat drew nearer to Godney, Merlin’s eye slid left and right, and he estimated that there might be ninety, perhaps a hundred households within the walls; and in the midst, rising above the peat roofs, was a hall with a newly-thatched roof that shone in the spring sun like spun gold. Some kind of designs were painted on the walls, though from this distance, Merlin could make nothing out except the rich blues and yellows and greens.

“So this is where the king of the Summer Country dwells,” commented Merlin.

Dydwch looked up, frowning. “Summer Country? Nah!” He spat into the lake. “This is the hall of king of the Fenlands. Where be’s the Summer Country?”

Merlin's mouth dropped open in surprise. He thought at first that Dydwch was jesting; but the sober expectation in his eyes revealed otherwise. Merlin said haltingly, "This is the Summer Country, all around us. From the border with Cornwall at Mai Dun and along the River Uscela in the west, to the border with Logris at the Afon in the east: that is the Summer Country."

Dydwch gave a skeptical grunt. "This Summer Country," he said, "be's it a big country?"

Merlin shrugged. "It is not the largest kingdom in the Island of the Mighty, but it is large enough, and mighty. Its king dwells at Badon."

Dydwch nodded. "Badon I knows," he said. "Big city, fine city. But I don't know this king in Badon, nor does any man here in the Fens. Here, Seddech is king."

Merlin did not have much time to ponder this sub-kingdom, nor the legality of its relationship to the kingship system of the Island of the Mighty, for now they were almost among the great pillars that supported Godney, and rapidly approaching a short jetty at the foot of one of the pillars. Merlin's eye traveled up the pillars. A flight of steps led up to a railed platform that hugged the foot of the stockade for the entire circumference of the town. And now that he was close enough to see it, Merlin observed a wide bridge that spanned the lake from what he presumed to be Godney's main gates to the wooded shore.

Dydwch tied his boat up beside several others and, without indicating anything to Merlin, began to climb the steps. Merlin hopped out of the boat and followed him. They walked along the platform at the top towards the land, until they came to the main gates. Heavy iron chains connected towers to the bridge, and Merlin realized that a twelve-foot section of the bridge could be raised in time of siege to deny attackers access. The drawbridge was currently down, however, the gates open, and a pair of guards stood on sentry duty in the opening. Dydwch muttered something to them that Merlin could not hear, then disappeared into the town. When Merlin tried to follow, one of the guards lowered his pike.

“Not now,” he said. “Dydwch tells the king of you; no stranger enters, till the king say yes.”

Merlin nodded, and turned his eyes away from the town and to the wooded shore. The sounds of strange birds and other creatures filled the air all around him. He watched a heron, on the shore, swallow a fish whole. A bulge appeared in its slender throat, slid down the neck, and was gone.

The minutes began to stretch, and the sun to slide slowly towards the west. Merlin took a walk about the perimeter of the stockade. The shore looked very much the same in all directions: grey forests of willows covering all the eye could behold.

When he got back to the main gates, a pair of fenlanders were waiting to escort him. They wore earthen-coloured tunics that came down to their knees, and their legs were cross-gartered. Each had an axe tucked into his belt, and carried a short spear. They each had dark, shoulder-length hair. One of them sported a thin beard.

They led Merlin through a world of timber houses—nothing was made of stone in this place. The streets were narrow, the houses low, so that wherever one stood within the stockade, the palace dominated the skyline.

Many of the buildings they strode past were businesses, fish-sellers or vegetable stalls, and many bronze- and iron-workers. Some of the wares were still displayed, and in passing, Merlin saw many fine pieces of work. Everything was decorated with intricate scroll-work, from hatchets to knives, urns to jewelry.

Outside the palace was a wide area, peopled by statues of strange-looking folk. Some were kings, Merlin thought as he passed them, but the one who stood closest to the palace was some sort of water-god, bald-headed with puffed cheeks and a portly girth, a girdle of rushes about his waist. He was surrounded by waif-like female figures.

The door to the palace was flanked by carvings of herons, whose beaks, touching as if they were kissing above the centre of the door, formed the lintel. The fenlanders escorting Merlin pushed on the door, and they passed inside.

The hall was circular in design, and in the precise centre was a large peat fire, enclosed by white stones, the only ones Merlin had yet seen in Godney. Benches with tables were arranged about the fire in two concentric circles. All around, wide windows gave views of the lake and the forest beyond, familiar to Merlin from his recent walk. On the far side of the fire, the king of the fenlanders sat upon his wooden throne, surrounded by his advisors. Dydwch stood at his right hand. Seddech wore a scarlet cloak and a crown of gold, ribbed all about like the fins of fishes. Merlin stopped before the throne and bowed deeply. "I am at your service, your majesty," he said.

The king of the Fenlands looked down at the top of Merlin's head for a while. Then he said, "I am Seddech, king of the Fenlands. Who are you?"

"I am Merlin Emrys, onetime prince of Cambria, king of Eicenniawn by marriage to Queen Boudicea."

Seddech said nothing for a moment, but his eyebrows rose a fraction of an inch, and then his eyes turned and bored into Dydwch. "Why did you not tell me it was a king you brought hither, marsh-wanderer?" he demanded, his voice rumbling like stones tossed together by a storm.

Dydwch stammered, "Dydwch knows not he be's king—he says nothin' all the way from Habren!"

"Not say?" roared the king. "Not say he was a king? What nonsense is this? How could he be a king and not say so? Did he not command you to bear him to this place?"

Dydwch's eyes were wide now. He said nothing, but shuffled his feet, and gnawed on his lower lip, and wrung his hands. He was showing more emotion, Merlin reflected, than he had shown in the last four days together.

"Pardon, your Majesty," interrupted Merlin, "but what Dydwch says is true. I did not reveal my identity to him . . . " His voice trailed off for a moment as he racked his brains for a plausible excuse. Then he hit upon one. "Such news," he said, "I could not trust to the ears of a marsh-wanderer. Such news is fit only for the ears of a king."

Seddech returned his gaze to Merlin, smiling. He seemed to be mollified. He asked, "Where is Eicenniawn? I have never heard of it."

"Eicenniawn is a land many miles to the north and to the east," replied Merlin. "If your majesty were to ride on a horse, it would take seven days to reach it, perhaps more."

Seddech thrust out his lower lip and wrinkled his brow thoughtfully. "I have never been so far," he said. "Why did you come alone? Why did you bring no servants, no wives?"

"I have only one wife, your majesty." Merlin smiled. "Boudicea is enough of a wife for any man, without more women. I am barely man enough for her alone. She stayed at home to rule the kingdom while I sought knowledge."

Seddech narrowed his eyes. "Leave a woman to rule a kingdom," he said doubtfully. Then he gave a great sigh and shook his head. "Your kingdom is very different from mine. But it saddens me that you have only one wife. Perhaps you would like to use one of mine while you stay here? I have enough to spare, if you are not staying more than a month or so."

He sounded so hopeful and accommodating that Merlin felt like a boor refusing him. "My people marry only once, my lord," he said, "and my wife would not understand your more than generous gesture. But I thank you."

The king grunted noncommittally. "What knowledge do you seek, Merlin Emrys?" he asked.

"I wish to know more of the Morforwyn," said Merlin. "I wish to know of Avalon."

There came a sharp intake of breath from a number of Seddech's advisors, and even from Dydwch, but the king himself did not respond physically. Instead, he examined Merlin closely for long moments, until Merlin began to feel very self-conscious, as if he were being sold. He returned the king's gaze, fixing his eyes on a point in the middle his forehead, and not daring to stir from where he stood.

At last, Seddech said, "I do not believe there is any deceit in you, although there is conflict. Abide awhile therefore in my kingdom, and learn what you can. Of Avalon, I can say only this: that it is a place cursed since before the days of my people, and no one ventures there who values his life.

You are welcome, Merlin Emrys, to the Fenlands. While you are here, share our table." He clapped his hands, and several servants stepped forward. "You will be accommodated in my palace, and wear other clothes, for these weeds are for traveling, and hardly fit for a king. Anything you wish for, my servants can fetch for you. We will speak further over meat and mead."

Merlin bowed again, and followed the servants out of the hall, wondering what dire circumstances could have earned Avalon so fearful a name among the Fenlanders.

XX

Merlin stayed with the Fenlanders for two years. In many ways, it was an agonizing time for him, for it seemed he was no closer to finding out about Excalibur's origins; and, though his knowledge of the Fens grew, he saw nothing that made him think that he had found Avalon or the Morforwyn. And visions of Boudicea and Gwenddolau haunted him in his sleep. He longed to return to Eicenniawn, but he said nothing, and slowly he learned more of the ways of the Fenlanders.

They were a taciturn folk, but capable of much merriment, whose songs were by turn mirthful and hauntingly sad. These songs, Merlin came to understand, reflected the landscape in which they lived: green and fertile in the summer, water-logged and treacherous in the winter. It was a constant source of amazement to him that this vital and enchanting people should be wholly unknown to the outside world. They were adroit craftsmen, forging all manner of household items from bronze and tools from iron, trading with Cornwall to get their ore. They had no agriculture worth mentioning, all their food coming from the marshes in the form of waterfowl or fish, or from the small islands from which they scraped a meagre vegetable harvest each year.

Merlin found that they knew little of the Morforwyn, and worshipped instead their ancestors, usually leaving a small plate for a departed grandfather or great-uncle at each meal. This did not mean that they did not believe in powerful non-human creatures—on the contrary, to a Fenlander, every tree, every stream was inhabited by its own particular spirit. Those who fished a particular stream many times came to know the soul of the stream well, and could read its mood and predict the outcome of fishing for the day, usually with uncanny accuracy.

But of Avalon, Merlin could discover nothing after almost a year of talking with the Fenlanders, and rowing out fishing with them many days.

At that time, he built himself a coracle, Dydwch himself lending assistance, and began searching the myriad of labyrinthine rivers and marshes for himself.

At first, Merlin lost his way frequently but, since he rarely strayed more than a mile from Godney, this was not very serious, and he came to know the locality well. When he was confident, he ventured a little further, and a little further, until he was secure roaming ten miles from Seddech's palace before paddling the coracle back whence it had come. He was equally cautious about venturing out in the summer months, putting his foot carefully forward, knowing the ground to be treacherous where it seemed most firm to the eye.

One night, when he had strayed too far from Godney to make it back in a single day, and had camped beneath the silky moon of August, he received a visit from one he had not seen in several years. He opened his eyes and found Morgana standing above him, her great cats curling about her. Her eyes were stern. Merlin scrambled to his feet.

"I am much amazed, Merlin Emrys, that you spend your time thus," she said. "Why do you dally among such backward folk as these, when great matters are at hand, which you have abandoned? Are you forgetful of our bargain?"

"I am not, my lady," replied Merlin, dropping his eyes. "I still seek Excalibur, but there are things I must know about its forging before I can go any further."

"And what might these things be, pray, that I have not already told you?"

"The Morforwyn. Where did they go? Why do we see them no more?"

Morgana hissed impatiently. "Leave aside these childish ponderings, Merlin Emrys, and find again the path that will lead you to Excalibur. That is what I need: Excalibur. Seek it, use all your powers. What you seek here is of no importance." She took a step closer to him, the moonlight shimmering through the thin stuff of her dress, so that Merlin could pick out the curve of her hips, the roundness of her breasts. "To those who do my bidding," she purred, "I can be a great solace; but to those who ignore me, it were better they had not been born. Remember this, Merlin Emrys, and find your path once more."

Merlin blinked, and she was gone. He was alone on the bank of a tiny island, the moon of the Summer Country silvering the waters and the spongy turf upon which he lay.

He did not sleep again that night, but watched as the stars slowly dimmed and the sun rose in the east. Then he stretched his limbs, and stepped back into his coracle.

Had he indeed lost his path? Was he here for a good reason, or was this all foolishness? Nobody here knew about the Morforwyn anyway. What was the use?

Suddenly a deep resolve grew in him. This quest had lasted for thirty years of his life, and for it he had abandoned wife and child, hearth and home, all the things that gave comfort to a man of his years. He would seek it no more. He would guide his coracle to the edge of the Fens, and make his way back, weary, to Boudicea and her embrace. She would understand his failure. She would be glad that he was back, even with empty hands.

Pondering these thoughts gloomily, he paddled his coracle without thought for a while, until suddenly before him rose an island. It rose like the back of a leviathan from the waters, it slopes grassed and entirely free of trees until the summit, where Merlin recognized the shapes of apple trees, heavy with their fruit.

He changed course, plying his boat parallel to the island's shore, seeking a place where the reed-beds gave him access to solid ground where he could land. His eyes flicked from the shore to the water ahead continuously.

The shore turned sharply at the tail of the leviathan. Here, the ground sloped up in a shallow gradient towards the crest of the hill. Merlin looked ahead.

There was another boat ahead of him; and in it sat a man with iron-grey hair, a fishing-pole in his hands. As Merlin watched, the man turned his head, saw him, and raised a cheery hand in greeting.

Merlin paddled towards him, bringing his coracle up beside his boat.

"Well met, old one," said Merlin. "I seek lodgings for the night; do you know where I might find them?"

"You can stay with me this night, if you like," said the man. Merlin noticed the thick muscularity of his hands and arms, the iron-like toughness of his jaw beneath the silvered beard. "My name is Pelles," he added.

"Mine is Merlin."

"Yes." He tossed his head backwards. "There's a spot to land your coracle there. Just walk to the crest of the hill. You'll find my house in the middle of the trees."

"Thank you."

"I'm fishing for lunch, but I shall join you presently."

Merlin nodded and paddled towards the shore. Sure enough, grassy turf sloped down to the water's edge and terminated but an inch above the waters. Merlin stepped out of his coracle and pulled it up onto the shore. The greensward rose gently before him, and the sun beat gently upon him as he climbed towards the summit.

Merlin snatched a glance over his shoulder. Pelles was approaching, a pair of bream dangling from a stick he held over his shoulder. He walked with a pronounced limp, Merlin observed, as he drew near. Merlin held out his hand to take the fish, and Pelles willingly surrendered his burden, though his limp did not lessen as they reached the summit and entered the shade of the apple trees.

"Apple trees," said Pelles, a smile on his face as he paused a moment and breathed deeply. "Where have you seen such fruit ere now, Merlin?"

"In Afallach," responded Merlin.

"Yes," said Pelles, without surprise, "in Afallach." He sighed. "But here they grow best." He reached up and plucked half a dozen apples from the nearest tree, and went on.

They were making for a wooden hut in the exact centre of the ring of apple trees. Pelles pushed open the door and entered, Merlin coming after him.

For a while, they were engaged in gutting and preparing the fish, but as the bream roasted slowly over the central hearth, Pelles drew them each a cup of mead. Merlin sipped it carefully, then drew a deep mouthful. It was rich and sweet, and the aftertaste, precisely like honey, glowed upon his tongue afterwards.

Pelles fixed Merlin with his eye. "You have come here," he said, "to learn about Avalon. Am I correct?"

Merlin could not fathom how this old man knew that, but he did not think to question him. "You are correct," he said.

"Good. I have waited for you long, although . . . there are some things for which I have waited longer, for which I still wait. First, you should know that this island is not itself Avalon. In times past, it was the gateway to Avalon, and a most holy place."

"What is Avalon?" asked Merlin.

"The dwelling-place of the Morforwyn," answered Pelles, "their retreat when Morgana's legions overwhelmed them. There, she cannot touch them, but thence they cannot come, until the gateway is opened once more."

"And how can that happen?"

Pelles hesitated a moment, and his eyes dropped. "There are some things that are beyond my knowledge," he said, "but I shall know the signs when I see them."

"Tell me of the Morforwyn," urged Merlin. "Tell me of Excalibur, and why Morgana rebelled against them."

Pelles reached out and patted his forearm. "This has been troubling you," he said. "Morgana can appear reasonable to those by whom she stands to profit. If you would know the true and full story, I can reveal it to you."

"Please do," said Merlin.

Pelles nodded gravely. "Then you should know that Excalibur, which you have sought so long, is a treasure past men's valuation; but combined with the other six treasures, its value passes the world. And one by one, Morgana has drawn these treasures to her."

"I know a little about the other treasures—the Siege Perilous, the Bridle of Gwynn and so forth," observed Merlin.

"Aye," answered Pelles, "but there is none but I can tell you their true story, for the druids do not know, and Morgana is as full of venom as an adder's tongue."

Merlin waited patiently; indeed, he thought, there was no need to rush. He smiled to himself: thirty years of seeking, distracted from time to time, but nevertheless, three decades of work. He knew he ought to feel more eager than he did; but it seemed as if, within this hut, time had ceased to have any meaning.

Presently, Pelles looked at him and began his story.

* * *

For many thousands of years, the Morforwyn lived together in peace and harmony, and great was the pleasure they took from the virgin land in which they dwelt, which they called Albion, and from their companions, the giants and dragons and other creatures that lived there before men came. Seven was the number of the men, and seven the number of the women, and their king was Arawn the Mighty, their queen Argante the Just. Happy were those days, when no dissension split the ranks of the Morforwyn, and they knew no envy. Then it was that they forged the seven Treasures: chief of them was Excalibur, but almost equal in beauty to it was the Siege Perilous, the throne of destiny, fashioned by Balor the Wise. So the long years, filled with bliss, passed; yet some few among them grew restless. Most of all did Balor desire to take his place upon the Siege Perilous, for he knew that it would confer great knowledge. But although he had wrought that treacherous throne himself, and set it with his own hands upon the loftiest peak in all the land, yet he feared its knowledge. There was the knowledge in him, which he sought to press down deep into the darkness of his soul, where he could ignore it, that absolute power belonged only to another, and in his heart he knew that with knowledge it would also bring madness.

Nevertheless, Balor grew jealous of Arawn over the long years, lest he should gain the knowledge of the Siege Perilous; so he cast spells about it, weaving his paces and signing the air with strange figures, until the mighty throne was hidden from all but him alone. Yet he took counsel with Morgana, as being closest to him in temperament, and she swore to keep this thing a secret between them.

But as the years passed, Balor grew ever more resentful of Arawn's leadership. "Why is it," he asked himself, "that he leads and I do not? Were we not created equal? Am I not endowed with qualities as noble and virtuous as his?" And even as these thoughts passed through his mind his eye strayed towards the Siege Perilous, and he would have sat upon it, but his heart misgave him. And so for a space more, things continued as they had always been; and to all outward appearances, Balor seemed as happy and content as the rest of the Morforwyn. But Morgana watched him closely, and perceived some of what went on inside his mind, and she said to him, "Why is it that my lord Balor has not made use of the Siege Perilous? Can there be some fear upon him?" And Balor was silent, for it sat ill with him that she should speak thus to him. And at length he said: "What use would be the gifts of the Siege Perilous? To know all is to be with the Creator, and what need have we of that, who sat at His table and sang His praises ere the world was begun?"

"What foolishness is this?" returned Morgana. "What certain word have we of this fabled meal before the beginning of days? It is a dream, a childish fantasy. But if there is One who made us, He desires us to use the Siege Perilous. Not to be with Him," purred Morgana, "but to be His equal, His comrade—*that* is His desire. Know you not this? He craves, in His loneliness, for a peer." And she smiled—he thought in kindness and encouragement, but in truth at the deceit she was weaving.

"Your speech is foolishness," said Balor. "You know not what you say." But her words had struck him deeply, and he pondered them for many days thereafter. And so, at the dead of night, he stole away from the other

Morforwyn, and betook him to the mountaintop where he had hidden the Siege Perilous.

"O, how events become greater than the thoughts which began them, swelling like a viper, heavy with its prey!" he cried as he stood there in the moonlight, the blue ice glowing all about him as with its own light. "When first I fashioned thee, I had in mind a thing of benefit for the world. No knowledge had I how afeard I might be to use thee." Then, remembering the words of Morgana, he shook himself as from a dream and declared: "Yet I shall take thee. Did I not create thee with these hands? Art thou not the manifestation of this mind? Why then should I not be His equal?" And so saying, he lowered himself onto the stone.

There came a noise, as it had been the earth tearing itself asunder, and a pain as of a thousand flames filled his body. And it seemed that his anguish could have no bounds; but when the agony was gone, Balor laughed, and the laugh echoed hollowly about the mountaintop. Then he saw that Morgana had followed him up the mountain, and stood there, bathed in moonlight, tall and majestical. And Balor was seized with a great desire to take her body. Rising from the Siege Perilous, he rent Morgana's shift so that her pale flesh was bared. Her breasts heaved, and her body yielded to him.

"My lord," she said, "I shall conceive for you a race of sons that shall conquer all of Albion."

"It shall be even as you say," answered Balor, as he bore down upon her. And that night he planted a seed in her, and then slept. But as he lay in his dreams, Morgana took a great icicle from an overhanging rock and wielded it in both her hands. She stood over Balor, naked and terrible, the blue light shining on her smooth flesh as she raised the weapon above her head.

At the last moment, Balor awoke.

"What is the meaning of this?" he asked.

"Thou hast the wisdom of the Siege Perilous," replied Morgana, a narrow smile revealing her teeth, "but thou art a fool, for I had it first!" And so saying, she plunged the ice sword into his heart, and his spirit went shrieking to the Underworld.

* * *

"I do not understand," said Merlin, after a pause. "How do you know these things?"

"Do you trust me, Merlin?" asked Pelles.

"I do," nodded Merlin.

"Then listen, and accept what I say." Without a pause, Pelles continued with his narration.

XXI

For the Morforwyn, as for men (Pelles went on), murder empties the soul, and the killer craves only more slaughter to fill the void, and so was it with Morgana. Her offspring, when it emerged, was a monster. One leg was shorter than the other, one shoulder lower, one eye recessed far back in its skull, the other bulging out onto the cheek. And worse, within a minute of its emergence, the breath left its frail body, and chant as Morgana could, nothing would restore life to the tiny frame. She took the creature to Arawn, and begged him to restore life to it, but he could do nothing.

"The power to breathe life into lifeless things," he said, "is no longer mine. Why have you done this thing? It was long forbidden the Morforwyn to engender creatures upon one another."

"Wouldst thou deny my love?" demanded Morgana.

"I would deny no one's love," answered Arawn; "but this was not a child begotten out of love—not for love of it, or its father. And where *is* its father? Where is Balor? Let him answer his wrongs before me also!"

"Dost thou think he will crawl before thee, craven and unmanned? Nay, Arawn, he will not. But now look to thine own—to thy people, thy subjects, thy lands, and thy treasures. For I shall return, and I shall bring war with me!"

Then Arawn knew that Morgana had murdered Balor, and his heart was heavy for the deed. Morgana, meanwhile, took herself into the remote mountains in the north of Albion, and there she bent all her powers upon the rock and ice, and brought forth great, monstrous creatures—giants of ice, with nerves and sinews of granite, not alive, for she had not that power, but animated, ready to do her bidding. And Morgana returned to the Morforwyn, bringing with her armies of these brutish creatures. Thus began the wars in which all the menfolk of the Morforwyn were slain. The Ladies of the Lake betook themselves to these fenlands, and there they hid the Treasures from view on the island of Avalon, biding their time for many long centuries, and all the while Morgana and her monstrous legions sought them, ravaging the country, until Brutus came.

Brutus was a Trojan, descended of Aeneas himself, and he brought with him the dispossessed lords and ladies of Troy. It was in the island of Albion that these Trojans proposed to settle and build up a kingdom to rival Latium. But when they arrived, the giants attacked their camps and new cities. A great war between the men and the giants ensued, and in the end Brutus drove them back. Morgana and the remnant fled into the north, and there she raised about her the realm of Annwn, and cast spells of protection upon it so that none might approach her unless she willed it.

So it was that men came to the island of Albion, and named it Britain, after their leader; and so it was also that the Ladies of the Lake gave into the possession of men all the Seven Treasures of the Island of the Mighty. Brutus divided the realm into seven, and to the king of each was given a Treasure, Brutus keeping Excalibur for himself and his descendants.

Morgana dared not move against men at first, but soon the time ripened, and she began to move about the Island of the Mighty. And she whispered into the ears of the kings, that they turned away from the Morforwyn, and the realm became a cold one to the Ladies of the Lake. So they withdrew again to Avalon, where still they dwell.

For many years, the sons of men guarded the seven Treasures of the Morforwyn; but no watch can be eternal. Those who first arrived on this island fought hard to keep it and the Treasures; but those who came after, the sons of their sons, fought not, and gave the Treasures a slighter value. Some were lost through foolishness. Conla, sometime king of Albany, surrendered the Bridle of Gwynn to his evil servant, Fraecos, thinking to use it as a wedding gift, for he was enamoured of the daughter of Geirrod of Annwn. Elathan's Veil of Gold disappeared with Gweir, erstwhile crown prince of Cameliard; it is said that he sits even now in the dungeon of Morgana's fortress of Caer Siddi, where he sings an eternal lament for his captivity.

The Siege Perilous remained long in Cornwall, until the fateful day that King Gorneu, the foolish one who would be wise, sat upon it, encouraged, no doubt, by the Lady of Annwn; and the crack which split it from side to side was heard in the furthest reaches of Orkney. The Cauldron of Garanhir was stolen by raiders from Eirin. When Bran the Blessed took it back, it was stolen again by one of Morgana's servants, a loathsome serpent. The Harp of Teirtu was lost when the people of Logris revolted against High King Belgabarad and sacked Caer Lundein. So, through pride or avarice or lust, the other Treasures of the Island of the Mighty were lost also, all except for Excalibur, the wondrous sword, and the sheath woven by Lady Argante. The others Morgana seized, but Excalibur was well guarded by the High Kings of Britain, until Cassivelaunos sent it away with Belinos; and where he laid them no one, not even Morgana, knows.

* * *

Pelles ceased, and there fell a silence between them that Merlin felt disinclined to break. He was thinking, about the Morforwyn, and the druids, and Excalibur, and Gwenddolau.

"Does this tale answer your questions, Merlin Emrys?" asked Pelles at length.

"Some of them," replied Merlin. "The druids, then, have only a glimpse of the truth—they know a part of it. They know that it is only Morgana who works in the realm of Britain; they have forgotten that there are others of the Morforwyn, the Ladies of the Lake."

Pelles nodded sagely. "What lies in the distant past is often taken as false by men of little imagination, and so, I fear, it is with the druids. They have forgotten the love of Argante, the music of Tylweth, the laughter of Rhiannon. Morgana demands blood, and that is what the druids remember, because her demands are constant."

"Then there is hope!" Merlin cried suddenly. "Gwelydd always said, and I have heard other druids repeat it, that life is a long scream, terminated by oblivion. But that is not true—at least, it is only that part of the truth that comes from Morgana. Oh, I have seen how those who are devoted to her behave, for I have evaded the princes of Morgannawg in their great hunt. But that is not all there is—there is love, and music, and laughter as well."

"Yes, Merlin, there is—but they must be freed."

"How? That I would know."

Pelles let out a great sigh. "That," he said, "I can neither say nor see."

Something in his manner suddenly struck Merlin. Perhaps it was a glint in the deep blackness of his eyes, a fellow-feeling. Merlin said, "Pelles, do you have the Sight?"

Pelles smiled, and Merlin could see that there was a secret in the smile, a secret to which he knew he could not yet be party. "Many are the things I see, especially here."

"Is this place special?" asked Merlin.

"You know it is, Merlin. You have known it since first you set foot upon this island. The druids imagine that the Sacred Hill of Afallach is the only Seeing Hill in the Island of the Mighty, but they are wrong—the Giants' Dance on the Great Plain, Pimlimon in Cambria, Hart Fell in Lothian, and here."

"Avalon?"

Pelles gave Merlin a friendly but admonitory punch on the shoulder. "Little have you listened to me, O Merlin who uses the Sight but not the Hearing! This island is not Avalon, but the gateway, the closed gateway, to Avalon. This is Caer Ban, the Bright Fortress, for bright it is indeed in the spring when the blossoms shine upon the apple trees!"

"Caer Ban," repeated Merlin.

"Or Corbenic, as the fenlanders would have the name."

"If I look now," said Merlin, "will I see where Excalibur lies?"

Pelles shook his head. "The power of the Sight is great, but not infinite," he said, "and it can be deceptive. It is possible to use the Sight, and see only a part of the truth, as the druids have only a part of the truth about the Morforwyn. And some things remain hidden, even from the Sight."

"Why?" demanded Merlin.

"Enough questions now," said Pelles firmly. "What you ask now cannot be answered by me, but only by him who sent me. And he has not spoken to me in a long while."

"But—"

"Enough," said Pelles. "The hour is late, and you have answers enough to ponder in your dreams."

Even before he had finished speaking, Merlin's eyes were closed; he was asleep seconds later.

* * *

That night, a dream came to Merlin. He saw a she-wolf, her cubs by her side, bathed in the silver light of a full moon. An eagle, dark against the stars, stooped out of the heights, its claws extended. It struck the she-wolf so that she somersaulted in mid-air before striking the ground in a heap of fur and limbs. The eagle alighted on the body of the wolf and folded its wings. The cubs attacked, but the eagle swiftly finished them off; a hawk swung from the circle of the moon, but the eagle rose upon its mighty wings and struck at the hawk with its talons. The hawk took flight, disappearing into a forest. The eagle turned back to the wolf.

The she-wolf lived yet, but she was weakened. She raised Her muzzle to the skies and let out a howl. There was blood on her lips.

Merlin sat bolt upright in the grey light of morning. Pelles sat exactly where he had been sitting the previous night; it looked as if he had never moved.

"What did you dream?" asked Pelles. Merlin told him quickly. "And what do you think it means?"

"Boudicea is in need," said Merlin. "I must leave this place. It is long I have desired to return to her."

"That may not be the best path," said Pelles. "The world is changing. For a while, at least, it will become Roman. Nothing, not even your love for Boudicea, can arrest that progress. But what is to happen here—that is something worth waiting for."

"What is going to happen here? When?"

"I do not know, yet. But I have been led here—"

"By the gods?"

Pelles smiled; it was the smile of an indulgent father towards a child who has not put his knowledge together properly. "Not by the gods, but, I think, by the One who made them. And here I shall remain, until I have seen what the One wants me to behold, until I have served my purpose, and can rest."

"Your words slip from my grasp," objected Merlin.

"I cannot help that," replied Pelles. "I know so little myself. But I believe that you should wait here with me."

"For how long?" There was a note of urgency in Merlin's rising voice.

"Again, I cannot say. You must trust me."

Merlin felt his will crumbling. It was strange that, knowing this man such a short space of time, he should trust him so utterly, be prepared to abandon wife, children, and kingdom on a vague promise.

"I wish this were the Sacred Hill," he muttered. "There is much I would seek to know at the moment."

Pelles indicated the door. "This hill is like Afallach, as I told you, and it resembles Afallach in being also a Seeing Hill. You have the Sight, Merlin. Go to my apple grove, and there use your Sight, if you wish to know what events are being set in motion."

Merlin leaped to his feet and dashed out of the hut. Outside, the air was warm, the grass beaded with dew. He could see mists hanging around the nearby willows, like a shawl about the shoulders of an old crone. He planted his feet in the centre of the circle of trees.

Nothing happened.

Merlin squeezed his eyes shut. He thought of his heart, pictured it in the eye of his mind. He saw the steady pulse as it pumped blood around his body, life-giving blood. He reached out from his heart, his fingers stretching outwards, and opened his eyes once more.

Pelles had joined him, and was sitting on a tree stump at the edge of the clearing. He was rubbing his lame leg, but now he looked up at Merlin curiously.

"What do you see?"

"Nothing!"

"Be calm," Pelles urged him, "and be open. Who can use the Sight, when he has already made up his mind what he is to do?"

"What should I do?"

"Do? Do nothing! Look—do not tell the Master of the Sight what it is you seek. He knows. Be ready."

Merlin noticed he was panting, and he slowed his breathing down until it came in and out like waves upon the shore. His heart kept time with his breathing. His body, his mind, and his soul were one. He reached out.

He saw Caermyrddin, its new king, Meldred, sitting upon a troubled throne. His own mother, Viviane, he saw reclined upon a couch. Her dark hair was shot through with strands of silver, and the veins stood out on the backs of her hands.

He saw the king of Morgannawg, dead and borne upon his bier, and Kenen smiling, the crown upon his head.

He saw the druids of Afallach. They were on the Sacred Hill, and had erected a pole in the midst of the clearing. A woman was bound to it, naked. He saw a knife flash.

Merlin came to his senses, kneeling upon the grass of Corbenic. His chest was heaving.

"Why?" he asked. "Why must the druids kill? Why must there be blood?"

"There must always be blood, Merlin," answered Pelles. "Blood is life, and the giving of it is an act of love. The druids do not understand this fully.

They would take out of fear that which must only be given out of love. But heed your vision: the druids sacrifice only on festival days, or in a time of need. What dark events do they respond to with a sacrifice of human flesh? Look again."

Merlin rose to his feet, sent a calming wave through his body, and stretched out his arms.

The visions came fast this time. He saw a great army, an army of Romans, marching towards the mountains of Cambria. The terrain was uneven —soaring mountains and swooping valleys—but the Romans marched over them in straight lines, their red and gold like rivers of blood cutting across Britain.

Then he saw Boudicea. Her face was bedaubed with war-paint, her hair flew like flames from her head. The glance of her eye was most fierce, and she clutched a spear in her hand. She was mounted upon a chariot, and beside her, in his own chariot, rode Gwenddolau. They were lit from behind by flames that sprang from the walls of a broken city. Smoke filled the air, and the wheels of the chariot crunched on the bones of men.

Merlin screamed and staggered backwards. When he opened his eyes, he found that Pelles had caught him and was supporting his head.

"I must go, Pelles," he said. He looked down at his body. It still quivered, as if cold. He raised his hands to his face, kneaded his eyes, then looked again. Carefully, he got to his feet. "I saw Roman armies moving," he said. "They march upon Afallach. And I saw Boudicea at the head of another army." The truth of the situation suddenly fell upon him. "Ah!" he cried. "The Romans have left Eicenniawn to attack Afallach; Boudicea has taken advantage of their absence to rebel. Can she win?"

Pelles was silent for a moment, then said, "There is no way of being certain. If the Romans spend much time subduing Ynys Mon and the druids, Boudicea might make great headway in the south."

"Then I must ensure that they do."

"How? Can you advise the druids? They have abandoned you, Merlin. They would not accept your help. *You must stay here*."

"And do what? Wait for you don't know what, you don't know how long?"

"All I can tell you is that what is to happen here is more important than Boudicea, Excalibur, or even the Island of the Mighty itself. If it happens and you are not here, you will regret it all your life, and perhaps the world will regret it more."

"All my hopes for Britain are pinned upon that boy—my boy, Gwenddolau. If I find Excalibur, it must be for him."

"Are you certain of that?"

Merlin did not speak. In truth, he was not certain, for the face of the young man he had seen bearing Excalibur in his visions did not resemble Gwenddolau's. "Who else could bear it? Meldred? Kenen? There is no one now worthy of bearing Excalibur within the boundaries of the Island of the Mighty, save Gwenddolau."

"Be patient, Merlin," said Pelles. "Stay and learn from me while we wait together."

"I must go to Eicenniawn," said Merlin plaintively. "Boudicea needs me: I am her husband."

Pelles took a deep breath, fixed Merlin's eye, and said, "And I need you also: you are my son."

XXII

Merlin was at first too stunned to speak. Long moments of silence passed between the apple trees. A thousand words crowded into his head, but each faltered on his lips. His mind reeled backwards over the years, and he saw before his mind's eye the vision that had come to him in his childhood, when he was sick. He had had a fall, and his mother was tending him and, as he had touched her hand, he had seen the silhouette of a man with a limp, who came to her bed in the dead of night.

He looked again at the fellow who stood before him. His frame was powerful, in spite of the limp, and his shoulders did not stoop. His jaw was firm, his nose aquiline, his eyes dark and ageless, like the depths of an ancient forest. How old was he? Merlin could not guess to within twenty years.

"Do you doubt what I have said?" asked Pelles at last.

"No," answered Merlin. "Strange to tell, but no, I do not doubt what you have said. I think I saw you once, in a vision."

Pelles nodded. "That vision I sent you."

"*You* sent me?"

"Aye. The Sight is a way of communicating—there must be one who shows, or reveals, as well as one who sees."

"I thought my visions came from the gods."

"Sometimes, they do." Pelles fell silent, and there were no more words for a space. Merlin moved over to the tree stump that Pelles had vacated, and slumped heavily onto it.

At length, he looked up, his eyes narrowed. "Why did you do it? Why did you seduce my mother? And why did you leave her?"

Pelles opened his arms towards his son. "Why did I do it? Can you ask me that, when you are before me? It is not the love of a woman alone that causes one to engender a son. I did it because I knew you would have the Sight, that you would be the greatest of the Seeing Ones."

Merlin's lip curled downwards. "Then you did not love my mother?"

Pelles drew a deep breath through his nose, expelling it through pursed lips. "Not everyone who loves a woman must see and touch her to love her," he said. "Of your forty years, Merlin, how many have you spent with Boudicea?" Merlin looked away. "Three children you have engendered upon her," he reminded him gently.

"Circumstances have kept me from Boudicea's side," Merlin said quietly.

"So they have for me. It is not always for the best that a child be raised near its father—there are certain freedoms it loses. This you know already —is it not a custom among your people to bring your sister-sons into your household, and send your sons out? What son does not wish to be like his father, or as much unlike as he can manage? I did not want to choose your path for you."

"And yet the path has never seemed like my choice," observed Merlin.

"The past never seems chosen."

"I don't want to debate fate and free will with you, father." The last word dropped awkwardly from Merlin's lips; he could not recall having uttered it before. To cover up his awkwardness, he added hastily, "I had my bellyful of philosophic conversation with Morfryn."

"He is a good man, if a little obsessed," observed Pelles.

Merlin frowned, turning his face up towards his father. "Who are you in truth?" he asked.

"In truth, I am Pelles, for now," replied the old fellow, "though I have known other names. Some of them I shall tell you, though not now."

"Why not?"

"Because it is not enough to reveal the truth; to reveal it at the proper moment and in the proper manner is the fullness of truth." His eyes took on suddenly a far-seeing look, like a sailor's, accustomed to gazing out over vast empty fields of water. "Great things are stirring in the world, perhaps the greatest that have ever come to pass." Merlin must have looked confused, for Pelles hastened to explain. "What we see in our loan-days, our days beneath the sun, is but a part of the truth. The fullness of the truth has yet to be revealed. This is so with men and women, and this is so with the great story of the world. Be patient, little hawk."

"That's no answer," grumbled Merlin ill-naturedly. "If Pelles isn't your real name, who are you truly?"

For the first time, a hint of sternness crept into Pelles' eyes, like granite glimpsed beneath moss on the slope of a mountain. He said, "I am he who is known now as Pelles. Do not seek to know more at this moment, Merlin, for you shall not. I have my reasons, and they are good."

For a moment, Merlin bristled. He got to his feet, his eyes hard as he faced Pelles. Then, suddenly, he laughed out loud, throwing his head back to guffaw at the sky. Pelles looked confused, his brow wrinkling as Merlin's mirth subsided.

"Forgive me, father," said Merlin, and now the word did not seem like a foreign one upon his tongue, "for now I understand something I heard often from my playmates as a child."

"And what is that, Merlin?"

"I could never understand why they were often so angry at their fathers. Once, the father of one of my friends forbade him do a thing, I forget what, and when my friend asked why he could not do it, his father answered, 'Because I say so.' And you have said that to me: you must in truth be my father!"

Pelles smiled. Then, all at once, they embraced, Pelles folding his son to him in a grip that was firm and warm. They parted, and began to stroll back towards the hut.

"As it is between a father and his son," he said as they walked, "so it is between a man and the world in which he lives. Some things are known to men, and others are not. Like others, my knowledge is unfinished, and will always be so in my days of breath. Like the druids, I lack the fullness of revelation. You and I, Merlin, we have the Sight. But we are never fully masters of the Sight—that was something even Llygat never properly understood. We see a part of the truth through our visions, but not all of it. Never all of it. Why is the yew tree in the courtyard of your grandfather's castle in Caermyrddin important?"

"The old yew tree?" said Merlin, startled. "It was the only tree that grew in the courtyard. I used to be a little afraid of it, its shadow was so sinister, till it was struck by lightning." He paused, his mind rolling back again over the years. "I remember that storm," he said. "I was in my ninth year, I think, and such a storm it was that no one in Caermyrddin could recall its like." He looked directly at Pelles. "Why *is* it important?"

Pelles shrugged. "I know not," he replied. "But I saw the brand of lightning split the yew tree, as it did the oak tree here upon Corbenic. I saw the yew split in a vision, and the oak split here with my waking eyes. And there was not a place in the Island of the Mighty left unchanged by that storm. But what did it signify? Why was it important? That revelation lies in the lap of time, to be revealed at the right moment, in the right manner."

"And it is for this that you wish me to remain here, this revelation?" asked Merlin.

Pelles nodded. "It pains me that I cannot cast my line closer to the right fish."

"If I stay," said Merlin, "I shall not be able to help Boudicea and Gwenddolau."

"Perhaps they will not need your help."

They had reached the hut now. Through the trees, Merlin could see the long slope down to the water, and his coracle, dark against the emerald turf.

"They are my wife and my son," he said. "I owe them my duty. I can choose no other path."

Pelles took a deep breath. "Perhaps all will not be lost," he said. He reached out and placed a hand upon his son's shoulder, and Merlin suddenly felt a new strength and resolve. Pelles said, "I will not say that this is the right path that you have chosen, nor that it does not matter. But the power to choose a path matters more in the end than what lies at the other end of it. Go, with my blessings, my son."

"I shall return," Merlin told him earnestly, "when Boudicea no longer needs my help."

Pelles nodded. "You came here seeking knowledge," he said. "Did you find what you sought?"

"I believe I did." Merlin smiled wryly. "I still have many questions, but I begin to understand why I have never wanted to join the druids."

"That is well," concluded Pelles. "May your path be straight, your footstep light!"

Merlin turned to go, but hesitated and looked at his father once more. "Father," he said, "will I ever find Excalibur, and place it into the hands of Gwenddolau?"

"Go," said Pelles again, "and do what you feel you must."

An hour later, Merlin was dipping his paddle into the waters of the fens, the early morning sun warm on the back of his head. He had left Corbenic so hastily that he had left his harp behind, and did not miss it until he had returned to Godney for his other belongings—they were few indeed. He thought about returning to Corbenic, but abandoned the idea when he remembered how difficult it had been to find in the first place. The need for haste was upon him. He waited anxiously in the town for Dydwch to return from one of his ventures, and then the old man rowed him once more through the fens—north and east this time.

"You'll not believe what I hears in Badon, Merlin," he said, as they rowed.

"What?" said Merlin, surprised at Dydwch's loquaciousness.

"That realm you're king of, what be's its name?"

"Eicenniawn."

"Aye, Eicenniawn, I thinks so. Well, Eicenniawn be's in revolt. A tavern-keeper in Badon is telling me. I tells him, how could that be, since we have the king of Eicenniawn our guest in Godney? He says it be's not the king who is going to war at the head of his army, but their queen, the queen of the Eicenni."

"Boudicea!"

"Aye, that be's the name. Boudicca."

Merlin's breast was churning so, he did not bother to correct the old man's pronunciation.

* * *

Dydwch deposited Merlin on the north-eastern border of the Fenlands, and pointed out a road that would take him towards Eicenniawn. It was a road that Merlin had never seen before and, although he made excellent progress, for it was well-paved and straight, he was seldom sure that he was going in the right direction. The landscape too was a Britain he had not seen ere now, with milestones to tell the distance between cities that had not existed twenty years previously, square villas surrounded by rolling fields, shrines to foreign gods. And yet the land seemed empty, and Merlin felt as if he were walking through a desert, where once there had been lakes and streams.

A sense of foreboding grew as Merlin passed east through Sarum to Venta, passing never a soul upon the road. The wind blew in from the east, like the blast of a furnace, the breath of a wrathful and avenging god. North he went to Calleva, the fortress of some Britonnic noble rudely wrested into a square shape for a Roman legion. But the Romans had since abandoned it, for there seemed to be very few soldiers about: the doors were barred, and Merlin could not enter. He spent the night under a dead hawthorn tree instead, and circled the wooden palisade of the city in the morning until he found the road that would take him east to Lundein.

Except that, now, Roman milestones told him that it was called Londinium.

Merlin hurried along now, resting seldom, like a horse scenting home on the evening air after a long day's ride through wastelands. This last leg of his journey took but one day and, as he neared Londinium, his heart grew heavy, for a dull red glow was smeared across the eastern sky like the rise of a mocking sun.

The road took Merlin to the crest of a shallow hill, so that he could look down into the Thames Valley. He came to stop, unable to move any further forward.

The river curled like a crimson snake to his right, or like a river of blood. Above it, Londinium was aflame. The mighty walls built by Lludd had been breached, the timber buildings within fired. Flames leaped skywards, and thick, oily smoke poured up, blotting out the heavens.

Merlin hurried down the incline towards the city. Now, he saw detritus on either side: broken wagons, discarded weapons, a wheel. And bodies. The first brought Merlin up short. It was a woman, no more than a girl. She wore the shreds of a woolen stola, the dress worn by Roman women. But her clothes had been wrenched from her, and she had met a bloody end. Merlin felt the earth swing vertiginously about his feet. His arm flailed about wildly for support, but he found none, and sank to the ground, his shoulders shaking with silent tears. He looked at the girl for a long moment, and thought about burying her, but then he saw the crooked form of another body, a little further along, and another, and another. He rose to his feet and walked, dazed, through the land of the dead, as the heat of the fires grew and the broken walls loomed higher before him.

At last, he stood below the dark walls, silhouetted by the fires within. The gates were broken, the roadway through them filled with smashed stones, splintered planks and other rubbish. But further along the wall was a breach, where the ancient masonry had been humbled. Merlin turned away from the impassable gate and climbed nimbly through the breach in the wall, alighting on the other side and dusting his hands off. He did not have a sword, but it did not take him long to find one: the body of a Roman soldier, disemboweled, lay across the street a hundred yards away. The stench almost overcame him, but Merlin endured it to pick up the gladius, the short

Roman sword still gripped in the outstretched hand. Merlin hurried on, holding his cloak over his nose and mouth.

Some of the fires were out now, the houses standing blackened and hollow and belching thick clouds of smoke. Sometimes, dark figures would scurry across the road before him, or else dart for cover at his approach. Once, he saw out of the corner of his eye a group of men and youths stripping bodies of valuables. On another occasion, he glimpsed a young man dashing from the gutted ruins of a goldsmith's shop, his arms full of necklaces and other treasures.

Merlin stopped when he heard the scream.

It was a woman's scream, and came from but a little distance away. It was accompanied by harsh male laughter.

Merlin dashed towards the screams, no longer thinking of the consequences. He raised his foot and brought it crashing into the wood panels of the door to a smouldering house and barreled through, planting his feet firmly and raising his sword.

Three Britonnic youths had surrounded a young girl. A fourth youth knelt before her and was struggling with her clothes, while she thrashed back and forth, cursing them in Latin while they jeered at her in Brythonic.

Merlin leaped forward, his head swimming. One of the youths lost his head without even turning around. A second caught the point of Merlin's gladius in his stomach, and curled noiselessly over the blade, his lips frothing with blood. Merlin hauled on the sword. It came free, but his victim lurched forward. Merlin took a step backwards to avoid him, and was off balance for a moment. The third youth had time to draw his sword and lunge at Merlin, but he over-extended, and Merlin swung the blade down onto his elbow. The youth cried out, clutching the severed stump of his arm, and scrambled away through the wreckage.

The fourth youth had scrambled off his knees, but now fell to them again, tears coursing down his cheeks, pleading for mercy in stammering Brythonic.

Merlin brought the edge of his blade crashing down on the top of the youth's head, and split it to the throat. He toppled over sideways.

Merlin closed his eyes, swaying a little. When he opened them again, the shattered, bloody world seemed a long way off, and there were voices in his head, like the clamouring of doomed souls in the Otherworld. Merlin looked down at the blade in his hand. It was smeared with blood and some pieces of bone and hair. Without wiping it, Merlin tucked the gladius into his belt and moved to the girl's side. He was master of himself again.

The boys had ripped her clothes from her shoulders, exposing her breasts to the crimson light, but they had not managed yet to pull them from her thighs. Merlin reached out to cover her up, but she screamed and scrambled away from him, her eyes wide and wild.

"I shall not harm you!" Merlin assured her in Latin. She didn't hear him, but kept babbling on, so he repeated himself, more firmly this time.

The girl ceased her babbling abruptly, and stared, her eyes still wide with fear, at Merlin. Her chest still rose and fell frantically.

"You will come to no harm while I live," Merlin told her. He pulled her dress gently back over her shoulders.

"You speak Latin!" The girl almost yelped. Her breathing became more regular. "You are not one of them?" she asked, her frame still shaking.

"Them? Who are they?" replied Merlin.

"How can you not know?" she said. Then, all at once, she convulsed, turned her head over, and vomited. Merlin waited patiently until she had finished, then placed his hands gently on her shoulders and drew her around to face him again.

"I am not one of the rebels," he said. "I have come this morning out of the west, and so know nothing about what has happened today save what I can learn from this wreckage. What happened?"

The girl's breathing gulped a few times, and she became calmer.

"They got here yesterday," she said. "They crushed the army—most of them are not here, but in the north. It was the queen, the bloody queen. She

. . . she wanted revenge, she said. And she had it. She slaughtered one after another of us."

"Of who?"

"Romans, of course, Romans. And the Britons who had accepted Roman rule. Anyone wearing a stola or a toga."

Merlin felt a gulf open up before him. "She just slaughtered them?"

"She sacrificed them, to her great goddess."

"Andraste," said Merlin. The girl nodded. "The goddess of victory, I know her." His mouth was dry; he remembered that no drop of water had passed his lips since he had entered the broken city. He ran his tongue over his parched lips and said, "Surely Boudicea did not give her approval to these deeds. These things were done by her men, no?"

The girl's eyes took on a pitying expression as they looked on Merlin. "She beheaded many of them herself," she said, "hanging the heads from her chariot. I saw her myself, surrounded by heaps and heaps of bodies, blood reddening her arms up to the elbows, and blood over her chest, and over her face." The girl's voice broke, and she covered her face with her hands. Her shoulders shook. "My father," she said, "they took my father. I could not look. But I went back, to find his body and give it proper burial. But who can find one body when so many lie in heaps about the forum?"

The faintness had come upon Merlin again. The shattered walls of the building, the lifeless bodies of the youths, the almost violated girl, all these images turned about and about Merlin's head in a crazy whirling dance.

The girl was still now, and peering up at him with curiosity. "Why do *you* weep?" she asked.

XXIII

Merlin took the girl to the Caverns of Sabrina and left her with a host of hollow-cheeked refugees. Then he turned his attention to reaching Boudicea. He still could not believe her capable of the horrors he had seen in Lundein.

By some fluke of fate, the stables had not been hit hard by the looters and the rebels, and Merlin found a horse, dark almost to blackness, stamping and whickering in his stall. The others had gone, and the doors were open, but as Merlin approached this dark beauty, he saw fire in his glance and knew why he had been left behind. The horse's nostrils flared and he tossed his head.

Merlin bit his knuckles for a moment, for although he was competent with horses, he had no special skill. Cautiously, he edged into the stall and spoke to him in gentle tones, cooing and using pet names, and he reached out, still keeping eye contact. The horse threatened at first, then shied away, then let Merlin touch his soft nose. Merlin spoke again, moving into the horse's stall and putting his mouth close to the great beast's ear. His words came softly, calming the horse's high spirit, and he fed him, for he had not eaten, Merlin reckoned, in a day or so. It took Merlin some time to locate fresh water, but in a short time, the horse was more contented and they were ready to leave. Merlin saddled him, swung himself onto the horse's back, and galloped off into the west.

In truth, the horse was glad to be given rein, for he had been cooped up for many days, and he fairly flew along the road westwards, sparks leaping from his hoofs, his long black mane lashing back into Merlin's face as he crouched low in the saddle.

Five or six miles from the gates of Londinium, a road branched off to the north, and along that road, an old legionnaire in the Caverns of Sabrina had told Merlin, Boudicea's rebels had marched, to meet the legions of Suetonius Paulinus. Now Merlin hurtled along the road towards the city of Verulamium, expecting at any moment to run into Boudicea's rearguard.

The sun was setting when he found them.

They had set up a kind of temporary fort, building the walls out of baggage wagons around the perimeter of a wide meadow. The sound of reveling came to Merlin on the night air as he reined in his horse, whose sides heaved as it stood there, forty yards or so from the perimeter.

"Good fellow," said Merlin, patting the beast's flank. "Rest now."

He dismounted, removed the saddle and bridle, and left it cropping the grass. He moved silently towards the improvised wall of Boudicea's fortress. They had camped, he saw, at the foot of a great hill, black against the darkening sky. And there was Paulinus with what legions he had been able to draw to him. Merlin could see that, following normal Roman practice, they had erected a temporary fort on the hilltop. The wooden palisade stretched all the way around the summit and, faintly, under the sounds of Britonnic reveling, Merlin could just catch orders barked back and forth in Latin.

Merlin moved like a shadow, silent as a cat. He could see a sentry posted on Boudicea's wall, crouching in one of the wagons, his eyes bright as he scanned the darkness. Merlin dropped and rolled between the wheels of one of the wagons, about ten yards from the sentry, then rose to a crouch, frozen for a moment, listening intently. Someone else was approaching.

"Here," said the newcomer, holding a cup of steaming liquid up to the sentry in the wagon. "May this give you cheer."

The sentry nodded his thanks and took a sip. Merlin's nostrils picked up the sweet aroma of spiced wine.

"What are you looking for?" asked the newcomer. "We're safe enough in here."

But the sentry shook his head. "There are Romans out there," he said. "Paulinus was expecting reinforcements and didn't get them. That's why he didn't march to help Lundein. Now Paulinus is on that hill behind us, and his reinforcements must be somewhere out there."

"If they had any wisdom at all," said the other, "they would run away. Perhaps they've heard what happened to Camulod and Lundein. If I were them, I'd march away from this place, and not stop until I reached the seven hills of Rome! Britain belongs to the Britons now."

They both fell silent for a moment, staring out into the darkness beyond the barricade of wagons. Merlin tensed his muscles, ready to rise and stalk off, but he never got that far.

Up on the hill, an orange light sprang up suddenly, silhouetting the wooden stockade and the sentries patrolling it. It leaped up, thirty or forty feet, dimming the early stars that had struggled to prick the canopy of night before the others. For a moment, the sound of reveling ceased, and all eyes turned towards the signal fire, for every man there knew what it meant. It was a message: send reinforcements.

"Well," shrugged the man who had brought the wine, "that makes your job easier: you can see the road as plain as day."

"What's that?" said the other, pointing. "A horse."

Merlin slipped away from them before they had decided on a course of action.

It was a simple task to find Boudicea's tent. It was the largest, it was in the centre of the army, and it stood in the middle of a circle of comparative quietness. There was no reveling about the queen's tent, only an intent and studious silence. Merlin emerged from the shadows six feet from the guards. They both gave a jump, startled. One of them lowered his spear.

"Who goes there?" he cried.

"Fool!" said Merlin. "Know you not your king?"

The warrior's eyes grew round. "Your majesty!" He and his companion snapped to attention.

"Well?" said Merlin. "Will you step aside, and allow me to enter?"

"One moment, my lord." The guard spun around and entered the tent. For a moment, nothing happened. Merlin could hear muffled voices within. Then he heard the guard declare, "Merlin Emrys, king of Eicenniawn, awaits your pleasure outside the tent, madam."

"Emrys!" came Boudicea's voice, and Merlin did not wait for permission to enter, but flew into her arms, his lips bearing down upon hers in a ferocious kiss.

"We did not expect to see you!" whispered Boudicea, reaching up to trail her fingers about his temple and cheek. "We had thought to hand Britain to you, the Island of the Mighty in the possession of the descendants of Brutus once more."

Merlin kissed her again. For a moment, a fleeting moment, a vision popped into his mind, of Boudicea standing in the midst of broken corpses, a curved knife in her hand, blood sticking to her hands and arms up to the elbows, while all around her flamed the ruins of a city; and now, he knew which city. The vision gone, Merlin pressed a smile onto his lips.

"I saw you," he said, "leading this army, and came with what swiftness I could." He gazed upon her with longing, but also with the breath of a frown touching his features, for now he could see that there was something different about her face. It was still proud and beautiful, but her skin seemed taut over her cheekbones and around her eyes, and her lips were grown harsh.

"O my love," said Boudicea. "I have so much to tell you. So many things have happened." Her voice dropped to a whisper. "Did you find Excalibur?" she asked.

Merlin winced, as if her words were a physical blow, and shook his head, lowering his eyes from hers. "The druids would not help me," he said.

"They will help no one now," said Boudicea. "They are all dead, the Sacred Grove destroyed utterly."

"Destroyed?" repeated Merlin. "All dead—everyone killed? Not one left alive?" It took a moment for Merlin to accept what Boudicea had said. He had known that Suetonius Paulinus was leading his legions against Afallach, of course, but the fullness of the event had not yet dawned on him. He had not parted from them on good terms, and yet their annihilation seemed cataclysmic. Merlin felt as if his insides had been scooped out and thrown to the winds. Amon and Dergen and Iorwerth—all dead.

"That is so," replied Boudicea. "This Roman, who faces us now, took his legions to Ynys Mon and destroyed everything he found. The Island of the Mighty must worship Roman gods. Except that we destroyed the Temple of Claudius the God in Camulod!"

She turned away from Merlin to send a servant for food and, for the first time, Merlin looked around at the interior of the tent. She had not been alone when he had arrived. Gwenddolau was there, and several of the councilors from Eicenniawn. There were no tables or chairs, just rugs and furs heaped against the walls of the tent. They had drawn a rough plan of the meadow in the dirt, and had evidently been discussing it when he had entered.

"Forgive me, please, my lords, this show of private affection," said the queen of the Eicenni.

"There is no need, your majesty," replied one of the councilors. "It is our privilege to be by when that which was sundered is reunited."

"We long have desired your presence, Emrys," added Boudicea, squeezing his hand.

"And I yours," replied Merlin. He blinked. There stood Gwenddolau, tall and noble-looking now that he was an adult, with a firm jaw and an aquiline nose; there, snowy-haired Segofax; there, others he knew from Eicenniawn's council: Ambiorix, Dumnacos, Lugotoros, and Verica, wise men all, sage of counsel, dressed in plaid with great swords hanging at their sides. And Boudicea, lovely Boudicea. For a moment, Merlin's mind skipped back to his childhood, to the little girl with the tangled hair who had played with him in the woods near Caermyrddin. Were these the rebels who had looted Londinium and put its citizens to the sword in the bloodiest manner? Merlin's head began to spin, and he must have nearly toppled to the floor, for the next thing he knew, Boudicea had caught him. There was a look of concern in her eyes. He wondered if any of the citizens of Londinium had seen that expression.

"Forgive me," he said. "One of my moments—it has passed now."

"What do you see, Emrys, when you look into the future?" asked Ambiorix.

"The same as I always see, brother," replied Merlin: "nothing. I see only what the gods send me."

A peal of raucous laughter erupted from close by outside the tent. Someone with a harsh voice sang a few lines of a lewd song before the noise petered out.

"The men certainly seem confident," observed Merlin. Several of the counselors laughed at this, and there was some general agreement.

"My lords," said Boudicea, regarding Merlin closely and with curiosity, "let us meet once more, at dawn; for the most part, we know what we must do on the morrow."

One by one, the counselors drained from the tent. Gwenddolau was the last to leave, hovering about the tent-flap and looking back at his parents for a moment.

"Goodnight, mother," he said, "and father." The last word stumbled, much as it had on Merlin's own lip recently.

"Gwenddolau," said Merlin, stepping forward and holding his shoulders firmly to take an appraising look at him, "you have grown into a man, and I have not been by you to see it happen."

Gwenddolau's eyes shifted from side to side. "Perhaps," he said, "after tomorrow . . . "

Merlin nodded. "Perhaps," he said. "If all goes well tomorrow, there will be much to do and discuss."

Gwenddolau pressed his lips into a restrained smile. "Goodnight, then. Much rests upon the morrow." The tent flap fell into place behind him.

There was silence for a while. Merlin did not turn to face Boudicea. A servant entered with the food, but he did not touch it.

"Merlin," urged Boudicea at last, "what did you see just now?"

Merlin drew a deep breath. "I saw nothing," he said. "But ere now I have seen what has transpired these last few weeks. And I think I know what will happen on the morrow."

"What have you seen?" demanded Boudicea, a look of hunger burning in her eyes.

Merlin turned to face her. "I saw your hands bathed in gore in Camulod and Lundein, and I saw you lying dead upon the field of battle." He spoke between gritted teeth, the words yanked from within as if by force.

Boudicea ran her tongue over her lips. "That I should die in battle," she said slowly, "is an honour, and no disgrace; and your vision might pertain to some later battle, rather than tomorrow's. In any case, to fly the field for fear of death is not becoming of a queen. Tomorrow, we have the Eagles at bay. The wolf shall drink its blood."

Merlin shook his head slowly. "No, my love," he said. "I do not believe so. If you fight tomorrow, you shall die."

"Then it is better that I should die a free queen of Britons than a slave," Boudicea snapped back. She paused, as if her next words were immeasurably difficult for her. "Will you fight with us?" she asked at length.

"Fight with you?" echoed Merlin. "Aye, if the fight is an honorable one."

"How can it be otherwise?" inquired Boudicea incredulously. "Our land has been invaded, our hearths and daughters violated." Her mouth became a thin, bitter line. "Has the hawk turned eagle?" she asked.

Merlin's mouth was open, as if he would speak, but no words came for a while. "Who is your enemy, Boudicea?" he asked.

"Who else but these Roman dogs?" responded the queen. "Have you been asleep, Emrys? Have you not seen the transformation they have wrought upon the Island of the Mighty?"

"I have seen a transformation," replied Merlin, looking on his wife as if doing so were an agony. "I have seen Lundein, the capital city of King Lludd, transformed into a smoking shell, her citizens into corpses, her daughters ravaged by her own people. Yet it was not the Romans—"

"It was a Roman town!" snapped Boudicea. "Not Lundein, but Londinium. We put it to the torch." She smiled uncannily. "I think we killed almost eight thousand people there. I wanted the priests, the priests most of all. When we sacked Camulod, I took the priests who had worshipped that mockery, Claudius the god, and I sacrificed them to Andraste on their own altar. It's a reckoning for Ynys Mon."

Merlin found himself suddenly shaking all over, though it was not cold in the tent. "What I saw was not a reckoning—it was savagery, it was brutality."

Boudicea's eyes narrowed. "It was war," she countered. "Is it so long since you fought at Mai Dun, Emrys, that you have forgotten what it is to have an enemy?"

"And have you hated so long, Boudicea, that you cannot tell the difference between friend and foe, the guilty and the innocent? Was the child I saw ravaged and disemboweled in a gutter your enemy? What of the women trembling in the Caverns of Sabrina even now, not knowing whether they are wives or mothers any more?"

"If they spoke Latin, they had no business on the Island of the Mighty," responded Boudicea.

"I speak Latin," said Merlin. "Am I a traitor? I am no less a Briton than you."

Boudicea's eyebrows dipped in the middle. "What words are these, Emrys?" she demanded. "You speak as one who has never had his home invaded by barbarians."

"I fought at Mai Dun," said Merlin. "I know what it is to face an enemy with naught but a yard of iron between the two of you. But these people in Lundein, you held no grudge against them, they had done you no harm."

"Only the harm of being here," answered Boudicea. "This is war, Emrys, the day-to-day practical business of war. You arrived at Mai Dun in time for a battle, which was over by the time the sun set. You didn't march with the army, forage with the army, listen to the reports of scouts and spies. When the battle is over, the war continues—and it continues against all those associated with the enemy. Our war is against an empire, and everyone who supports or feeds off that empire. If we lose the battle tomorrow—which, the gods forbid!—I can expect no more of the Romans. Have you ever seen a man crucified, Emrys? Have you heard the nails break the bones in the palms of his hands, or the gurgling of his lungs as he drowns slowly in his own fluids, hour after slow hour? Do you think the Romans blameless in this, Emrys?"

"I know the Romans are capable of cruelty, but—"

Boudicea turned, unlacing her bodice, and dropped it from her shoulders, exposing her back. What once had been fair and smooth was now crisscrossed by scars, and white welts had risen all over her fair skin. Merlin caught his breath

The Queen of the Eicenni had been flogged.

XXIV

Merlin gaped at Boudicea's wounds. He reached out gingerly to touch them, trace the shapes across her back. She turned to him again.

"We refused to pay their tribute," she said, "and they flogged me—*me*, the Queen of the Eicenni."

Merlin winced, as if he felt the lashes himself. He said, "Did they . . . do anything else to you?"

Boudicea shook her head, her lip curled savagely from her teeth and her eyes wicked slits. "They did not violate me, but they raped our daughters. And Catus Decianus, that glorified tax collector, watched and laughed and drank wine, while his junior officers used the princesses of Eicenniawn as they wished. He watched. His eyes were upon the girls the whole time, and mine upon him. I think he was aroused, watching it. Aroused, but impotent, or else he too would have taken his turn." Now Boudicea was trembling, her teeth gritted as she ground out the syllables. She looked up, and smiled suddenly, a bitter, twisted smile. "But he will watch nothing more," she said. "I cut out his eyes and fed them to ravens before I flayed the skin from his body and cast him to the wild beasts outside the walls of Camulod!"

Merlin felt his gorge rise. He sank onto one of the stools near the table, passing a fluttering hand over his brow. He could think of nothing to say. And Boudicea waited.

He looked up at her. There was defiance, he saw, smouldering in her eyes, like the heart of a mountain of fire.

"Where are the girls now?" he asked.

Boudicea's face changed. She looked at Merlin as one would look at a foreigner, wholly unfamiliar with one's own customs. She said, "Do you think they would choose to live on, to bear into the world brats of Rome?

They took poison, and I swore unto them, as they died, such a vengeance as Rome would never forget! O Emrys, would that you had been there!"

Merlin looked away from the savage beauty before him. He felt as if his body had been drained. The slightest breeze would have brought him low. "Would that I had never left your side, as once we dreamed!" he said quietly.

"Do you weep, Emrys?" inquired Boudicea. "Turn that water into fire, that your wrath may blaze forth and turn all the Romans into ashes!"

But Merlin was not listening to her. "This is a world of blood," he said, thoughtfully fingering the blade of the knife that had been brought with his food. "Would that I too were quit of it." A nerve pulled in his cheek, and the lightness was buoying up his head again.

"This is the world," responded Boudicea, "that we live in. The only way to survive it to be strong."

Her words pulled Merlin back into the world. He turned to face her, his mouth twitching upwards ironically. "I have heard that before, from another Britonnic queen," he said.

"I am no Cartimandua," said Boudicea coldly, "but I understand our world."

"There has to be something else," said Merlin, "something more."

Boudicea spread her hands wide. "Where is it, Emrys?" she demanded. "Where do you see it, this other way? If I saw some way to turn aside from the path that lies before me, I would take it. But it is they, the Romans, who have paved this path, and I must follow it to the end."

"But this is a path that never ends," said Merlin. "How can it end, if you will not stop following it?"

For a long while, Boudicea said nothing. Her chest heaved with passion. At last, she said, "If you can show me the way, Emrys, I will take it. But I think you will not find it before tomorrow, my hawk, and tomorrow the forces of Boudicea of the Eicenni must meet those of Suetonius Paulinus of Rome." She paused. "Will you fight with us tomorrow, or no?"

"Fight in a battle you cannot win?" asked Merlin.

"Mai Dun was a battle you could not win."

Merlin did not speak. His eyes rested on the food that had been brought for him—some bread, onions, cheese, a few slices of roast pork. He picked up the knife and examined the blade for a few moments, his mind turning and turning upon something, he knew not what. "Perhaps," he said slowly, "this is not the time to fight."

Boudicea's nostrils flared. "Then you will not fight?" she said. "You will skulk away—"

"No!" cried Merlin. He rose from his seat. "Boudicea, listen to me. You are queen of the Eicenni, and you are queen of my heart. Listen to me now! You have won your victory. The Ninth Legion is no more, the towns of Camulodunum and Londinium are leveled. That is our revenge. Our daughters can rest easily, knowing that they have been avenged. But now, we need not fight on. We could negotiate a peace."

"Negotiate?"

"Aye," answered Merlin. "Is that so dishonourable? We are in an excellent position to negotiate—we can ask for all we desire."

"We have the Romans at our mercy," said Boudicea.

"You have said it!" replied Merlin. "This is the power of mercy: granting them their lives, we make them beholden to us."

Their eyes met, and Merlin saw that hers had softened for a moment; but then they become hard, like garnets. "Where is the man in you, Emrys? Are you turned all woman, and must *I* swear revenge and bring *my* wrath upon the heads of these interlopers, who scourged me and raped and killed our daughters?"

Merlin's breath came in ragged gasps now. "I cannot excuse what the invaders have done to us," he said; "but is not the revenge you have had enough? How much blood will it take to wash away the welts upon your back? And not just Roman blood—Britonnic blood too." Merlin held out his hands, palm-upwards, towards her. "These hands too are stained with Britonnic blood. I killed some youths that were trying to rape a girl in Lundein. Britonnic boys, trying to rape a girl born in Britain, and raised in

Lludd's city. I have raised a sword against my own people, and spilled the blood of my brothers, and I would not do that again. But if we continue along the path you have chosen, that is where it will lead. If you win tomorrow, how do you think the citizens of Camulod or Lundein will obey their new queen? Stop now, my love, or you will become that which you detest!"

Boudicea's eyes dropped, and for a moment she did not speak. Merlin wet his lips with his tongue. *She is almost with me*, he thought.

But then Boudicea looked up, and her eyes were a pair of flints. "A queen may rule by fear where love is lacking," she said. "If fear is the readiest way to obedience, I shall rule by fear."

"Why choose fear?" asked Merlin. "You once would have chosen love —when you and I ruled Eicenniawn, you ruled your people with love. Could you not see it—that they loved you, that they obeyed you because they knew you loved them. Would you lose that?"

Boudicea looked shaken. For a moment, it seemed as if she would fly weeping to his arms. But then, something flashed in her eyes, some memory perhaps, and her nostrils flared. "No," she said, almost snarling. "No, for fear is strong and I must be strong to rule my people. They are fishermen and marsh-wanderers all. How can they know what is best for them? Only I can know that, and so I must have their obedience, by whatever means I can get it. And love is not efficient—fear is the readiest way."

"What change is this?" cried Merlin. "This is no woman talking—this is a she-wolf!"

The edges of Boudicea's teeth showed, sharp and white, as she said, "Then, little hawk, you must take flight and be gone from this place as swiftly as you may. This is a world where wolves survive. There is no triumph for the lamb."

They faced each other, breathing hard, their eyes burning, while long seconds drew out between them.

"This is not the girl I loved," said Merlin, "nor the woman I married."

"It is both, Emrys, and always has been. How have you missed it all this time? Life is brutal, and you can survive it only by being more brutal than those who surround you. But this you certainly did know—you did not hesitate to feed Cartimandua the poison I sent you."

"Death was a blessedness to that despairing woman," said Merlin.

"But you would have poisoned her anyway, because you are strong, like me."

Merlin shook his head. "I am not strong," he said. "I have killed men —those that threatened me or mine. But to massacre women and children and men with no weapons—if *that* is strong, then I am not strong."

"They would do no differently to me, were I in their power," countered Boudicea. "And did do no differently—flog a queen, and rape her daughters! What else can they expect, but the most brutal treatment?" Boudicea shook her head vigorously. "No, Emrys, we live in a wilderness, surrounded by wild beasts, and we must behave like them to survive; and when at last we come to die, we shall know that life was not a thing that happened to us, but which we took by the throat and shook until there was nothing left!"

Merlin's head was swimming again. He looked at Boudicea as if seeing her at the bottom of a deep pool, gone beyond retrieval. "Life is a long scream," he said, "terminated by oblivion." He took a deep breath. "I shall fight tomorrow, but not as king of the Eicenni. I shall fight beside them, but I cannot lead them any more. If they are to go where you want them to go, it is you must lead them, and not I."

To Merlin's surprise, Boudicea's face sagged at this. "Then this is the end?" she said. "The end of our love?"

"No," answered Merlin. "That will never end. If I lived half a thousand years, I should still love you until the last minute of the very last day of my life. But our life together is over, since you have chosen this course." With that, he turned upon his heel and strode towards the tent-flap; yet reaching it, he hesitated, and looked back, and still he marveled at her beauty and wondered if anything ever again would seem to him to be beautiful. "Will you not change your mind?" he asked.

"If I did so, I should not be Boudicea," she replied; "and how should you love a woman who was not Boudicea?"

"Then farewell, love. I shall fight in your army, and if chance will have it I may save my queen's life, I shall. But henceforth, there can be no accord between us."

The tent-flap fell between them; Merlin thought he heard her cry his name, but the sounds of the camp were loud and various, and he might have been mistaken.

* * *

Once he had been engulfed by the clamour of the camp, Merlin paused. He looked up at the hill where the Romans were encamped. Still the signal fire blazed, blotting out the stars. He could see the sentries moving about on the palisades.

An image, as familiar to him as it was disturbing, inveigled its way into his mind: a she-wolf, dead upon a field, and eagles tearing at its flesh. He knew what it meant, and would with all his heart that such a fate could be averted.

But then another image supplanted it: a boy-king, surrounded by the waters of a subterranean lake, the fiery blade of Excalibur raised above him. The philosopher king.

Merlin looked left and right, and plunged in among the nobles' tents.

It did not take him long to find Gwenddolau's tent, pitched close to his mother's. Merlin sent the guard inside, and waited to be admitted. A moment later, the guard returned, and Merlin entered.

Gwenddolau was sitting on the edge of his cot, rubbing sleep out of his eyes. He had thrown his plaids about him hastily, and blinked up at Merlin.

"Father?" he said. "What would you with me?"

Merlin dropped himself onto the cot beside his son. He looked upon the man whose growth from childhood he had missed, who now seemed so grown. And he was at a loss for words.

Gwenddolau waited patiently. He yawned.

"Gwenddolau," said Merlin, "we have never really spoken as father and son."

"We have not had the chance, father," replied the other.

"I haven't much time," said Merlin. "A few hours from now, the swords will be drawn." Gwenddolau nodded. Merlin seized him by the shoulders and spoke earnestly into his face. "It must not be allowed to happen," he said.

Gwenddolau's eyebrows came together, much as his mother's had done. "Why ever not?" he said. "Do you think we will lose?"

"I am certain of it," answered Merlin.

"How can you be certain?" wondered Gwenddolau. "I know you have a gift for prophecy, but are not the visions you receive ambiguous? What is it you have seen?"

"The carcass of a she-wolf, being devoured by eagles." Merlin waited for a response. Gwenddolau waited for Merlin to explain. At last, Merlin said, "The she-wolf is your mother. She has always been a wolf in my visions, since we were both children in Cambria."

"Have you told this to my mother?"

"I have tried to tell her," said Merlin, "but she will not listen."

Gwenddolau blinked a few times to banish the last vestiges of sleep from his eyes. He said, "And if someone told you not to do something because you might die, would you heed that person?"

Merlin hesitated. "It would depend who the person was," he answered slowly, "and what the deed." Gwenddolau waited. "If it was a deed that needed utterly to be done," Merlin went on, "and no one else would do it, I should not hesitate to give up my life."

Merlin knew he had lost the point already, and Gwenddolau confirmed it: "Then you cannot expect my mother to lay down arms because she is taking a soldier's risk."

"There is no risk; it is a certainty."

Gwenddolau changed the subject. "I think we would all be better off if there were no prophecies," he said. "I mean that with all respect to you, sir, but prophecies cloud simple issues. The Romans invaded our land. The Romans must be stopped. We will do it tomorrow, or we will die in the attempt. Prophecies do nothing but eat away a man's courage."

Merlin sighed. "I believe I can negotiate a truce," he said.

Gwenddolau's face twisted. "If we delay," he said, "Suetonius will receive the reinforcements he has signaled for. We *must* fight on the morrow! There will never be another time."

"If we can negotiate," said Merlin, "we might be able to get the Romans to leave us alone."

"Aye, for a price," responded Gwenddolau wryly. "For a tribute, which sooner or later we will neglect, and sooner or later some other Emperor will bring his Eagles across the sea to demand it."

"You are a keen reasoner, my son," observed Merlin.

"I believe I inherited that trait from my father," answered Gwenddolau. "But, father, you cannot mean what you say. The Romans have taken what is ours. You cannot negotiate with a thief—if you could negotiate with him, he would be a merchant, not a thief. The edge of the sword is the answer, father. What else could there be?"

"There is another path, I am sure," said Merlin.

"Where is it? Where does it begin? Through what lands does it pass, and whither is it bound? I see no other way, father, but the way of spear and shield. But that is not wrong. It is honourable, it is right."

"There is more to being a High King than killing and slashing. The High King must fight because he is a man of peace, not a man of war. Excalibur's blade is to heal, not to hack."

"What has the High King to do with anything, father?" asked Gwenddolau. "He is in Rome, a captive." He shook his head, beginning to be impatient. "Give me no more warnings or prophecies, father. We must fight tomorrow, because not to fight means living as slaves."

"These are your mother's words," said Merlin, the first hints of a coldness spreading through his body.

"They are good words," responded Gwenddolau hotly, rising from his cot and striding to the brazier. The coals were warm, and he held his hands out over them. "There can be no truce," he said. "When the Romans leave, there will be peace. Until then, look for nothing but blood. If no other Briton will fight tomorrow, then I shall, even if I must die."

"Gwenddolau—" began Merlin.

But his son interrupted him. "Was this why you came here, father? To persuade me to turn my back on my friends? To persuade me to fly my enemies? What did you want of me?"

"I want to bring peace to my people, not a sword," said Merlin.

"Now is not a time for peace, father. Now is a time for the sword. There must be blood. There must always be blood. The gods demand it, and it runs through our lives as surely as the rivers course through our land."

Merlin rose to his feet. "Perhaps I am wrong," he said. Gwenddolau said nothing. "I had hoped . . . " His voice trailed away, and he looked up wretchedly at the stern picture of his son, standing beside the brazier.

"Father," said Gwenddolau, "why would you spend your life looking for a sword, when you would not use one?"

"It is a good question," replied Merlin, "but I have no answer. I have lost my way."

"But the way is clear for me," said his son.

"I see that." For some reason, Merlin was thinking of the pale, wild wanderer that led him to Morfran's hut through the snows of Cameliard. "Follow me," he had said, "and I shall steer you to a safe harbourage." But where was he now?

For the first time in his life, Merlin felt old. Turning, he shuffled from the tent without another word.

* * *

Some time later, some carousing warriors happened upon the quivering form of a dark-robed man. He was muttering and twitching as if possessed by a dark god, and the warriors left him to himself, and continued their reveling elsewhere.

XXV

Half an hour before dawn, when the grey light glowed along the eastern horizon, Boudicea called her officers to a final conference. Merlin watched them from nearby, his face impassive. Some of them snatched a glance in his direction; most did not notice him. Through the long, cold hours of night, Merlin had wondered what he should do. He had considered making an appeal to them all, an appeal to lay down arms and depart for Eicenniawn. But there was no sense in such an appeal. The Romans would have no mercy on those who surrendered, Boudicea was right about that—the crucifixions would line the roads from coast to coast. A deep brooding had grown upon Merlin, for he felt certain that the victory would be cast away by the Britons.

And then, he wondered, who would there be to wield Excalibur? And what should his own role in the battle be?

Something seemed wrong with the world. Boudicea's kingdom would be no gentler, no more loving, than the Empire of the Romans. And the Romans, if they won, would instigate a series of massacres and reprisals to punish the people of Britain for the insurrection. In short, whatever the outcome of the battle, Britain would lose, and her people suffer. And Merlin had had his fill of that.

Merlin closed his eyes and, somewhere in his mind, he could see the faces in the tent, and hear their voices.

"What is the situation this morning?" Boudicea was asking. "Did the reinforcements reach Paulinus?"

"No," replied Dumnacos. "And the situation is good. We estimate their numbers are almost ten thousand, the Fourteenth Legion and the remnants of the Twentieth." Dumnacos smiled grimly. "We outnumber Paulinus at least three to one."

“There is one other legion, the Augusta, led by Poenius Postumus,” said Gwenddolau. “That beacon Paulinus lit last night was obviously a summons to Postumus, but he has not arrived yet.”

“That is why we cannot abandon the barricade at our perimeter,” said Boudicea. “We cannot allow Postumus’ forces to join up with Paulinus’. This day will decide everything: we will crush Paulinus, then turn about, and do the same to Postumus.”

Lugotoros pointed with a stick at the diagram of the battle, still etched in the floor of Boudicea’s tent. “Here is the hill,” he said. “We expect Paulinus to stay there until Postumus turns up. So, we will fire flaming arrows into his camp, until we provoke his attack. The meadow narrows between the hill and this forest. We will drive him backwards and crush him between the hill and the trees.”

“And the last serious threat to the sovereignty of the Island of the Mighty will be gone,” concluded Boudicea.

One of the guards stepped inside and bowed to Boudicea. “Suetonius Paulinus, the Roman commander, is upon the field, and craves a parley with you, my lady.”

“He is afraid,” said Boudicea. “He knows we have him at an advantage, and now wishes to come to terms.”

“Then let us go and accept his defeat,” said Gwenddolau.

“Let us go and listen to what he has to say,” agreed Boudicea; “but let us crush these Romans anyway. Where was their mercy at Bran Dun? Then we should use none here—this day brings us victory or death, and we should allow no more to the Romans.”

The vision faded, and Merlin blended into the ranks. The generals, led by Boudicea, filed out of the tent and marched towards the vanguard. Merlin followed unseen.

The Romans had spread themselves in a single line of gold and scarlet before the Britonnic hope. In the precise centre, flanked by standard bearers, resplendent in their leopard-skins, Suetonius Paulinus sat astride a magnificent horse of such perfect whiteness that it seemed composed entirely of light. He himself was tall and wide-shouldered, his white hair thinning without receding, his eyes dark in his weathered face. With a start, Merlin recognized him. At first, he could not place him, but then he remembered the general who had sat next to Cartimandua in Cameliard and accepted Coroticos and Grwhyr as his prisoners. He sat on his horse with a bored and unimpressed expression on his face, as if he were awaiting someone who was late for an appointment. But Merlin sensed something else in his posture: a tenseness about the shoulders, perhaps, or a tautness in the muscles of his face. He was hiding it well.

Boudicea and her generals emerged from the host of the Britons and fanned out to stand defiantly before the might of Rome. Boudicea's fists were on her hips, her cloak thrown back to show off her gold-hilted sword.

Suetonius Paulinus's eyes moved sluggishly and lighted on her. He glanced up and down her length once, and said, "Is this the rebel Boudicea, self-styled queen of the Iceni, murderer of the citizens of Camulodunum and Londinium?" He spoke in Brythonic, heavily accented, but precise and perfect.

"I am Boudicea, Queen of Eicenniawn, liberator of my people from the thieves and brigands who have occupied our land without invitation." Boudicea thrust her chin out defiantly: she was not fooled by this Roman.

"H'm." Paulinus twisted his lip as he looked down at her. "I had expected you to be taller."

"Have done with your words swiftly, Roman," said Boudicea. "We Britons are warriors, unaccustomed to womanish gossiping. We long to feast the ravens!"

"H'm," said Paulinus again. "How different we are! Now I do not enjoy battle at all. To plan one, and to see it brought to successful accomplishment, as I did so recently to those priests of yours—druids, I believe you call them?—that is very satisfying. But the actual business of hacking and slashing—butchers' work merely." Paulinus sighed. "Well, Rome has brought civilization to the whole world, saving this blasted heath. I suppose it will take a little longer here. A bitch will always be a bitch, even if you give it a golden collar."

Paulinus ceased, and no one spoke again for a while. Then Boudicea said, "Is this why you have come here, Roman? To insult the queen of the Britons?" She drew her sword with a metallic swish and held it aloft so that the rays of the early sun flashed on its blade. "Here is my voice!" she cried, so that all the host could hear her. "I will not speak foully of you or any Roman, save to list your deeds, which said of any other man would be insulting. But truly it is said that you cannot insult a thoroughgoing villain." She leveled the sword at Paulinus. "Come within the reach of this my blade, Roman, and you will see how harsh is the singing of a Britonnic queen! State your business, but spend no extra words, for they are all in vain. It is deeds, not words, men will remember, a thousand years from now."

"Very well, then," replied Paulinus in the lilting syllables of his patrician accent. "I have come to accept your surrender." He raised his voice so that it carried far back into the Britonnic host. "If you surrender now, there will be no reprisal. We will execute this unnatural woman, this mannish spirit, Boudicea, and her generals, take into custody your weapons, and do no more. But if you defy us . . . " He clenched his fist slowly, as if some enemy were enclosed within. "If you defy the might of Rome, we will destroy you, every man, woman, and child on this field, as you put to the sword the inhabitants of Camulodunum and Londinium."

There was a stirring among the Britons, a hum of conversation, some defiant, some afraid. When the clamour died down, Boudicea spoke.

"You have spoken, Suetonius Paulinus. Now hear me, Boudicea, Queen of Eicenniawn. You do not belong here. You were not invited here. You are thieves and brigands, and we will treat you as such. Do not expect mercy from those you have dispossessed, and raped, and robbed. Your position here is hopeless: your reinforcements have not arrived. Pray to the stammering, gammy-footed fool whose altar you erected in Camulod, if you like, and see what help he can send. For every man in your army there are three warriors of Britain, who have killed Romans before. Before the sun reaches its zenith this day, you and your cohorts will lie dead upon this field!"

"H'm." Paulinus looked down at the ground and spat, then up at Boudicea. "So be it," he said. "Three to one, is it? Well, the odds were worse in Gaul, and against Hannibal. Fight if you like, rebel, but if I were you, I'd lay a little wager on the Romans. That way, at least you'll gain something from today's events."

Suetonius Paulinus shook his reins and turned the head of his horse away from the Britons, who began to jeer and fling insults at him, as he dwindled slowly in the green of the vast meadow. For the first time, they saw that the Romans had left the crest of the hill and arranged themselves across the narrow neck of the meadow. The scuta, the great square shields of the Roman legionnaires, were all out, and formed what looked like a solid wall of bronze across the field.

Boudicea turned to her army, climbing into the chariot that had carried her out of the east, all the way from Bran Dun.

"You have heard the Roman speak," she said. "You have heard them speak before but, for seventeen years, you have seen what these Romans do: they sit in their bathhouses, scraping each other and eating dormice, and they talk, and talk, and talk in their Senate, and they take little boys into their beds. And for seventeen years, we have laboured for them, ploughed and harvested for them, paid taxes to them so that scarce a denarius was left us to purchase food from their over-priced markets. Seventeen harvests we have turned over to these invaders.

"There will not be an eighteenth!"

There was a roar of approval from the host. Boudicea waited for it to die down. Eventually, she held up her hands for silence, and spoke again.

"I do not wish to inspire you to hate these men, for I know that hatred is already in your hearts. I do not wish you to fear for the future of your families—I know that you already fear for them under Roman rule. I do not wish you to be ashamed of the past—any man might be enslaved once. But a Briton will not remain so. A Briton will break the chains of his bondage. A

Briton will strive for his freedom, or die! I am not queen over the burden-bearing Egyptians, like the old emperor's hussy, Cleopatra! I do not rule the peddlers and traffickers of the east, the Assyrians, as Semiramis did. I am no Messalina, striving for supremacy with a whore, nor no Mistress Domitia Nero, painting my face and singing to the lyre. I am Boudicea, and I am queen of all free Britons!"

Again, the roar of approval, like the roar of the sea on a stormy winter night.

"I do not offer you certainty of victory," said Boudicea. "War is never certain, and it is true that there are those among us who will not see the end of this day. But is it better to live in slavery, or die free of shackles? That is what I offer you, children of Britain: not certainty, for only a coward craves certainty. I offer you freedom! I offer you Boudicea! And I offer you Britain!"

The cheer again went up from the host and, this time, Boudicea did not wait for it to die down.

"What is it, then, my brothers and my sisters? Will you follow me to your freedom?" She waited a split second for an answer, and then cried: "Let us go, then! Let us go to victory or death!"

"Victory or death!" shouted the host, and they surged after her in one massive block.

The earth shook under the hoofs of the Britonnic horses, and the sky rang with the shouts and war cries. The chariots drew ahead of the foot soldiers, Boudicea in the lead, brandishing her sword over her head, her mouth stretched wide in a scream of violence and death.

The gap between the Romans and the Britons narrowed. They were sixty yards apart when a voice snapped out orders in Latin. The voice could barely be heard over the tumult of the Britons, but it was heard, and relayed quickly through the cohorts. In one movement, eight thousand arms snapped back, and the points of eight thousand spears flashed in the light of the young sun.

As the Britonnic host poured down the field, the sides narrowed, and they were forced into a tightly-packed wedge.

The first volley of spears sailed through the air and into the line of chariots. Horses rolled forward, spinning the charging vehicles up into the air and down into piles of smashed wood. The charioteers and warriors inside were flung to the earth, some of them already dead, with spears through their bodies. The sound of screaming, tortured horses filled the air.

Miraculously, a few chariots rumbled clear of the wreckage, and came on, the great host on foot surging behind them.

A second volley flew from the Roman hands and smashed into the Britonnic foot warriors. It made a sound like a mighty wave striking a rock. All along the line, Britons tumbled and fell, and those behind them, and those behind them. The charge staggered, like a wave breaking upon a shallow beach.

Still they came on, but slower now, for the survivors had to pick their way over the bodies of the dead and wounded.

The few remaining chariots smashed into the Roman wall. They slowed to a halt. Legionnaires surrounded them and ground them like grist in a mill. The wall closed again.

The Britonnic generals were regrouping around Boudicea's chariot. She was shouting orders to them, and some of the foot-warriors were gathering around them too. But somebody called out to the queen and pointed.

From either side of the legion came a new movement. Two great arms of mounted soldiers, wielding long swords, broke cover and thundered down upon the remnant of the Britonnic charge. On the flanks, some of the Britons froze, preparing for the impact.

The Roman cavalry plunged into the Britonnic flanks, swinging their long swords in great circular motions. Some of the horses went down, impaled upon Britonnic spears. But the long swords swung, and the Britons fell, and Boudicea's host was squeezed like an apple in a vice.

The Roman infantry began to move forward, keeping a perfectly straight line all the way along. The cavalry broke off the engagement, retiring to the sides of the field.

The Roman machine bore down upon the Britonnic host. The scuta pressed forward, the gladii stabbed out, and if a legionnaire fell, another stepped in to replace him. Slowly, but surely, the Roman cohorts pressed the Britonnic host back.

The cavalry galloped back into the fray, charging along the Britonnic flanks and keeping them confined to a narrow area.

Then the Britons gave way, turning and fleeing from the field. They ran headlong, tossing aside their weapons and shields, intent only upon flying the scene of slaughter.

They stopped when they reached the barricade of wagons. A few struggled through but, in the pause, the Roman cavalry swept through, slashing left and right.

The Britons were caught between the cavalry and infantry, and the two now began to systematically squeeze the life out of Boudicea's rebellion.

On the edge of the field, on the margin of the forest, stood an apple tree. Its branches were heavy with fruit, its leaves thick. From the depth of its foliage came the sound of something, man or beast, emitting a great wail of soul anguish. From its branches clattered an object: it was a sword, bright as the morning, but smeared with blood.

Merlin Emrys looked up to the skies. The sounds of the battle bounced back from the summer clouds, as if the clouds themselves were striving one with another. Merlin was streaked with blood and dirt, and his face twitched, his eyes darted here and there.

Below him, spread out in the field, was the slaughter of the Britonnic host. He had seen Boudicea throw her arms wide, a Roman pilum buried between her breasts; he had seen Gwenddolau pitched out of his chariot, his head striking a rock upon the field of slaughter.

With a shriek that no one marked, Merlin flung himself into another tree, and then into another, until many forested miles lay between himself and the death of the Britonnic host.

Merlin ran. Elm, beech, oak, ash, all flitted past him, left and right. The branches of the forests of the Island of the Mighty whipped past him, rending his clothes and gashing his flesh, until the clothes dropped from his body and he ran naked and wild-eyed.

Behind him, snapping at his heels like a pack of hounds, came images: a giant made of wicker, flaming, while men and women trapped inside clawed and screamed for escape; the square formations of Romans, crawling uphill towards the carnage of Mai Dun; Cartimandua on her throne, gloating as her warriors drove sword or spear through the slumbering forms of the Cambrian host; his own hut in Afallach, belching flames into the night as the druids stood around it, torches in their hands; and Boudicea.

Boudicea, throwing her arms wide, the point of a spear buried between her breasts. But also Boudicea, the wreckage of Londinium or Camulodunum in conflagration behind her, up to her elbows in blood, her eyes and nostrils wide as her knife came down into the throat of one victim after another, until eight thousand men, women and children writhed in their own blood at her feet.

Merlin flew through the forest; he howled. Night followed day, day night, and weeks turned into months, and Merlin knew not whither he ran.

One day, he threw himself down in a glade. Above him, the sky was overcast, threatening rain. There were apple trees around him, grey and gaunt. They had shed their leaves, and stood now, waiting for winter's death. Merlin sobbed.

"Sweet apple tree," he said, "sweet your branches which bear precious fruit and hide me from the wrath of Boudicea! I strove for a woman's pleasure against an army, shield on my shoulder, sword at my thigh. But now I shall sleep alone in the forest. Dead, dead, they are all dead, and cold in the earth, and no lord will speak well of me now. No entertainment for me in my sorrow, no harp played by bard, or horse stamping in the courtyard, no lover to visit me. Alas, that death did not visit me long ago, long before it visited every friend I have!

Sweet apple tree, that grows by a river,
Your branches shaded us in our youth as we played.
Calm my mind then, happier my days,
I did not sleep then up to my thighs in snow.
Icicles in my beard, naught but wolves for company.
Fair was the maiden, slender and queenly!
Now she is in the earth, sorrow to my soul,
There will never be another."

Merlin rolled over in his misery, wet leaves clinging to his hair, and he slumbered. When the sun rose the next morning, he leaped to his feet with a yelp, and galloped off into the forest.

XXVI

Meldred, king of Cambria, dipped his fingers in cold water and wiped them off on a napkin. He had just finished his midday meal in his day-room, away from the fuss of the great hall of Caermyrddin. He pushed away his plate—immediately, a servant whisked it away—and rose from the table, taking a few leisurely steps towards the window. The shutters had been thrown open to let in the warm July air. The sun on his face felt good, and he could smell a little salt on the breeze that blew in from the south.

Dafat, his woolly-headed steward, hovered in the doorway. Meldred knew what he wanted. But in the thirteen years of his reign, ever since the capture of his father, Grwhyr, Meldred had never been late for anything—not for council, not for judgements, not even for the feasts that his wife organized from time to time.

There was a noise in the courtyard below, the clattering of hoofs in the gateway, and Meldred looked down, curiously. It was Donacht, his Master Huntsman, returning from a two-day trip. A few of Caermyrddin's nobles rode in with him, a few with hawks on their gloved hands. Last came the servants, bearing several deer and a boar, their heads lolling absurdly beneath the poles on which they were slung. Donacht leaped from his saddle and immediately began issuing orders about the storage of the meat.

A distant trumpet sounded, and Meldred's eyes rose to the coast road. His wife, Ganieda, was returning from her journey to Cydwelli, where she had been visiting a cousin. Her guard marched before and after, and in between were the two carts loaded with food and possessions that supplied her on the road and in the court away from home. Meldred smiled. Ganieda always traveled modestly.

Another commotion broke out in the courtyard below, and Meldred saw that the hunting party had brought back some live creature with them.

Meldred could see a mass of whitish hair, scrawny nut-brown limbs, but nothing more certain. It looked human, but its stooping posture and loping gait belied that definition. Curiosity building in him, Meldred left the day-room, Dafat following in his wake, and entered the hall at the same moment that Donacht entered.

"I have returned, your majesty," said Donacht, dropping to one knee before Meldred.

"Welcome," said Meldred. "We thank you, Donacht. We saw the quarry you brought home from above."

There was a twinkle in Donacht's eye as he rose to his feet. "That is not all, your majesty. Look."

Some servants brought in the creature. It was, or had been, human, but living in the wild had reduced it to savagery. It was naked, its body brown and lacerated with white scars, its hair and beard tangled and white and so voluminous that the only other discernible features were an aquiline nose and dark, hawklike eyes. The servants had tied its hands together, and led it on a leash, as one would a performing bear. It stood in the smoky hall of the king of Cambria, gazing about itself at the tapestries on the wooden walls, and the vaulted ceiling, dark with years of soot.

"This is the wildman, sire," said Donacht, "that your people have heard these several months."

"Where did you find it?" asked Meldred, marveling at the creature.

Donacht shook his head and scratched his ear. "That's a strange thing, your majesty," he said. "We found him asleep upon the grave mound of your father's sister, Viviane. We tried to steal upon him unawares, but he awoke—may the gods never grant me quarry again, but I swear we made no sound—and off he dashed into the undergrowth, where no man could follow him."

"But you tracked him down at last? However did you manage it?" asked Meldred, coming close to the wildman in fascination.

"With music, sire," replied Donacht. "It seems to love music."

"Fascinating!" Meldred studied the face. "Perhaps we can teach it to dance," he mused. He frowned. There was something about the shape of the nose, something vaguely familiar; and when the wildman looked up into his eyes, he took a step back, they seemed so deep, so penetrating. "What does it do?"

"It talks a deal of nonsense, lord," answered Donacht.

"Is it amusing nonsense?" asked Meldred. Donacht shrugged. Meldred reached out to prod the wildman's shoulder, but it hissed at him.

"Wretched, wretched am I!" cried the wildman. "Dark was the lady, dark of hair. O, little pig, listen to me! I saw a battle, a great battle, upon the earth, in the heavens, all around me! Blades are red, swords are swift—men playing ball with the heads of the warriors of Britain! This is no lie—the she-wolf rose against the eagle! They will not go home, not from the tumult of battle. Ah, wretched soul that I am! I used to sit in the hall with a fair woman at my side, a slender and queenly woman, and drink from golden goblets. What am I now? I have been wandering, wild in the wild—the owl sings in my ear, not bards, and a wolf is my companion, not a prince. Woe is me, woe upon me for ever and ever!"

Meldred shied away from the creature, his eyebrows almost meeting over his nose, his lips curled from his teeth.

"Put him in the guardhouse," he said curtly, and the guards hauled the wildman away from the royal hall.

At that moment, Ganieda entered, and Meldred forgot for the moment about the wildman.

* * *

The wildman stayed for many months in Caermyrddin. Winter came and went, the wildman chained to the wall in the guardhouse until he was brought into the hall for the amusement of Meldred's friends. On those occasions, they would pose him questions about the future, and he would answer cryptically, and they would find sport in trying to interpret the symbolism of his replies. Sometimes, if music was playing, the wildman would cock his head on one side and listen, enraptured. Once, he bounded across the hall and snatched a harp away from a bard. For long minutes, he crouched over the instrument, and the bard quaked with fear while dissonant chords shuddered out. Then the wildman launched into the strangest melody anyone had ever heard: it began with great violence, the notes crashing one into another like waves against a sea-wall. But eventually the sea-like sounds were ground between pounding, stony chords, and a strange, airy melody took over, full of unexpected changes in tempo. Light notes, like the wind, breathed over the strings, getting faster and louder until they whirled about the hall in a frenzy, and then were still.

The wildman handed the harp back to the bard. It was perfectly tuned, and remained so until the bard died, many years later.

In the summer, Donacht built the wildman a hut in the courtyard with a barred window, through which passersby could look in at him. They had attempted to cut his hair and trim his beard, they had tried to put clothes on him, but he had rejected all help of that sort, taking the food he was offered but doing nothing more in the way of becoming civilized. From time to time, he chanted nonsense from his rude home. Another year came and went, the guards brought the wildman food, but few looked at him any more.

"Perhaps," mused Meldred one day to Dafat, "we should release him."

"No, lord!" cried Dafat, emphatically. "We cannot do that."

"Why not?" asked the king, surprised.

Dafat shifted awkwardly. "He has a talent for divination, my lord," he said.

"Yes, I know," said the king impatiently. "He has stood before my friends on many occasions, making obscure prognostications of all sorts. But they don't mean anything."

"Begging your pardon, sire," said Dafat, "but the kitchen staff swear by his word. They do, sir. He prophesied the storm in August that clogged up the millwheel and broke a tooth so that the stone couldn't be used for a week. And he foretold that Blodwyn would find a husband, and she so old and not too fine-looking, if I may say so, sire. And she did, as you know, and very happy they are. Then there was the knife I lost last May—well, he knew exactly where I could find it, didn't he?"

"A talent for divination, eh?" said Meldred. "Well, bring him to the hall. Let us hear him divine one more time."

* * *

Half an hour later, the king sat in his hall, having finished with a few pieces of official business from earlier in the day. He watched the last disputants leave the hall with some satisfaction. Their case had been a tricky one, but his druid had remembered some precedents. He cast his eyes about the hall and, seeing that he was finished, he said, "Bring us the wildman. Let us hear him prophesy."

A servant brought Meldred a cup of Gaulish wine, a little boar-meat, its skin blackened with roasting, and some bread, and he ate and drank for a little while in silence. At length, some servants returned to the hall, the wildman bound between them. They tugged him over to the dais. He seemed intent on the ceiling, for some reason, as if the blackened rafters held the secret of his life.

Meldred waited a few moments, and then said, "Well, wildman, what do you see in my future?"

The wildman's eyes snapped down and met his.

"Oho, little pig!" he exclaimed. "Not easy, my sleep, for the tumult of sadness upon me. Two score years and ten have I borne this pain; a sorry figure I, may the king support me as I need." He sighed. "I saw Gwenddolau, splendid lord, gathering spoils upon the field of battle, but he is silent under the earth now. I saw the she-wolf in her battle frenzy, blood and eagle feathers on her lips, blood on her paws, and where is she now? Where was the hawk when the she-wolf was brought down? Far, far away, and he screamed in his loneliness, that he did." His eyes took on a glassy look.

"The eagle and the dragon," he said faintly, "the dragon and the eagle. They will fight, and then they will lie down together and sleep. A hundred years will pass, and another hundred years, and another, and another . . . and where the eagles then? They have flown, flown away, and the dragon is old, he cannot defend himself. There will be uproar in the land when father fights against son. The land will know it, and the land will feel it, and the men of Logris will taste death at the hands of men from over the wide seas."

Meldred screwed his brow into a twisted shape. "What does he mean?" he asked. "Can anyone interpret? Can you, my love?"

Ganieda had just entered the hall, beautiful and golden-haired, her gown of green and yellow clinging to her voluptuous form. Meldred looked on her with pleasure as she approached.

"I, my lord?" said she, reaching up to give him a light kiss. "I know nothing of the ravings of madmen, I am glad to say."

Still smiling, Meldred reached up and plucked a leaf out of her hair. He dropped it to the floor and said, "Now you are perfect." He kissed her gently on the forehead and on the lips.

The wildman shouted with laughter. Wide-eyed, Meldred spun around to face him.

"Good friend," said Meldred, "what mean you by this laughter?" But the wildman continued to laugh uncontrollably, and made no reply. His impatience rising, Meldred said, "What are you laughing about? Tell me why you assail my ears thus, and I shall release you."

The wildman's laughter subsided at once. "You took me from my forest home," he said, "you took me from my friends of fur and feather, bound me with leather thongs and thrust me into a cold and darksome prison-house, and you wished to hear an oracle. Very well. Answer me this riddle." And the wildman began to sing:

"Ambition obeyed friendship
And evil was turned;
Friendship bowed to lust
And goodness was spurned.

Two in one or one in two:
Neither to the other
Long remain true.

Solve me that, O wise king!"

"I cannot solve that!" cried the king at once. Turning to his guards, he barked, "Lock him up again!" They stepped forward and seized the wildman's leash and pulled it towards the door so that he staggered, but he held his ground, and sang out once more:

"Words are as clouds
And none will do better;
From poison comes sweetness,
From honey the bitter.
Two in one or one in two:
Neither to other
Long remain true."

"Either tell me at once in plain terms the meaning of your laughter, or else return to your cage; speak no more in riddles."

"Pain to you and grief to me—that is the price of plain speaking!" sang the wildman, dancing around in a circle. Stopping, he fixed Meldred with one impassioned eye and said, "There once was a king who conferred the highest honour on a friend who then betrayed him, then the worst punishment on one who nevertheless remained loyal. What do these two subjects deserve?"

The king shrugged. "The first punishment, the second reward. The king is a poor judge of character."

The wildman straightened up, lifting his nose in the air like a lawmaker sitting in judgement. "Thou hast adjudged the case aright!" he declared. "Today, you punished your friend by plucking him from your lady's hair and trampling him on the floor—the leaf was your friend, for it fell upon your wife's head to reveal the adultery she was committing with your steward in the orchard, not a quarter of an hour ago!"

There was a yelp from the wildman's audience, and Ganieda hissed, "He lies!" Turning to Meldred, she said, "My lord, believe not the ravings of a madman. He would do anything to achieve his freedom."

King Meldred looked levelly at his queen for a long moment; then he said, "Lock him up. We do not doubt the queen's loyalty."

The wildman began once more to hoot with laughter as the guards dragged him away.

"The bars of the cage, little pig, the bars of the cage!" he cried, his voice receding as they dragged him away. "We cannot break loose, and the yew tree in the courtyard was struck with lightning on the world's great day!" There was a sound of scuffling, and the wildman reappeared in the hall. The nobles shied away, and Ganieda stepped behind her husband.

"Look to your wife, O king!" shouted the wildman. "Fair she is and golden-haired, but the spear will pierce your side, and it is borne by your best friend!"

The guards seized him and dragged him away. The nobles exchanged wondering glances.

"Leave us!" bellowed King Meldred, his fists clenched.

Ganieda whirled on her husband as the nobles filed out. "Surely," she said, "you cannot believe him!"

"My dear," replied Meldred, kissing her again on the forehead, "I have already said that I doubt not your loyalty. But once the word *adultery* is mentioned in a royal court, it is a hard one for the people to forget. We must crush this rumour." Ganieda did not speak. Her shoulders and her chest were heaving with indignation. "Do not fret yourself, my love," said the king. "I have a plan."

XXVII

Dafat paused in the doorway of the hall and looked up at the clouds that were louring overhead. Rain was hammering the grassy courtyard into muddy pools in what appeared to be thin lances of water. From somewhere behind him, over the gloomy mountains of southern Cambria, thunder boomed.

In spite of the rain, Dafat's spirits were high. He even laughed a little, disguising his mirth as a cough into the sleeve of his tunic. The body of the queen was sweet, and he thought of her, just a few days ago, lying in the shade of the apple trees, her pale thighs open for him, her flesh soft and yielding under the pressure of his hands, but her breasts ripe and firm against his lips. The final ecstasy had brought a blush to her cheeks that the king had mistaken for love of him. Dafat smirked again, and wondered for a moment what it was he wanted. He would never be the king, he knew that. He was not tupping the king's wife as a prelude to rebellion. But her body was sweet, and he derived a certain satisfaction from the knowledge, every time he poured a cup of wine for Meldred, every time he tested the king's plate for poison, every time he shooed away unwanted bards or supplicants, that the queen's bare legs had been wrapped around him this morning or last night.

He did not know why the queen made love to him. If he had been forced to offer an opinion, he would have said that she found him attractive. But it did not occur to him to wonder.

Dafat threw his hood over his head and strode out into the storm. The rain was pattering upon the wildman's cabin like some primitive drummer out of the hills. He reached out with one hand to steady himself against the wall, and tilted his head sideways to peer through the barred window.

The wildman was squatting, naked, in the corner. A bone, stripped of most of its meat, lay on a pewter plate nearby, and a reddish beaker was overturned not far from it. The wildman looked up at Dafat, peering from behind long, matted strands of bleached hair.

"You've done me an ill turn, wildman," said Dafat, throwing back his hood so that the wildman could see his face. "I should have let the king release you, days ago, when he wanted to."

"I drank wine from a fair glass with grim lords of war," said the wildman, his voice barely audible over the pattering rain and the buffeting of the wind. "The dark rider comes, driving the foreigners back to their ships. Who will he be? Bright the blade that he wields, through stone under water. Bitter rage contending for the hill by the fen. Death, death, death, death, death. But the cup of life pours out for us!"

"Death, that's it," said Dafat, peering closely in at the wildman. "Tell me how I will die, old fool."

The wildman stopped talking. He was, Dafat noticed, shivering quite uncontrollably. But now he ceased shivering and, in uncanny stillness, looked up and pierced Dafat to the soul with his dark eye.

"What you ask is unwise," he said, "for no man should know of his own end; truly, it is denied those with the Sight to foresee their own deaths."

"If you are a true seer, look, and tell me what I ask."

"The king's steward will fall from his horse," the wildman said, and promptly fell asleep.

Dafat adjusted his cloak over his shoulders, pulled the hood back up over his head, turned his back upon the wildman, and returned to the hall, where the cuckold waited for the answer to the question.

* * *

The next day was dry. A mist that hung about in the morning was burned off by mid-morning, but the puddles remained, drying out slowly over the long hours before noon.

Shortly before noon, a warrior emerged from the hall. He sported a thick yellow beard, and a scar ran down one side of his face. A patch covered the eye. He wore plaids, flowing robes over a scarlet tunic. A gold-buckled belt circled his waist, and from it hung a thick sword.

The warrior strode across the courtyard until he came to the wildman's cabin. He bent slightly to peer through the window.

"They tell me," he said, in a gruff voice, "that you have the gift of prophecy. I must know—will I die in battle, as befits one of my rank, or will I be dishonoured by death in a bed?"

The wildman looked up at the warrior. "I see the hanged man," he said.

The warrior's lip curled away from his teeth. "Hang? Curse you, you wretch!" He kicked the door of the hut so that the walls rattled. "I shall die no traitor's death!"

"You will hang," said the wretched clairvoyant. He coughed and, in his coughing fit, the warrior stormed away from him.

* * *

Early the next morning, ere the light of dawn crept over the fortress of Caermyrddin, a wind out of the west picked up, tangy with the scent of salt. When the sun rose, the weather got little warmer, in spite of the bright skies across which clouds raced like horses in a cavalry charge. The wildman craned his neck to see the sky out of his window, watching the airy shapes all morning long.

When it was almost noon, a heavily cowled peasant, pitchfork in hand, strode from the gatehouse to the wildman's hut and bent down to look inside.

The wildman's eyes descended from the clouds to the peasant's face. He could see very little of it, but the end of a sharp nose and the twinkle of a pair of eyes. He looked across at the hall. The king and queen had emerged. The queen had put a hand up to her crown, so that it would not blow off, while the king's cloak streamed backwards from him, like the wind itself, given physical shape.

"Long have I laboured in the fields of King Meldred," said the peasant. "My back is sore, my limbs ache. Tell me, for it is said you know things that have not yet come to pass, shall I die of old age, or is it another death I should look forward to?"

The wildman looked at the king and queen for a long while, then up at the peasant. "Fear death by water," he said. "You shall drown."

The peasant gave out a triumphant cry and threw back the hood. "You old fool!" he cried, for it was Dafat. "It was I who asked you, each of these three days past, how I would die. And you gave me a different answer each time. Can a man die three different deaths? You are no prophet—you are a fake, a humbug!"

The king and queen were close now, and triumph lit Ganieda's eyes. "Listen to this false prophet!" she said. "Could he ever lead you so far astray as to think me disloyal to you, my husband and my king? It is nonsense he has spoken, and always has been. He made up what he said about me so that he could escape into the woods again."

"We certainly seem to have cast doubt upon the truth of what he said," observed Meldred.

"Put him to death," said Dafat, peeling off his peasant's disguise to reveal his more accustomed clothing beneath.

"Nay," said the queen, "seal him up where he can have a view of the forest, but never get to it."

Meldred narrowed his eyes at the queen. "That were a cruelty indeed," he said. "How can you wish revenge against so pathetic a creature as this?" He turned to look at the wildman. "Perhaps, if he stays here, he will recover his wits." He raised his voice so that all in the courtyard could hear him. "The wildman spoke untruths! The queen is innocent!" He turned to Donacht and added, "See that he is fed and kept, and *comes to no harm*." Donacht nodded and bowed as the king and queen turned to enter the hall, Dafat at their side.

* * *

Another year passed. The wildman was not trotted out for King Meldred's guests, as had been his wont, and few looked through his barred window to obtain his prognostications. Sometimes, his voice rose, high and shrieking, and the people of Caermyrddin made the sign of the evil eye; but they forced their eyes ahead, and tried not to look at his hut.

Another year went by. Nobody looked in at the wildman, except Donacht, the huntsman, who took pity upon him in his misery. But then, early in the springtime, when the wind out of the west was still sharp with early morning chill, there was a great commotion in the hall. Women wept, and in particular, the queen's voice was raised in lamentation. The king stormed out of the hall. On the steps, he stopped and turned back.

"What, strumpet? Dare you weep for him to my face?" he cried. He stomped across the courtyard to the wildman's hut. Donacht rushed to intercept him, thinking the king meant to do him mischief. Meldred stood before the wildman's hut, his chest heaving, his lip curled downward, his eyes fuming.

"Your majesty?" said Donacht.

"Dafat is dead," said the king. He turned his eyes upon the huntsman. "Did you know?" he asked pointedly.

"No, lord; your word to me is the first I have heard. Peace upon his soul!"

"I don't mean about his death—he deserved to die, and may his soul rot, one grain a day, until the end of time!"

"Then—"

"I meant," said Meldred, taking a deep breath, "about him and my wife." Donacht looked still uncomprehending, and Meldred explained: "We were returning from Cydwelli this forenoon. Our path took us over a narrow wooden bridge across the Tywi. As Dafat began to cross, a snake slid across his path. His horse shied, and he was cast from it. As he tumbled down the riverbank, his foot caught in the fork of a low tree branch, and he hung with his head in the water."

A woman's screams shattered the air, and Donacht whirled round to see the queen led between two guards from the hall. Her face was red with weeping, and she struggled ineffectually with the guards.

"He was cast from a horse, hung from a tree, and drowned in a stream," said Meldred. "The wildman's prophecy was true. Release him."

Donacht reached to his belt, took the key and turned it in the lock. Meldred reached in and hauled the wildman, none too gently, from the hut and spun him into the sunlight, where he stood blinking, his shoulders hunched.

"Go!" cried Meldred. "I said you could go if you prophesied aright, so go, and the curse of the gods go with you!" Turning to the guards, he said, "Put that woman in here. Here she stays, awaiting my judgement."

As Ganieda passed by, the king reached out and tore her dress from her shoulders, flinging it far away across the courtyard. She stood, cringing at her nakedness, shivering with fear and sorrow, in the doorway. The king thrust her through. "There," he said. "Since you do not seem too particular who you spread your legs for, let the commoners gaze on you all they like!" And he himself turned the key.

Donacht followed the wildman as he hobbled through the gate. The wildman's face turned left and right in wonder, his eyes still blinking. But once he entered the forest, there was no keeping up with him, and no one at Caermyrddin ever saw the wildman again.

XXVIII

Merlin ran on through the forests of southern Cambria. Flames licked at his heels as he ran on, flames pressed in on him on either hand, and flames blazed up ahead of him. He spun in circles. There was no path ahead, and none behind him either. So he ran—ran through the flames, leaped over the flames, rolled through the flames. He jabbered at the flames to make them go down, beat at them to extinguish them, blew upon them to put them out, but they leaped up, angrier and fiercer than ever. In the end, he spread out his arms and stood still, thinking that the flames would consume him, and at last all would be over. But the flames burned him, and did not consume him, and he remained alive, and he ran once more.

Then, one day, through the crackling and roaring of the flames, he heard music, and it was like water upon his soul. He leaped for it, he lunged towards the sound. The flames burned and charred, but he grit his teeth and endured it. He reached out with sooty fingers toward the sound of the singing, while the flames roared and leaped all around him.

Merlin swam through fire: the wicker man blazed, his house in Afallach blazed, the Cave of Knowledge blazed while Suetonius Paulinus looked on. The flames danced and wavered before him, forming the faces of Cartimandua and Boudicea, his grandfather and Cathbhad the bard.

Through the flames came a pale, wild traveler, cloaked in dark colours, a staff in his hand. His beard was grey, his eyes so pale that Merlin almost took him for a blind man. The contrast between the paleness of his face and the darkness of his robes burned Merlin's eyes like the flames, but not so fiercely. Merlin had seen him before.

The pale wanderer reached out to Merlin. "Come," he said, "there is a path through the flames. You must trust, and love."

Merlin reached out and took the pale wanderer's hand. In his other hand, Merlin could see, he bore a golden chalice.

"Do you see a path?" asked the pale wanderer.

"No, just flames, as high as trees," replied Merlin.

"Then let me lead you."

"Where are we going?"

"Home," said the pale wanderer. And he thrust himself into the flames, which drew aside, and when Merlin passed between them, his skin was cool, although they leaped and roared angrily on either hand.

At the end of the path was a hill; and on the hill, a criminal was being put to death.

* * *

Merlin's eyes snapped open. He knew a coolness, and a calmness, which had been lost to him he knew not how long. Over him hovered the face of the pale wanderer, kindly concern stamped upon his features. His face was framed by the blue sky. Merlin could tell, though, from the motion beneath him, that he was on a boat. He wondered briefly if he were dead, or if he were captured by enemies; but the effort of thinking was too much, and ere long he slipped once more into a delicious, cool sleep, in which he dreamed of water soothing his body like balm.

* * *

When Merlin awoke again, he was lying on his back in a small stone-built chamber. A fire was burning in a central hearth, shedding its warmth deliciously over all of his body. In an instant, all the events of the last few years clamoured in his head: he saw, as vividly as the room about him, the spite of Ganieda and the wrath of Meldred; the forest, and the wolves and pigs among which he had dwelt; Boudicea's arms flung wide as she pitched from her chariot. He pressed his eyelids together, but tears squeezed out anyway. Turning his face to the side, he tried to bury it in the pillow upon which he reclined.

"Boudicea, Boudicea," he moaned. But he said no more. He thought of Boudi, her eyes bright in the hall of his grandfather, as they spoke together of the sword of kings, and of the tall, lithe woman into which she grew, fierce and queenly, his wife and his one love.

Merlin felt a hand on his forehead, and cool water, and he opened his eyes once more. Beside him was the man he had seen earlier. Had he been on a boat? But it was also the man of his vision, the man who had met him in the snows of Cameliard, and who had come through the flames to bring him home.

"You are the pale wanderer," said Merlin. "I have met you before."

"I know," replied the other simply.

"Are you a god?"

The smile did not leave the other's face; it became more loving, more protective, though. He said, "No, but I have looked on His face, and so some little of His glory might still be there. But I am clay, like you."

Merlin looked about him at his surroundings. The early morning sun shone through the window, and he could see the glassy lake and the trees beyond. He looked at the man. He was about fifty or sixty years old, his skin olive-coloured, and his hair dark, shot through with grey. He wore a coarse tunic of grey stuff, that hung to his ankles, and was fastened about the middle by a girdle of hemp. He looked very different from the pale, wild wanderer from Merlin's visions, yet this was he.

Beside Merlin's bed was a low table, and upon it rested a golden cup. It was of a very simple design, but lovely proportions.

"What place is this?" asked Merlin.

"You are in a place called Corbenic," answered the man. "Is it known to you?"

Merlin nodded. "It is the home of my father."

"Pelles," said the man.

"Is he here?" asked Merlin eagerly.

"He is," replied the pale wanderer. "He will join us presently. Please rest in the meantime."

"Who are you?"

"My name," answered the man, "is Joseph."

The name sounded strange to Merlin's ears. "You are not of Britain," he said, "nor, I think, of Rome."

"You are correct; yet in my early life, I served Rome. I am from Arimathea, a city very far away from here."

"I am Merlin Emrys," said Merlin. "I was once a prince of Cambria, and a king of Eicenniawn, but that was long ago, long ago, and I can barely remember it." His memories threatened to rise up in him again, and he said hastily, "What brings you to these shores?"

"My Lord led me hither," answered Joseph. "How did you lose your kingdom?"

Merlin frowned. "Carelessness, I suppose," he said quickly. "Are you not lord in this place?"

Joseph laughed merrily. "I am no more Lord here than I am anywhere. Here, we are all servants of the Lord."

Merlin's pulse quickened. "Is then the High King restored?"

"I speak of no worldly king," replied Joseph, "but He who is above all earthly power."

Merlin sank back on the pallet. "I thought I was healed," he said, "but things still seem strange to me." For a few moments, he was lost in thought; then he spoke again. "How long is it, I wonder, since last I knew myself?"

"You have been here, sleeping and raving, for two days," answered Joseph. "Your father tells us that it is eleven years since last you and he parted company."

"Eleven years!" breathed Merlin. He could feel the burden of the years pressing heavily upon him once more. "So many, and so wasted!"

"Nothing is wasted," Joseph assured him. "Come." He reached for the golden cup that stood beside Merlin's bed. "Drink of this cup, the cup of life."

Joseph raised Merlin's head with one hand, and used the other to raise the chalice to his lips, so that Merlin could sip what was within.

Merlin screamed. It seemed to him that his limbs were forcibly pinioned. Above him, the sky was dark. He was in a high place, looking down at a crowd of people who stood in the rain, gazing up with love and sorrow, some with guilty triumph, at him. His arms were spread wide, secured by nails through the wrists, and by ropes. Blood ran from his wrists, and from his head, and from gashes on his back, but the rain took the blood and washed it down the hill in all directions.

But the worst pain was in his chest. He could barely breathe. He felt as if he were drowning, or as if a great weight had been placed upon his chest. His breath came in shallow, laboured gurgles, and he strove to speak, to gather enough breath to speak just once to the people ranged out at his feet.

He opened his lips, and words came unbidden to them: "My God, my God, why have you forsaken me?" he cried.

Lightning flashed; it clove in two a yew tree. Then the vision faded, and Merlin was back in the stone-built room on Corbenic. He looked up at the pale wanderer. And all at once, it was as if a darkness was lifted from his soul, beating its leathern wings upon the air and screeching with fright as it departed through the window. And in its place, an incredible sweetness, like the scent of a newborn babe, filled the remotest corners of Merlin's soul. He felt comfort like a hearth in winter, bed after a long journey, rainfall after long drought. For the first time in many years, Merlin brimmed over with calm and happiness and delight.

"What power is in the cup?" he asked.

Joseph took a deep breath. "No one knows, for certain, Merlin," he said. "It was in this cup that I collected the blood of my Lord, thirty years ago. Who drinks from the Grail is one with the Lord, and where the Grail is, no man shall go hungry."

"A gift of the gods!" breathed Merlin, looking on the cup with wonder. "It is like the Cauldron of Garanhir, which multiplies the food cast into it, and can give motion to the lifeless."

Joseph nodded. "Life after death," he said, "and an eternal banquet—that is what my Lord has promised me."

"I don't understand," said Merlin.

Joseph continued to smile, a beatific smile that seemed to inform every particle of his being. "It is not always wise to understand all things," he said. "Is not that what the story means about—what name do you give her?—Morgana? And the Siege Perilous? Nevertheless, there are things that will become clearer to you, with time. But now, you must rest." He rose and called over his shoulder: "Rachel!" A young girl entered the room. She had dark hair and a dark complexion, like Joseph's, and she was lovely of face, with an unsurpassed and chaste beauty. She inclined her head before Joseph, who said to her, "Please return the Grail to the tabernacle."

She picked up the cup and, holding it before her with reverence, left the room silently.

"Now rest," said Joseph, leaving. Merlin heard his voice outside, singing a song about a star in the east, until it faded with distance.

Merlin breathed in and out deeply, and reflected for a while upon the strangeness of this place, which combined blood and peace, before slipping back into a restful and dreamless sleep.

* * *

The next time he awoke, he found Pelles sitting beside him, in the seat recently occupied by Joseph.

"Father!" said Merlin.

"My son!" exclaimed Pelles. "You have returned!"

Merlin sat up in the bed, and scrutinized his father's face. He hadn't changed.

"You were right," said Merlin, hanging his head. "I should have stayed. Can you ever forgive me?"

Pelles reached out and smoothed Merlin's hair. Some strands fell forward, and Merlin saw with something of a shock that they were snowy white. Pelles said, "Much has happened since you left; but you are here now. It is not too late." He reached behind him, and produced a largish object—the harp that Merlin had left behind in Corbenic, before his madness, before Boudicea's revolt. Merlin took it with wonder.

"You kept it!" he cried, delighted. Then, setting it down, he looked once more at his father. "Tell me what has happened," he urged.

Pelles drew a deep breath. "God has come among us," he said.

"You mean the pale wanderer, Joseph?" asked Merlin.

"No." Pelles shook his head, slowly but definitively. "No, Joseph is not God, but he brought God, and now God dwells among us, in our hearts, where he has always dwelt, though unrevealed."

Merlin felt dismayed. "I don't understand," he said. "I'm beginning to wonder if I ever will."

"Come with me," said Pelles, "for easier it is to show than to tell."

He rose and held out his hand. Merlin took it, and allowed himself to be hauled out of bed. He was wearing a short tunic and breeches, both of a neutral brown colour, and there were shoes tucked under the bed that he slipped onto his feet before he ventured out into the sunlight.

Joseph and his people had wrought a transformation upon Corbenic. The apple grove still remained, and Pelles' hut, but there were other huts, perhaps a dozen in all. In their midst stood a great tower, cruciform in plan, with high windows in every wall and a door facing east. People moved about between the buildings, and Merlin could see gardens further off down the slope, tended by still others. The buzzing of bees filled the air.

"Who are these people?" asked Merlin. "Some of them look like Britons, but the others—I have not seen men or women who resembled these before."

"They are from a land far away from here called Judea," Pelles explained. "They came with Joseph but, you are right, my son, that some are Britons too."

They had reached the tower. Carved above the door on the lintel was the shape of a fish. From within came the sound of singing, and Merlin stood for a moment, his motion arrested by the beauty of the song. Then he began to listen to the words, and a frown drew his eyebrows together. The song was about a maiden, and a man who chose her for his mother, stealing upon her like the dew on the grass in April: matchless the lady, peerless the son. Merlin understood it not, but tears prickled the backs of his eyes on hearing it.

Merlin swallowed, his throat moving up and down heavily. "Mother and maiden," he said quietly. "How can that be?"

"Much that we thought could not be," said Pelles, "is indeed. That is the news for which I have so long waited here. So long. Death itself has been reversed, and God Himself—not the gods, but the one true Creator, He who stands behind all other beings we have called gods—God Himself, I say, has taken on the form of a man and offered himself as a sacrifice."

"Why?" asked Merlin. "And how?"

"You will see," Pelles assured him. He pushed on the door and they entered together.

The design was simple. A window in each wall gave light onto the central space, in which stood about two dozen people who had their backs to the door. At the western end was what appeared to be an altar, and from it Joseph, dressed in robes of white and green, had taken the Grail, holding it out for the people to see. Behind the altar knelt two young women, their hands folded before them, their heads inclined. One of them, Merlin saw, was Rachel. The other, equally beautiful, he had never seen before.

"On the night that he was betrayed," said Joseph, "Our Lord broke bread and drank wine, saying, 'This is my body and my blood, which will be given for you, that sins might be forgiven. Do this in memory of me.'"

Joseph raised the Grail to his lips. Then, one by one, the people walked up to him, bowed, and sipped from the Grail. Merlin watched as this happened. A young woman stepped up to Joseph, bowed, and took the Grail. She lifted it to her lips and sipped.

For a moment, Merlin was on a storm-benighted hill, a place of execution. The woman he had been watching was nailed and strapped to a tall cross, and blood was streaming from her hands, her feet, and her side.

A moment later, the vision was gone. The woman made a sign, like the evil eye, but covering her chest, and knelt down, her head bowed in contemplation. After a few moments, she rose and left the building, greeting Pelles with a nod and a smile on the way out.

The same happened to each person that sipped from the Grail.

Merlin turned to Pelles. "I don't understand any of this," he protested.

Pelles beckoned him out of the building, and together they walked down the hill, away from the huts and between the gardens to the expanse of grass that, in the winter, fringed the lake. It had evidently been a wet summer, for the ground was miry and full of puddles a few feet away from them. Pelles sat down upon the ground, and Merlin did likewise. For a long while, Pelles seemed content to gaze out over the fens, a look of far-seeing contentment upon his face. Then he said, "The Ladies of the Lake have returned. The doorway between Britain and Avalon has opened, and the remnants of the Morforwyn have issued forth."

Merlin gasped. "Is it true?"

Pelles nodded. "Sometimes," he said, "they are here on the island of Corbenic. Sometimes, they are elsewhere. They do not intrude in men's affairs. There is still that to come for which they are waiting, but they are in readiness now."

"Father," said Merlin, "I am still bewildered by all this. I have spent long years doing the gods alone know what, and my brain is weak. Would you please help me by speaking clearly? Small words would not go amiss."

Pelles laughed, and thumped his son on the shoulder. "Very well, then," he said. "Here, in plain terms, is the truth. The Morforwyn are truly the gods of your people, set upon the Island of the Mighty long ago to guide the men of Britain. They were nearly averted from their task by Morgana's greed, but now they are back. And they have been brought back not by an army, not by their own powers, but by the hand of God Himself."

“That’s what I don’t understand,” said Merlin. “Which god?”

“Which god? *The* God, the only true God, He who made the Morforwyn and shaped this world out of chaos.”

“There is but one God,” said Merlin quietly, suddenly realizing what Pelles was telling him. “It was in Plato, and Cathbhad spoke of it once, but there is only one God.” He looked up at his father. “What, then, are the Morforwyn,” he asked, “if not gods?”

Pelles drew a deep breath. There seemed suddenly something ageless about him, and his eyes looked as if they had seen all ages of men. He said, “The Morforwyn are not mortal men, nor are they God, for there is only one God. They are themselves, the long-lived ones, whom some call gods.”

Merlin became sceptical. “And how do we know about this God?” he asked. “What is His name? What must we sacrifice to Him?”

“Now you speak like a druid,” chided Pelles. “But, since you ask, the answer is simple. You must sacrifice yourself.”

Before Merlin had a chance to register his confusion again, they were interrupted by the arrival of Joseph of Arimathea.

XXIX

Joseph of Arimathea had divested himself of the robes in which he had just been celebrating the ritual of the Grail, and now he wore the same loose-fitting grey tunic and hempen girdle he had worn before. Hitching up the skirts of his tunic, he lowered himself onto the ground beside Merlin and Pelles.

"God's greetings to you this fine day, my friends," he said. They returned their greetings to him. After a while, he said, "How do you find things here in our community, Merlin?"

"This place is a pleasant one," said Merlin, "and the folk friendly. But I am still bewildered."

"So have we all been," admitted Joseph. "For many thousands of years, we have been beguiled. But that has happened now which has brought everything into sharp focus."

Merlin shook his head. "That doesn't help," he said.

Joseph patted him on the shoulder, like a teacher correcting a student of whom he was fond, but who was rather slow-witted. He said, "There is no reason that you should understand yet. But if it will help at all, I shall tell you the whole story."

"I think it would help."

Joseph thought a moment. "It is my story," he said, "but it is also the story of another, one far greater than I."

"Tell me," urged Merlin; and Joseph began.

* * *

I was born (said Joseph), in the Roman province of Judea, in the city of Arimathea, two days' journey from Jerusalem, the holy city of my people. In Arimathea, I am called Yusef, but one's name changes as one travels.

My father was a merchant and, although I dreamed of the faraway places to which his caravans carried his merchandise, I had no head for figures. My father tried to teach me the ways of a merchant, but eventually concluded that I would be bankrupt within a year and sent me to a House of Study in Jerusalem.

After travel, the love of my early years was the written word. Indeed, in my spare time, I collected not the books of the Laws which were my daily professional concern, but books describing the wonders of distant lands. I fear I was a very poor pupil. My master, Nicodemus, often despaired of me. But in truth, I found our laws to be too mathematical. Life did not seem to me to be a simple matter of sin and retribution, virtue and reward. Something was missing from our lives, though I could not say what.

My people live and die by the Law. In our holy books, we read that we were once held in slavery by the nation of Egypt. God spoke to a man called Moses, who led us out of captivity, and He gave Moses the Law. The Law is a wonderful thing, and every boy I grew up with respected, venerated, even loved the Law. And so did I. But, as I say, the Law was just too arithmetical to be appealing to me. I am afraid I neglected my studies.

One day, Nicodemus summoned me. I must have been in my twenties. He began quite bluntly. "You will never make a scribe," he said. I asked him why, although I already knew the answer. "You are more of a poet than a scribe," he said. "You seek truth, but you do not find it in the Law."

"Are you accusing me of rejecting the Law?" I asked, suddenly startled.

"No, Yusef," replied Nicodemus patiently. "But you obviously don't see God in the Law: you want to see His face directly."

I think I was offended by his remark at the time—not because I thought he was wrong. I had long suspected that to which he was giving voice, but this would be my second failure. I'd make no merchant, and I'd make no scribe. Looking back over the years, I can see that Nicodemus had actually discovered one of my talents, and was trying to put me to good use, but at the time I could not see it.

“To look on the face of God—don’t we *all* want that?” I demanded stubbornly.

Oddly enough, that remark took him by surprise, and he reflected upon it for a few moments before making his reply. “The Law is my staff,” he said, “my shield against my enemies, my comfort in a harsh world. A world without law is hardly worth living in. But I am not here to defend the ancient traditions of Judah against the likes of you, Yusef. I have a proposition for you.” I waited. Nicodemus went on, “You and I both know that you will never make a scribe; but you have a natural facility for language, and the Governor, Valerius Gratus, needs an interpreter. I can get you the job. Would you like it?”

I was taken aback for a moment. “Me?” I said. “Work with a Gentile?”

Nicodemus shrugged. “The Romans are here, and have been for nearly eighty years. I think you should be safe, so long as you don’t eat with him or marry his daughter.”

I considered the proposition but, in truth, I had already decided. Nicodemus was right—I did not have the makings of a scribe. And I knew that Jewish men who worked for the Roman authorities were well paid. The next day, I visited Gratus, and he gave me the job. I did well. Before long, Gratus had made me his liaison with the Sanhedrin, our Great Council.

There came among my people at this time a man blessed by God with what you, Merlin, call the Sight. His name was John, and he warned us to be on our guard, for the Messiah, the Anointed One, was at hand. My people have long awaited this Messiah. Our prophets tell us through our scriptures that the Messiah will save us from oppression and bless all nations. John, this prophet, told us that the Messiah was already here, among us. Most of my friends and colleagues in the Sanhedrin thought that John was a lunatic. How could the Messiah be among us, and we not notice him? they asked. The Messiah was supposed to be a king, leading a great army. He would liberate us from the Romans. Our own king, Herod, was clearly not the Messiah. Who else was there?

One day, I had to visit the Sanhedrin on the Governor's business—Gratus had gone back to Rome, and a man called Pontius Pilate had replaced him. Pilate was unpopular with the Sanhedrin. Arriving in Jerusalem, he had carried with him graven images of Caesar, a practice my people abhor. Within a few months of his arrival, he had plundered the Temple treasury to build a water-pipe into Jerusalem. He had been particularly brutal in his reprisals when the people of Galilee protested the theft, crucifying large numbers of men he called rebels. The Sanhedrin had complained of him to Caesar, and it seems that Caesar admonished him, for he certainly committed fewer atrocious acts after that. He seemed to me, always, to be a man on the edge of a cliff, looking into the chasm and feeling the pull of gravity upon him. You can imagine that, during his governorship, I was not as popular with the Sanhedrin as had been my wont. Still, no one was openly hostile to me.

On this particular occasion, a man was brought before the Sanhedrin who had been blind, but to whom sight was now restored. This was, you see, one of the signs by which we were supposed to recognize the Messiah.

"How was your sight restored?" demanded Caiaphas, the high priest of the Sanhedrin.

"Worshipful one!" cried the blind man, prostrating himself before the high priest, "it was the man called Yeshua!"

This sat ill with the members of the Sanhedrin, and they muttered ill-temperedly among themselves for a few seconds at the mention of His name.

"How did this man Yeshua cure your blindness?" asked Caiaphas.

"Worshipful one," said the man again, still cringing, "He put clay on my eyes, and bade me go wash it away. I did, and I saw men, who looked like trees walking!"

There was another buzz of comment from the Sanhedrin at this, but Caiaphas remained aloof, and held up a hand to silence them. "When did this happen?" he asked.

"Yesterday, my lord," answered the man who was not blind.

"The Sabbath," observed Caiaphas. Then, after a pause, he went on, "And what do you say about him, since he has opened your eyes?"

"He is a prophet, lord!" replied the man.

Caiaphas smiled a thin smile. "How can this man be from God," he asked slowly, "If he does not keep the Sabbath? If he does not observe the day of rest decreed by God Himself, how can he be the messenger of God?"

The man did not answer. He opened his mouth to speak, but looking about him, thought better of it. Caiaphas motioned for him to be taken away, and some of the temple guards pulled him to his feet and dragged him backwards from the temple.

"Since the time of Moses, the Lawgiver," said Caiaphas, "when God Himself led our people out of their bondage in Egypt, this council has preserved and implemented the laws that He gave us. And now, are those laws to be overturned by the son of a carpenter?"

There was a roar of denial from the members of the Sanhedrin, and I could feel the anger at the deeds of this Yeshua growing among them. And yet I heard one say nearby, "Yet how can a man who is a sinner do such signs?" I turned, and looked into the eyes of Nicodemus, my old teacher.

* * *

Joseph paused in his narration, and leaned forward a little. "Merlin?" he said. "You look thoughtful."

Merlin nodded and looked up at him. "This Sanhedrin sounds familiar," he said. "They sound like our druids."

Joseph smiled, rather sadly. "The old ways are passing, Merlin," he said. "The Sanhedrin and Afallach are old ways of finding a way. A boy cannot but regret the passing of his youth; but to become a man is an event for celebration, and it greatly outweighs the regret he feels."

"Please continue," said Merlin, and Joseph went on.

* * *

The weeks passed, turning into months. I heard frequently about Yeshua, but I paid the stories little heed, for I was busy with my duties for the governor, and in any case, what I had heard about the man smacked of heresy. Nicodemus' words had left me confused more than anything. My duties kept me mostly away from Jerusalem. For about thirty years, the Roman governors had made Caesarea their residence. Caesarea was a splendid city, rebuilt in a magnificent fashion by Herod the Great and named after Augustus Caesar. We Jews did not like to acknowledge that Herod as our king—he built many pagan temples, and had once, in a fit of jealous anger over a child who had been prophesied a king, slaughtered many children. But Caesarea remained a beautiful city, and I was happy to be there.

And it was in Caesarea that I first came face to face with Yeshua.

I saw him at the side of the ocean. I had a day free and, as I had grown up far from the ocean, I made my way thither and, for many hours, I watched the boats going to and fro across the bright water. I saw some merchant ships set sail—for where? Paphos? Ephesus? Syracuse? These were places unknown to me except when named by the captains of my father's vessels and, looking out over that shimmering table of water, I yearned once again as I had not since childhood to travel out across the water or the desert and see foreign lands and talk with foreign folk.

Then I saw Him. He was surrounded by a large group of people, standing upon the shore among the fishing boats. All eyes were upon Him, all ears were open to Him. And I stood there and listened too.

"Do not labor for the food which perishes," He said, "but for the food which endures to eternal life, which the Son of Man will give to you; for on him has God the Father set his seal."

One in the crowd said to him, "What must we do, to be doing the works of God?"

Yeshua answered them, "This is the work of God, that you believe in him whom He has sent."

Then another said to Him, “What sign will you do, that we may see, and believe you? What work do you perform? Our fathers ate the bread in the wilderness; as it is written, ‘He gave them bread from heaven to eat.’”

Yeshua replied, “Truly, it was not Moses who gave you the bread from heaven; my Father gives you the true bread from heaven. For the bread of God is that which comes down from heaven, and gives life to the world.”

“Lord,” someone cried out “give us this bread always.”

Yeshua looked at them and smiled; and it seemed to me that his smile was tinged with sadness. “I am the bread of life,” He said; “he who comes to me shall not hunger, and he who believes in me shall never thirst. I am the living bread which came down from heaven; if any one eats of this bread, he will live for ever; and the bread which I shall give for the life of the world is my flesh.”

There was a murmur of protest from the crowd then, and one, a Pharisee, said, “How can this man give us his flesh to eat?”

“Truly,” replied Yeshua, “unless you eat the flesh of the Son of Man and drink his blood, you have no life in you; he who eats my flesh and drinks my blood has eternal life, and I will raise him up at the last day.”

There was more grumbling from the crowd at this, and some got up and left. As they passed by me, I heard one remarking, “This is a hard saying; who can listen to it?”

But Yeshua knew what they murmured, and said to them, “Do you not see? There are those who hear but do not hear, and see but do not see. This is why I told you that no one can come to me unless it is granted him by the Father.”

“Is he talking about me?” muttered one person nearby. He got up, shook the dust from his robes, and went about his business. Very soon, there were no more than a dozen about Yeshua—a dozen and me.

Yeshua turned to those who were still with Him. “Do you also wish to go away?”

One of those who remained said, “Lord, to whom shall we go? You have the words of eternal life; and we have believed, and have come to know, that you are the Holy One of God.”

“Well have you learned, Kephas,” replied Yeshua. “To you are granted the keys of heaven. And all of you will share to some measure in the glory that is to come. For all of you will carry the good news to all corners of the world, that there may be none from this day until the last judgement who can say, ‘I did not know.’” He paused, and looked directly at me. At me! Merlin, Pelles—He saw me, and walked towards me, and He spoke to me directly! He said, “You, Yusef, you shall play your part too.”

“Me, lord?” I threw myself to the ground before Him but, after a moment, I felt His gentle hands raising me up.

“Yes, you,” He said. “But your part is not to play yet. Not yet. So go now, about your business, for you did not leave when the others left. But do not forget what you have heard.”

“I have heard little that I understand, lord,” I told him earnestly.

“Now is not the time for understanding,” answered Yeshua. “Yet there will be a time for that too. I tell you truly, we shall meet again, and again.”

“Farewell, lord,” I said; and He gave me His blessing, and I left.

XXX

Joseph fell silent. Merlin waited for him to continue, impatient to hear the rest, but Joseph did not speak for a while. At last, he said, "How sweet the air smells today in this spot! This is a blessed land indeed!"

"But, my lord," said Merlin, "this man, Yeshua—what did he mean? How could you do what he commanded you? I understand less than I did before!"

Joseph nodded understandingly. "Many felt that way," he said, "and many deserted Him then, at a time when I thought He had most need of friends. As for what he meant—well, that is something to be experienced, not explained."

"If it can be experienced, it can be explained," replied Merlin doubtfully.

"Not necessarily," answered Joseph. "Can love be explained?"

"I see," said Merlin, still not quite understanding. "Please, on with your tale, I beg you!"

Joseph's face clouded a little at the memory, and he said, "For a time, things were bleak—as bleak as they could be. But now, as He said, I understand."

* * *

Over the next few weeks, I stole secretly to listen to this man Yeshua preach, whenever I could. I became conscious of a change in the way I perceived others. Before, I had feared my employer, Pontius Pilate; now I pitied him, and longed in my heart to soothe the anxiety he felt perpetually. Before, I had feared Caiaphas, the leader of the Sanhedrin; now, I was more —how can I say?—disappointed with his behaviour. Not that I would ever say anything to him, but I felt constantly that he was falling short of a standard of behaviour that he knew about, but willfully ignored. Of Nicodemus, I grew even more fond, and we spent much of our time together, talking of history, of the Law, and of Yeshua. "Think not that I have come to abolish the Law and the prophets," Yeshua said one day; "I have come not to abolish them but to fulfill them."

I did not fully understand that. He certainly seemed to be abolishing a lot of our traditions, or attempting to. This became evident when Pilate moved his household back to Jerusalem, shortly before the Passover, the main religious feast of our year. It was customary among my people to sell small sacrifices in the temple forecourt, to people who could not bring their own. Over the years, moneylenders too had gathered in the forecourt, so that those without the means could still purchase sacrifices. Seeing this, Yeshua was apparently struck by the hypocrisy of lending money in God's temple, and overturned the tables, raising his voice in anger at the moneylenders and chasing them out of the forecourt. It seemed so different from what one normally heard about Him, that it struck me as odd, and I wondered if it was even true, seeing that I heard it only second-hand, from a centurion reporting to Pilate shortly after it had happened.

"Caiaphas will not like that," Pilate observed wryly, when the centurion had finished his tale. He stood for a few moments, lost in thought, tapping his front teeth with a stylus. Noticing my presence—I had not been dismissed—he said sharply, "Well, Joseph, you're a Jew. What do you think?"

"I think you are right," I replied. "Caiaphas will take it as a personal affront."

"The people love this Jesus," mused Pilate, taking his seat behind his desk and drumming his fingers on the surface, "but the Sanhedrin hate him. What to do, what to do." His voice trailed away into indecisive silence. "Do you think he's the Christ, Joseph?" Pilate asked me at last. I noticed that he had, without thinking, used the Greek word for *anointed one*, rather than the Hebrew *messiah.*

"He is a good man," I said. "His teachings will change the world. If He is the Messiah, He is different from what most of my countrymen have expected, all these years. We have expected the Messiah to be a great king, accompanied by a grand army."

"Come to liberate your people from the shackles of Rome, eh?" concluded Pilate with another wry smile. "Hard to see how a carpenter's son will be able to do that."

"It is foretold," I said, "that the Messiah will be born of a virgin."

Pilate looked up sharply. "I have heard a rumour that this is so of Jesus. They are saying that his mother has never known man, but that Jehovah himself engendered the child upon her."

I was taken aback by this, for it was a word I had never heard spoken of Yeshua yet; but I said nothing.

Pilate put his head in his hands. "Prophecies, stories, dietary laws—what is one supposed to do with a people like this?" He looked up. "Joseph," he said, "I want to know more. I want to know what this man is like. Go, seek him out. It should not be hard to find him. Listen to him, and tell me what you think of him."

"I shall, your Excellency," I said, pleased more than I can say at the prospect of doing for a duty what hitherto I had done as a secret pleasure.

It was even easier to find Yeshua than Pilate had supposed, for he was dining that night with my friend Nicodemus. Although I had seen Him often, this was the first time I had actually met Him since our encounter in Caesarea, and I felt strangely shy eating with Him. But Nicodemus did not have my scruples, and when we had eaten a little, he said to Him, "Rabbi, we know that you are a teacher come from God; for no one can do these signs that you do, unless God is with him."

"Nicodemus," said Yeshua, smiling, "can you read all the signs aright? Truly, I tell you, unless you are born anew, you cannot see the kingdom of God."

Nicodemus blanched, as if he had looked upon his own death, and said to Him, "How can a man be born when he is old? Can he enter a second time into his mother's womb and be born?"

"Unless you are born of water and the Spirit," replied Yeshua, "you cannot enter the kingdom of God. What is born of the flesh is flesh, and will perish, even as the flesh perishes; that which is born of the Spirit is spirit, and will live for ever."

"But how can this be?" asked Nicodemus, and I was amused to see that my old teacher was confused.

Yeshua smiled—I cannot picture His face now, except smiling—and answered him, "Are you a teacher of Israel, and yet do not understand this? We speak of what we know, and bear witness to what we have seen; you have seen what has happened in your lifetime, here, in Israel, but you do not receive our testimony. If I have told you earthly things and you do not believe, how can you believe if I tell you heavenly things?"

"We are born of the flesh once," said Nicodemus slowly, "but that birth is sinful—our second birth is the birth of the spirit . . . "

"Go on, Nicodemus," said Yeshua, smiling, all patience.

"The spirit cannot perish. The spirit lives for ever. The second birth is an everlasting one."

Yeshua nodded, and broke some bread. "But no one can ascend to Heaven but he who has descended from Heaven, the Son of Man. And the Son of Man must be lifted up, that whoever believes in him may have eternal life."

"Are you the Son of Man?" asked Nicodemus.

"Nicodemus," said Yeshua, "you have seen what you have seen: the blind see, the lame walk, the hungry are filled. Ask yourself, who can do these signs? Believe what you have seen, Nicodemus, and you will know the answer to your question."

I had seen what I had seen, and I knew that I never wanted to leave the side of my master. But when dawn broke the following morning, I went back to Pilate, and told him what I had learned of the prophet from Nazareth.

"Is he the Christ?" asked Pilate.

"Either He is the Messiah," I replied, "or else He is mad. And I do not think He is mad."

"There is a plot afoot," Pilate said, "to capture him and put him to death."

I felt a sudden coldness clutch my heart. "Caiaphas?" I asked. Pilate nodded. I went on, "But to put a man to death lies not within the power of the Sanhedrin. That is for the Roman authorities only—only you can sign a man's death warrant, Excellency."

"I know it," replied Pilate with a heavy sigh. He did not speak for a long time, his hands spread out on the desk in front of him. At last, he said, "Please do not mistake me, Joseph, I do not believe in this Messiah. I don't think I even believe in the gods of my own people. I met Augustus Caesar once. It's hard for me to believe he's a god now. But what I believe is immaterial. If the people love this man Jesus, I have a problem." He paused for a long while, his cup of wine untasted before him on the desk. "My job here is to govern a province on behalf of Caesar. Do you know why I do this?"

I shook my head. In truth, I did not know why one man would covet another's property. Pilate explained, "Money. Rome grows rich on the labour of her provinces, from Germany in the north, to Judea in the south, and Iberia in the west. The whole of the known world renders unto Caesar what is Caesar's due. What ails Caesar is what costs him the most money. And rebellions cost us money. How many legionnaires, trained to peak condition at a cost inestimable to you, are lost each time a province rebels? What of the weapons that are lost, the pila that must be beaten straight once more, the new weapons forged to replace those broken? And to ensure no further rebellions, whenever one takes place, many men must be crucified. You think we Romans like to crucify our prisoners, because we do it so often. Let me tell you, it is expensive to crucify a man. The soldiers must be paid, the prisoner fed in prison, sometimes lawyers paid to plead his case or judges to hear it. We lose the labour of the man afterwards. Rebellion is a great inconvenience, a massive expense. I would do anything—anything, do you hear me?—to prevent a rebellion. If an innocent man has to die to prevent a rebellion, I shall not hesitate to sign the warrant."

"But His *death* will cause a rebellion!" I protested.

"The people will rebel if he dies," said Pilate, his voice flat and dead, "but the Sanhedrin will cause a rebellion if they capture him and he does not die. Either way, I am a dead man."

I looked at Pilate, and saw him once more with the pity I had recently been able to muster for him. I thought of the complaints that the Sanhedrin had sent to Rome following the business with the graven images and the temple treasury. After the last incident, he had received a message from Tiberius which had put him out of sorts with the world. I knew that, whichever path he chose, it would lead to his doom. And suddenly, in that moment, I realized that, in spite of all their pomp and pride, all their legions and their fortresses, their fine clothes and food and exotic dancers, this was the situation that all the Romans were in. For us, Yahweh had always provided an alternative path, one that would not lead to destruction. It was hard to see sometimes, and almost always hard to take, so that the taking of it seemed as hard as death itself. I thought of the protests of my fathers while Moses led them through the desert away from Egypt. But there was always that second path. And I knew that there must be one now.

"Excellency," I said, "the Sanhedrin must move fast. If they wish Yeshua to die this Passover, they must arrest Him tomorrow night, and execute him on Friday. They cannot delay until the Sabbath, for that would be unlawful. Let me find out where He sups this Passover, and see if I can help Him to escape. If the Sanhedrin never captures Him, that would solve your problem."

There was a sudden light in Pilate's eyes. "It would," he said slowly. "Can you do it?"

"I think I can," I said. Another thought occurred to me. "If He is captured anyway," I said, "perhaps you can turn the people against the Sanhedrin? They would not dare to oppose the will of the people, if the people supported Yeshua's liberation."

But Pilate was ahead of me on that. "Yes," he said. "Hasn't it been customary to offer to liberate a prisoner at the Passover? I could offer to release Jesus, with the permission of the people." He rubbed his hands together, delight in his eyes. "I would be the darling of the people of Jerusalem, and the Sanhedrin would not dare to oppose me. Go, Joseph, and find this prophet. Rome and Judea both depend upon you!"

* * *

But, strangely enough, it proved difficult to find Yeshua that day. Preparations were being made for the Passover, and the holy city was alive with servants going to and fro, even some masters, the markets were busy, and finding one man—even *that* man—in such a hurly-burly proved impossible. I had my own preparations to make too, and made them whilst seeking Yeshua out. I returned home at sunset, disappointed, but determined to renew my efforts in the morning.

* * *

"Did you find Him?" asked Merlin, after a long pause.

Joseph shook his head. "Not until it was too late," he said.

"What happened?"

"He was betrayed," answered Joseph, "by one who was like a son to Him. He knew it, and knew that Judas was going to Caiaphas, and He let him go."

"Did He *want* to die?" said Merlin incredulously.

"No," answered Joseph, emphatically. "To Him, death was an abomination, an utter evil, a disease, a curse brought onto the human race by separation from God, and that error has infected every man and woman who has ever lived. No, He did not want to die. But He knew that it was His destiny to do so."

"It is the destiny of all men to die," observed Merlin.

"Yes," answered Joseph, "but the rest of us deserve to die—there is not one of us but he has some sin lurking near his heart. Yeshua was the blameless sacrifice. He was the Messiah.

"I did not find Yeshua that day, but I heard a rumour of His capture, and made my way to Pilate's palace. It was already too late. The crowds had left. Pilate had offered the men and women of Jerusalem the choice of releasing Him, or Barabas, a notorious bandit." Joseph shook his head in disbelief. "They had chosen Barabas," he said.

"And so He died," said Merlin, and the matter seemed closed.

"And so He died," repeated Joseph; "but that was not the end of the story. Yeshua was crucified, a punishment usually reserved for the basest criminals. I finally caught up with His progress as He was carrying the tree of His execution up the side of Golgotha Hill. I stood beside Nicodemus, and wept, and watched.

"I heard Him make no sound. Not when they drove nails through his wrists, not when they dropped the cross into the slot that would keep it upright, not when Caiaphas and the other Pharisees mocked him from the foot of that terrible tree. Once, He spoke, and He said, 'Father, forgive them, for they know not what they do!' Another time, He cried out, 'My God, my God, why have you forsaken me?" And then He yielded up His spirit.'"

XXXI

I cannot properly convey to you the depth of my desolation at that moment. The heavens opened, and a rain such as no man has seen since the Great Deluge fell upon the earth. Deep thunder rolled above the clouds. In the temple, they say, the tabernacle veil was torn in two. The earth shook, and tombs opened up. All around, I could hear the voices of women keening and men lamenting in loud voices. Nearby, a young centurion looked up at the devastation, and said, "Surely, this man was the son of God!" I looked about, but Caiaphas was gone. No one from the Sanhedrin had remained until the uttermost moment, nobody except Nicodemus. Seeing me, he staggered towards me, his face streaming, either with tears or rain, I could not tell.

"We cannot leave Him there!" Nicodemus cried out to me, raising his voice over the storm. "Let us go to Pilate, and beg the body of Yeshua for burial; to leave Him unburied would be a great sin!"

I nodded my consent, and we hurried off, but I could not venture any words as yet—my throat was thick, and I could not even tell if I still had the power of speech.

But I could not remain in silence for long. We passed in through the great gates of Jerusalem, into the holy city that had welcomed the Son of Man a week ago with adulation and songs, and which had so recently expelled Him to His death, and I fell upon my knees, and I howled like a beast, my throat open and my face turned to the sky. Nicodemus did not try to hurry me along, but waited for me, his eyes full of understanding, one hand upon my shoulder.

"O Jerusalem!" I cried. "I fear you will rue this day! Your people will be scattered, and not one brick will remain upon another for this day's work!"

"Come," Nicodemus urged me; and rising, I followed him.

We found Pilate in the palace, sitting before a bowl of water, looking down at his hands. Suddenly aware of our presence, he turned to face us, and I gasped, for in his face was a bleakness such as I have never seen in the face of a man.

"Joseph," he said distantly, "I don't think water will ever clean my hands. What can an Empire do? What can a man do?" He looked up at me. "He would not say anything about the accusations against him," he said, "not a word. I kept pressing him to defend himself, but he would not. What kind of a man was he? Did he *want* to die? All he would say was, 'For this I was born, and for this I have come into the world, to bear witness to the truth. Every one who is of the truth hears my voice.'"

Pilate said nothing for a few moments, but stirred the water with his forefinger, listlessly. "What is truth?" he asked. "What is truth?" He looked up at me again. "Do you believe in portents, Joseph? Do you believe that what men dream at night can come true? My wife dreamed last night, and as I sat on the judgment seat, my wife sent word to me. 'Have nothing to do with this righteous man,' she said, 'for I have suffered much over him today in a dream.' Perhaps he truly is the Christ." He breathed out heavily, scooped up some water, and dashed it over his face. "I fear my hands will never be clean," he said.

I did not know what to say to him for, in truth, I held him partially to blame for what had happened. But Nicodemus spoke from behind me: "The mercy of Yahweh is infinite," he said. "He will forgive even you, if you desire it."

"I don't know if I desire it," replied Pilate. "I have failed. I wish only for death."

All the pity I had felt for this man came rushing back at this, and I was suddenly reminded of the arrogant governor who had brought graven images of the Emperor into the holy city of Jerusalem, and who had rifled through the temple treasury for money to build a water pipe. It was a matter of a few days that had wrought an utter change upon him.

“I beg you, Excellency,” I said, stepping forward, “to grant me a boon, if it seems good to you.”

“What is it you wish, Joseph?” he asked.

“The body of Yeshua,” I replied. “I have a plot of ground, which I was going to use for my own tomb. I would like to inter Yeshua there.”

Pilate regarded me for long moments, uncomprehending, unseeing, even.

“My lord,” I said, “let no hatred fall upon a dead man; for a man’s deeds should perish with his death.”

Pilate looked up at me, his gaze blank, as if the soul had fled his body. He said nothing, so I plunged on: “I know, Excellency, how eager you were that Yeshua should not be crucified, and how much you said to the Sanhedrin on his behalf, now begging, now angry, and at last how you washed your hands, and declared that you would by no means take part with those who wished Him to be put to death.”

Still, Pilate gave me no reply. He looked on me as he would have looked on the birth of a child or his own death, with complete indifference.

“For all these reasons,” I concluded, “I entreat you not to refuse my request.”

“Go,” replied Pilate, in a dead voice, “and take him. Do as you will.”

“We thank your Excellency!” I said, bowing low before him; and Nicodemus and I rushed off, back to Golgotha. We passed by my house on the way, and I collected some myrrh, which I placed in a cup that had belonged to my father, and some aloe, and then we hurried off.

The tempest was beginning to blow itself out as we climbed the hill to the place of execution, and the low and bloody sun came through the clouds in angry shafts. Still, though, a great wind buffeted the top of the hill, and we had to lower our heads against it.

The Romans had taken down the crosses, and a small crowd, mainly of women, was weeping over the body of Yeshua. Once again, my heart was stung by grief, and I could not move.

Nicodemus set down the box containing the aloes, and put a tender arm across the shoulders of the oldest of the women.

"Lady Mary," he said gently, "let us bury your son."

Mary, the mother of Yeshua, looked up at his words, and the sight of her face brought me at once to my knees, and I wept for this lady of sorrows as I had not wept since childhood.

What happened next is indistinct in my mind. Somehow, we took His body from the cross, and carried it to my tomb. I remember anointing His body with the myrrh. Blood was still flowing from His wounds and, on a sudden impulse, I collected the precious liquid in the cup. Then I wept again.

The world was dark when we emerged from the tomb. Together, Nicodemus and I and the companion of Yeshua called John bar Zebedee rolled the stone into place over the entrance. Then we made our way to our homes. I went to bed, and sank into a dark sleep full of vexatious dreams.

* * *

I remember little of the following day. It was the Sabbath, so I did not work that day; but neither did I go to the temple. All hope seemed lost, the Law a travesty. I lay upon my bed as if sick, staring at the ceiling, wondering if there would ever come a time again that life would seem good.

That day passed into night, and the night brightened to another day. Still, I could barely move. I had not eaten in over a day, but there seemed little point in sustaining my body, when the world had sustained such a loss.

In the afternoon of that Sunday, there came a heavy rapping on my door. My servant answered it, and I heard him pushed aside. The sound of heavy boots tramped along the passageway to the door of my chamber. It burst open, and a pair of Pilate's legionnaires entered.

"Joseph of Arimathea," said the centurion in charge, "you are to come with me at once to the Governor."

I was very weak, and could barely move; but I rose from my bed, the world swimming about me, and tried to accompany them. Seeing my infirmity, two of the soldiers supported me, and together we marched through Jerusalem towards the Governor's Palace.

Pilate was not alone. Several members of the Sanhedrin were with him, and Caiaphas rounded on me at once.

"Where have you put the body?" he demanded.

I was still dazed, and at first understood nothing of what he was saying. "What body?" I asked.

Caiaphas beat a fist upon the table in his impatience. "Do not play games with me, Yusef," he said. "I mean the body of the false prophet, Yeshua."

"I placed Him in my tomb," I replied.

"Yes, and where is he now, then?" demanded Caiaphas.

I blinked. "Unless life has been restored to His body," I said, "and He has found the strength of three men and removed the stone from the entrance to the tomb, I should say that He is still there."

Caiaphas' teeth showed as he curled his lip back from them in a snarl. "Is that what you believe?" he asked.

I became troubled. "Is the body gone?" I asked.

"Do not pretend you do not know," countered Caiaphas.

"Yusef." For the first time, I noticed that Nicodemus was present. "Yusef, you must recall that Yeshua predicted that He would die, and rise from the dead on the third day."

My eyes grew round. "And today is the third day," I breathed.

"And you," said Caiaphas, "have removed this man's body from the tomb in an act of rebellion against the Sanhedrin and the Law of Moses, that came from Yahweh Himself!"

"I did nothing to Yeshua's body save place it in my tomb and anoint it with myrrh," I replied. I looked up now, and met Caiaphas' eye. "But if He is truly risen from the dead, what a price will you pay, Caiaphas, who conspired in His death!"

"We have heard enough!" declared Caiaphas. "Treason, blasphemy, heresy! These are the charges against Yusef of Arimathea, and you have all heard them proved here, today. Pilate, I demand justice!"

But now it was Pilate's turn to be angry. "Caiaphas, you will not touch this man!" he yelled, and it seemed the marble pillars shook with his vehemence. "Already, one innocent man has died for your jealousy. I will not assist you in making a second. I must insist that you leave this place at once. And if I learn that my servant Joseph is harmed, if I should even hear that he has met with an accident, you yourself shall pay with your head!"

"Your Excellency—" began Caiaphas.

"Enough!" cried Pilate. "I have spoken, and I have spoken with the voice of Tiberius Caesar! Be gone from this place!"

The priests and scribes scurried from Pilate's presence like scolded dogs. Nicodemus went last. "Yusef," he said, "let us talk, when we both have leisure."

I nodded, and stood alone before Pontius Pilate, waiting for him to speak. He was quivering with wrath, I could see, and needed a little time to calm down. At last, he looked at me and spoke. "Somebody," he said, "has removed the body of Jesus from the tomb into which you placed it. Since it was your tomb, and you requested his body, and you interred it, you are the prime suspect. Joseph, you have been a valuable servant to me, and your advice has been good, but I swear, if you removed that body, I shall see you crucified as your friend Jesus was!"

"It would be my honour to share my Master's death," I replied. "But by the God of my fathers, I did nothing to Yeshua's body but inter it. If it has been stolen, it is by another; if it has arisen, then He was indeed the Messiah."

"Let me be frank with you, Joseph," said Pilate, stepping up close to me. "I don't believe all this nonsense about the Christ. I'm a politician. And whether Jesus was the Christ or the Son of God Himself, I don't care—the disappearance of his body will cause revolution." He gave an ironic snort. "Didn't he once say, 'I come not to bring peace, but a sword?'" I nodded. "Find his body, Joseph, and bring me the names of the conspirators who removed it. And carry out this order as if your life depended on it—for it does."

I inclined my head, and walked out of the palace. When I got outside, I drew some water from a well, dashed it over my face, drank long and deep, and thought about what I should do.

Nicodemus might know something, I thought. Then there was John, and Kephas, and Mary, Yeshua's mother. I might seek them out. Nicodemus would know where to find them.

And yet, part of me hoped that it was futile. Part of me wondered if Yeshua had not indeed risen from the dead. There were rumours that a man called Lazarus had been restored to life after he had died and been placed into a tomb. And one of Pilate's centurions claimed that Yeshua had restored life to his servant. But who was there to restore life to Him who restored life?

I set off in search of Nicodemus.

I had not gone far when a pair of temple guards stepped out in front of me. Their spears were leveled at my breast. I turned to flee, but another pair had cut off my retreat.

The next thing I knew, the butt of a spear came crashing into the backs of my knees, and I fell over backwards. Pain exploded in my side as one of the guards kicked me. Then another foot smashed into my ribs, one into my groin, and another into my face. That was the last thing I remember, for at that point, I passed out.

XXXII

When I came to myself, I found that I was in the most filthy, squalid conditions imaginable. It was a prison cell, the only contents of which were a hard bed with moth-eaten sheets and a bucket. The light came from far over my head. I could see blue sky through a grating, but I could not reach it. The place smelled of rot and rodents.

At first, I rattled my door and called for my jailer, but no one came, and I was reduced to silence, sitting on the bed, rubbing my bruises, and wondering who had brought me here.

Five times the sun brightened the slab of light above me; five times, I saw stars stab the veil of night; but it seemed that ages of the world passed in the filth and excrement. At last, however, I heard footsteps, and saw the glimmer of torchlight. A key rattled in the lock, and the hinges creaked as the door swung open. Caiaphas stood there, his nose wrinkled in distaste.

I stood up, my fists clenched at my side. "Release me," I said.

"No doubt you think that your friendship with the Gentile governor is enough to secure your release," answered Caiaphas calmly, his voice muffled for he held his hand in front of his face to fend off the stink. "Pilate thinks you have gone on a journey to Arimathea."

"What do you want?"

"The body of Yeshua," replied Caiaphas.

"I placed it in my own tomb," I said. "If it is no longer there, I do not know where it can be found."

"I don't want to kill you, Yusef," Caiaphas said. "After all, Pilate wants you alive, and I wouldn't want to offend Pilate. The reason you are not dead is that I would like to be able to produce you, should Pilate insist. But don't think you can escape from this place by any means other than revealing to me the location of the body of Yeshua the heretic. Eventually, Pilate will forget about you. Eventually, and probably quite soon, Pilate will be replaced. There is no hope for you, save telling me the truth about the whereabouts of the body of this false prophet."

"Then here I must remain in patience," I said, "for I cannot tell you what you want to know."

"Very well," said Caiaphas and, turning on his heel, left the prison cell.

And I remained in the stench and the refuse, I don't know how long. I know at least one night passed, for the light above my head was reduced to blackness, and I looked with longing on the stars that pricked the firmament, utterly beyond my reach.

And then, in the midst of the night, a great light suddenly filled my cell, and I scrambled to my feet.

There, standing before me, was Yeshua; and in His hands was the cup in which I had collected His blood.

I fell to my knees at once, my heart gripped with fear. "My Lord!" I cried out.

But Yeshua raised me up. "Yusef, Yusef, do not be afraid," He said.

"My Lord," I said, "I thought you were dead."

"I was, Yusef. Behold." And He showed me His hands, the wrists drilled through by the nails of the crucifixion, and His feet likewise, and a great wound in His side, where a centurion had stabbed Him to prevent Him from lingering on into the Sabbath. "The blood of the sinless one has been shed, but death had no power over him," Yeshua explained. "Follow me, for my path leads to eternal life."

"What do you wish me to do, my Lord?" I asked.

Yeshua held out the cup to me, and I took it. "Drink," He said.

I looked down at the contents of the cup. "Lord," I said, "this is your blood."

"Did I not say, whoever eats my flesh and drinks my blood will know eternal life?"

"But I did not think—"

"You did not think I meant it?" A smile played over His lips. "Do not fear. Love. Trust. Drink."

I looked down at the cup, and saw that it did not appear to be blood any more, but wine, and I drank deeply. Afterwards, I felt refreshed, as if I had awoken after long sleep.

"This I have done for you," said Yeshua. "This is my blood and my body. I have given it to you under the appearance of wine and bread, for no man should grow happy to drink the blood and eat the flesh of his fellow. And yet, it must be done."

"I do not understand, Lord," I said. "Why?"

"Now I am in you, and I have made the sacrifice that reverses death. As death had no power over me, so now you, united with me, cannot die, but will live for ever."

"I will never die?"

"The flesh must die, Yusef, but the spirit will live on. And the day will come when my Father in Heaven will raise up a new body for you, as He has this for me."

"What must I do, Lord?"

"Take the Grail," said Yeshua, putting my hands around the cup. "Return it to the people who wrought it. Because of what you have done, it is now the greatest treasure they could possess. Lead that people out of darkness, Yusef, and into my light."

He held my head in His hands, and said, "Rest now, Yusef, for you have need of much strength." He kissed me on the forehead, and I fell into a deep sleep.

When I woke up, I was still in the cell, with blue light filtering down to me from far above. He was not with me, and His light had gone. A moment later, though, I heard a key in the lock, and a magnificently-dressed Roman entered my cell.

"My name is Vespasian," he said, "and long have I sought you, Joseph."

* * *

“Vespasian!” cried Merlin in surprise.

“Yes, the Emperor of Rome,” answered Joseph.

“Is he emperor, then?” said Merlin. “I met a legate called Vespasian once, a good man, though my enemy. He commanded the forces that defeated us at Mai Dun. Could it be the same man?”

“Emperor Vespasian was a legate during the invasion of this island,” answered Joseph.

“I prophesied to him,” Merlin remembered, frowning. “I told him his son would be healed by . . . I don’t remember.”

“His son had fallen sick indeed,” Joseph confirmed, “for he had contracted leprosy. None of the healers of Rome, skilled Greeks learned in the lore of Galen, could cure his disease. Then, one day, Vespasian heard from a merchant that there had been a great healer in Judea, a man called Yeshua, who healed miraculously even though he had been crucified, many years before.”

“Many years before?” said Merlin in surprise.

“Yes, many years before. It was not days, not even years, but decades that I spent in my cell, though it all passed for me as one sleep—that was one of the blessings that my Lord Yeshua bestowed upon me through the miracle of the Grail.

“Vespasian himself came to Judea, seeking any relic of Yeshua that might assist him in the healing of his son. He wanted, for one thing, to properly inter Yeshua’s body, and so he sought me out, thinking that I knew its whereabouts. It was a long search, for no one was alive who could remember where I was imprisoned, and Vespasian grew wrathful, but at last he learned where I had been bestowed, and he came to me and released me.

“And how the world had changed while I had slept in the arms of my Lord! Jerusalem had been destroyed, its people wiped out or scattered. Forty years, I learned, had passed—like the forty years my people had spent in the desert with Moses, after they had been freed from slavery in Egypt.

Everyone I knew was dead. But I went with Vespasian to Rome, and there I lifted the Grail to his son's lips, and cured him of his disease."

"That's what I saw," said Merlin, "all those years ago."

"You have a gift," observed Joseph with a smile, "a blessing from the Lord."

"And then you came here?" Merlin prompted him.

Joseph nodded. "This is the home of the Grail. Here it was fashioned, years and years ago, and here it returns to rest, and it is become the master of all the treasures of this island. I did not come alone—I brought with me some of my countrymen, whom I met in Judea or Rome, and their families. We took ship with a merchant." Joseph smiled. "It gladdened my heart, to feel the boards churning with the waves beneath my feet! It was a desire that had long been upon me, to see strange lands! I thought I might never live to travel. But all things are possible to the Lord. We came at length to this island, and I knew that this was where I would stay. And here we have been ever since, here on the island of Corbenic."

For a great length of time, no one spoke. Merlin wasn't even thinking about Joseph's story. He was enjoying the warmth of the sun on his skin, the deep green of the wooded shade across the lake, the silver plumage of a heron that stood on one leg among the reeds.

"Do you understand now, Merlin?" asked Joseph.

"No," answered Merlin, "but I don't think it matters. I feel very much at peace. I could stay in a place like this. I could stay among friends like these." Merlin looked across at Pelles. "You say the Morforwyn have returned?"

Pelles nodded. "The Ladies of the Lake have returned," he said. "You will see them, soon, though they come and go as they please and will not be bidden."

Merlin stretched out on the grass. The sun lay like warm velvet on his arms and face. "What must I do?" he wondered.

“Do?” repeated Joseph. “Before you can do anything of any value, you must first learn who you are. Stay with us, Merlin, and at length, your path will become clear to you.”

“I have been seeking a path all my life,” said Merlin.

“Cease your search, and a way will open.”

But Merlin was asleep.

* * *

Over the next few weeks, Merlin got to know the other members of the community well. There were Britons among them, but most had come with Joseph from Judea, and their names were strange upon Merlin’s tongue—Rachel and Leah, the Grail Maidens, and Shakhr and his sister, Tumadir, Judith, Uzziah, Esther, Manasseh, Sarah, Eliakim.

Merlin’s recovery, after his initial healing, seemed slow and by infinitely small degrees. Dawn never seemed to bring a radical improvement in his health. He slowly resigned himself to the fact that he was getting old. When he passed by a looking-glass once, he noticed that his hair was now snow-white, his beard growing long, his face seamed with wrinkles, and deep shadows gathering under his eyes. He looked more closely. Ah, but his eyes! he noticed. They were still bright. They had lost none of their lustre. Ten years of insanity had not dulled them.

Some of his time he spent in contemplation, and he thought of his life and losses. He knew his mother must be dead by now, and he had seen the sweetheart of his youth fall in battle. No son remained to him, and no daughters. No friend or relative from before his illness survived save Pelles. There was no one left who would call him Emrys. Now he truly was Merlin.

But he thought too of the future. There was that within him that bade him not to despair of finding Excalibur. There would be a king, the philosopher king, as he had suspected all those years ago, after his sojourn with Morfryn. At night, he dreamed of the philosopher king—his hair brown, his eyes blue as the ocean, he saw the boy standing upon an island on a dark sea, the sword above his head. After one such dream, he sat upright in bed, the cold air prickling his face, his chest heaving. He muttered to himself, "Surely God will not allow me to die before I have achieved this quest!"

The days passed, and summer grew to fullness, and Merlin talked with the followers of the Christ, and ate with them and, at length, began to worship with them. He even allowed Joseph to baptize him, immersing him in the waters of the fenlands as, they said, Yeshua had been immersed in the waters of the River Jordan. He did not feel any different after the ritual was over, but he was aware, in his inmost soul, that his relationship with the world was changing. It was as if his soul were inclining somewhere new—as if it were returning home.

But one thing troubled him, and one evening, he mentioned it to Pelles.

"You say that the door to Avalon has been opened now," he said. "How can this be, if the gods of old are false?"

"When our Lord walked upon the earth," replied Pelles, "He told Joseph and his people that He came not to abolish the Law, but to fulfill it. Likewise, He has come not to abolish the old gods, but to fulfill their meaning and their mission."

"Their mission?"

"Nothing is lost," said Pelles. "The gods of old were placed here by the One God, and their story is concluded by Yeshua. There will come a time, perhaps, when the Morforwyn mix no longer with men; then, perhaps, men will begin to speak differently, unjustly, about them, as it is the custom of men to speak unjustly of those things about which they have only a dim memory. But for now, it is well to remember that there is nothing ill or well about the Morforwyn. Being placed in the world, they have the power for either good or evil, and only as they have chosen are they good or evil themselves. In that, they are no different from men."

"Then I am troubled, father," said Merlin. "In what way *are* they different from men?"

Pelles smiled. "Is it not enough that they do not grow old?" he asked.

Merlin pondered these words long, and at last, he said, "Shall I ever meet them?"

"They have their own business to attend to," said Pelles. "But I think you will."

Merlin rose from his bench and walked across the room to the window. He still leaned upon a stick, though he was almost whole by now. Outside, the trees were turning gold, and the sky was dark with approaching night.

"The Romans are on the move again," said Merlin. He could not see beyond the trees, and yet he could, dimly: there were shapes moving, columns of men wearing Imperial scarlet, great square buildings over which flew the golden eagles of Rome. "The world is passing me by, father," Merlin said quietly. "I grow old, and have achieved nothing. Britonnic fortresses in the North and in southern Cambria now bear Roman names, and are called cities. Caermyrddin, they tell me, is now the Imperial sea-port of Moridunum. I hear what Joseph says, and the others that came with him from Judea, and his words are good. This is the way to live a life: turn the other cheek, love your neighbour. A man who does this is a good man. But the world is not Christian, and my land is enslaved, and I sit here doing nothing, and the time will come, soon, when I am too old to travel far from the hearth-fire, too old to wield a sword."

"There are greater skills than sword-wielding," observed Pelles.

Merlin smiled, and drew the shutters closed. "I beg your pardon, father," he said. "I was whining."

"Come," said Pelles, rising from his seat, "let us join the others. "Sion, they tell me, is opening a cask of mead this evening. We Britons, I think, can show these Judeans a thing or two about winemaking!"

He and Merlin left their hut together, and made their way to the hall where they ate and celebrated as a community. Pelles walked a little ahead of Merlin, hobbling with his accustomed limp. For the first time, Merlin began to marvel at his father. Quickly, he performed a calculation in his mind, and concluded that Pelles was somewhere between seventy and eighty summers old. And yet here he was, limping along beside him, as sprightly as a man in his prime.

Someone was running towards them from the assembly hall. It was Rachel, one of the Grail maidens, whose quiet beauty Merlin much admired. Her dress, of the purest white, seemed to glow in the twilight as she drew to a halt before them.

"Come, quickly," she said. "The Morforwyn are here!"

XXXIII

Merlin and Pelles hurried down the grassy slope after Rachel. The night was chilly, the air crisp and cold. In the rest of Britain, it was drawing close to Samhain.

"Behold!" said Pelles.

Merlin looked ahead. Coming towards them across the lawn were six of the most beautiful women he had ever seen. They moved as if upon air, and their garments of white samite moved as if in the breeze of faraway countries. There seemed always a light playing about them, and power and joy were in their faces.

A crowd had gathered about the Ladies of the Lake, and the voices rose to meet Merlin and Pelles. But the chief of the Ladies raised her eyes, blue as a summer sky, and fixed them on Merlin.

Argante came forward to meet him, and Merlin threw himself flat on his face before her, his arms outstretched in a posture of obeisance.

"Merlin," Joseph of Arimathea chided him gently, "arise, and do not fear these messengers of the living God!"

His feelings whirling about in his chest, Merlin scrambled to his feet and faced the Morforwyn as they approached. It was hard to remain upright —their mere presence commanded submission.

"Merlin Emrys," said Argante, chief of the Ladies of the Lake, "long have I desired to speak with you, but our imprisonment has prevented me."

"Imprisonment, my lady?" repeated Merlin.

Argante exchanged a glance with Pelles that Merlin could not fathom. "Aye, imprisonment. It was my word. Will you walk with me, Merlin?"

Together, they walked off up the gentle incline towards the community of Corbenic. Merlin felt like a terrier, trotting to keep up with the strides of a wolf-hound. He could not take his eyes from her face. She seemed to glow, with a light that came from within her. Her golden hair wafted out behind her like a train borne by invisible attendants.

All at once, Argante, Queen of the Morforwyn, turned to Merlin and said, "What was dim is now lit, is it not?"

Merlin hung his head. "Many things are still obscure to me, my lady."

"More than a thousand years have passed," said Argante, "since Brutus came to these shores, and took from my hands Excalibur, the sword of kings. In all that time, we had faith that meaning would be given to our deeds, and now it has."

"So long, lady!" said Merlin in an awed voice. "Can it be you have waited so long?"

"We have, Merlin. And the years have weighed upon us. Time brings grief to all, even those who do not age. Perhaps especially to us."

Merlin said nothing. Argante gazed upon him, holding him in the twin lights of her blue eyes while moments, years, whole ages seemed to pass. Merlin felt the weight of many centuries pressing upon his shoulders while those eyes fixed him. Centuries of grief, of separation. It occurred to him for the first time that it might not be agreeable to live for ever.

"The world has changed," said Argante, "in the creeping years since we were forbidden entry into it. Those who fathered our sons and daughters lie in their long sleep."

"But now you have returned, my lady," observed Merlin. "What shall you do?"

"Look to the future, Merlin," the Lady of the Lake urged him. "Tell me what you see."

Merlin closed his eyes. "I see a child," he said. "He is the son of a king, and raised amid the lakes and streams of the fenlands." Merlin frowned. "No, there are two children. This other is in the arms of an old man, who hurries with him away from a dark fortress." He opened his eyes.

Argante smiled. "There are deeds enough for all of us, Merlin," she said, "but they will take long to accomplish, by the account of men."

“I grow old, Lady Argante,” said Merlin. “My time is surely growing short.”

Argante’s smile remained, but took on a sad cast. She said, “Men are but the creatures of an hour. But you will complete your task, will you not?”

Merlin did not answer at once, but turned the eyes of his mind inward, to contemplate his own heart. At last, he said, “Yes, my lady. I shall complete my task. But how and when are matters dark to me.”

“All that matters is that you undertake them,” Argante told him. “Let Him who is above all determine the outcome.”

Merlin gave a bashful smile. “You are hardly what I thought you would be,” he said. “I have been seeking you all my life, and I expected you to be different.”

“How?” asked the Lady of the Lake.

Merlin searched for the words, but they did not come, and he ended up saying, “I don’t know. I don’t think I ever had an idea of what you would be like. I didn’t even have a false idea. My thoughts were unformed, like the ocean. But you are surprising to me, and I don’t know why that should be.”

All of a sudden, Merlin’s whole frame seemed weighed down. He felt as if his limbs would no longer support him, and he sank to the ground, gazing out over the water to the trees of the opposite shore. “O my lady!” he cried, “will I ever find Excalibur?”

Argante did not reply, but continued to look upon Merlin. Feeling the warmth of her eyes, Merlin returned her gaze. It seemed to hold him in its twin beams, and the passage of time seemed to hold no meaning.

“You have been with my sister in her realm,” Argante observed, “but you have never seen mine.” Merlin dropped his eyes, but Argante reached down and raised him to his feet so that she could look through his eyes and into his soul once more. “There should be no guilt in this,” she reassured him, “for the way to my realm was closed but lately. But come now, and see what *I* offer.”

She turned and led him onwards, up the slope, and Merlin followed after. But a moment later, his step faltered. The sky and the grass seemed to shimmer about him, as if two worlds had slid past one another, mixing like the wakes of two ships bound for different ports whose voyages intersected each other.

Merlin looked around in wonder. Before him stood a great walled city, at the foot of which were apple trees in blossom. Within the city walls, roofs and towers reached for the heavens. Beneath Merlin's feet was a path, and it led to massive silver gates, etched with the spreading designs of apple trees beneath starry skies. To his left and right, he could see other paths meeting his own, and all leading to the gates of silver.

"Where is this?" he asked.

Argante turned to face him, and framed by the glorious scene, she seemed even more beautiful than before. "This is Avalon," she said, "the blessed island of the Morforwyn. Look well upon it, Merlin Emrys, for this is the pattern of the realm you shall forge in Britain, a realm that men will never forget."

Merlin dropped to one knee, not as a worshiper before a god, but as a warrior before his queen. "I am at your command, my lady," he said. "What would you have me do?"

Argante moved in close to Merlin, and her smile was like the rays of the sun. "Return to your quest," she said, "and pay no heed to my sister's empty promises."

"I shall do it at once, my lady!" cried Merlin, leaping to his feet.

But Argante laughed, a musical sound like a bourn at the spring thaw. "Merlin Emrys," she said, "well have you been chosen. But this is not a quest to be rushed into, like a child leaping into a pond, even after so many years. What will you do?"

Merlin pondered the question a moment, then answered, "I think I shall attempt to pick up the threads in Afallach."

"The Romans left little undestroyed in Afallach," observed the Lady of the Lake.

“But there may be other things left, which will set my feet on the right path, other clues. And the Roman destruction may have unearthed that which the druids forbade me to see—books, clues. And—” Merlin broke off. He wondered what it was he was going to say. At last, he concluded, “And I should like to look out one last time, now, from the crest of the Sacred Hill. So much has changed, my lady—I feel I would be able to see far more.”

“Arise, Merlin Emrys,” said Argante, lifting him to his feet so that he stood, doting, before her. “Stay a little with Joseph and Pelles before you leave upon this quest, for there is much you can learn from them. Before a man can accomplish the great deeds of his life, he must understand himself; before he can understand himself, he must understand his time; before his time, he must understand his world. And much has been missing from your world—the greatest part of it, perhaps. The Sight has shown you the way, but dimly. So stay a little while in Corbenic. Speak with Joseph. Speak with me. Speak with your father. Learn, and put your knowledge to use in your quest.” She paused, and looked at him more closely. “How do you feel?” she asked.

“Young,” answered Merlin at once. “I am not, I know, but I feel young, as if I could stand alone against the forces of evil and overthrow them all!”

Again, Argante’s musical laugh. “Sweet Merlin,” she said, “You feel as we all do, now that Corbenic and Avalon have come together. This release of ours has shown us all the path that we must take. Come, let us return to Corbenic.”

In a moment, they were back on Pelles’ island, the new community behind them, the green slope down to the water at their feet.

“What do you know of the Grail, my lady?” asked Merlin. “Is this the land in which it was fashioned?”

“It is,” answered she. “And many are the years since it was fashioned, and its maker thought little as he wrought it on its future greatness, for it has become the master of all the Treasures of the Island of the Mighty.”

Merlin’s brow furrowed. “Why then must I seek Excalibur?” he asked.

"Not Excalibur alone," replied Argante, "but all the treasures must be restored. There is one more age of greatness for the men of the Island of the Mighty ere night falls. And when the time comes, the Grail will lead all the treasures away from the Island of the Mighty, and the new age will have begun."

"The new age?"

Argante breathed in deeply through her nose, as if drinking in the fragrance of the sweetest of roses. "The old age, the age of the Morforwyn, is passing away. Can you not tell? We are in our twilight, Merlin. The age is about to begin of the God who became man. For a while, a short while, we will be here together—the Grail *and* Excalibur, Yeshua *and* Argante; and then the Morforwyn must take their treasures beyond the world. Why do you weep, Merlin?"

"I weep for the age that is passing, madam," answered Merlin.

"Do not grieve; it is a matter of honour when a girl becomes a woman, or a boy a man. These things must be. And for us, this is a return home, a rest at last from the weary matters of this turbulent world. But come, now, let us rejoin the pale wanderer and your father, and rejoice that we have seen these days, for there is a glory to come!"

They walked together for a few moments down the slope. The sun was setting, and clouds of midges hung in the air over the reeds. Merlin said, "My lady, you did not answer my question. Will I ever find Excalibur, think you?"

"The sword is for the king," answered Argante. "It is for him to bear. Seek you out the king, and let *him* find it."

And Merlin felt as if he had emerged from darkness into light.

* * *

Merlin intended to leave almost straight away, but in the community of Corbenic he knew a deep satisfaction such as had been missing from his life until then, and he could not bring himself to go. He brought in the harvest with them, fished with his father, traded with the fenlanders and renewed his acquaintance with King Seddech, though Dydwch had died some time ago. He did not spend much of his time alone, and was not often troubled with visions. But when he had been with the community for a little over two years, he began to feel restless, and he sat long in the midst of the apple grove of Corbenic, willing visions to come to him and show him the way to find the High King. But nothing came, and the months passed by, and another winter closed in, and on the darkest night of winter, when preparations were underway to commemorate the birth of Yeshua, Merlin resolved to be gone in the springtime. The next morning—a day of blue skies and fresh snow, and crisp air between—he shared his decision with his father.

To his surprise, Pelles nodded. "I think you are ready, my son," he said.

"I had thought you wanted me to stay," said Merlin, puzzled.

"It was to meet Joseph, and hear the good news of the God-Man, and to welcome Argante and the Morforwyn when they were released, that I wanted you to stay. But now, it is time for you to walk the path you long have sought."

Even so, Merlin stayed through the next summer, for it seemed good to him to land fish with his father and talk long into the night with Argante and Tylweth and the Ladies of the Lake. He helped the community with their harvest, and it was not until the end of summer, when the leaves were beginning to look pale and brittle upon the branches, that Merlin bade farewell to Joseph and Pelles and the Christian community of Corbenic.

"Farewell to you, Merlin," said Joseph.

"And to you also," said Merlin, embracing him and his father next. He drew a deep breath. "I shall miss the merry laughter of this place," he reflected.

"Then you must take the joy that has been in your heart here with you wherever you go," said Joseph.

Merlin gave a short sigh. "I fear," he said, "that this joy will seldom make me welcome amongst men."

Joseph nodded sadly. "Alas, there is a kind of man abroad who cannot share a joy, but must crush it. But that does not diminish our joy, nor still our laughter."

"Such a one is Morgana," added Pelles. "Beware of her, Merlin. She is a fearsome adversary."

"Yet fear her neither," interjected Joseph. "You have a Lord now who has banished fear, and replaced it with love."

Merlin laughed. "I shall seek to reconcile your various words of advice," he said, "and I shall return when I may."

"Go, then," said Joseph, "and God go with you."

Merlin stepped into his coracle, struck out with his paddle, and soon the Christian community of Corbenic was lost to sight.

It took Merlin two days to reach the edge of the fens, and a further day to find a road. Once upon it, he made his way north, stopping in the city of Corinium that night. All places were named now in the Roman fashion—when he mentioned Caer Lloyw, no one seemed to understand him. Even to the native Britons, it had become Glevum.

He was late setting out the next morning, for he had to buy some provisions, and so he did not reach Glevum that day. When night fell, he left the road and curled up under a hawthorn bush, pulling his cloak over him for a blanket. The night air was cool, but not cold, and Merlin slumbered drowsily, warm under the wool of his cloak, while overhead, the fiery pageant of the stars danced majestically through the night.

At the darkest hour of the night, he awoke suddenly. The stars were different from when he had gone to sleep. All drowsiness seemed to have drained from him, leaving his senses as sharp as a needle. He sat up and looked about him. At first, he could see nothing, and hear nothing.

Then, from quite close by, he heard the low purring of a large cat.

A moment later, someone struck a flint and lit a torch. In the orange light, Merlin saw a woman, flanked by men in black and red form-fitting clothing. The woman walked towards Merlin, her eyes half shut, and she lowered herself beside him.

Morgana.

XXXIV

No one spoke for a long time. The two men with her bore torches, and the orange light played intimate games along the deep line of shadow between her breasts. The outline of her leg, curving slightly towards the thigh, was picked out by a crimson glow along her dark silk dress. Her eyes had locked Merlin in their gaze. At last, she said, almost teasingly, "It is long, my Merlin, since last we spoke, is it not?"

Merlin felt a black miasma rising in him, and fought to push it down. It seemed to have claws, and to be gripping his heart with piercing talons. He rubbed his chest, saying, "I have been busy, my lady."

"Yes, I know," answered Morgana. "Though we have not spoken, I learn many things about you. I know, for example, about those humiliating years of madness that you spent wandering about in the wild, naked, with your beard covering your manhood. And I know that you fought with Boudicea against the Romans—that was foolish, by the way. How could that silly girl ever have prevailed without Excalibur?" Morgana shook her head in pity, or rather an insolent mockery of it. Merlin felt a new sensation in his chest—a convulsion, as if his body were in rebellion against the sentiments Morgana was feigning. "Now, what else was there? Ah yes, I know about the time you spent in Morgannawg, and how you fled from Afallach, and under what compulsion, and I know you murdered the queen of Cameliard. Now, *that* was a deed of note!"

"Why do you mock me, lady?" demanded Merlin with sudden vehemence. He leaped to his feet and faced her, breathing heavily. She seemed to be some subterranean goddess, thrusting up through the rocky earth to wreak mischief upon its inhabitants.

Merlin took a step backwards, but planted his feet firmly, ready for whatever she could throw at him.

Morgana threw her shoulders back. The wind tugged at the silken fabric of her dress, which streamed out behind her body, so that the curve of her breasts, the sweep of her waist, the insides of her thighs were picked out in sharp relief, illuminated by the torches. Merlin felt as if he were on the edge of a precipice and she at the bottom, coaxing him on: the long, ticklish fingers of gravity were pulling him gently but remorselessly towards her. To sink into her embrace—how easy it would be! How delightful to feel her body folding about him, wrapping him up and drawing him into her warmth! Merlin's breathing became shallow, his fingers unclenched and reached out towards her.

"Mock you?" said Morgana. She took two paces towards him, her hips sliding under the silk. "How should I mock you? You have proved your worthiness by this deed, and many others. You are worthy of my bed, and for the throne beside mine!"

"My lady," stammered Merlin, "surely honours me more than I can ever deserve."

Morgana closed in. She placed her hands upon his chest, slid them up and around his neck, her eyes holding him ever in their gaze. He followed the curve of her dark eyebrows outwards and around the eyes, along the high cheekbones, picked out with soft shadows, to the lips, parted and moist. Her thighs closed with his, her breasts were soft against his chest.

"Be like us," said Morgana. "The gift is mine to grant you of undying life, as I have these good men. One of them is Kenen, king of Morgannawg, whom you know; but the other fought beside great Alexander in Asia. Think of what you could do, had you this gift! Kiss me, love me, and take all that I can give you. Without any of these silly worries about death stealing upon you unawares, think what quests you could accomplish! Why, you yourself could carry Excalibur against these Roman invaders! Accept the kiss of the goddess."

She paused; her lips were open slightly, and he could see her tongue within, poised. He began to cock his head, ready his own lips. He looked up into her eyes.

They were black and empty, like pits from which men had quarried all that could be brought. That was the abyss into which Merlin was being drawn! Night, starless and without end, a trackless wilderness, stretching through gloomy darkness to the edge of time and space.

But there, above the gloom, shone a piercing light. Merlin lifted his eyes and saw the Grail, and all the wasteland was lit up with its radiance. The edge tipped, and the blood of the sacrifice spilled onto the world, and green life shot forth in abundance.

Suddenly, it became easy. Morgana and all her vain promises were exposed before him. He reached up and unlaced her hands. "Undying life," he said, "but perpetual torture. Is that what you want for me, Morgana? And if our bodies came together here, but here and in this place, what then? Our bodies would be satisfied, but what soul could call itself delighted by a loveless embrace? For there is no love in you, and a life stretched out along all time, but devoid of love, is a living death. I would not be what you are for a host of swords. Silly girl though she was, Boudicea was the woman I loved, and I shall never love another. If I lived for ever, as you promise me, I should but have the longer to regret her passing."

"Folly!" spat Morgana. "Naught but folly! Sentimental rubbish! Boudicea is in her grave. It is the worms that enjoy that delicate body of hers now, not you. You must move in the real world, Merlin, here and now, as you say. Our need for Excalibur is real. With your knowledge and my power we could easily find the sword, and the Island of the Mighty would be whole again, and not a province of the Empire."

"I will speak with you no longer," said Merlin, stooping to pick up his harp and sword. "There can be no agreement between us."

"Greater men than you have accepted the gift of my body," said Morgana, "but it is surely nothing but folly to reject my offered help!"

Merlin slung the harp over his shoulder and fitted the sword into its sheath. He held his traveling cloak over his arm. His eyes flitted over to the men who had arrived with her.

"My lord Kenen," said Merlin, "what have you done to prove yourself worthy of the love of the queen of Annwn? I killed a sad old woman, who had grown tired of a life of murder and betrayal. To what depths of conduct have you stooped?"

"Kin slaying," purred Kenen. "The murther of a brother, and the murther of a father. The father accounteth but little—he was dying whether I would or no. But I did it for the act itself."

Merlin turned back to Morgana. "Do to me what you will, Morgana," he said. "My soul's my own. I would not be as you are, even if I could buy Britain's freedom with it."

Morgana gave a harsh laugh. "Can he who has the Sight so lack vision?" she mocked. "You reject this help because you do not see what it can do for you, even as you reject my body for the mere memory of the skinny loins of that Cambrian slut."

Merlin clenched his fists and his teeth. He could feel his nails digging into his palms. But he did not move. He saw her now for what she was: a tawdry, unlovely, barren, miserable, wretched shell of a woman, desperate to stretch out an existence that gave no joy, nor even any real pleasure.

"Had I the power, lady," said Merlin, "I should take you out of your misery and our danger." He gritted his teeth and squared his shoulders. "Since I have not, do what you must to me: kill me, and be swift about it."

"*I* kill you?" said Morgana. "Nay, my dear Merlin. Out of love for my followers, I grant the greatest of honours to them. Kenen!" He stepped forward smartly, drawing his thin sword as he did so. "Your duty calls."

"Duty, my lady?" said Kenen, flexing his sword blade in his hands. "Nay, 'tis my pleasure."

Merlin shook his sword so that the sheath flew from it, and crouched into a ward. Kenen's teeth flashed in a grin. His poise was perfect, like an illustration from a manual: his sword arm extended, the blade sloping across his body, his other hand out for balance, his knees bent slightly for mobility backwards and forwards.

"What say you, Merlin?" purred Kenen. "Come, bird, come."

Merlin shook his head. “I seek no battle,” he said. “It is you must come to me.”

Kenen lunged, a smart movement, his left arm flicking backwards as the blade flashed forward. Merlin dodged to his right, parried, and held the blade a moment. But his blade was heavier than Kenen’s, and he could not move so quickly. In a second, Kenen had danced out of the engagement. Merlin stepped forward, extending his sword as he did so. But Kenen whirled around and flicked the point of his sword across Merlin’s upper arm. Merlin cursed, retracted his blade, and retreated a few steps.

But Kenen did not allow him a respite. He lunged again, the orange glow from the torch outlining his dark silhouette. Merlin parried, but before he could counter-attack, Kenen had disengaged and thrust again. Merlin defended. Kenen thrust again, and again, and again, and all the time, Merlin retreated from him.

Finally, Kenen feinted a low attack, and Merlin’s blade swept down to parry on his right, but Kenen’s sword dipped and rose, and the point pierced the fabric of Merlin’s tunic. He felt the steel pierce his skin, felt its coldness between the muscles over his heart. He gasped, and stood for a moment, stilled with shock.

Kenen withdrew the point and stepped back. Reaching into a pocket, he took out a lace kerchief and wiped the blood from his blade before sliding it back into the sheath.

Merlin’s hand fluttered up to his chest, like a wounded butterfly. He looked down at a dark stain on his fingers. His legs felt weak. He took a few tottering steps towards the backs of Kenen and Morgana, but he could go no further. He pitched forward onto his face beside the hawthorn bush, and his fingers clutched the cold earth.

* * *

It was dark and cold in the cave. The clammy breath of a subterranean god sighed constantly over him. Merlin scrambled to his feet. The pain in his shoulder was a dull throb. Outside the cave, through the craggy mouth, he could see stars, and he knew that Gwelydd the Arch-druid awaited him there with his acolyte, their cervine mounts pawing the ground or tossing their great antlers at the moon.

Why had he entered the cave? wondered Merlin. Why had he yielded? There was a chattering all about him, like the rattle of dry bones, words that were no more than wind over fields of corpses.

"Come and rest," said a voice, deep, rising from within the earth. "You are old, and have walked for many years along many paths. You have lost all those whom you love. Now it is time for you to join them. Come and rest."

Merlin looked down at his hands. They were not withered, but neither did they possess the plumpness of youth. And veins stood out sharply under the skin. The hairs that covered the backs, all the way up to the first knuckle-joints, were white. With a sigh, Merlin knew that Gwelydd had died, an old man, and that the acolyte with him had most likely been cut down by one of Suetonius Paulinus' soldiers.

"This is the way that all go at last," said the voice; and Merlin was uncertain whether the voice came from somewhere in the cave or beyond it—or even from within himself. "Set down your burden, and rest. Join those who have come before you."

The weariness of the journey came suddenly over Merlin, and it seemed an easy thing to just lie down and let unconsciousness overwhelm him. "Who would care?" he wondered. "Who would even know?"

Merlin sank to his knees but, even as he did so, he caught sight of the panorama of stars outside the cave. One of them in particular was brighter than the others: bright and strong and moving, ever so slightly, across the sky. Curious, Merlin rose and walked to the mouth of the cave.

* * *

Merlin opened his eyes, and found that he was lying on his back, covered with the scarlet cloak of a Roman soldier. The wooden floor beneath him was moving, and he could hear the creaking boards of a wagon as it rumbled along a paved causeway. Over his head, Merlin could see a white canvas canopy. He was surrounded by various pots and pans, axes and adzes, lamps and ladles, basins, bottles, and bowls. Merlin levered himself up on one elbow, but pain shot through his shoulder and he fell back onto the pelt that had been spread upon the floor of the wagon for him.

"Good morrow, friend," said a man's voice. Merlin screwed his head round to look at who had spoken. He sat with his back to Merlin, his eyes fixed on the scrawny backs of the horses that were drawing them along the road. "I hope you were traveling to Glevum, for that is where I am going." He spoke Latin, Merlin noticed, and sounded like a Roman. A small talisman, which Merlin recognized as the Roman god Mithras, dangled from the canopy of the wagon. Merlin mumbled something incoherent in reply to the question. "My name is Martin," said the Roman.

"I am Merlin."

"I am happy to make your acquaintance, Merlin," returned the other. "The fellow who gave you that wound—did he rob you? Or did you travel only with a light burden?"

Merlin cast his mind back over the previous night's events. "I doubt it," he said. "I had nothing to steal, save my sword and my harp."

"Both of which I have recovered," replied Martin. "They lie beside you." Merlin reached out, and his hand found the smooth wood of his harp. "It is most fortunate for you that I happened along," said Martin. "I am no surgeon, but I learned enough, during my years in the legions, to bind up a man's wounds so that he will not bleed to death. But they did not rob you? A curious matter, curious indeed."

Merlin reached up under the cloak and touched the dressing on his wound. He pressed gently, and felt a stab of pain shoot through his chest and shoulder. He gave a sharp intake of breath between clenched teeth. When the pain had ebbed away, he felt a little nauseous.

That blade must have missed my heart by the breadth of a moth's wing! he thought. Does Morgana think then that I am dead? If so, her eyes will be elsewhere, and that is to my advantage.

The cart rumbled on. Outside, Merlin could hear a column of soldiers passing, their boots tramping on the pavement with mechanical unity.

Much may be done, he concluded, as the cart passed through the gates of Glevum and into the city.

* * *

Martin the merchant drew his wagon up at an inn and, while an ostler took care of his horses, he and a boy from the inn helped Merlin up some narrow steps and into a bed in a room at the top of the house. Merlin lay on his back, staring at the ceiling, while outside the door, he could hear the muffled conversation of Martin and the landlord. Merlin didn't try to listen, though he could have heard every word clearly, had he wished. He was planning. He would use the very roads that the Romans had built to get quickly to Afallach. He could be there in a week—less than a week, if he could somehow obtain a horse.

The door opened and Martin entered. He sat on a stool beside Merlin's bed. "I have instructed the landlord's daughter in the changing of your bandages and the washing of your wound. It is deep, and will take at least a week to heal—longer than that to heal properly. In a week, though, you will at least be mobile. I am to remain three days in Glevum, and then I am moving on to Viroconium. I have paid the landlord for your food and board for ten days, however, so you can stay here until you are recovered."

"Why would you do this?" asked Merlin, puzzled.

"Wouldn't anybody?" responded Martin, equally puzzled. "You needed help."

"I would not have expected help from a Roman," said Merlin. He thought to himself, I have killed more Romans than I have spoken to; but he said nothing aloud.

Martin rose from his stool and walked to the window. For a while, he looked out at the busy streets of Glevum. Then he said, "You are an ancient people, whereas we Romans are relatively new. You must be patient with us."

"Patient!" exploded Merlin. "You invaded our land—stole it from us, put our priests and our wives to the sword!"

Martin seemed to be wrestling with some ideas deep down inside of himself. "Invasion and conquest," he said, "are the natural condition of the world. Your ancient heroes, Belin and Brennios, conquered Rome, many centuries ago. At least, so I have heard from Britons with whom I have spoken. But Rome wishes to put an end to the constant cycle of invasion and death."

"It seems like an odd sort of method," remarked Merlin.

Martin returned to the bedside and sat down. "It must seem so to you, now, so soon after our arrival." Martin gave a great sigh. "Oh, Merlin! If only you could see this province, a hundred, two hundred years from now—I think you would see that becoming a part of the Empire was the best thing that ever happened to Britannia. From now on, Rome will protect you from your enemies. And one day, when the Empire is large enough and strong enough, there will be no enemies left."

"I shall not live to see it," said Merlin.

"Neither shall I," replied Martin. "And the chances are that some emperor or other—another Nero or Caligula, the gods forbid—will retard our progress towards that goal. But the goal is nevertheless worth striving for. It's worth striving for, even if we never attain it." He rose. "I go now to eat my supper, but I shall have something sent up for you. If you earn your living by using that harp, I would suggest that you do not return to it for at least three days. In the meantime, rest."

Merlin slept soon after; and in his sleep, he was visited by another vision: the sword Excalibur, buried in stone and water, drawn forth from its long hiding by the philosopher king. But his hair, Merlin noticed, was cropped close in Roman fashion.

XXXV

As Martin had said, he stayed but three days in Glevum, and then began to pack up his wagon to set out upon the road once more. Merlin was able to get about by himself, though Martin refused to let him load up the wagon. So he stood in the doorway of the inn, leaning heavily on a staff, and watching Martin stack his unsold goods and tie them down.

"I wish all the blessings of my people, and of God in Heaven, upon you, Martin," said Merlin. "What you have done for me is no small thing."

Martin looked almost embarrassed at Merlin's words. "It was a small inconvenience, no more than that," he said dismissively. "I have never met a Christian before—it might help me to have your God's good will, in case you are right."

Merlin laughed. "And yet, to me" he said, "your inconvenience means everything—life, instead of death."

"To save a life," replied Martin. "What is that, but what a mother does for her child twenty times a day before it sees its fifth summer? Farewell, Merlin. Should you stay in Glevum two months longer, you shall see me again. I make a great loop, as far east as Ratae, and as far south as Corinium, before I return to Glevum, and there are many stops on the way, many smaller cities and fortresses. So I shall be two months at the least, perhaps more. If you are still here upon my return, I shall look in upon you, and see that you are well. If you have gone already about your business, I wish you well."

Martin shook the reins of his team, and his wagon rattled off along the street towards the north gate. Distant thunder rumbled among the nearby hills, and the first few drops of rain fell in dark, glistening drops on the pavement. Merlin cast his eyes disconsolately up for a second, and then returned to the interior of the inn.

He ventured down into the common room of the inn that night, and earned a few coins by playing his harp. The crowd in there was a mix—Romans rubbed shoulders with native Britons, and Merlin began to learn the songs of the legions. He sang songs of love and lust for the locals, and of sun-drenched southern slopes for the Roman officers, of girls with dark hair and dark eyes, and the blue waters of the Mediterranean, while the rain drummed on the horn-windows and cloaks steamed before the fire. Thus, over the days that followed—dark days, for rain set in and would not release the land from its oppression—Merlin was able to make a living from both peoples.

Some nights, the innkeeper's child, a boy with tawny hair and dark eyes, ran in loops through the crowd in the common room. One of the Roman officers made him a wooden sword, and he brandished it with delight night after night.

"That's a fine child you have," Merlin observed to the innkeeper.

"Aye, that he is," replied the innkeeper. "There's much of his mother in him." Merlin looked up at him, and he could see the pride in his eyes, shining like a beacon on a dark night. Merlin's eye traveled from the innkeeper to the barrels of ale and casks of Gaulish wine, and then back to the innkeeper again.

"Why are you here?" Merlin asked him. "You are not a Briton. Why do you stay in a land that is not your own?"

The innkeeper stirred and rubbed the outside of his thigh. "I came here," he said, "with Vespasian's legion, and I was wounded at Mai Dun, so that my military service was brought to an end there. But I married a Briton, the gods be kind to her soul." He gave a small sigh. "I love this land," he said, "partly for her sake, and partly for my own, but mostly because it's in the blood of my son. I couldn't go back to Gaul. It's a land he's never seen, a tongue he cannot speak, ways he doesn't understand—and no more would I, should I return there after an absence of over thirty years. This is where he belongs—and, because of him, where I belong."

Merlin turned his eyes back to the tousle-headed ruffian, who was exchanging witticisms with a knot of old men.

"That I can understand," he said. "Your boy is the future of Britannia. The future of the Island of the Mighty. Both at once." He drained his cup and retired for the night.

* * *

Within a week of Martin's departure, Merlin was recovered sufficiently that he was not in constant pain, and he began to plan his trip north. He moved about the city in search of the items he would need. Glevum was a different place from Caer Lloyw, and Merlin realized that his memories of the place, now thirty years old, were not much use to him. The Roman military presence was strong—almost every street corner was guarded by a legionnaire, his eyes wary, his grip firm upon his pilum, and the patrols tramped constantly along the streets even after the sun had gone down and the gates had been locked for the night. The streets were as straight as thought, intersected at right angles, and the round houses of the native dwellers were relegated to the unprotected area outside the walls. Within the city, the buildings were square, some made of stone or brick, some of them even two stories, like the inn, and in the centre of the city was the marketplace—except that the citizens called it the *forum*, after the Roman fashion. To Merlin, it seemed like an alien land, and a sadness came upon him, for he did not see how the Island of the Mighty could ever be as it was again.

It was at the forum that he was able to purchase a map. He knew the land, of course, and had traversed it many times. But he knew that the Roman roads would greatly facilitate his journey north, and he pored over the vellum that night by the light of half a dozen candles. He was sure that he could make the journey, once he began, in six days—eight if he took it in a leisurely fashion, or if something unforeseen should happen upon the road. The road from Glevum would take him to the fortress of Deva, where he would turn west along the coast. There, he would leave the Roman world behind him. Deva was but a frontier fort and, he learned from a traveler, the road within fifty miles of it a mere dirt track. The Romans had made no incursions into the north of Cambria, but Merlin knew the land. He began to provide for the journey.

* * *

That night, Merlin lay long in his bunk, writhing for the pain in his chest, which the damp weather enhanced. Then, in the midst of the night—he knew not whether he slept or waked—the things around him changed, and it seemed that he stood in the cave, the same cave he had seen so often in his visions. The wound in his chest throbbed, and he raised a hand to rub it; but he found that he had claws instead of hands, and they rubbed at scales as hard as bronze. He looked down at his body, and saw that he was scaled all over, and that great leathern wings stretched out on either side. He looked left and right about the cave, and saw that it was filled with water, and that in the midst of it was an island, and buried almost up to the hilts in the rock of the island was a sword, *the* sword, Excalibur. At a rumbling noise, Merlin looked up, and he saw part of the cave ceiling split apart and tumble downwards. He held up his wings to fend off the falling rock, but they had become frozen—they were iced over, like frost on a December morning. The wind howled about him, and ice gathered on his limbs, and above him the rocks formed a chamber like a tomb. The chamber rose, a great tower reaching up to the heavens; and then it collapsed in on itself, and the whole structure came crashing down on Merlin's head.

He sat bolt upright in bed. Outside, rain pattered on the windows, but he could see little in the room. He could feel the boards of his bunk beneath him. He rubbed his hands together, and knew that they were hands of flesh and blood and sinew, not scaled talons. What did it all mean?

Merlin lowered himself back down onto the bed, and the pillow cradled the back of his head. He lay awake long, pondering the meaning of his vision, and finally slept once more in the dark hour before the rising of the sun.

* * *

At first light, Merlin rose and broke his fast. He hurried off to the forum, wincing a little with the pain over his heart. When he got there, it was already busy, the vendors vying with each other, street entertainers juggling or cavorting.

Since Merlin could not afford a horse, he had resolved to buy a pair of stout walking shoes, and he searched through the stalls for a pair that would serve. He had just paid the vendor when he caught a glimpse through the crowd of something black: a broad-brimmed hat, with a pale face and curled hair beneath it.

Merlin caught his breath, and turned his back on the figure. Kenen. He knew it was Kenen. Then where was her ladyship? Slowly, cautiously, Merlin peered over his shoulder. The figure in black was nowhere to be seen.

Perhaps, he thought, he had imagined it. After all, Morgana had left him for dead beside the road. Kenen could not be seeking him. Some fantastic coincidence had brought him and Kenen to the same place at the same time, but it was exactly that: coincidence, never to be repeated. If it was even Kenen in reality, and not just some passerby in a wide-brimmed hat.

Nevertheless, Merlin was shaken, and made his way back to the inn with many uneasy glances over his shoulder.

* * *

But that night, as Merlin was enjoying a mug of ale in the common room after his evening repast, he felt a blast of cold air as the door opened, and the conversation lulled for a moment as a newcomer strode up to the bar.

"Well, *there's* a sight!" said a voice from nearby.

"Must be from out of town," commented another.

"A long way out of town," added a third dubiously.

Merlin had his back to both the door and the bar. Curiosity building in him, he set down his mug and turned to look at the newcomer. The stranger's back was turned to him, but it was clearly Kenen: the swagger of his walk, the self-assured angle of the chin, even when seen from behind, the casual attitude with which he rested his hand on the pommel of that slender-bladed sword—it was Kenen, and no mistake. And the venom of his personality pervaded the room like a foul smell. Comments upon his appearance swiftly ceased as, one after another, the tavern's customers realized that danger stalked in this man's shadow.

Merlin instinctively turned his back to the newcomer. His insides were quivering. He looked at the hand that had just set down the mug—it was shaking visibly. There were many people in the room—his singing had attracted customers—and so he was fairly sure that he had been hidden from Kenen's view by the crowd. Quickly, he finished his ale, mumbled his apologies to the drawer, and hurried off to his room.

He stood for a moment, listening to the pounding of his heart in his ears, his hand upon the wound Kenen had given him a few short weeks ago. Outside, a fitful wind drove bursts of rain against the horn-windows.

What was there to do? With all his soul, Merlin yearned to know why Kenen was here in Glevum. With all his soul, he yearned to be himself away from Glevum and Morgana's men.

Merlin's eye alighted upon the brazier the innkeeper had set up in his room, and the stack of unlit charcoals beside it. Merlin picked up a few of these, his mind racing. Resolve gripped him, and he crushed some of the charcoal with the pommel of his sword. Then, taking the powder that resulted from this operation, he kneaded it liberally into his hair and beard. Drawing his knife, he examined his appearance in the blade—the sword, he knew, was too dull to give any kind of reflection. He smiled. The darkening of his hair had made him unrecognizable.

Quickly, he stained his eyebrows. He looked a little like a man whose hair was just turning grey, rather than one whose hair had become white some years since. He crossed to the water-basin that stood on a table beside his bed, and scrubbed his hands for a few seconds—the stuff was sticky, and it took a few minutes to remove the stain from his hands completely. That reassured him—if it clung so obstinately to his hands, it would stay in his hair.

Merlin stepped over to the window, and removed the horn screen. The street below was dark, but the cobblestones shone faintly. Merlin climbed to the window-sill. He dangled his legs out, then slipped off, landing lightly on his feet. He rose, brushed himself down, and re-entered the inn from outside, like a new customer. He made his walk a little more shuffling, sloped his shoulders somewhat, and slapped a coin upon the bar, ordering ale in the best local accent he could muster.

He spoke loudly enough for Kenen to hear, but Kenen did not respond. Nonetheless, Merlin could not relax. He felt as if his innards were tied up in a knot. Once, when the innkeeper's boy ran up to Kenen, brandishing his sword joyously above his head, Merlin thought he would cry out. Kenen reached out towards the boy—Merlin saw his signet-ring quite clearly—and ruffled the boy's tawny hair.

"Thou wilt make a fine soldier, when thou art grown, boy," said Kenen, sounding for all the world like the boy's fond uncle. Then he went back to his conversation with one of the locals, and the boy dashed off elsewhere.

Merlin remained in the common room for over an hour, watching Kenen. Some of the locals spoke to him, but none suspected that he was the minstrel in whose songs they had commonly taken such delight. Merlin started no conversations, but listened attentively to what Kenen said. Throughout the entire hour, he never once mentioned Morgana by name, nor Merlin, nor did he say anything that would imply he was searching for him.

His conversation was entirely of harvests and the weather and the condition of the roads.

When he had drunk two mugs of ale, Merlin left the common room. He shinned up onto the roof of a low lean-to beside the inn, then slipped in through the still open window of his room.

What did it all mean? Morgana thought him dead, so Kenen was not following him in Glevum. There had to be some other explanation—coincidence was no longer convincing. Merlin reached up and pressed his fingers gently against his wound. The sword had passed so close to the heart: it was a stroke of good fortune that he had not been killed.

But then another thought occurred to Merlin, and it chilled the marrow in his bones. Perhaps, rather, Kenen's thrust had been the most accurate that human hand could have managed. Had Kenen perhaps *intended* to miss? If that were true, then Morgana knew he was alive, and Merlin was a marked man. He was leading her to Afallach, and the secrets he expected to uncover there.

He had to leave now, under the cover of night, when it would be easy to cover his tracks. But already, the night had worn on, and dawn was but an hour or so to come. He must be swift.

Merlin gathered his possessions into his pack, slung it on his back, stacked a few coins—more than enough to satisfy the innkeeper—on the table, and dropped himself out of the window and onto the street.

It was deserted.

Merlin moved through the blue streets and passed like a shadow along the rigid thoroughfares to the north gate. It was locked, of course, but he found a way up onto the battlements, where he crouched in the shadows, unseen by the sentries as they passed their way along, eyes turned resentfully up at the drizzle. When they were gone, Merlin rose, found a suitable spot, flung himself into a tree, and snaked down to the ground outside the city.

Merlin walked briskly, and the damp, cold air seeped through his clothes, through his skin, and into his bones. His joints seemed to creak as he plodded along, like badly oiled hinges. The eastern horizon glowed greyly, and he could make out shapes all around him as the sun awoke from its wintry slumber.

The city dropped behind him and, as the road bent slightly, slipped completely out of sight. Merlin paused, looked up and down the road, then dashed across the open space beside the road and into the forest. The light was getting stronger, and he could see a few leaves here and there in the forest's canopy that had turned prematurely brown. Merlin turned and cast his eyes along the road in both directions, but no one was to be seen either way.

A noise, like the snorting of a pig, broke out close by, and Merlin spun round to see a raven glaring directly at him. It made the snorting noise again. It was almost as if the wretched creature was laughing at him. But before Merlin could respond in any way, the bird spread its wings and flapped up into the top branches of a tall and spreading elm.

A sudden urge rose in Merlin to destroy the bird. He looked around quickly, seized up three or four stones, and cast them, one after another, at the insolent creature. One whizzed through the air past its head. Another struck the branch on which it stood, sending white chips of wood spiraling into the gloom of the forest.

Merlin stood, panting as if he had made some great exertion, his eyes fixed upon the raven. It had not moved, but watched him with dark, malevolent eyes. Then, suddenly, it opened its scissor-like beak, let out a great "Caw!" and spread its wings. In a moment, it was gone.

Merlin leaned over from his waist, supporting his body by bracing his hands against his knees, as if he were going to throw up. It was a ludicrous notion, he knew—the bird was a bird. But there had been that gleam in its eye that suggested Morgana to him, and he had felt the urge to destroy it for her sake, for all creatures in the world that reminded him of her should meet their destruction at his hands.

Merlin shook his body out, as if getting rid of a cloying evil that had enmeshed him. He struck off northwards through the undergrowth, his eyes pale and turned upwards in the forest's gloom.

XXXVI

Merlin soon found the River Sabrina, and followed it north, skirting the border between Logris and Cambria for the first few days of his journey. Sometimes, the clouds would open and rain would slant down upon him and the river, as it slid lazily southwards. The air grew colder as he plied his way north, and he wore the hood of his cloak up always. From time to time, he caught glimpses of the foothills of the Cambrian mountains.

He found lodgings most nights, for settlements were strewn along the course of the Sabrina; but one night, when he knew he was due to reach Viroconium on the following day, he camped out beneath the bare sky. The night was cold, the air damp, and though he wrapped himself up in his blanket, it was hard to sleep, and he stayed long awake, staring out at the darkness.

He must have slept fitfully, for it was when he snapped awake that he became aware that he was not alone.

Nobody was close by; but when he reached out with the Sight, he could sense others, perhaps two or three hundred yards away. Silent as a shadow, he rose and, moving from tree to tree, came by concealed ways some distance south along the river. Before he had gone very far, he heard voices. He sat down, and strained to hear them.

"Argante," he said solemnly in his heart, "assist me in this—Yeshua too. If you can hear me, allow me to hear them!"

A gust of wind blew in Merlin's direction, and it seemed to clear the air of all obstacles. He could suddenly hear them as if he sat with them.

"Thou art but young in the Lady's service, Kenen," said one voice. "Thou art excused thy heresy. But speak not so again, I prithee."

“I only say,” answered Kenen’s voice, “that I have given up much to serve the Lady—home and throne, and wives too. I would I could be sure it were all worth the giving up.”

“Assure thyself,” said another voice. “Thou shalt not miss thy wives, when thou tastest of the willing dames of Annwn. And the power of a king —what is that, to the power thou hast as the Lady’s minion?”

“Very well, then,” said Kenen, “I shall not despair.”

The third voice laughed; a hollow sound, like a void. “I did not bid thee not despair. I tell thee, friend, despair is thy lot now, despair thy constant companion, thy friend, the strength of thine arm. What I say is that there are compensations enough that the despair seems but a trifling expense. The bawd’s price is a trifling sum, if he lead thee to Helen of Troy!”

There was some laughter at this, and Merlin turned away, returning to the place where he had been slumbering.

They *were* following him. There was no doubt of that now. How could he throw them off his scent?

Quickly, he gathered what he could of stones, branches, moss and dead leaves, and built them into the semblance of a human body, covering that with his blanket. He pulled out a few pieces of food—some dried meat, half an onion, a small hunk of hard cheese—and consumed it swiftly. Then he tied his harp onto his back and padded down the wooded slope to the edge of the river.

This land must be pleasant in the summertime, reflected Merlin, as he paused on the firm earth beside the water’s margin. Lowering himself into a crouch, he leaped lightly into the river, the splash of his entry drowned in the general rush of the current. He gasped at the sudden cold up to his waist, then slowly lowered himself until the water came up to his neck, and waded out to the edge of the reeds. He could make out little in the darkness, but he sensed that hills surrounded him, and willows came down to the edge of the water, and—

A noise and a fluttering startled him out of his reverie. He had unwittingly waded past a mallard’s nest, and the distressed bird had erupted from it with a sound to open tombs. Merlin dropped his head beneath the water's surface, and pushed himself away from the bank. He glided through the icy underwater world for a few seconds, then drifted to the surface.

The duck had ceased her clamour, and was settling down to roost again. All other things seemed quiet. But the current had caused Merlin to drift a few yards south. He turned his face to the north and struck out again, making long and easy strokes against the current.

How long he swam in that fashion, he could never recall, for minute slid into minute, stroke into stroke, until it seemed that he had never done anything but swim through the utter darkness of the river, and never would do anything else. But at length, he began to notice an aching in his arms, and a distant roaring ahead of him. He changed course, making for the eastern bank, and in a moment found himself on a narrow strip of shingle in the crook of the river's arm, dripping and panting. Looking upstream, he could make out a faint whiteness that he recognized as rapids, and knew that he would have been unable to swim much further.

It was evidently not long until sunrise, for he was beginning to be able to make out the shapes of trees around him. But he began to shiver, his teeth to chatter. Autumn was almost over, and the air was chill about him. He was weary almost past caring whether he lived or died now, and die he felt he surely must if he did not get his clothes dried out before beginning his journey once more.

He became aware of a pair of unblinking golden eyes staring at him out of the darkness. He returned their stare, and realized suddenly that he was looking into the eyes of a mature she-wolf that had come down to the water's edge to lap up some water.

The creature watched him for some length of time, and he her, and then, as if a decision had been made abruptly, she padded over to him and lay down beside him. Merlin nestled into the soft warmth of her fur, feeling her radiance spreading through his own body, slowly but surely. She worked her muzzle under his neck, so that his head rested on her shoulders. In a moment, cradled in her warmth like an infant at its mother's breast, Merlin slept.

He awoke in the grey and misty light of early morning. Rising to his elbow, he looked at the she-wolf. She returned his gaze.

"I thank you, sister wolf," said Merlin.

She rose, lowered her muzzle to his hand, licked it quickly with a pink tongue and, before he had time to see what had happened, disappeared into the forest. Merlin was left on the narrow beach, staring in wonderment after her.

His clothes were damp, but not dripping wet, and he began his journey again soon afterwards. For the rest of the day, until he reached Viroconium, he felt no more presence of pursuers behind him.

* * *

It was early afternoon when he reached Viroconium. Caer Guricon used to be the fortress of the Horse People, the Cornawfi, they who, in ancient times, had carved away the turf of a whole hillside to form the image of a galloping stallion out of the chalk beneath. Now it too had turned civilized. Merlin paid his last few silver coins for lodgings at the first inn he came to, and as soon as the door was closed behind him, sank into a sleep from which he did not rise until the next morning was well advanced.

Merlin stayed in Viroconium for several days, earning enough money by his harping to pay for some provisions. The next stage of his journey, in which he would thrust himself between the brooding mountain ranges of central Cambria, would most likely be the most arduous. The Sabrina would still be his guide, winding between dark peaks into the west. There were no roads and, although he had visited the region, many years ago, he remembered it poorly. He knew only that he should strike west, then north when he came to Cereticiaun Bay.

He set out on a grey morning in early November, his pack replenished with items he had bought at the forum in Viroconium. His face was set and grim, and he was ready for the worst the weather could throw at him.

The mountains reared up on either side of him, their heads wreathed in clouds, narrow burns cascading down their sides. Merlin saw no one, nor came across any settlement larger than a sheep-fold. At mid-morning on his third day since leaving Viroconium, snow began to fall, and soon the world all around him was grey, the air full of swirling flakes.

The day was dark, so there was little knowing the hour; but he reckoned that it must have been late afternoon when he happened upon a nearly derelict shelter built in the lap between two grey hills. Merlin put his shoulder to the door and threw himself inside. It must have been used by some shepherd or other, for a neat stack of peat stood in one corner. Merlin quickly lit a fire, taking off his outer garments and spreading them out to dry. He ate, shivering in the smoky shelter, and contemplated the journey to Afallach while the world outside drew on to blackness.

When the next day dawned, Merlin donned relatively dry clothes and emerged into daylight.

The world was garbed in white. Great white plains sloped up to the mountain-tops, the branches of the trees stretched out with white-robed branches, the roof of the shelter was white with the mantle of yesternight's fall. The sky above was white, its bulging threatening still more snow. Only the river, sliding between the snowy banks, picked out its course with dark waters.

Merlin spent a few moments staring west along the river's course. It was probably another two days' journey, in this weather and over such terrain, before he struck the coast. He looked back the way he had come.

Far off, almost too far to see, three black specks moved slowly against the utter whiteness of the landscape. Merlin felt his stomach lurch, as if it were trying to tie itself up in knots.

Without wasting a moment, Merlin strode off into the west. It was heavy going, for the snow had fallen thickly the night before. His only consolation was that his pursuers had also to make their way through snow.

He should have known that they would pick up his trail again. He chided himself over and over as he trudged through the snow. His ruse could not have delayed them more than an hour or two. He would have to be a much cleverer fox than that to shake off these hunters.

Morning turned into afternoon, and each time Merlin looked back, they were still there. Another river tumbled down from the heights of the mountains, and he stood for a while, thinking about the path he must take to Afallach. Then he followed the course of this new river up through the treeless white plain, his steps ever ascending laboriously as he went. The wind up here was a very devil, buffeting his damp clothes against his skin, so that there was no chance of being warm, and kicking up the snow in little whirling funnels. Behind him, the world was spread out like a map, and over its surface crawled the three tiny black spots.

The afternoon wore on, and snow began once more to fall. Merlin's progress slowed. His eyebrows, moustache and beard were thick with ice, his nose red with cold, and his fingers numb. He suddenly got an idea.

Where the river turned, a narrow crevice opened up in the bank. Merlin climbed down to it, and found that he could, with some squeezing and wriggling, fit into the crevice. The snow would conceal his footprints, and would soon fall over his cloak, concealing him completely from anyone on the river bank. Once Kenen and his other pursuers had passed him by, he could slip out and fly in the opposite direction.

He waited. The snow covered up his cloak, and he shivered, for it was as cold as death where he sat. An hour passed, and Merlin sat as still as forgetfulness, cold filling him to the marrow.

Then he heard a voice and, a few moments later, the crunching of boots in snow. Merlin closed his eyes. The snow had been falling constantly since he had pushed himself into this crevice, and he knew it must have concealed his footprints. They would not see him, unless they looked directly at him. He sent up a prayer from his heart: "There is no apple tree, O Lord, to conceal me from the eyes of those who hunt me. Send therefore darkness over their eyes, that they see me not!"

The tramping of the boots came closer. It seemed to Merlin that it echoed in his very ears, that it merged with the beating of his heart and became the pulse by which the world lived.

Then he realized that it *was* only the beating of his heart that he was listening to, that they had passed on without, apparently, having seen him.

Merlin waited, his ears alert to the sound of every falling flake of snow. He became conscious of a strange pain in his chest, and realized that he had been holding his breath. Slowly, cautiously, he drew in a breath, and let it out. Then another.

They were gone. He was certain. He pushed himself out of his hiding place, and shook the stiffness from his limbs. He climbed up the bank. The footprints of his pursuers were still visible, though they were beginning to be filled with snow. They led up the side of the mountain, alongside the river, and disappeared into the growing darkness. Smiling to himself, Merlin turned and began his descent of the mountain. He did not know how long they would follow that false trail, but it would give him a few hours, at the very least, and more if he walked on through the night.

When he got back to the valley bottom, he resumed his original course westward. The waters were slow now, for most of the width of the river was ice, but he could hear it distinctly, and when night fell, the sound was his guide.

Three more days he trudged westward, and in all that time he never saw his pursuers. At the end of it, the river he was following emptied itself into the wide sweep of Cereticiaun Bay, and Merlin knew that the most difficult part of his journey was over. He turned north. The snow did not fall here, and his progress was good.

So it was that, nine days after leaving Viroconium, footsore, hungry, and cold, Merlin came at last with great relief to the village of Aber Alaw and took his repast at the inn there.

* * *

Merlin slept well that night, and did not get out of bed until the watery sun was high in the sky. Then he rose, broke his fast, and emerged into the bright air of an early winter day. Light snow covered the ground, and the inhabitants of Aber Alaw, who had risen hours earlier than Merlin, were in the midst of their daily business. Merlin noticed that most of the buildings had been rebuilt recently, within the last ten years, and the village seemed smaller. Suetonius Paulinus must have left very little standing or breathing after his visit.

Merlin left the village behind him and followed the path he knew so well to Afallach. It was overgrown, hardly a path at all any more, and the only footprints in the snow that he could see were the slots of deer.

At last, the Sacred Hill rose before him, but Merlin's heart quailed to see it.

The apple trees were gone. Scorch marks, still visible even after thirteen years, told unmistakably what had happened. The crest of the hill was an unbroken arc, treeless, bare, forlorn. At its foot, the caves in which the druids had dwelt stood open to the elements, snow and old leaves piled high over the threshold.

With a heavy heart, Merlin followed the overgrown path around the hill until he came to the Cave of Knowledge. The lintel had been shattered, and lay in fragments, with other pieces of debris from the roof of the entranceway. Merlin climbed over the pile of dirt and rocks, and stood at last in the old study, his breath steaming. The interior was full of old leaves and cobwebs, but surprisingly undamaged. The doorway to the sleepers was still intact.

But he had not come for book knowledge, and so he turned, clambered back over the pile of debris, and emerged once more into the sunlight.

"Who are you, and what do you want?" demanded a voice.

Alarmed, Merlin spun round, and found himself face to face with an old, bearded man in a grey cloak. His eyes were closed, and Merlin could see scars about them, deducing that he had been blinded at some point in the past. A golden sickle was tucked into his belt.

There was something familiar about the man, something about his features; and suddenly, Merlin knew him.

"Aled!" he cried. "Is it you?"

The old man gave a start, and his hand fluttered upwards towards Merlin's face. There was a faint smile upon his lips. "Merlin," he said. "You have come at last. Well, she said you would."

XXXVII

Merlin leaned heavily on his staff, his fingers tightening about the gnarled wood, but he made no movement. The wretched man before him had raised his face a little, as if he were listening intently, his darkened eyes turned towards the sky.

"The years have not been kind to you, my friend," said Merlin, at last. "Your years are not much more than mine, and yet you look very much older. Is it so hard, serving the Lady of Annwn?"

"When the legions swarmed over Ynys Mon," said Aled, his nostrils flared and his teeth gritted, "it was the Lady of Annwn who lifted me from the jaws of death. She gave me my life—the kiss of the goddess."

"Hardly," responded Merlin. "She extended what was already yours."

"A quibble," retorted Aled. "The difference is insignificant. There is no one else to serve. Look around you, Merlin. You can love who you want, you can help the poor, the infirm, the destitute, and what is your reward? A life of misery and a knife in the back, a slit throat, the rope's end. Life is a long scream, terminated by oblivion—well was it said by Gwelydd, all those years ago."

"If I believed that," said Merlin, "I should choose oblivion."

"It will come, soon enough, choose it or no. But in the meanwhile, Morgana's way is the way of the real world. You must submit to reality, Merlin. Did not Morgana destroy utterly all the other Morforwyn? Are not the menfolk slain, the Ladies of the Lake vanquished? It is the strong who succeed in this world, Merlin. Those who are not afraid to shed blood. We must be strong."

Merlin laughed. "Is this the wisdom of Morgana?" he said. "Is this the wisdom of the druids? I would have believed you, Aled, many years ago, but now I know different, for I have met them. I have spoken with Argante, Queen of the Morforwyn, and I have trodden the secret way of Avalon."

"It is not possible," said Aled, his voice quavering. "You are lying. Why have they not shown themselves before now?"

"A way has opened to them," said Merlin, "a way that was closed until a short time ago." He smiled. "We live in a different world now," he finished.

Aled's nostrils flared sarcastically. "You are delusional, Merlin," he said. "If the world is different, it is harsher. Look around you, Merlin, and see what happens in your world. We have need of greater strength now—the kind of strength that comes from Morgana."

"Or perhaps greater love," suggested Merlin.

Aled snorted derisively. "You are a sentimental fool, Merlin," he said.

"Perhaps I am," admitted Merlin, moving at last away from the cave's entrance and into the sunlight, "but I would not trade my sentiment for your fear."

Aled's staff lashed out. A resounding crack echoed from the hillside as Merlin intercepted it with his own.

"Why do you think I fear anything?" demanded Aled in a snarl. "He who has Morgana as an ally need fear nothing."

Merlin shook his head. "No, Aled," he said. "Fear is Morgana's weapon, the chains with which she enslaves those who follow her. And she uses it as liberally on those she calls her friends as on her enemies."

"What is it you seek, Merlin?" asked Aled. "Peace?"

"Perhaps," answered Merlin.

"Strange," commented Aled, relishing the sounds of the words, "that a man who seeks peace should do so by seeking a sword." He placed himself before Merlin, blocking his way, and holding his staff at the ready. For some reason, his blindness did not make his threat less menacing.

"Aled, there are many things I do not expect you to understand about me, and now is not the time to explain them all. I beg you not to bar my way."

"Beg me? Why not command?"

"For the friendship we once shared, I would not command, but beg you."

Aled snorted with a flat-sounding laugh. "Why should I move, Merlin? I shall bar your way whichever way you choose." Merlin turned and tried to get around him, but with one step he barred his way once more. "You see, Merlin? Sometimes, it is necessary to resort to violence. Behold me: I am weak and blind, aged past my years. You are strong. You could batter me down easily, and do as you pleased. You could do it—but if you did that, you would be as I am now, as Morgana is and wants you to be. There is no room for the weak in this world, Merlin. Strike me down. Be strong. Take your place."

"You mistake me much," said Merlin in a low voice, "if you think I will not use violent means to achieve peace. 'I come not to bring peace, but a sword,' my master said. And so say I: move aside, or taste death." Merlin let drop his staff and drew his sword, holding the point out towards Aled.

Aled stood his ground. He seemed to grow in stature, expanding before Merlin so that his shadow was cast over him completely. He seemed to eclipse the sun. Merlin tightened his fingers on the grip of his sword, and pressed the tip into the soft flesh at the base of Aled's throat.

"I warn you, druid," said Merlin, "do not provoke my vengeance!"

For a moment, Aled bristled. Merlin could see the corners of his mouth turn down. The fingers of his free hand clenched.

Then, all at once, Aled shrank to his normal size, and more—he began to be a wizened, sniveling old man. Merlin gazed with disdain down the blade of his sword at what Morgana had made of a once proud man. The point dropped, and Merlin strode past him and along the path towards the summit of the Sacred Hill. Behind him, Aled screeched, "Coward! Would you draw on a blind man? One that cannot see your blade, but only feel it at his throat? Is this your way, Merlin? Is this the way of Merlin? To threaten the old, the infirm, the helpless? Sorry I am you were not killed years ago, in your flaming hovel! But you will die yet! You will die! The Lady will find you, and she will show you what true strength means!"

Aled relapsed into a coughing fit, bowed down towards the ground and spitting upon the earth. Merlin shivered for fear and pity, and turned a corner.

A wind was blowing out of the west, and it was blowing the light covering of snow along the ground and into drifts eastward of the path. Merlin climbed. He had expected to be wearied with the climb—it was almost twenty years since he had trodden this path. But his step sprang, and he could feel a kind of youth flowing through his body as he neared the summit of the hill.

"What do I expect to find here?" he wondered, smiling at his own folly. To have come all this way—to have evaded the servants of Morgana, and bandied words with her minion, and not to know what he was after! It was insane! "And yet—" he thought, "and yet I think I shall know. It is not the knowing that achieves the quest, but the readiness to do the bidding of the Lord."

The summit of the hill lay before him, bare except for a few withered saplings, and grey grass, flattened by the wind from the Eirish Sea. It was not a place of luxurious fecundity, as it had been in the past. Merlin felt a deep sadness in him, like the sinking of lead in his veins. Would he even be able to see from here? He stepped out into the forlorn centre—the World Centre, it had been, and now nothing marked it but the charred and shattered stump of the Sacred Tree, no higher than his own chest, and the well, clogged with blackened leaves. Slowly, he turned about, seeking with his heart, his mind, his soul, stretching through the mist-shrouded land as if with long fingers.

"God of Light," he prayed, "visit me and reveal to me that which I should know, which all my life has been hidden from me!"

Fire. He saw fire, and blood, and the plumed helmets of the Romans moving back and forth, lighting the trees, putting to the sword the druids that fluttered before them. He saw Aled, running from a young legionnaire. The legionnaire stopped, looked up. A raven swung out of the flame-rent air and into his face. Aled ran on.

Merlin reached out further, beyond Afallach, to the edges of the Island of the Mighty.

He saw a fortress of glass—Caer Siddi, Morgana's fortress in Annwn. How it caught the light of the sun, broke it up and twisted it, throwing it in a thousand fragments here and there! And below the fortress was a cave, and in the mouth of the cave, a man with a sword.

"I have it!" cried Merlin. He opened his eyes, and the vision flew about his head, and off into nowhere. He pitched over backwards, striking the stump of the World Tree, then sliding into a sitting position.

"I have it," he said again, more quietly now. Then he began to chuckle softly. Excalibur was beneath Morgana's very feet, in the cave below her own fortress in Annwn, and she knew it not!

"But how to get there?" said Merlin, rising to his feet. "No man has found out Annwn but Belinos. How did he get there? Did he leave a chart, a log, anything?" Merlin closed his eyes and held out his arms. He drew in a deep breath, filled his lungs, ready to receive another vision.

Nothing happened.

"O come, Lord of Visions!" he cried. "Come to my poor eyes and open them! Where can the *Prydwen* be? Give me a clue, anything!"

A shape emerged from the darkness, vague, hardly anything but a shadow upon a shadow.

"What is it?" Merlin asked.

Shapes were visible in the darkness, and he could see that he was in a cave. Was it the cave in which Excalibur rested? he wondered. But he could see nothing clearly, nor could he move from his spot.

He looked down. And it seemed to him that his limbs were wrapped with ice, as an apple is with its skin. And it seemed to him too that a year passed, and another, and more and more flew by, until centuries had passed him in their headlong career, and still he was clad with this impenetrable armour of ice. He strained his muscles, flexed his fingers, but nothing would move.

He heard a cracking sound, and another. He drew in a breath, filling his lungs so that his chest swelled. The ice encasing his chest cracked, fell in shards away from him, tinkling on the floor of the cave, and he rose from his recumbent posture and strode across the floor.

The mouth of the cave lay before him, and he emerged into daylight, blinking as the fragments of ice dropped from his body and rattled down the slopes of a great mountain.

The world lay below him, green and fertile, filled with castles and cities and mighty warriors, and all of them looked to him.

"Yes," he said to them, "it is I, Merlin the Kingmaker! I shall find a king, the greatest of all the kings, and I shall place into his hands Excalibur, the sword of kings!"

But in that instant, he was back upon the crest of the Sacred Hill of Afallach, with the western wind blowing snow upon him, and a mad, blind old druid somewhere below him in the blasted forest, and he knew that he must leave Afallach, and never return to it.

Merlin left, and the World Tree, shocked by Merlin's collision with it, finally fell into a mess of wood chips.

* * *

Merlin wasted no time, but set off south again, his only thought to get to Glevum and begin searching the coast, inch by inch, until he discovered the *Prydwen* and the charts he prayed would be within it. It would be the work of many years, he knew, but he knew too that, eventually, he would find it.

The years stretched ahead of Merlin, and he saw himself, alone and forlorn, clothed in rags, plying his way slowly along the coast of the Summer Country and Cornwall. Many years it would be; and how many were left to him? He thought of Joseph, so far from his home of Arimathea. How old was he? But the Grail had sustained him for forty years in prison, and it had given him the strength to live beyond his mortal years. Could Merlin buy some extra time by returning to Corbenic periodically and drinking from the Grail?

No. The answer came to him swiftly, almost a voice in his ear. The Grail was not something to take, but to receive when offered. There must be some other way.

Merlin remembered something Joseph had said to him shortly before his departure from Corbenic. "The Lord," he had said, "does not test us beyond our abilities." Well, if it was within his abilities to find Excalibur, he would find Excalibur; if not, he would lay the ground-work for someone else.

"The point is," he muttered, as he strode along the lanes of Ynys Mon, "to be ready to do His bidding."

He stopped suddenly in his tracks. He did not know why. Nothing he could see or hear had bidden him stop. But something prickled the hairs on the back of his scalp, and it was with infinite caution that he peered around the last corner at the ferry that would take him across the straits to the mainland.

Morgana had just stepped off the ferry, with three of her men. One of them was Kenen.

"Kenen, stay here," said Morgana. "If he leaves Afallach, he must use the ferry to regain the mainland. You two come with me. He must be in Afallach now. I shall go ahead."

Merlin must have blinked, for otherwise Morgana had simply vanished. The cawing of a raven broke out overhead, and Merlin rolled into a ditch for cover. A moment later, he heard the tramp of boots along the path. He cowered lower in the ditch, his ears alert.

"'Twere simplest to kill him," said an approaching voice. "Had we but done the deed ere this, as we have had a thousand chances on our road here, we should e'en now be resting in comfort in Annwn."

"Thou hast heard the Lady's commands," replied the other, almost level with Merlin now. "I know not her reasons, nor would I question them. There is that he knoweth, and that we seek, and that is all *I* need to know."

Their voices faded, and Merlin waited.

Only Kenen left. Merlin peered over the edge of the ditch. No one was around. He rose to his feet and, sliding his sword out of its sheath, peered once more around the corner.

Kenen was pacing up and down before the ferry, his movements as fluid as a cat's. The ferryman sat on the edge of his craft, his fingers twined before him. His eyes were raised distrustfully towards Kenen.

A steep bank rose on the landward side of the path, roughly to the height of Kenen's head, overgrown with twisted old bushes and a yew tree. Kenen paced within a foot of the bank.

Silently, Merlin left the path and pushed through the old, dry brambles beside it. He moved slowly and with great caution, his eyes darting this way and that, his ears pricked.

The sun was setting behind him, lighting up weirdly-shaped clouds with a blaze of blood. Merlin looked down at Kenen, his pale face lit by the ruddy glow.

Merlin rose, ready to leap.

In that instant, the ferryman saw him. Merlin heard a sharp intake of breath. Kenen heard it too and looked, puzzled for the moment, at the ferryman. Then he turned to seek the source of his surprise.

Merlin jumped. He landed with his full weight on Kenen's chest. Kenen grunted. His arms flew wide, and he buckled under Merlin's momentum. Merlin raised his fist, and brought the pommel of his sword crashing down on Kenen's head. Kenen went limp. In a moment, Merlin was on his feet.

He hesitated a moment, the tip of his sword over Kenen's throat. One quick movement would finish him. But the moment stretched, and Merlin could not do it. The point of the sword dropped, and Merlin shook his head, disappointed.

He whirled about and turned on the ferryman. "Will you take me to the further bank?" he demanded. The man shook his head, shrinking from Merlin as from a viper.

"Then get off the ferry," said Merlin, "and I shall steer myself."

He held out his sword threateningly towards the poor man. He really bore him no ill will. It was hardly surprising that he should fear Morgana. But he had no time to negotiate. The man hopped down from the boat, and Merlin pushed it into the swift waters of the straits.

Almost immediately, the current took the craft and pulled it against the rope that tethered it to either shore. Merlin sheathed his sword and heaved on the line, and the boat crept out into the midst of the straits. Darkness was falling, and the southern shore looked like a black dragon stretched out in the gloaming.

The prow of the boat crunched on the sand at last, and Merlin hopped down. A moment later, he had dissolved into the woods of northern Cambria, and escaped Morgana's men once more.

* * *

He slept that night in the forest, but when day broke, he started moving up once more into the mountains. As on his northward journey, the weather started to close in as he reached higher altitudes. The wind from the Eirish Sea, which he had noticed on the Sacred Hill, now set in, and brought with it waves of snow that dashed themselves against him as he climbed along the narrow passes.

It was on the second afternoon of his journey through the mountains that he saw three black specks moving like insects after him.

Merlin strode on, redoubling his steps in an effort to put more distance between himself and Morgana's men.

He was climbing the side of the westernmost of three mighty peaks. Below him, a forest of pine trees lay like a blanket across the valley that swept down to the northern peninsula of Cambria. Above him, the snow-capped peak glowered with dark wrath. He felt unutterably small, dwarfed by the landscape, put to flight by the might of Annwn.

Late in the afternoon, the path took him around a corner so that he saw the wide, sweeping valley whose northern slope was formed by the mountains he had been climbing. The Sabrina meandered along its bottom, the whole scene covered by snow. His path wove downwards into the trees, some three or four miles away.

Even as he watched, a dark shape emerged from the forest and began to climb along the path towards him. Another followed it, and another. He did not need to guess what they were. He knew that Morgana's men were before him now, as well as behind.

There was only one way to go: up. Merlin cast about for an easy ascent. Not far off, an icy rill tumbled down from the heights of the mountain. It cut its course through a cleft in the mountain, jagged and full of thrusting and juttied outcrops. Merlin set his hand and his foot to the rock-face, and began to climb. It was slippery with ice and snow, and his progress was agonizingly slow. His fingers cried out with the strain of hanging on, and his heart thumped against his ribs. The world swung away beneath him, wet and very far away.

It was almost nightfall when he found himself clambering onto level ground. It was grassy, and opened out into a shallow, sparsely wooded basin, in the midst of which lay a long, narrow lake. Beside the lake, like broken teeth, stood the remains of an ancient fortress, and suddenly Merlin knew where he was. This was Dinas Eryri. He looked down. Beneath his feet, legend said, had once lain the Addanc, a terrible serpent whose vile offspring, dragons as white as death, and red as blood, still slept in an icy subterranean lake, awaiting the hour at which they would be released, and unleash their terrible wrath upon the Island of the Mighty.

"Oh, what unfortunate chance has brought me to this place?" Merlin cried, turning his face up to the churning heavens.

Snow was falling, whirling in the wind all about him now. It had gathered in deep drifts against the shattered walls of the old fort. He looked around and, suddenly, he could see all things, though still they lay in darkness. At his feet, the great mountain ranges of northern Cambria stretched out in ragged ranks. He could see the glistening of the waters between Cambria and Ynys Mon. He could see the estuary of the Sabrina, far to the south. He could see the frigid waters that divided the Island of the Mighty from Gaul. He saw it as it was: asleep, covered with darkness. But he saw also something else: great buildings of granite and marble rising from the misty hills, wide paved roads stretching their fingers between the mountains and along the valleys, until the entire kingdom was crisscrossed with them, mighty fortresses, wrought from square-cut stone, bristling with spears and red plumes, repulsing every foreign invader. He saw, spread all around him like a map, the victory of the enemies of Britain.

Merlin cast his eyes down the precipice he had just climbed. Part of the way down was still lit, albeit dimly, and he was sure that six pale faces were turned up towards him, intent on their pursuit.

Suddenly, he flew into a frenzy, as if the wind had got into his veins and driven him to wildness.

"Well, come then!" cried Merlin, whipping out his sword and brandishing it over his head. "Come and kill me! You wouldn't do it before! I care nothing for you! Nothing! Come, death, and welcome! What can you do to me—I, who desire what all men else fear?"

"Oh, this is very good, very good," said a voice, dripping with sarcasm, from behind him. "Well done, Merlin. You have climbed into a place from which there can be no escape. Now, it only remains that you tell me everything you know. Everything, mind."

Merlin turned slowly, his sword-point dropping. He had seen the whole world from up there, but he had not seen until now Morgana.

XXXVIII

The wind howled with a bitter voice about the mountain-top, and snow whirled about, gusting into Merlin's face. He did not move. His sword arm hung loosely at his side—he was ready to use it, but did not want to threaten. He took a sideways step so that he could see when Morgana's men reached the top of the cliff, without taking his eyes off their mistress.

"You would have me at an advantage," he said, "if you wanted to kill me. But if you kill me, you could not find out what I know. And I would rather die than reveal anything to you." Merlin smiled. "I am worth more to you alive than dead."

"You remind me of what I already know, Merlin," replied Morgana. "But there are signs to be read from a corpse, by one who knows how to read them." She walked towards him. Snowflakes swirled around her—they seemed to emanate from her, and funnel around her, upwards as well as out and down upon the ground. Merlin looked up. There was no snow from the sky—it came all from her; and he remembered the stories of how she had dwelt among the icy regions of the Island of the Mighty in the early days, long before the coming of Brutus.

There was a noise at the cliff's edge, and Merlin saw Kenen scramble over the lip and onto level ground. Another followed, clad just like him, and another, until all six stood, panting, their swords drawn.

"But, Merlin," said Morgana confidentially, stepping right up to him and turning her face up so that her breath was warm on his face, "there are things men fear more than death."

Merlin's blade swiped upwards, and he took Morgana by the shoulder, whirling her around and pulling her to him. He pressed the edge of his sword against her throat.

"Lay down your weapons!" he barked.

But even as his voice rang out, he felt a slackening of her weight against him, and something feathered beat against his face. Merlin staggered backwards. He raised his hand to batter it away, and a raven swung away from him to the ruins, where it perched atop an ancient doorway.

Morgana's six guards flew at Merlin, their blades singing a grim song as they drew them from their sheaths. Blue light ran like liquid fire along the keen edges. Merlin readied himself, arm out for balance, blade crossing his body, the tip at the level of their eyes.

"God protect me!" he prayed quietly, his teeth gritted in readiness. "Yeshua guide my hand!"

In a flash, it seemed to him that he could see two worlds at once, almost identical. Sound receded, the howling of the wind and the cries of the men like noises heard underwater. He saw the nearest of the men swing his weapon at him—but he saw it before the man swung.

It was the Sight. He could see what would come to pass, an instant before it happened. Merlin's heart sang. Long had he sought mastery of the Sight, but now he saw that was vanity. This was what he had unknowingly sought: a perfect coexistence with the One who sent him visions.

Merlin ducked and swung, catching the man in the stomach with a slicing cut. Blood flew, and the man fell over backwards, clutching his belly, his legs kicking in his death agony.

The next aimed his swing at Merlin's head. Merlin made a quarter-turn, and the blade sliced through the air, past his shoulder. He swiped backhanded at the man. His head spun through the air and off the mountain, into black emptiness.

Another was upon him, raising his sword to make a downwards stab. Merlin reached out with his left hand and seized the man's wrist. He drove his sword into his stomach up to the hilts, so that the point thrust through his back. Merlin shook him off.

Kenen was next. Merlin lunged, caught him in the shoulder, and felled him at once. Kenen rolled away, and tumbled down the crack in the mountain's side by which they had all ascended. There came a dull thud, and a cry of outrage and pain.

Merlin leaped over the prostrate forms of his other victims, and slashed at the remaining pair. They turned about and fled, Merlin in hot pursuit, until they reached the ruins.

A wave of ice-laden air exploded from the ruins, and hit Merlin full in the face and body. So strong was it that he was lifted from his feet, and thrown into the heap of cooling bodies of Morgana's men. He scrambled to his feet.

Morgana had resumed her human form, and snow and ice were whirling about her in waves, as if in some bizarre, abstract dance. The ice bowed down before her, caressed her limbs and hair, flew from her to do her bidding.

Merlin felt a dull shock in the pit of his stomach, as if ice had formed in the innermost part of his body. He pushed himself onto his hands and feet, reached out and picked up his sword. Morgana was readying herself to send out another wave of ice towards him. Merlin jumped.

Ice struck the ground where he had squatted moments before, and threw up a shower of freezing particles, high in the night air. Grey frost covered the bodies of the three men Merlin had slain.

Merlin was behind an outcrop of rock. The ice had missed him, but still he felt cold and heavy. From somewhere, he could hear Kenen moaning with pain, and he wondered what was wrong with him—it was a small wound he had given him. Perhaps the fall had hurt him.

"This is a small matter, Merlin!" cried Morgana, her voice rising in pitch. "What you know, I too can know—I can sit once more on the Siege Perilous, and know all that I need to know!"

Ice crackled in Merlin's beard as he parted his lips to speak. "If you can do that," he said, "then why have you not done it ere now?"

A sudden shock reverberated through the rock that had been sheltering Merlin, casting him backwards in somersaults. The sword skittered away from him. Ice pattered all around. Much of it struck Merlin's clothing and stuck there. Merlin rolled, twice, three times, and leaped behind a boulder. Another blast of ice exploded at his heels.

Behind the boulder was a cleft in the rock. It was climbable. Merlin's mind raced. He turned his face back towards the ruins. "You are afraid, Morgana!" he called. "To use the Siege Perilous once brought madness; to use it a second time would bring death."

Quickly, as quietly as he could, he scrambled up the cleft in the rocks. Morgana's ice blasted the boulder to pieces moments after he had departed. He reached the top and scrambled over, rolling two or three times down the shallow incline beyond it.

He was on a narrow shelf of rock, and on the further side of it, darkness —a drop of ten feet or two hundred, he could not tell.

But there was a way down—a narrow winding path, which looked almost man-made. He cupped his hands about his mouth. "It is not alone mortal men who fear death," he said. "They fear it who have no life beyond the grave, who come to nothing after it!"

Morgana sighted him quicker this time, but the ledge of rock gave him better protection. Shards of ice and rock flew over his head and into space.

Merlin stood and revealed himself to her. "It is not for men, Morgana, that life is a long scream, terminated by oblivion!" he cried out, and his voice shook the mountain-top. "That has been your lie to the druids. But for you, the lie is true, is it not?"

Before she could respond, Merlin dashed away along the narrow path.

Morgana made no answer, but the snow and ice hurled itself in all directions, screaming like a fell beast.

Merlin reached the bottom of the path. It brought him to the ruins, on the opposite side to the rill by which he had climbed to this high place. He could not flex his fingers. Ice had formed over his clothes. He could barely move his lips.

"Who fears death, Merlin?" screeched the Lady of Annwn. "I lived a thousand years, and another thousand years, and yet more years beyond reckoning before Brutus came to this island. I have never known death, and

I never shall! But fear it or fear it not, Merlin, the hour is come for you to taste it!"

A great cracking noise sounded off to Merlin's left, as if the mountain were splitting right down to its root. With a massive effort, Merlin limped forward to the nearest of the shattered walls and peered around.

The cracking sound came again. Rocks were springing from the outcrop that had recently sheltered Merlin from Morgana's ice, like water dancing from a spring. Merlin looked on, his heart quailing within him.

It was not merely *like* a spring—it seemed to *be* a spring, for water flowed from the fissure. But the water was solid. It took on a form, and grew before him, inch by glistening inch: two rough legs, a thick torso, a craggy head. It was as if an invisible sculptor were carving the shape of a crude man out of ice at the speed of thought. But Merlin knew what it was: it was an ice giant, like those Morgana had summoned out of the ice of the northern mountains to fight against the Morforwyn, thousands of years ago.

"I had the power all those years ago," she said, "and I still have it. Arawn was a fool not to use it more often. He told me he had no power left for my son, but behold—what he lacked, I possess! I have the power to bring forth life!"

The ice giant advanced through the ruins of the fortress. It seemed to know already its mistress' mind, orders it would carry out unflinchingly and without deviation. Mindless physical power rippled through its limbs, its mighty torso. It towered before Merlin. It glistened in the dim light, muscles of rock and ice, eyes dull. In its hand was a great club. It raised the club.

Merlin ran. He ran around the edge of the cliff, away from the ruins. The ground shook as the giant's club pounded into it. Shards of rock flew—Merlin felt one nick his ear. He spun around and faced the giant.

At that moment, the ice hit him again, right in the thighs. He felt the coldness flow outwards like death, consuming him. He looked down at his hands. Ice was forming over the skin. His lips were frozen shut. He put all his effort into moving his feet and, sluggishly, one of them dragged along the rough ground, and he inched away from the giant.

It swung again—a lateral sweep this time. Merlin pitched over, and the club swished harmlessly overhead. He found himself among the debris left over from the giant's genesis.

Death. Death was all that was left to him. If he allowed Morgana to interrogate him, he knew he would reveal all, and a dark age would begin for the men of the Island of the Mighty. The enmity of the Romans was nothing compared to the darkness and the cold that Morgana would cast over the whole realm. And so death it must be.

Merlin scrambled up and away from the giant, which was lumbering towards him on unsure feet. Merlin had his back to the outcrop, and the abyss opened before him out of which the giant had issued. The giant was within range now. It had its club in both hands, and was raising it for a mighty blow.

It must be now or never, Merlin thought. He was ready to die.

In his last effort, Merlin cast himself from the edge and into the darkness. Above him, the giant's club shattered the rocky outcrop, and tons of rock tumbled into the breach. A cloud of dust went up from the wreckage, unfurling along the ground towards the figures of Morgana, her men, and the ruins.

Kenen pulled himself to the top of the cliff, his face ashen with the pain and the effort. He rested his back against a rock and surveyed the scene of wreckage. He was clutching his elbow tightly to his body, for his fall had dislocated his shoulder, and the slightest movement sent shockwaves of pain through his whole body. Gritting his teeth, sweat springing on his brow in spite of the cold, he staggered over to the pile of crumbled rocks that lay where Merlin had stood moments before.

There was no hole now, no abyss. And Merlin was gone, irrecoverably gone, and certainly dead. Kenen, finally overcome by the pain, fell to the rocky ground, where his comrades examined his wound and pulled his arm back into place. The pain woke him up for a moment, and the mountain shook with his scream. Then he fell once more into a faint.

Morgana looked down at the wreckage. There was nothing in her eyes, nothing at all. A moment later, she had vanished, but a raven was winging its way through the night into the north. Shortly afterwards, Kenen and his comrades were gone too. The ice giant remained on the mountain still, unmoving, until it fell into a senseless pile of inanimate matter.

* * *

Merlin hurtled through the darkness. He could hear, he could smell the debris falling with him through the pitchy dark. The ice still encased his limbs, the cold seeped through his veins into every corner of his being.

He stopped falling. His body was too numb to say for sure whether he struck something, or something caught him. But after a while, he was at rest.

He could not move. From the smell, he knew that he was in a cave, and it was cold, bitterly cold. Ice had formed over his whole body now. His heart slowed, the blood thickened in his veins.

Is this death, he wondered, or do I but sleep?

But his eyes were open, and before him, ere his eyes closed, a vision came to him—nay, was sent to him by one who loved him well, of that he was sure. For now he knew why he had been granted this gift, which some called a curse of the gods.

It seemed to him as if there appeared before him a cup, fashioned from the purest gold; and the cup was lifted by an unseen hand to his lips, and he drank, and was nourished.

Then Merlin knew a warmth spreading through his body and his soul, as if he were burning within. And though all was ice without, Merlin knew within a comfort such as he had never known before.

And Merlin slept.

Author's Note

The story of Merlin originated with an amalgam of various different stories made by a twelfth-century bishop called Geoffrey of Monmouth. Geoffrey had popularized King Arthur in his book *The History of the Kings of Britain*, but with his *Life of Merlin*, he took the character who had been the focus of only an episode in his earlier work, and gave him a lengthy biography. Geoffrey took the story of the servant who tests Merlin's prophetic powers by three times asking how he will die from Jocelin of Furness' *Life of St. Kentigern*, and the story of his madness from early poems concerned with the Irish wildman Suibne. These stories have been collected in the excellent anthology, *The Romance of Merlin* (edited by Peter Goodrich, Garland, 1990). About sixty years later, a Frenchman called Robert de Boron incorporated these stories into his own account of Merlin who, he claimed, was the son of the Devil, born to counteract the effects wrought by Christ's resurrection (*Merlin and the Grail*, trans. Nigel Bryant, D. S. Brewer, 2001).

A few years later than this, an anonymous French author wrote a vast and rather rambling account of Merlin's life called *The Story of Merlin*. This was part of a huge prose compilation called the *Lancelot-Grail Cycle*, or the *Vulgate Cycle*, depending on whose account of its writing you read (*The Lancelot-Grail Reader*, ed. Norris J. Lacy, Garland, 2000). *The Story of Merlin* tells how, when an old man, Merlin was besotted upon a girl called Niniane, who learned all his magic arts and finally used them against him, sealing him up in a cave from which he could not escape.

The time scheme had always seemed odd to me. How could Merlin have been born shortly after the Resurrection, as Robert de Boron claimed, and still be a contemporary of Arthur? In the Vulgate Cycle, we read how Lancelot had descended in a direct line of eight generations from Joseph of Arimathea. Reckoning a generation at twenty-five years, that places his birth at around AD 225, not 475, as would be reasonable for a contemporary of Arthur. I've attempted to solve this chronological problem by placing Merlin's story in the first century and his sojourn in the cave in the middle, not at the end of his story, though it is, of course, at the end of this book. He will wake up in time for Arthur!

Joseph of Arimathea is mentioned in all four gospel accounts of the Resurrection, but in the early years of the Church, many rival accounts arose which were, over the course of time, deemed to be less accurate than these —the apocryphal gospels. One of these is called *The Acts of Pilate* or the *Gospel of Nicodemus*. It tells the story of Joseph's imprisonment on account of his burial of Jesus' body, and his later release by Vespasian. This tale was greatly expanded upon in the Middle Ages, first by Robert de Boron, then by an anonymous author whose *History of the Grail* formed a part of the *Lancelot-Grail Cycle*. According to these accounts, Joseph was fed by the Grail in prison, and later brought it to Britain. Dan Scavone, in an article called "Joseph of Arimathea, the Holy Grail, and the Edessa Icon" (*Arthuriana* 9.4, 1999, pp. 1-31) has argued (conclusively, I think) that the object on which the Grail was based was actually the Edessa Icon, a shroud imprinted with the image of Christ's body, which Joseph took with him to Edessa, Turkey. The story that Joseph went to Britain comes about because of a misreading of the name of the royal palace in Edessa, which was called Britian. My account of Joseph of Arimathea, therefore, is historically bogus, and is based instead on Robert de Boron's account. As I have already pointed out, my aim is to produce a novel based on the legend, not the history.

* * *

Once again, I'd like to thank my wife, Adrianne, who has been, and still is, the best proof-reader and friend any man could have; my sons, Kit and Jack; and my friends and colleagues who read and suggested, over many beers, many revisions, especially Nate Williams and Harry Carrell. Since they have all done what they can to save *The Hawk and the Cup* from error, any flaws that remain are my own.

PERSONS AND PLACES IN
THE HAWK AND THE CUP

ADDANC: (uh-THANK) Type of dragon created by Morgana

AFALLACH: (AH-vuh-LAK) The principle stronghold of the druids on Ynys Mon

AGOR: A fisherman of Habren, father of Gwyden

ALED: An acolyte in Afallach; a maker of ink

AMON: Archdruid of Afallach; successor to Gwelydd

ANDRASTE: (an-DRAS-tay) Brittonic goddess of victory

ANNWN: (AH-noon) The Otherworld, the realm of Morgana

ARAWN: (uh-RAWN) One of the Morforwyn, consort of Argante; he forged Excalibur

ARGANTE: (ar-GAN-tay) One of the Morforwyn, consort of Arawn; she wrought the sheath for Excalibur

AULUS TULLIUS BRITANNICUS: Tribune of the Ninth Cohort of the Ninth Legion Hispania

BELIN: Previous High King of Britain; twin brother of Brennios; together, they fought against and defeated Rome

BELINOS: (bu-LEE-nus) Friend of Cassivelaunos and king of the Summer Country

BOUDICEA: daughter of Cydwelli of Dinas Morfan, queen of Eicenniawn and husband of Prasutagos

BRAN DUN: Bran's Fort, a minor fortress on the north coast of Eicenniawn.

CAER CAMULOD: Principal fortress of Eicenniawn

CAER EBRAUC: (KAIR uh-BRAWK) Principal city of Cameliard

CAER LLOYW: (KAIR HLOI-oo) City in the Summer Country

CAER LUEL: A city in the north-west corner of Cameliard

CAER LUNDEIN: Principal city and fortress of Logris; principal court of the High Kings of Britain; see also Londinium

CAER RHYDD: (KAIR RITH) City in Eicenniawn, ruled by Segofax

CAER SIDDI: Morgana's fortress in Annwn

CAER WENTA: Capital city of Eicenniawn

CAER WISC: The principal stronghold of Cornwall; known to the Romans as Isca Dumnoniorum

CAERLEON: (ker-LEE-uhn) City in southeast Cambria

CAERMYRDDIN: (ker-MER-thin) principal southern fortress of Rhydderch

CAMBRIA: The two peninsulae west of the River Sabrina (modern Severn), a land of mountains and valleys

CAMELIARD: (kuh-MEL-yard) One of the seven kingdoms of Britain, north of Logris and south of Albany

CAMULODUNUM: Roman name of Caer Camulod

CARTIMANDUA: (kar-ti-MAN-du-ah) Queen of Cameliard

CASSIVELAUNOS: (Kas-i-veh-LAU-nus) previous High king of Britain, the last to bear Excalibur

CATHBHAD: (KATH-vad) Bard to Rhydderch of Cambria

CATUS DECIUS: Roman procurator of Britain

CERETICIAUN BAY: (KE-ruh-TIK-yawn) The wide bay between the two great peninsulae of Cambria

CLOTEN: Former king of Cameliard and husband of Cartimandua

CORBENIC: Caer Ban, the Shining Fortress; island in the Summer Country, gateway to Avalon and later the home of Joseph of Arimathea

COROTICOS: Son of the former High King Tenvantios and rightful High King of Britain

CYNGEN: (KUN-gun) First husband of Cartimandua

DAFAT: (DAH-vat) Steward to King Meldred of Cambria

DEHEUBARTH: (du-HOI-barth) Region of central Cambria

DEPET: A ship's camptain from Morgannawg, prisoner with Merlin

DERGAN: Druid of Afallach, who teaches memory

DINAS ERYRI: (DEE-nus e-ROOR-ee) The palace of Bran the Blessed, situation on top of Mount Eryri, the tallest mountain peak in Cambria

DONACHT: (doh-NAHT) Master Huntsman of King Meldred of Cambria

DUBGLAS: River in Lothian

DUN GUINNION: Principal fortress of Albany, built on the River Dubglas

DYFED: (DUH-ved) Region in the southwest of Cambria

EICENNIAWN: A region in the east of Logris, chiefly fenland, ruled by Prasutagos

EIRIN: (AIR-in) The large island west of Britain

ERYRI: Mountain in the north of Cambria

FELOCATOS: (fuh-LO-ca-toss) Druid and lover of Cartimandua

GANIEDA: (gan-YEH-dah) Wife of Meldred and queen of Cambria

GARANHIR: (guh-RAN-heer) One of the seven male Morforwyn, god of feasting and revelry, creator of the Cauldron of Plenty

GLEVUM: Roman name of Caer Lloyw

GLYNN: Lord of Deheubarth

GRWHYR: (GREW-heer) Son of Rhydderch; king of Cambria

GUTOR: Fisherman of Habren, husband of Gwyden

GWELYDD: (GWEL-ith) Archdruid of Ynys Mon

GWENDDOLAU: (gwen-THO-lai) Son of Boudicea and Merlin; also the name of Merlin's great-grandfather

GWENUTIOS: (gwe-NOO-tyos) Cartimandua's third husband

GWYDEN: Goodwife of Habren, wife of Gutor and daughter of Agor

GWYNEDD: (GWIN-eth) Region in northeastern Cambria

HABREN: Fishing village at the estuary of the River Sabrina, on the northern coast of Cornwall

HESET: Steward and Butler to the King's Pantry in Morgannawg, now a prisoner

IEUAN: (YOO-an) Master of Spears in EIcenniawn

IORWERTH: (YOR-werth) Druid of Afallach, teacher of rhetoric

ISCA DUMNONIORUM: Roman name for Caer Wisc

KENEN: Eldest prince of Morgannawg

KHEFTEY: Prince of Morgannawg

IORWERTH: (YOR-werth) Druid of Afallach, teacher of rhetoric

LINDUM: Roman name for Linnuis

LINNUIS: Stronghold in northern Logris

LLYGAT: (HLUH-gat) Druid of ancient times, who possessed and learned to control the Sight

LOCRIN: Second High King of Britain, youngest son of Brutus and husband of Gwendolyn, after whom Logris is named

LOGRIS: The principal kingdom of Britain, stretching from the River Sabrina in the west to the Humber in the north

LONDINIUM: Principal city and fortress of Logris; principal court of the High Kings of Britain; see also Caer Lundein

LOTHIAN: Kingdom north of Hadrian's Wall

LYONESSE: Archipelago off the coast of Benwick

MAELGWN: Lord of Gwynedd

MATHREU: Former lover of Cartimandua

MELDRED: Son of Grwhyr

MESHA: Prince of Morgannawg

MILWYR: (MILL-wur) One of the warriors of Coroticos

MODRON: King of Morgannawg, taking his name from the son of Morgana and Balor

MORFORWYN: (mor-VOR-win) The gods and goddesses of the Britons. They were fourteen in all, seven men and seven women.

MORFRYN: (MOR-vrun) A hermit living in Cameliard

MORGANA: One of the Morforwyn, the fourteen gods and goddesses who fashioned the realms of Albion, Eirin, and Benwick in the time before the arrival of Brutus and the Trojans; she rebelled against the other Morforwyn.

MORGANNAWG: Kingdom situated within Cambria, on the south coast

NORTHGALIS: Region in northeastern Cambria

PELLES: Hermit living upon the island of Caer Ban

PRASUTAGOS: (PRAS-oo-TAH-gus) King of Eicenniawn and aged husband of Boudicea

PRYDWEN: (PRUD-wen) Ship belonging to Cassivelaunos, in which Belinos took Excalibur before the battle with Julius Caesar

PWYLL: (poo-UHL) Lord of Dyfed

RHYDDERCH: (RU-therk) late king of Cambria, father of Grwhyr and grandfather of Merlin Emrys

RUDGLANN: City in Cambria

RUTHIN: Servant of Grwhyr

SAMHAIN: (SAH-wen) The festival of the druids that marks the beginning of winter, celebrated on the last day of October

SEDDECH: (SEH-thek) King of the Fenlands in the Summer Country

SEGOFAX: Lord of Caer Rhydd

SEKHREY: Captain of the Guard in Morgannawg

SESMET: Prince of Morgannawg

SHESEP: Prisoner in Morgannawg

SUETONIUS PAULINUS: Roman governor of Britain

TASGETIOS: Boudicea's druid

TYLWETH: One of the local goddesses of Britain, not properly one of the Morforwyn; she is a water spirit, one of the race like the Greek naiads, created by Tyronoe

TYWI: (TUH-wee) River in southern Cambria

WERERYET: Prince of Morgannawg

WYSG: (oo-IZG) River in Cambria, bordering Morgannawg on the east

YNYS MON: (I-nis MON) Modern Anglesey, the home of the druids

About the Author

Mark Adderley was born in the railway town of Crewe, England. Like many of his contemporaries, he grew up devouring the novels of C. S. Lewis and, later, Ian Fleming and J. R. R. Tolkien. It wasn't until he was studying at the University of Wales, however, that he discovered a passion for the Arthurian legend that has now lasted . . . well, a very long time.

During his studies in Wales, Mark also met an American woman, Adrianne, whom he married. Moving to America, he got, in not very rapid succession, four children and a PhD in medieval literature from the University of South Florida. He has lived in Florida, Georgia, Montana, and Missouri, and now teaches writing and humanities at Wyoming Catholic College in Lander, Wyoming.

Also Available from WestBank Publishing

The Hawk and the Wolf

The Matter of Britain: Book One

Britain, the Island of the Mighty, stands on the brink of war with the Roman Empire. Excalibur is lost—the sword forged by the gods in the dawn of days, which has been passed down through the generations of High Kings. Can Britain stand without the help of the gods? Young prince Emrys, nick-named Merlin, knows his destiny is to find the lost sword of power, for the gods have given him a special gift to see into the heart of the world. He knows the rebel goddess Morgana will kill him to take Excalibur and become Queen of the Island of the Mighty, with a promise of days dark and bloody. In this fast-paced and violent tale, the world seems poised upon the brink of two possibilities: darkness and death . . . or the age of Arthur.

Coming Soon

The Hawk and the Huntress

The Matter of Britain: Book Three

Her home and family destroyed by Saxon invaders, young Nymve of the Cornawfi pursues her enemies relentlessly, bow in hand. She has nothing left; but the mysterious stranger who saves her life tells her that she is the possessor of a strange and daunting power that will enable her to influence kings and change the destinies of nations, a power he calls the Sight.

Set in an age hundreds of years after *The Hawk and the Cup*, *The Hawk and the Huntress* depicts the turmoil left in the Island of the Mighty when the Romans leave, and the Saxon barbarians invade. Seers and kings, warriors and goddesses abound in this exciting and violent novel. And at the centre of it all is Nymve, huntress and horse-tamer, prophetess and advisor to the High Kings of the Island of the Mighty.

Made in the USA
Charleston, SC
01 September 2010